PENGUIN BOOKS

NIGHTINGALE

Fiona McIntosh is an internationally bestselling author of novels for adults and children. She co-founded an award-winning travel magazine with her husband, which they ran for fifteen years while raising their twin sons before she became a full-time author. Fiona roams the world researching and drawing inspiration for her novels, and runs a series of highly respected fiction masterclasses. She calls South Australia home.

PRAISE FOR FIONA McINTOSH'S BESTSELLERS

'A blockbuster of a book that you
won't want to put down.'
BRYCE COURTENAY

'McIntosh's narrative races across oceans and
dances through ballrooms.'
SUN HERALD

'This book is fast-paced, beautifully haunting and filled
with the excruciating pain of war.'
WEST AUSTRALIAN

'A fine read . . . The moral ambiguity McIntosh
builds into the novel gives it a depth that takes it beyond
a sweeping wartime romantic thriller.'
SUNDAY HERALD SUN

'McIntosh weaves a diverse cast together,
and you gain an appreciation for her depth of research.'
BOOKS+PUBLISHING

'A captivating saga of love, loss, and the
triumph of the human spirit . . . Fiona McIntosh
is an extraordinary storyteller.'
BOOK'D OUT

'A perfect blend of romance, action,
mystery and intrigue by one of our best
known and popular authors.'
NOOSA TODAY

FIONA McINTOSH

NIGHTINGALE

PENGUIN BOOKS

PENGUIN BOOKS

UK | USA | Canada | Ireland | Australia
India | New Zealand | South Africa | China

Penguin Books is part of the Penguin Random House group of companies
whose addresses can be found at global.penguinrandomhouse.com.

Penguin
Random House
Australia

First published by Penguin Group (Australia), 2014
This edition published by Penguin Books, 2021

Cover photography by Piotr Krzeslak/Shutterstock
Cover design by Louisa Maggio © Penguin Random House Australia Pty Ltd
Text design © Penguin Random House Australia Pty Ltd
Typeset in Sabon by Penguin Random House Australia Pty Ltd
With thanks to D.I. McIntosh and family for the photography on p.vii

Printed and bound in Australia by Griffin Press, part of Ovato, an accredited
ISO AS/NZS 14001 Environmental Management Systems printer

 A catalogue record for this
book is available from the
National Library of Australia

ISBN 978 1 76104 238 6

penguin.com.au

*In memory of Trooper Darcy James Roberts
of the 1st Australian Light Horse Regiment*

Killed in action on 6 August 1915 at Lone Pine, Gallipoli

PART ONE

I

MAY 1915

Claire watched the morphine work its magic beneath the flickering lights she'd now become used to. The soldier's body began to relax immediately and, although he had not cried out once, his features slackened as relief arrived through the sting of a needle. She let out a breath on his behalf, glad that he could drift away for a while, and reached for the pencil to record the dosage. It was only in this moment, as she considered the date, that Claire became fully aware she had been on the hospital ship for nearly a month, plying the waters in the triangle of Turkey, Greece and Egypt.

She had finished her nurses' training in Britain and had already been working full-time for two years in one of the top teaching hospitals there. Claire had left Australia, where she'd lived from ten to seventeen, only to sail back to the England of her birth, believing if she could move among the familiar places of her childhood, she might be able to recapture that wonderful, naive happiness she recalled. Claire's yearning, however, had turned out to be more about the people who had populated her childhood than the places. And all of those people she belonged to and remembered with love were now dead. No one waited anxiously for her return in Australia or Britain, nor for a telegram or letter – not even for news on the grapevine of her wellbeing. So she'd gladly volunteered to leave England to nurse soldiers embroiled in this terrible war.

Assuming she'd be sent to France, she had instead found herself on a Greek island with a daring team of medicos who defied the woeful conditions, climate and food supply to set up the tented hospital known formally as Australian General Hospital 3, or 'Mudros'.

That had all changed in April when the Allies' push for the Dardanelles had become a reality and she once again cast aside fear to join a legion of tanned, joshing young men who had volunteered from Australia and New Zealand for an adventure on the other side of the world. They were doing their bit for King and country, planning to return to their farms and simple lives with heroic tales of war, but theirs was an empty daydream.

In the galley, waiting to be taken for surgery, a young man's laboured breathing turned to a familiar death rattle that Claire's nursing ear was finely attuned to. She quickly hooked the medical notes onto the end of the bed of her sleeping soldier and hurried to the struggling youngster's side. There'd been no time to even learn his name. One of the other nurses looked over in enquiry but Claire shook her head. He would be gone in moments. She took his hand because his gaze seemed to be staring far away. 'Say sorry for me . . .' he whispered. She was mostly lip-reading. 'Tell Mum —'

Mum was the last word he uttered from cracked lips before he sighed and the Cornish light she fancied she'd spied in his pale blue eyes was smothered like a candle flame. His plea to apologise to his mother sliced through her thin resolve to toughen up. Claire wondered sadly about that mother at home, waiting for her young son's letter, which would be replaced by a bland telegram from the army bringing the devastating news.

Who might the army contact if something happened to me? she wondered fleetingly.

Claire reached for the slim oval identification disc the soldier wore around his neck on a leather cord. Her finger reverently touched the initials and surname that had been pressed out from the aluminium above his infantry number, unit and religious persuasion. It was the only way she could honour him in this solemn moment. *E. W. Cornish*, her fingers traced as she shook her head. How appropriate. Claire closed the young soldier's eyes and momentarily shut her own in a soft communion of farewell, and her thoughts were drawn to the first morning of their arrival in Gallipoli.

———————

The Turks called it Gaba Tepe. The maps called it No. 2 Beach. But for those on board the converted passenger ship *Gascon*, the region was already nicknamed Anzac Cove. On the night of April 24, *Gascon* had been part of a fleet including battleships, minesweepers, tugs and troopships that eased out of Mudros Harbour to glide stealthily several hours later, just prior to 4 a.m., and station several hundred yards off the beach. British ships had then disgorged two divisions of Australians. Beneath the moon's phosphorescence that gilded the dark waters, young braves of the colony had descended rope ladders and clambered into small craft that were towed closer by tugs, before British naval crewmen rowed them to shore.

A grey dawn had lifted the veil on the so-called surprise landing that had called for lights out and no anchors. But the silence had been shattered as alert Turkish troops, nestled near-invisibly on the hilltop, had opened fire with machine guns. Sunrise had given way to a morning of spectacular courage by the ANZACs, who were being peppered with equally determined firepower by the small defending force.

Claire could remember how she'd lifted heavy, borrowed field glasses to a view of dauntingly high cliffs. Her world narrowed to the flash of gunfire exploding from the arid, grey-green bushes of scrub that clung to the incline while the ANZACs swarmed the hill face. Smaller shells rained on the surrounding waters like hail, bouncing dangerously close to the ship as the Turks tried to prevent the British artillery booming from nearby, the sound of those guns reverberating through her chest. Cordite spiced the air with its burnt smell and from what she could see by squinting at the foreshore, the men were being ordered to leave the wounded where they fell.

Claire tried not to focus on any individual. It was too painful to see men trapped, cowering mid-ascent beneath small overhangs and in tiny crags. Even so it was carnage beyond any nightmare. Well-armed Turks with the high ground and perfect views could aim accurately and strafe their gamely ascending attackers with what must surely be German-supplied machine guns, cutting down a generation of young men, weighted heavily by their gear, trying to hold ground they'd occupied earlier. 'The Turks have little more than antiquated muskets, so we're anticipating only lightly wounded,' they'd been told by the head doctor.

Lightly wounded? Claire thought, watching in silent horror as men, some of whose boots had barely left their print on damp Turkish sand, fell, fatally injured.

The mules were crazed with terror and the screams of injured animals joined the cacophony of explosions, gunfire . . . and the groaning, dying men who began arriving on the ship by the late afternoon.

That was day one. By the time they returned there was better organisation on the ground but the casualties were so many it had been heartbreaking. On the next return voyage into Gallipoli the full horror of war had wormed beneath her best defences and Claire was convinced there was no glory in it for either side. By the end of the first fortnight of her new routine she had tuned out to the firepower sounding its rage around her; instead she closed in on the daily battles in the wards beneath *Gascon*'s deck and the relentless fight to save organs, limbs and lives.

Rosie Parsons, a fellow nurse Claire shared accommodations with, now arrived alongside her, tucking a few wayward reddish curls back behind her nursing veil. She reached for some bandages from the nearby cabinet but squeezed her friend's arm. 'I'm sorry about your baby-faced soldier,' she said, staring down at young Cornish. 'He doesn't look old enough to join up.'

'I'm sure he wasn't. He can barely be seventeen.'

'You all right?'

Claire nodded and took a sighing breath. 'Good,' Rosie continued, 'because Matron's looking for you, by the by, but right now we're both needed in surgery.'

Claire signalled to an orderly that her patient had succumbed to his injuries before hurrying down the corridor to where theatre was likely in full emergency.

'Maybe the Turks don't know what a white ship with red crosses on it means,' Rosie bellowed over her shoulder as another mortar rocked the waters around them. She sounded disgusted. 'Now I'll never get to the Heliopolis Club in Cairo for that Pisco Sour that Victor promised he'd make me.'

Claire gave her a look of admonishment when Rosie glanced back at her with a wry smile. Rosie plotted her life in blocks of weeks that revolved around her entertainment schedule and social calendar in Alexandria or Cairo whenever they got leave. There were times when Claire wished she could make her life that straightforward and simply enjoy the good times. 'Maybe they've taken offence to us firing on them, in their own country.' She bit back on anything else that threatened to spill; it made her sound like one of those objectors.

Men were dying in concentrated numbers while as many were destined to barely survive their horrific wounds or to wake up more miserable than they'd felt before surgery, like this soldier, whose head she reached to stroke in the hope he might feel her soothing touch somewhere in his dreams.

'How is this man, in the prime of his life, going to recover mentally when he wakes and realises his legs have been amputated?' Claire asked.

'I can't answer that,' Rosie replied with a grimace as she prepared her tray of equipment, 'and I can't let myself think about it.' Despite the hardness of her words, Claire had seen the sorrow in her friend's eyes.

The *Gascon* had four hundred cots but Claire suspected twice that number of beds wouldn't be sufficient for the casualties and demand for transport away from Turkey. But those decisions were not hers and, rather than struggle with logistics she could not control, Claire lost herself in her work, moving from patient to patient, never knowing their names or where they hailed from – only the nature of their wounds. She was assisting a new doctor, and a freshly qualified nurse was helping her hold a man still who was not fully sedated while the surgeon dug shrapnel out of the corner of his patient's eye.

'Be still, there's a good fellow,' the English surgeon said in a mild tone.

'Will he lose his eye?' Betty wondered aloud and Claire gave her a look of admonishment.

'He can hear you,' she mouthed and on cue the blond-headed boy, surely not even out of his teens, cried out; he was another one begging for his mother and Claire blinked away how sad that made her feel.

'I can't say if he'll lose the eye,' the doctor continued softly, matter-of-factly, 'but looking at the mess of his shoulder, I suspect he will lose his arm. We'd better prep for an amputation.'

Claire wished she could shoosh the doctor too but dared not. She deliberately kept her face blank and recorded everything she could. He belonged to Bed 200 and his name, he had told them, was Billy Martin. He was just eighteen. Billy began to cry, tears leaking to sting his wounded eye further and drip across his spotty cheeks.

'Don't take my arm off,' he pleaded. 'I have to help run our farm. I've only got sisters.'

Claire glanced at the doctor.

'Give him the chloroform,' he instructed.

She stopped herself from remarking yet again on the absence of the more sophisticated equipment that they'd been promised, but the surgeon seemed to read her thoughts and gestured towards the bottle. 'You'll have to learn to be quick and deft with the chemical, Nurse . . .?'

'Nightingale, sir. Claire Nightingale.'

He smiled. 'Nurse Nightingale, eh? Most appropriate.' She'd heard it dozens of times since her training began at the Eugenie Nightingale School in London. 'Pretty. It suits you,' he said, less predictably. 'I'll need you to administer the anaesthetic daily from now on when I'm on duty, Nightingale. I'd feel more comfortable if one person I trust takes on the job and does it how I want it. All right?'

She nodded.

'Have you had much experience with anaesthetic in the colonies?'

'I actually did my training in London, sir.'

'Ah, very good. At St Thomas's, I presume?'

'That's right.' She paused, hoping he wouldn't refer to her surname again – an odd coincidence but nonetheless identical to the London hospital across from Westminster. 'And later at the Royal Hampshire County Hospital,' she added, watching him place a dressing across Billy's eye.

'I thought we had only Australian nurses on board.' He frowned, indicating for her to take over the bandaging.

'It's a long story,' she murmured, glancing at Rosie with a slight

9

shake of her head, who, though working alongside a different patient, was nearly touching shoulders with her and could easily join in this conversation. Claire didn't want her life story explained to the surgeon.

He shot her a puzzled glance but couldn't pursue it. Time was short and he began readying himself for the bigger, uglier task of his patient's arm. 'Now we'll fix up the rest,' he said kindly. 'I suspect we're going to be seeing a lot more head wounds today.'

'Why, sir?' Betty queried, keen to catch the surgeon's attention.

'These poor wretches don't seem to have tin helmets. The Australian army had better hurry up and supply their boys with some or there'll be plenty more eyes, ears, noses, jaws lost.'

Claire looked up anxiously from where she had helped Betty cut off Billy's shirt and isolate his arm. Her companion was drenching the left side of his body with iodine. 'But we're not equipped for anything reconstructive,' Claire warned.

He shook his head as though helpless. 'All we can do is patch them up and move them on, Nightingale. This boy will be sent to Cairo and then, I hope, to England where they'll be able to do a better job. If I thought that shoulder could wait, I would, but he's already had hours of filth and flies in that wound. See this?' He pointed and pressed where Claire saw a brownish-red swollen area. 'Press it,' he said to her, ignoring Betty.

Claire hesitated, not enjoying being singled out by him but intrigued by the chance to improve her skills.

'You've got to learn to recognise this. It's going to come in repeatedly and if my nurses can be my eyes around the ship, it will be an enormous help.'

She reached over with awkwardly gloved hands – the new advance – that made it impossible at times to make use of that all-important sensation of touch that she relied on. She pushed on Billy's blistered skin and felt a slight crackly sensation.

'Can you feel it . . . the gas?' the doctor continued. 'In these conditions it thrives. I'm guessing the triage team didn't consider him an emergency. Sadly, they've left him too long and the infection has got too much of a hold.'

Gangrene, Claire thought. No need to say it in front of Billy.

'He's becoming feverish, doctor,' Betty said.

He sighed. 'Another sign. And this infected area will enlarge rapidly. We really do need to get his arm off immediately.'

Claire turned away again, this time to drag over a small rolling table with surgical scalpels and knives. Behind her Billy groaned and began to beg in a soft slur that the doctor just 'fix up' his shoulder as best he could. Claire took a slow breath and reached for the brown bottle and mask.

'Your war will be over soon, Billy,' she murmured to reassure herself more than Private Martin, who was no longer listening.

———

Back on the ward, Claire drew her wrist across her forehead before vigilantly washing her hands once again. She moved towards a new patient, flicking away droplets of water and recalling how her long-fingered hands, with neat, oblong nails, had been the envy of the other girls in her year at St Catherine's in Sydney, which she'd attended briefly. She smiled wryly to herself now; today her hands were raw from the constant disinfectant and carbolic soap, whose sulphurous smell clung to the makeshift ward like an invisible overseer.

'Get some air,' she heard a voice say behind her.

She didn't have to look around to know who it was. 'I'll be fine, Matron.'

'That wasn't a suggestion, Nurse Nightingale,' the older woman said, eyeing her over tiny horn-rimmed glasses. 'Nurse Parsons has already been sent up for a break. It's time you took one too.'

Claire had come to respect their head nurse. On that first night, when they'd begun excitedly mobilising from their tented hospital onto the *Gascon*, she'd given her nurses a welcome with her most stern face on.

'. . . *and there's to be no fraternising with the ship's officers. The captain has requested that colonial nurses eat separately!*'

Matron, Claire had learned, only sounded like a stickler; she bent the rules constantly to make sure they helped as many wounded as they possibly could. Claire obeyed her senior and headed up the stairs. The sound of mortar shells and artillery got louder the higher she ascended. The smell of carbolic switched to cordite, and black smoke, like drifts of gloom from various explosions, hung above the tiny bay. She wondered when the captain of the *Gascon* ever imagined the officers and nurses might fraternise. There was barely time for anyone to scribble letters home. Developing romantic relationships was the last notion on anyone's minds right now, she was sure.

The scene above was worse than below. Walking wounded helped their fellow diggers stagger down the short beach that was now a chaotic casualty clearing station, swarming with soldiers and alarmed animals that intermittently escaped handlers or pens and were capable of hurting themselves and further injuring already hurting men. Wounded diggers took their chances under fire and in a raggle-taggle line made their way towards the shore, ignoring regimental medical officers, who were also undoubtedly finding proper assessment near impossible. Their ticketing system had clearly been abandoned. To Claire's knowledge none of the nursing team had viewed a priority red ticket recently; besides, near enough every soldier seemed to qualify for that category.

She massaged the muscles above her shoulderblade and arched her back to stretch out the soreness that nagged from shifting around prone men daily. Day, night, afternoon, evening . . . it was a seemingly interminable round of blood-soaked dressings and despair. Each time the *Gascon* sailed away with its hundreds of casualties Claire knew there were dozens of desperately hurt men left behind at the clearing station on the beach. Too many of them would die before the three-day turnaround gave them access again to full surgical help.

Even so, some evenings they'd sailed with seven hundred injured or sick, dropping off the least grave at Mudros before going on to Egypt – to Alexandria, where ambulances, quality facilities and specialist staff attended to the most seriously hurt men, who may then be transported to Cairo for even more sophisticated help.

Cairo! What a city. It was only weeks but it felt like a lifetime ago that she'd witnessed the enormous orb of sun sinking behind the Great Pyramid of Cheops. Claire recalled in vivid clarity how, in the diffused half-light of that golden-pink evening, she had allowed one of the turban-headed donkey boys to assist her onto the saddle of his patient beast before guiding her to the opulent Shepheard's Hotel. Sunset cocktails had been flowing and she could remember the frisson in the air of imminent departure for most of the men present. Even now Claire could stretch her thoughts and almost taste the cooling hum of infused fresh mint tea that she'd sipped on the terrace behind the wrought-iron balustrade overlooking the frenetic activity of Ibrahim Pasha Street. And if she reached for the happy memory far enough, she knew she could reconstruct the feel of the famous hotel's wicker armchairs pressing against her grey nursing uniform and hear the echoes of laughter bouncing off the stucco façade as she and Rosie were entertained by some officers from the 3rd Light Horse Regiment.

So handsome in their dress khakis, they were surely the smartest of all the Australian divisions with those tall boots and spiral strap leggings and spurs. One of the men had allowed her to try on his slouch hat, making sure it sat on her head in true, rakish light horsemen style. Three finger spaces above the left ear, two finger spaces above the left eye and a finger space above the right eye. 'There,' he'd said, having adjusted it perfectly, his tanned face stretching into an appreciative grin. 'Now despite the fact that you're a gorgeous blonde who is surely going to give men in the trenches unhelpful daydreams, you're now an honorary member.' Its ostentatious but nonetheless striking white emu plumage at the back had danced in the soft Cairo breeze of a mild night that teetered, in late April, with the promise of summer around the corner.

Though the hotel was built in Opera Square and on the pulse of the city's heartland, Claire had decided it was spiritually a world away from the ramshackle cluster of brothels, restaurants, cafés and cinemas that cluttered around it, luring soldiers with coin to spend and an itch to scratch. Despite all the warnings from their troop leaders about the dangers of fraternising with the local women of the Wazzir district – or 'Wozza', as the Aussies called it – she had noticed that the streets were thick with Australians, New Zealanders and British keen to escape into someone's arms – or fists – for a happy distraction.

She could picture the donkeys queued up kerbside, vying for space with fruit sellers or men who'd trained their monkeys to hop onto willing shoulders for an unusual photograph, which of course Rosie had to have to send home. Jugglers, card sharps, nut sellers, trick cyclists and gambling touts – even women selling themselves from balconies desperately tried to catch the attention of fit young men on leave with mainly one thing on their minds. That all felt like a century ago – a different world . . . another lifetime almost.

Matron arrived by her side and the aromatic memory of mint tea faded.

'Is there any triage occurring down there?' Claire asked, nodding at the beach.

'Think you could do better in that hell?'

'It wasn't a criticism, Matron. I'm sorry, I —'

'And mine wasn't a serious question. I feel as helpless as you do.'

Claire gave a sad smile. 'I would like to try, though.'

Matron blinked slowly. 'We don't put women ashore.'

'Think of me as another soldier. Better, think of me as an extension of you, Matron. I know you could make a difference down there and I also suspect you'd love to get a better idea of what's happening too.'

Matron's eyes smiled, although her mouth forbade the warmth to touch its tightly pinched line.

'Let me try,' Claire pleaded. 'We can actually ticket some of these men and organise their care better. Right now they're all taking matters into their own hands.'

'I am aware of that, Nightingale.'

'They're dying, Matron.'

Her supervisor sighed. 'They'll die here too.'

'Yes, but at least they'll die hearing a woman's voice speaking kindly to them. Most of those boys need a mother as much as the morphine. A tender touch can do a world of good to their state of mind.'

'You're as soft as you are daring, Nurse Nightingale. I hope you don't have to face the Western Front lines because that romantic soul of yours is going to be badly scarred.' Matron paused. 'What is it about you, Claire? I can tell you about each of my staff: why they became nurses, why they volunteered for a war zone, why they do what they do. Most of them had the calling or felt the need to be doing something meaningful with their lives. But you remain an enigma to me. I like you very much, you're a brilliant young nurse, but sometimes you strike me as a ghost.'

Claire laughed, puzzled. 'A ghost?'

'Indeed. You move among us sometimes as if invisible, not wanting to leave a mark.'

'Sometimes I do feel like that,' she admitted, further impressed by her elder's insight.

Matron smiled and her expression was filled with kind concern. 'Why would you ask to go ashore when you know it's so dangerous?'

She stared at Matron, slightly flustered. 'It's my job. Surely we —'

'No need to patronise me, Nurse Nightingale. I've got three decades on you and deserve honesty.'

Claire's shoulders slumped. 'I lost another patient this morning. He didn't even have stubble on his chin he was so young.'

'They're mostly heartbreakingly young. Why did this one make such an impression on you?'

She folded her arms in a protective gesture. 'His eyes reminded me of childhood summers in Cornwall with my father – happy times.' Claire sighed in memory. 'And then I saw his tag and it told me his surname was Cornish.' She shrugged apologetically. 'It was as though it was a message to me. I started to think about his mother.'

'Most unwise. Didn't we teach you that?'

'Easy to learn, hard to put into practice. And even more unwisely, his death got me thinking about my own family.'

'And?' Matron pressed.

'That the few people I love are no longer alive. And it occurred to me that should I die in some foreign land like young Cornish, it really wouldn't matter to anyone.' She watched Matron's expression turn fractionally exasperated as she opened her mouth to respond but Claire hurried on. 'No, it's true, Matron. There is no one hoping to hear from me. I move from place to place, belonging nowhere and to no one. The person I'm closest to is Rosie Parsons and I met Rosie six weeks ago. I'm twenty-five, Matron; don't you think it's odd that in a quarter of a century I have no one who might be touched in any way should I die?'

'Claire, how very bleak of you.'

She gave a sad smile. 'Sorry. But you did insist.'

Matron squeezed Claire's wrist with concern. 'And being adventurous soothes this mood?'

'No, but I am a logical choice for a dangerous task. The most I have to lose is my life, and as no one cares about it, I'll endanger it willingly if it saves another person who matters to someone.'

'And is this why you took up nursing, Claire? Did you go into this vocation simply so that you would have people to care for?'

'I . . . I don't know.' She hesitated, caught by the insightful sugges-tion that she suspected was true. 'More likely it's because of my father, whom I adored. We were a team; he used to say I was his favourite girl and that no woman would come between us.' She hesitated and then gave a rueful smile. 'Of course one did, but that's by the by. My father fought and survived the Boer War, then came to Australia, where I'd been sent to live with cousins because my mother had passed away when I was a child, and he died far too soon after his return from disease . . . but I believe more especially from a lack of good nursing. If we can get to these men faster —' Claire gestured across Anzac Cove, 'and perform triage with more expedience, maybe we can save them losing limbs or dying from injuries out there on foreign land.' She shrugged. 'It's about more professional nursing.'

'I see. You're a crusader,' Matron said, adding levity to her tone and a smile.

Claire shared it, glad to leave the dark years of her early teens behind. 'I'm happy to take that role,' she replied.

'Well, Claire, I want no heroics today. You are simply to help where you can in the brief period you'll have but essentially you are to observe and report.'

Claire's eyes widened. 'You're letting me go onto the beach?'

'I have a message to get to the medical officers from the sur-geons here. You can go with the messenger. Whatever you can achieve in the time there is up to you. But I do agree it will help if we get a nurse on the ground. Focus – I want valuable information coming back with you.'

Claire's smile shone as brightly as her gaze. 'Thank you, Matron.' She turned to fetch some supplies.

'Nurse Nightingale.' Claire spun back as a roar from the nearby HMS *London* signalled the unleashing of some firepower. 'This is a very dangerous business, you know. I'm breaking orders but only because you've broken my heart a little with your romantic notion of nursing. What you need is some real romance.'

Claire grinned. 'Well, I doubt I'm going to find it here, Matron.'

2

Jamie made a silent promise that he would never complain about flies again. They had been annoying during the swearing-in parade of the 9th Regiment of the Australian Light Horse at Morphetville, on the outskirts of Adelaide city, but nothing like Turkey.

A lone sniper bullet cracked uselessly above him and a fleck chose that moment to target his eye. 'Bugger,' he muttered, rubbing at the grit that instantly felt like a rock beneath his eyelid. The thorny scrub had become so dry over the last few weeks it was now brittle. He blinked rapidly, hoping his tears would loosen the annoying mote, and reflected that despite the sniper fire it was a relatively quiet day, given the carnage of the previous week. He was leaning back against the parados of the trench and unless a mortar came straight at him he considered himself relatively safe for breakfast. It was odd how mortar coming from the left or the right could be pinpointed, but if it was like an arrow coming at you, then *you* were its breakfast. He found this twist on the thought darkly comic and smiled privately.

He peered into the tin of jam he'd opened minutes earlier and his amusement died. 'I can't even tell what fruit's in this,' he lamented, staring at what had got to his treat before him.

'It's all good, mate,' his neighbour said, reaching over to dig his spoon in where a horde of flies had gathered so thick that the pressure pushed at least a dozen of them into the thick, sticky conserve.

His companion sucked the spoon clean with an appreciative sigh. 'There you go, mate. Fuckin' apricot,' he confirmed, grinning as he swallowed the glob. Jamie noticed that Swampy didn't seem to care that flies were in his eyes or that they were sucking at his sweat on his receding hairline. He'd bounced back from his bout of dysentery too; Swampy just accepted. He was probably the perfect recruit. Never complained, mostly cheerful, and always ready to bait his fellow digger and amuse those around him.

Why had they thought Johnny Turk would be a pushover? They'd just assumed they'd be an untrained rabble of shepherds or farmers, and certainly not as well equipped as the ANZACs. What had meant to be a triumphant, surprise attack had been resisted brilliantly and forcefully. Now both sides had worn each other down into a stalemate of trench warfare and neither Turk nor ANZAC could dislodge the other.

The greater challenge was surviving the despicable conditions of heat, illness, insects, poor hygiene, lack of water and food . . . and rapidly diminishing ammunition.

They had sailed from Port Melbourne in February, arriving into Egypt mid-March, where it was soon agreed that being a mounted division made them unsuitable for the push for the Dardanelles. But the decision was made to leave the horses in Egypt and deploy to Gallipoli, only arriving this month to hear the horror stories of the amphibious landings the previous month and the heroics that ensued.

'Stretcher-bearer told me the figure's now knockin' forty thousand,' Swampy remarked, rolling a thin cigarette. He licked the paper with a dry tongue through cracked lips that he stuck his smoke to and then lit. The nickname Swampy truly suited him. Jamie had gathered that he'd been a vagrant at the time of his recruitment but somewhere in his past he'd been a brilliant horseman. Jamie had stopped wondering what had gone wrong in

Swampy's life. He was happy that he was among them and no longer offended by his poor manners.

'You're lying.'

Swampy shrugged and scratched his lice-riddled chest. 'It's what I was told, mate.'

'I don't believe it,' Jamie said, but he was the one lying. He did believe it. The Turkish counterattacks had decimated entire divisions of the ANZACs but the Turks had paid a terrible price as well. The seemingly endless skirmishes took lives on both sides daily, as did the sniper fire. Just yesterday they'd lost one of their favourites, a popular 36-year-old called Archie Cammelle. Everyone pronounced his last name 'Camel', so it was only a short leap to call him Humpy. It was Spud, Jamie's closest mate, who'd found Humpy, dead on the latrines; a lucky sniper's bullet had caught him clean through the temple and he'd simply sagged where he'd sat on the timber boards, which barely covered and certainly didn't mask the foul reek of the drop hole.

Spud returned from that very place now, dragging with him a terrible whiff of the latrines. 'I just took a crap with the lieutenant,' Spud said, sounding chuffed.

Jamie laughed. Spud was reliably amusing without trying.

'What's funny?' Spud should never have told Jamie that his mother reckoned he looked like a potato when he was born. In fact, everything about Harry Primrose was entertaining – from his surname for such a block of a man, to his nickname because he did look a bit like a potato (a King Edward, Jamie thought), to his pale skin and the pink splotches that were erupting in this warmer weather, to his deadpan expression that was the key to his accidental comedy. 'Bloody bugs,' he said, not waiting for Jamie's answer and scratching his crotch. 'I think I'll just pour petrol over my dick.'

The men chuckled and chimed in with a few other ripe suggestions for what Spud might also try. His friend sat down, leaned back against the wall alongside Jamie, his vast size-thirteen boots looking like a pair of laced twin monoliths soaring up from the duckboard floor of the trench. Jamie was half as tall as their twelve-foot high trench; Spud probably stood six inches shorter than Jamie but his stocky frame was muscular. 'Years of being a shearer,' Spud had boasted as he'd flexed his biceps when they'd met on Christmas Eve while clearing out the stables at their training barracks.

'Not going home?' Spud had opened the conversation.

'I'm happy to tend the horses. Someone has to.' He grinned. 'How about you?'

His shorter, barrel-chested companion had offered a hand. 'Harry Primrose. You're a bit dedicated, mate, aren't you? I volunteered to stay because they've ordered extra rations of food and beer for the boys left behind.' He winked. 'What's your name, then?'

'James Wren.' He lifted a shoulder with embarrassment. 'My family calls me Jamie.'

'Where's home?'

'A place called Farina in the Flinders Ranges.'

'Ah, right. Got a girl?'

He caught his breath at the unexpected query. 'Er, sort of, well . . . not really.'

Spud looked at him with quizzical amusement.

'No. I did.' He hesitated. 'But I don't want any girl waiting for me.'

'Does she understand?'

'I'm not thinking about all that right now. I don't know what I feel other than I wasn't ready to put any sort of ring on her finger. I just want to do my country proud.'

'Stupid bugger. Don't you know that every fella needs a girl dreaming about him when he goes off to war? And who are you going to dream of? Your granny?' Spud chortled. 'Come on, Heartthrob. Let's at least make these girls happy with us,' he said, cocking his head towards the horses.

It had been a wet Christmas Day and the camp had turned into a mud pool; the humid conditions of New South Wales were an unpleasant contrast to the dry summer of the Flinders Ranges. They discovered they were both South Australians and footy lovers and shared a loathing of each other's clubs. It's all they needed in common to become best mates. Jamie had started calling his new pal by an appropriate nickname and Spud had done the same for him, although Jamie could wish his was anything but the one Spud had given him.

Spud was talking footy now, he realised. '. . . didn't lose a single match last year, Heartthrob, just you remember that. And then you make sure you recall last year's Grand Final when your blokes gave it up like the ladies they are.' Before Jamie could respond, his friend had added, 'Champions of Australia, mate.'

Jamie sighed. 'Guess there's no one to play in any matches this year,' he noted, offering Spud the jam that his mum had sent in a parcel.

Spud pulled a spoon out of his pocket and dug it into the tin, then smeared jam onto a half slice of stale bread that he produced from another pocket. 'They may play this year but I reckon they'll have to suspend the comp after it.' He bit into his breakfast, speaking as he chewed. 'There'll be no teams, no crowd – we'll all be dead.'

'Don't be morbid, Spud. I plan to survive.'

'You will, Heartthrob. Not me. I've been unlucky all my life.' He didn't sound bitter. 'These bastard flies,' he spat. 'I'm eating them now.'

'It's all these corpses. We've got to do something about it.'

'I am,' Spud said. 'I've made a bet with Swampy. You know Johnny Turk on that bush, whose face is turned our way?'

Jamie blinked.

'Well, I reckon he'll be purple by tomorrow but Swampy

reckons it's a couple of days yet. I've got my last bit of tobacco riding on that one. Knackers is happy to lay down his new fruit cake from home that he'll be black in four days.'

It was a macabre pastime but the gallows humour helped to not only pass the hours between surviving to another dawn, but keep the fear of death or terrible injury away . . . and the increasing thirst. It wasn't the pathetic lack of food that got the men down so much as the spartan supply of water. Jamie was sure that if you offered the men a dixie of fresh water to a loaf of bread or pot of boiled potatoes, they'd take the water each time. But the water had to be sailed in, hauled up the cliffs in carts and then hand-carried in pots by soldiers, dodging machine-gun strafing and sniper bullets. He began to wonder how they were ever going to manage when the summer really kicked in. The worst months beckoned; dysentery was rife and surely going to get worse. Poor Kenny Pidgeon was sleeping by the latrines, his running belly was so bad. He'd lost perhaps two stone already and was too weak to make the journey over the ravines to the medical officer. Jamie had shared his water rations with the ailing man yesterday. Spud hadn't approved, giving him a lecture that every man must take care of himself first. Jamie didn't bother arguing that he'd been raised differently. If Kenny didn't improve over the course of today, he was going to carry the sick man to the medical tent on the beach.

He pointed towards no-man's-land. 'Those bodies are going to make us all sick. It's why the flies are so thick.'

'There's talk of clearing them,' Spud shrugged.

'Really?'

'Yeah, I heard about it during my crap. They're hoping to organise some sort of truce. The lieutenant called it, um, an armistice. Guess we'll hear about that soon enough. Is it time yet?'

Jamie glanced at his pocket watch. 'Few more minutes,' he said, in no hurry to go on sniper duty.

'Enough time for another cuppa if one's going,' Spud said.

As his friend left, Jamie nodded and carefully returned his father's watch to the safety of a pocket. The old man had given it to him when they'd driven their horse and cart to Quorn in the mid-north of South Australia and the railway line that would take him into Adelaide. They'd had to overnight at the large Transcontinental Hotel across from the station and Jamie recalled the packed public bar, brimful of laughing young men, all of them heading in the same direction as him, most of them standing with male members of their family. It had felt strange to be alone with his father amidst the laughter and jollity and he was unsure of what to say. His father sipped his drink quietly, standing at the furthest end of the bar, neatly licking the creamy froth of the cold beer from his lips.

'You'll be all right, won't you, Dad?'

'We'll be fine,' he answered in his usual dry tone. 'You go do your duty. You can pick right up where you left off. Fencing repairs never end, as you well know.'

Jamie nodded, sipped his beer mournfully, wishing he could share in the fun of the others around him or drag a smile from his father . . . some show of emotion.

'How was your young lady?'

Jamie looked up, surprised by the question. 'Oh, you know, she likes the idea that I'm going to be in a Light Horse Regiment but she's not happy about having to wait.' He gave a single shoulder shrug. 'I mean about getting engaged. She isn't fussed about the ring yet, but says she wants to tell everyone that we are planning to get married.'

'Does she make you happy?'

Jamie hesitated. This was a most unusual conversation to be having with his father.

'Does she make you laugh?' his father continued. 'Do you think about her when you should be thinking about your tasks? Does the sun remind you of her smile, the wheat fields of her hair?' He poked Jamie's chest lightly. 'Does it hurt in here when you are apart?'

He met his father's hard stare and knew it was a moment for honesty and still he couldn't give it. 'I don't know.'

William Wren's mouth twitched, the vaguest of smiles beneath his bushy moustache. 'No need to rush in then, son. How did you leave it?'

'I said it was best to wait until the war was over. See how we both feel.'

His elder nodded. 'You'll have seen plenty by then and no doubt be changed by it. You'll know yourself a lot better.'

His father's remark sounded cryptic but he was clearly speaking from experience, having served in the Boer War. Jamie had let the comment sit between them until his father's beer glass was empty. He drained his own.

'Right,' Wren senior said, glancing at his pocket watch that Jamie never saw him without, except when he pulled on a nightshirt and turned in and then it sat at his bedside, ticking away the hours to 5 a.m. when his father habitually rose to beat the worst heat of the day. 'We might as well go to the platform. The train is about ten minutes away.'

It was as though their movement towards the pub's door was infectious because a stream of men began to flow behind them in the direction of the weatherboard station and its platform. Women in their Sunday best long dresses and broad-brimmed hats were standing beneath the shade of the huge Moreton Bay fig in the forecourt, more out of habit than need, for it was not a hot day. He could hear an occasional soft sigh of laughter but mainly the women were subdued.

He'd followed his father around onto the platform, checking he had his ticket, which they'd bought the previous evening, safely stashed in his pocket. People gathered beneath the verandah awning and he could hear last snatches of advice from fathers to sons, while the womenfolk predictably began to drag out handkerchiefs. His mother had offered to make the journey to Quorn but Jamie had preferred to enjoy a final family meal in the home he'd been born in and to remember his tall, slim mother in her apron, near the stove, forever producing delicious food from her range for her five hungry men.

It had been backslaps and fierce handshaking from his elder brothers, who made jokes about the French women who were going to fall in love with him, reminding him to keep score of the hearts he broke and the Germans he killed. He'd ruffled his youngest brother's hair before going out on the verandah to watch him ride off to school, his dog Bingo chasing after him, barking.

Finally it was just him and his mum. They'd stood by the large, scrubbed pine table in their kitchen. After the activity of a noisy breakfast, all he could remember hearing in that wrenching moment of farewell was the solid tick of the clock above the mantelpiece surrounding the Metters wood stove; the clock seemed to be marking time with his heartbeat as he reached for his slouch hat, signalling it was time to leave. His mother had wiped her hands nervously on her apron as he stepped forward to hug her. She had accepted his squeezing embrace, hung on to him far longer than she normally would when saying goodbye, and when his mother finally let him go she had reached out to caress his face. He couldn't remember the last time she'd been so openly affectionate, but her large brown eyes were damp and he realised she was smiling with an effort.

'Now you take care of yourself, Jamie Wren. And you come home to us?'

He nodded, swallowing away the sudden claustrophobic sensation in his throat.

'I need you to promise me,' she insisted.

'I promise, Mum. I'll come home.'

27

'Not in a box, mind. It will be all my birthday gifts for the rest of my life to see you walk through that door.' Laura Wren had stepped back then, her hands gripping his arms that were slack either side of his broad chest. She nodded, as though fixing a final image of him in her mind as she shifted a swatch of his mid-brown hair to get a better look at his eyes, which she'd said on occasion reminded her of unshelled macadamias, the delicious nuts that she'd only eaten once but had never forgotten, their richness encased in burnished green-brown shells. 'You're a good boy, Jamie. Don't fall for some French girl, either. We need you here.'

Curiously, saying goodbye to the one border collie not working this morning was the hardest farewell of all for Jamie. She leapt up from where she'd been waiting patiently since breakfast, and gave him her special grin, mouth open, tongue lolling, tail thumping the boards. He'd won her as a pup at the local tombola night three years earlier. William Wren had said if he was going to bring home another mouth to feed, he'd better make her earn her keep and so Jamie had been given the task of training the fluffy black-and-white pup that simply wanted to chew everything or sleep. She was so small he called her Pipsqueak. Years on she had become a valuable working dog, one of their best, but from today she'd have to get used to his brothers issuing her commands. Her expressive, chocolatey eyes suggested that she already knew.

'I'll be gone a while, Pippy.' She panted her understanding and stroked a paw across his bended knee. He took it, gave her a scratch beneath her chin and then leaned to kiss her head, glad his father wasn't around to see it. 'Look after them all, Pippy, and watch out for those snakes in the tall grass, all right?'

He'd got lost in his memory of farewell and it was his father being hailed by another man that dragged him back to the present. William Wren was shaking hands and nodding at Jamie. His companion cocked a thumb over a shoulder to where another young man was kicking at a stone, among a group of women. Jamie didn't want to talk to anyone or be introduced. He suspected his father had already guessed this.

He let his gaze be drawn to the north where his family lived and stared at the tracks that ran across the dry, rusted earth and tricked his eye into believing they met at the base of the range, purple in the distance with highlights of gold slashes. It was as though a careless painter had daubed odd splotches of yellow paint and yet he knew those he loved were beyond that rise of craggy hills where the scudding drifts of frothy clouds seemed to part right where his family's property was. A small misshapen oblong of piercing blue sky opened right above where he pictured the homestead, Bingo probably barking at a sleepy lizard from his vantage on the wide, shady verandah.

He heard his father clear his throat and blinked away from his sentimental thoughts. The other fellow had drifted away and William Wren was pushing something into Jamie's hands.

'You'll need this,' he said brusquely.

Jamie had stared at it, confused. 'Won't you?'

His father had shaken his head. 'I can tell the time from the sun.'

'So can I.'

'Not to the minute and you're going to need this to make sure you keep good time for when you're on duty.'

'Dad, it's precious. Too —'

'I won it playing cards.'

Jamie remembered now how shocked he'd been to hear this. 'I thought . . .'

'Yeah, well, you know what Thought did, son. It's not mine. Originally belonged to a fellow called Bailey. He was a good man, useless at cards, though, and best he lost to me because I was his mate during the war. I always intended to give it back but he took a bullet to the belly from an Afrikaner musket.' Jamie remembered how his father's voice had taken on an uncharacteristically wistful tone.

Jamie weighted the silver watch in his hand now, recalling how it had felt then on the station platform, with the pressure of his father's hand on top of it. 'It kept me safe and now it's going to keep you safe and bring you home to your mother. She knows you have to go, son, but it doesn't make it any easier for her.'

'How about you, Dad?' he'd found the courage to ask as the train wheezed into the station and everybody seemed to move at once.

'I'll be fine. Your brothers can manage.'

'I didn't mean that. I meant —'

'I know what you meant,' his father interrupted in a gruff voice, fixing him with a stare. In that pause Jamie understood that even this conversation was hard for him and about as close as Jamie might ever get to revealing William Wren's closely guarded emotions. 'Take the watch. Keep your head down. I know you'll make the Wren name count for something over there.'

Whistles had blown and doors had begun slamming closed. His father hadn't hugged him, but he'd shaken his hand tightly and hadn't let go quickly, William's lips thin and working hard to keep all words contained behind them. Jamie had turned and felt his father squeeze his neck gently in the way he used to when Jamie had been a boy. The affection in that heartbeat had been unmistakable.

'OP time, mate,' Spud said, kicking his boot and dragging him fully into the present. 'When you write next, tell your mum I love her jam.'

All the men took regular turns at the observation post at the parapet. Their only defence was sandbags at the lip and the Turks had the high ground, so periscopes were their only way of assessing the enemy camp.

'Come on, let's head to the shooting step. See if we can't catch us a couple of Turks.'

Jamie buttoned the watch away and with it his memories as he fell in step. Swampy and Dickie Jones pushed in front of Spud.

'Hey!' Spud said, shoving Swampy.

'Let them go. Age before beauty, eh?' Jamie mocked.

'Beauty was a horse, mate,' Jones chortled.

'Oh, so you *can* read, Jones? That's a surprise,' Jamie remarked.

Just then a bullet cracked into the sandbags above Spud. 'I swear they can see me,' he growled.

Impossible though it seemed to Jamie, the smell of decaying corpses was even worse here than further back in the trench they'd just navigated. The zigzag design hadn't made sense at first but it soon became evident that if the Turks did overwhelm one end of the trench, the enemy couldn't see past more than a few feet.

These tiny salients, jutting out into no-man's-land, cut so close at times to the enemy trench that they could hear the Turks talking. He'd heard rumours that in other places the trenches were close enough to touch a Turk's head. It made no sense if you could shake hands with your enemy. Was there any point to this war? One fellow from the opposing trench, with some sort of penny whistle, was beginning to play his instrument alongside Jamie's harmonica most evenings. It made beautiful, haunting music and the pipe's mellow timbre complemented Jamie's melodies; its owner was clearly adept, weaving lovely notes and trills around the mouth organ's slow, sad meanderings.

'Play us a jolly tune,' Swampy was always asking but Jamie didn't seem inclined. It didn't feel right to him, given how many dead lay all around them. But the Turkish piper and he understood one another, and their combined breath wove songs of regret and sorrow that did feel right on behalf of the fallen.

Jamie watched Dickie Jones take a trench-fashioned periscope, which comprised a broken piece of shaving mirror attached to a length of timber, and gingerly position it just above the parapet. Swampy meanwhile took position on the fire step with the trench's single periscope rifle and began sighting through it. Spud was standing right below them, giving Swampy a bit of a baiting.

Jamie tuned out and began to wonder if his father secretly worried about his middle son's safety. Maybe his mother had been right all along that his father loved his sons as much as she did. *He just doesn't know how to show it to you boys*, she'd said on several occasions.

Jamie heard the sound of the shell arriving but barely had a couple of seconds to register that Spud and the others couldn't. In that heartbeat of realisation, death arrived laughing at them. The explosion rocked the land around them like the jellies his mother used to unmould on his summertime birthday in February, arriving quivering to the table in a rainbow of colours that were now echoed in his dazed vision. His sight cleared into the stunned silence that followed the explosion before sound too gradually filtered back and so did his wits.

He was buried to his shoulders and most of this end of the trench, where they'd been joshing just seconds earlier, had entirely collapsed. He could taste the sand from the bags, spitting and coughing, and as he blinked away the initial stupor he realised he was staring straight at the sightless eyes of Swampy. He could see his mother's apricot jam still clinging to the side of Swampy's slack mouth, except his body was no longer attached at the shoulders. Meanwhile the slumped form of Dickie Jones, still holding his periscope, was in the near distance.

Spud was nowhere to be seen.

Jamie half ran, half staggered. The other two were dead and there was no time to mourn them because Spud was alive but badly injured; he needed to get his friend down to the beach and onto that hospital ship.

'Spud?'

'Yeah,' he croaked from where he was slumped across Jamie's back.

'How are you?'

'How d'ya reckon, ya mug? I'm just bonzer! Let's go dancing later.'

Beneath the weight of Spud and his private escalating fear, Jamie still laughed. 'Well, you feel like a whole sack of potatoes right now.'

It was Spud's turn to chuckle but it sounded dry and sad. 'Oh, mate, this is bad. I can't feel anything. Did my legs get blown off?' he groaned.

'You're all there, Spud. Just hold on.'

Sniper fire began to crack nearby as they became the new sport for the Turkish trenches.

'Ah, bugger! I know you're using me as cover. Shoot the short bloke first,' Spud accused in a weak groan.

Jamie bent his knees to lower Spud beneath an overhang for a few moments of respite. He was panting but could tell Spud was breathing with a struggle.

'Spud?'

His friend gave a grunt. 'What?'

'Are you dead yet?'

They both began to laugh . . . the sort of out-of-control laughter like children have at someone who just made a farting sound. It felt good to release the tension but it cost them both. Jamie was aware that other soldiers, clambering up with water or supplies, were crouched in crags and gullies around them, also avoiding the sniper bullets and staring at the lunatic spluttering, bleeding duo, but he knew if he didn't laugh with Spud right now, he might just sit back and cry.

'We're going to the field hospital, Spud, and I'm getting you on that hospital ship. All right, mate? No more talking. I need my strength to get to the bottom and not fall or get shot in the process. You need yours to stay alive. Ready?'

'Heartthrob?'

'Yes?' Jamie could hear his friend's seriously laboured breathing now.

'Tell Mum it was me who broke her granny's vase all those years ago, not Eddie, and that I'm sorry.'

Jamie paused, the muscles in his thighs complaining loudly beneath the weight; he was grateful for his rigorous training with the Light Horse Brigade, which had taught him to push through the burn of muscles and to keep moving at all cost. 'You tell her, Spud, when you get home. Now, be quiet. Save your energy. Ready?'

Spud didn't answer and Jamie didn't wait for his approval. He pushed off, moving as quickly as his burden and the terrain would permit, not a thought in his head – it was like a white light had flooded his mind; a searing white of emptiness with only the burn from his body begging to unload the cargo, and a distant voice that only he could hear now bleeding into that space with urgings to look at his boots. Concentrate on each footfall and the potential traps beneath. Time, space, his whole life distilled to where he would place his next stride – left, right, straight ahead? Watch that crevice, look out for that bush, don't get too close to the edge, stay close to the edge, follow the main ravine down to Anzac Cove. He couldn't see the beach from here, especially from his crouched stance, but he knew it was there, knew how to reach it. *You've done this descent enough times!* Suddenly his inner voice sounded like his father. *You fetch water every other day from the beaches. It's no different. Zigzag, Jamie!* His father yelled as a sniper found his range and a rifle cracked on the heights and its bullet whizzed at him, ripping through his uniform, and he felt the sting of it against his calf. He'd been grazed. Lucky. *Control is everything*, his father used to say when teaching him to ride, even though Jamie had been eager to gallop. *Take her one step at a time.*

He wouldn't fall, he wouldn't trip, he wouldn't give up . . . he wouldn't let his mate down. He thought of Pippy and how tirelessly she worked because he asked her to. It didn't matter how hot the sun blazed, or how many hours they were in the field, Pippy wouldn't stop because Jamie needed her. And Jamie wouldn't stop now because Spud needed him and no Johnny Turk was going to have the chance to shoot him in the back. He thought of the music he played most nights with his enemy and wondered if that soldier was shooting at him right now.

His thoughts were roaming. *Stay focused.* 'Spud?'

Nothing.

'Spud!'

'It's your shout,' Spud mumbled and Jamie helplessly began to leak tears around his grim smile.

'Hang in there, Harry,' he whispered, more for himself as he encountered a familiar nullah he had negotiated so many times previously. 'We're halfway, mate.'

3

The noise of shelling and rapid gunfire this close was disorienting as well as terrifying. Claire was momentarily paralysed the moment she set foot on the beach, as though her feet had taken root. The smell of tar and wet timbers of the hastily erected jetties broke through the familiar aroma of smoke that permeated the hospital ship. The soft late spring breeze brought the earthy whiff of animal dung and, curiously, soap. She blinked at the men who were laughing and bathing in the water, some drying themselves with their shirts and others racing each other down to the water as though they were at the seaside.

The scene around her was surreal. Groans from the wounded and dying mingled with the braying of mules and voices of joshing soldiers, while a dislocated man's voice on a megaphone barked orders that she presumed someone was following. In the distance and over the last few minutes the shelling had suddenly gone quiet and all she could now hear was the soft, infrequent crack of gunfire. She could swear a bird was singing somewhere too. It was like hell's version of a holiday resort. And cheese . . . why could she smell cheese?

A Turkish shell obligingly landed thirty yards from where she stood, exploding in the water to snap her from her stupor. The shock of watching explosive, unexpected death arrive so callously made Claire gasp with horror.

Her guide, Gupta, who was clearly used to these scenes, pleaded with a frantic gaze at her. 'Please, madam,' he urged, his head shaking in that Indian way. 'Please,' he repeated, herding her off the makeshift jetty towards the cliff face and its relative protection to the shamble of tiny awnings that she gathered were serving as the field dressing and clearing station. Claire quickly gathered her wits.

'I'll be fine. Gupta, get help for those men in the water; one may bleed to death if he's not taken onto the ship immediately.'

'I have to —'.

'I know. But him first. Promise me, or I'll go and get him myself.'

'I promise, madam. I'll go now.'

Looking around, Claire could see it was a shambles. She'd already calculated that there was seemingly nobody in overall command of the embarkation of wounded men at the jetty, which now explained the increasingly steady stream of the walking wounded making their own way onto the hospital ship. Others, less mobile, waited – bleeding, dying – to be ferried out to the transport ships that were also anchored offshore and each evening would make the sailing back to Mudros and then on to Egypt. These ships were rapidly earning the nickname of deathships because there was no medical officer on board, no nurse, and no medical supplies, despite the pledges. Reports were that many were dying from infection or hemorrhaging on the voyage. It all felt so hopeless.

There was no sign of the medical officer when Claire finally arrived into the thick of suffering at the base of the cliff and knelt immediately in the sand to gauge the situation of the wounded man nearest her. Half of his jaw looked to have disappeared, blown away by shrapnel. At the sight of her, a single tear leaked from the man's eye, snaking into his hairline. She nodded and smiled to cover the misting in her eyes. A weeping nurse helped no one. She checked his identification disc.

Charles, she read. 'Charlie?' she guessed and he nodded awkwardly. 'I'm Nurse Nightingale. I'm going to help with that pain and then I'm getting you onto the hospital ship. All right?' He nodded again, wearily, as though just her words of intent brought the relief he needed.

Claire quickly assembled her syringe, pulled out a vial of morphine and within moments Charlie Packer floated away to a new place in his mind where there were no bombs or blood, hunger or thirst. She caught the attention of a stretcher-bearer. He ran up. She scribbled a note, glad she'd had the forethought to pack these few items, detailing what had been administered, and pinned it to Charlie's chest. She'd have to tell Matron that they needed safety pins, pencils and cards down here so adequate triage could be organised; they also needed someone on the jetty making sure the most urgent cases were loaded first. 'This man needs immediate attention.' The bearer nodded and yelled to a companion in a language she didn't understand. 'He'll need to go straight to theatre,' she insisted.

Claire looked around and felt the weight of fear press on her chest as there were dozens of men lying on the sand in equal need of attention. She blanked out everything around her except the man she was working on and became lost in her work and rapidly began to marshall anyone within shouting distance for help. Men on rest hours, surprised, horrified, perhaps even vaguely delighted to see a woman in their midst, came to her aid and cheerfully carried out her orders.

Claire inwardly rejoiced at the feeling of being in control at last – not of people, but finally of her situation. It felt uplifting to be in command, achieving, giving directions and not hovering in a mire of despair as it often felt on board. Claire experienced her sense of purpose returning and knew her presence, no matter how short, was going to make a difference and ultimately save some lives today.

Within a short time she was known as Nurse Claire, even caught herself laughing with a couple of the less gravely injured who assisted her with writing out notes, pinning them to men and then helping with forming the queue to the jetty in order of urgency.

'You can hold on, can't you, Johnno?'

'For you, Nurse Claire, I could fly to the moon.'

She smiled. 'Your shoulder's dislocated. I can put it back in, but —'

'I'll be right,' Johnno said. 'Just light my smoke first. You can see to me later.'

Claire lost track of time and patients but it felt like only moments had passed before a senior officer tapped her on the shoulder.

'Nurse Nightingale?'

'Er, yes?' She stood from where she'd been kneeling to dress a shocking burn to a man's face. As she straightened, she felt the tightness in her back complain; it had probably been protesting all morning. The smell of burnt flesh was still cloying. The young soldier would be maimed for life but he would live to see his girlfriend in Bathurst.

The officer frowned at her. 'Thank you.' It sounded heartfelt but uncertain. 'But you shouldn't be here. It's too dangerous. I'm . . . confused.'

'Claire,' she said, wiping her hand and offering to shake his.

He did so. 'You're doing triage?'

'I tagged along with the messenger. I know this breaks the rules but Matron wanted to get a proper sense of what's happening here on the beach and how we might help streamline things for you. I volunteered.'

'Happening? Chaos, death, destruction . . . lunacy. I don't think our generals can keep the death toll secret any longer. I won't let them. What's happening here is beyond all reasoning. I wonder if they'd send their sons.'

She nodded. 'Matron forbids us to think like that.'

He blew out a long sigh. 'I'm sorry I wasn't here – I was getting a message out to the *Queen Elizabeth* about this hellhole but I'm afraid their focus is squarely on gaining ground. The evacuation procedure is wildly insufficient, to say the least. Hundreds of men are dying that we could likely save if the system were better, but of course you can see that for yourself.' He shrugged an apology. 'Thank you for coming. Your presence alone will make a huge difference.'

'Better get back to it,' she said, bending down to tend to a soldier.

Another bullet snapped a small branch from a scrubby bush to his right. Ten more steps and he'd be out of range. Impossibly, he began to run. He had handed himself over to instinct and the tiny corner in his mind that was pure animal took over. With a guttural roar, he ignored the crush in his chest as his ribs were compressed by Spud's dead weight and he was charging, feinting left, then right, even jumping once over a furrow. No matter what, he pushed on. He was out of firing range, but didn't want to think about whether Spud had been hit. Droplets of sweat stung his eyes and he tasted the salt leaking onto his lips. Almost there. *Push!* his father urged from far away. *Keep your head down, stay safe, come home. Not in a box, mind.* Echoes of the Flinders crowded in on his empty headspace. The sound of magpies warbling to each other; Pippy barking joyously, simply because she was alive; colours brighter, deeper, richer than he could describe gathered in a rainbow to remind him of home – purples, yellows, reds and endless blue. He would see it all again. He would kiss the ground at Farina one day.

The numbness that had reached down his arm mocked him. Where was that coming from? Had he been hurt? That's right, his shoulder. Don't reach my legs, he pleaded. Let me get to the beach, then you can take all of me.

He could no longer feel anything on his left side, although his legs mercifully kept moving by instinct, but now his vision was blurring and surely tricking him. That couldn't be a woman on the beach – he had to be hallucinating. No, it was surely an angel.

Was that sand beneath him? Was that the shore? Gunfire had faded, he could hear no more artillery but his senses had narrowed entirely to the sketchy, blurry vision of an angel in the midst of the carnage.

Perhaps they had both died? Was heaven collecting them? His legs finally crumpled and he sagged, Spud rolling off his back as the angelic figure noticed him.

———————

Claire realised she didn't even know the officer's name and was about to ask when she suddenly saw behind him a lurching figure with a face entirely covered by a crusted layer of blood and dirt. He was staggering towards the tent. Looking in far worse shape, however, was the soldier he had somehow balanced across his back. Their gazes met as his knees buckled and the wounded soldier toppled off into the sand. Claire rushed towards them.

'Help me, please,' Jamie begged before he collapsed. It took a few moments before he found his voice again, shaking his dark head as if to clear a muddled mind. 'We were buried. He's badly wounded but he was conscious not long ago,' he rasped.

Claire and the medical officer dragged the fallen man closer to the casualty station.

'Are you hurt?' Claire asked, moving back to speak with the heroic carrier.

He ignored the question, eyes riveted on his friend. 'They all said he was a goner. I don't want to believe that, not Spud.'

She shielded her eyes and looked up the escarpment of unforgiving terrain. This soldier had somehow carried a man twice his own weight downhill over the most treacherous landscape in heat, all the while being shot at . . . She licked her lips, feeling her own thirst, unable to imagine how lightheaded he must be feeling. 'What's your name?'

'Jamie Wren.'

She smiled sadly at him. 'Claire Nightingale. You're very brave.'

He looked at her now and his broken expression beneath the dirt on his face touched her. 'He's my best mate.'

Claire nodded. 'The doctor's with him. Wait here.'

Jamie didn't wait, though. He struggled to his feet, shambling behind her. Claire peered into the tent. 'Do we have any water for this man, please?'

No one reacted. She glanced at the doctor's water canister at his hip and undid it. 'Forgive me – this man needs a sip to recover.' She handed it to Wren. He glanced at the doctor who nodded and only then he accepted it.

'Thank you, sir.'

As he reached for it she saw him wince and knew he was hurt.

'Is he dead?' he asked as he handed her back the can, wiping his mouth with his sleeve, heedless of the blood on his hands.

Claire's concerns deepened.

'No,' the doctor replied. 'But close enough, son.'

Claire watched her soldier's expression remain unchanged but within the darkest of warm brown-green eyes she saw the flicker of hope dashed.

She imagined the power brokers on the ship staring at maps from some safe vantage and making decisions – poor decisions – with young men's lives. If they were here – if they could see it, experience it for themselves – they'd surely evacuate all these men, her inner voice raged.

A groan from their patient captured their attention. The doctor looked at Claire and shook his head slightly over the top of Wren's bent head as he leaned over his mate. The doctor stood, moved away quietly to someone whose life he had a better chance of preserving. Claire knew she should do the same.

'Hey, Spud, you silly bugger. You caught one.'

'Yeah. Caught but not out, mate.'

'No, not out, Spud.'

She tuned out to the desperately sad conversation and stepped away with the doctor.

'Not worth taking him on board?' she whispered.

'He'll be gone before you reach the jetty.'

She took a deep breath, saw Gupta arriving and turned back to touch Wren's shoulder. 'I must go, but —'

'Just a moment longer? I don't want to do this alone.'

There was something so heartbreakingly touching about the plea that Claire had nodded before she could censor herself. 'Let's move him over here. It won't hurt him, I promise.' She didn't believe the man called Spud was feeling much at all. 'What's his name?'

'Harry Primrose,' Wren answered and his look defied her to smile.

She did with a soft gasp of a laugh. 'Gosh, you two must take some stick. Wren and Primrose.'

'Yeah,' he said and his eyes lingered on her.

'Nurse Nightingale?' It was Gupta.

'Just a moment please, Gupta. What happened?' she said, trying to keep Wren talking.

He explained.

Harry's lids fluttered open again and Claire could barely believe it when his expression broadened into a wide smile, wrinkling the mud that caked his face. She recognised the sudden lucidity that often pre-empts death. Harry was about to leave them. 'Cor, mate, is this a trick of the eye or are you the luckiest bloke in hell to have found a gorgeous girl?'

'Luckiest blokes both of us, Spud.'

'Bugger me. I'd ask you to marry me, nurse, if I wasn't about to head off,' he wheezed.

'Don't, Harry,' Wren pleaded.

Claire swallowed. It was far harder to watch a man die with his mate at his side than if she were alone with him. Wren back-handed away some tears.

'I'm checking out, Heartthrob. I told you I wouldn't make it. But you will. Keep playing those sad songs and stick around.' His breathing became even shallower. 'Are you holding my hand, mate?'

Wren nodded through watering eyes. He sniffed hard.

'Are you holding my other hand, nurse?'

She took it immediately. 'Yes, Harry, I am.'

'Put my hands on my chest,' he urged. 'I can't feel anything.'

They did so and their fingers touched.

'He scrubs up well, nurse. You'll see. Most handsome of all us fellas. You'll fall in love with him like I did.' Spud was struggling badly to string his words together. It would be just moments now. Claire ignored Gupta's anxious pacing nearby. 'See you at the big pub in the sky, mate. Kiss him, nurse. You know he's a bloody virgin. That's gotta change . . .' Harry sighed his last breath quietly as he chuckled to himself.

Wren blinked, seemingly holding his breath.

'He's gone, Jamie,' Claire said gently.

It was excruciating to watch this man, who couldn't be a lot older than her, wrestle his emotion back under control. It wasn't seemly for Aussie blokes to cry – she knew that. She took his hand, not sure if it made things worse. 'No more pain,' she whispered and his gaze lifted to hers. It was only then, holding his hand awkwardly linked with Spud's, that she saw fresh blood trickling beneath his sleeve, running in tiny rivulets through the mud.

'Jamie, you're wounded and I need to see how bad it is.'

'I'll be fine,' he muttered.

She was on her feet moving around Spud and insisting Jamie undo his jacket before he could protest again.

'That isn't going to heal itself,' she breathed, staring closely into the jagged tear in his skin on his broad, tanned chest. The rip ran from the top of his shoulder to beneath his arm. 'You actually covered this up before you left?'

'You don't leave your uniform.'

A moment of dawning arrived; that was what had nagged at her. 'You're from the Light Horse Brigade, aren't you?' she said, suddenly recognising the distinctive uniform.

He nodded miserably. 'I'm 9th Regiment.'

She smiled sadly. 'I used to know some of the officers from the 8th. Always thought you were the smartest dressed in the whole army.'

'They suggested just lying him down in the trench. At least descending that bastard cliff made me feel as though I was trying to save him.'

She squeezed his wrist. 'No one could have saved Spud . . . you need to know that. But what you've done is open up this wound further,' she said, trying not to glance at his taut belly and the out-line of his ribs. As with every other man here, the diet of bully beef and hard biscuit was taking its toll. 'It has to be rinsed out, checked for grime, foreign bodies, properly sutured.'

He looked back at Spud as if needing to remind himself that the recent events had indeed happened. 'Don't worry about me. Look after the others.'

'I will. But you do need that wound seen to, or it risks gangrene, and the next time you see me I'll be the one administering the chloroform so the surgeon on board the ship can take your arm off. Is that what you want?' Her voice had hardened.

His gaze narrowed. 'You're tough.'

She shook her head and immediately let go of the tension in her tone. 'Not tough enough, my matron complains,' she sighed. 'I've just seen too much horror in the last few weeks and seen too many limbs amputated and tipped into the sea for the fish to feed on.' She stood. 'I'm really, really sorry about Harry.' Claire nodded at the wound. 'I must go or Matron will hang me out to dry but promise me you'll get that seen to. Better still, just follow me down to the jetty and walk onto the ship. Everyone else does. Right now you can walk on, have your wound dressed and be back with your unit.'

He didn't move.

She pleaded silently that he would but tried her best to sound matter-of-fact. 'It's your decision. Bye, Jamie. Good luck.'

'Er . . . Thanks, Claire.'

She turned back. 'For what?'

He shrugged. There was nothing to say and as she started to turn away again, he spoke. 'Spud lied. He's the virgin,' he said, clearing his throat. 'I just let him think I was so he didn't feel alone.' He fixed her with a stare from out of the bomb-blasted mud that seemed to cut through all the noise and activity, all smell of blood and sweat and seaweed, and penetrate into her heart, she was sure. 'I think of all ways to go, he was happy to have died holding a pretty woman's hand.'

The intensity of his stare, in which the sun lit golden glints in its green depths, caught her unawares and her throat constricted as she felt a quickening in her chest, as though something new had come alive. Across the invisible yet suddenly taut frisson that linked them, she also felt the exchange of pain and loneliness, wished in that moment she could just hold him, reassure him, feel his heartbeat against hers.

'I . . . I wish I could do that for every man here,' she said, sounding awkward. Could he read her thoughts from the way he was looking at her so deeply? Was she blushing? Wren reached for his slouch hat, which she hadn't noticed on the ground nearby, before he nodded his thanks again and she was reminded of what the surgeon had said about tin helmets. *Please save this one*, she cast out.

'Well, as rude as it sounds, I hope I don't see you again,' she said, trying this time to sound jaunty.

'I'll risk it,' he said and gave her a crooked grin to mask the hurting wound he was obviously trying to hide and the sorrow he couldn't.

Jamie watched Claire Nightingale walk down the beach with one of the Indian stretcher-bearers hurrying at her side, and impossible though it seemed to him, overriding his grief was a sense of intoxication. It could be the shock, the heat, the blood loss, thirst . . . but he was sure it was simply Claire Nightingale.

His mind catapulted him back to being four years old and the day his father lifted him onto his first horse: a beautiful dappled grey he called Chalkie. The thrill of sitting on her back and in his own saddle had made him feel like a king on his throne, and when his father had begun leading her around it was so exciting he'd begun to cry. But that day had paled by comparison with the morning he'd ridden Chalkie alone, taken her out for her first gallop alongside his father and elder brother. He'd felt the first delicious stirrings of independence and with it came a sense of adventure. He'd been six. By twice that age kissing Sarah Potter behind the sheds had come close to being right up there with winning Best in Show with Chalkie when he was ten, but then kissing Beth Fairview and stroking her breasts through her thin summer frock five years

47

later really did make him wonder if life could ever deliver a better prize. It had. Beth had let him go even further at nineteen but neither of them had ever shared that fact with anyone. That ungainly, inexperienced and yet utterly incredible moment in her treehouse, with only the magpies warbling across the vividly golden plains to sing them through a rite of passage into adulthood, was their secret. And then along had come Alice from her good family with her good manners and had claimed him away from all other women. It was as though he'd been under Alice's spell because he'd become lazy, happy to go along with her ideas and her long-term plans for them both. She'd even taken him into her bedroom when her family was away and allowed Jamie to share the breathless, bone-shaking thrill of stolen pleasure to convince him there would never be a moment to match for his entire life.

And yet, while he'd given himself physically to her, even maybe mentally in accepting she would be Mrs James Wren one day, emotionally his heart had remained aloof. Alice was too controlling. It wasn't sinister, it was just bossy Alice, who knew best, wanted a big country wedding and a big country house, precisely two children – a girl and a boy, who'd be schooled in Adelaide, privately, of course. It was a healthy, normal desire, Jamie knew that, but still he felt cornered. He didn't want a big country wedding, he could live in a cottage, he wanted a full nest of laughing Wren children who would go to the local school, learn to ride, be taught their father's and uncles' and grandfather's work on the land. But he'd never mentioned this to Alice; he'd run away to war instead.

Their families were both well off and they were undeniably a good match on paper, but it wasn't until his father had queried the relationship that he'd realised all he really felt towards Alice was duty. His ability to love her to the exclusion of all else was not in the equation; in fact, he didn't love her in that pure sense of how he knew he should. He loved his family, he loved Pippy, he loved Spud.

All more intense and loyal than anything he felt for Alice.

And that rare touch on his neck from his father on the day he left Quorn, the single unexpected communication of unspoken affection, could, in his most desperate moments, trump all else. It had the capacity to motivate him, make him want to survive – and if he did survive, he would fling his arms around his father and hug him, no matter what he thought.

And so he hadn't been ready in this moment of hell – in this place of cruelty and blood, of sorrow and hurt – for an angel to materialise and touch him physically, emotionally and even spiritually in a way no other had. Claire Nightingale, golden bright hair pulled back from angular features, with her grey glance like summer rain and her timely squeeze of his wrist with a long, pale hand in his darkest hour, had given him an ethereal moment of awakening. Spud in his final gasps had hit on it without even knowing the truth of his words as Jamie Wren's heart had given itself over – he could fall in love with Claire Nightingale in a heartbeat, and in a way that he could never fall in love with Alice.

He turned back just as they were covering Spud with a blanket. Jamie blinked as the pain of loss warred with the pain of realisation that he'd never understood what it was to be in love . . . until this moment. This is what his father had been referring to when he'd asked those questions in the pub.

He knelt by Spud's body, wiping his eyes again as tears sprang. Jamie pulled the blanket back so he could look at Harry Primrose for the final time. He took his friend's limp, callused hand and squeezed it. 'I'll miss you, mate, especially all those things we said we were going to do when we got back to Egypt.' Jamie sniffed, determined to say something that felt important. 'I'm not sure how I'll get through the rest of today without you, let alone tomorrow. But I'll stay alive, I promise. You've given me something to live for, Spud, because without you I'd never have met her. You're right, I should have just asked her to marry me.' He gusted a mirthless laugh at how ridiculous he must sound chatting to a corpse.

He saw boots arrive beside Harry's head. 'We have to move your bloke to the cemetery with the others. Sorry, mate, we need to make room – there'll be this many again by sundown.'

Jamie didn't want to let Spud's hand go because then it would be final. He'd never see Harry's potato-shaped face again, never discuss whether ants think, or fish sleep, or argue his friend's point that Port Adelaide could beat all the best that the VFL could throw at the single South Australian club, or whether SA Brewing produced a better ale than Coopers, or whether he had noticed that old men have hair growing out of their ears.

Jamie leaned down and kissed his dead mate on his mud-encrusted forehead. 'Sleep now,' he said, echoing something he'd heard his broken-hearted father say when he'd had to put down his dog. William Wren always was better with animals than he was with people.

'What about the chaplain?' Jamie asked.

The soldier looked over his shoulder. 'He's working his way here.'

'Can I wash off the mud?' he asked, gesturing to Spud's slack expression.

'Sorry. We can't spare the water . . .' He must have seen Jamie look towards the sea as he continued, 'and frankly there's no time and it's a risk just gathering it from there.'

Jamie nodded sadly and heard the words 'dust to dust' in his mind. What did it matter if Spud had dirt on his face? So did most potatoes. He gave Spud's hand a final squeeze and said, 'Bye, mate,' before sniffing and standing.

The pain of his injury was cutting through the grief now. He could feel the pulse at the site of his wound beginning to pound, knew he should get it seen to but didn't want to queue up with everyone else.

Jamie looked up the incline to Walker's Ridge where he needed to be.

What do you want? The question blew into his mind without warning.

I want to see her again, he answered, remembering Claire's long-limbed, straight bearing and how she seemed to float across the sand.

He didn't think twice. Jamie Wren walked away from Harry Primrose, away from Walker's Ridge, and headed for the jetty. He came across a weeping man, no more than fifteen steps from it, who was wounded in the leg but trying to support another bloke who looked to be gravely injured – a shocking gut wound.

'He's my brother,' the man wailed to no one in particular. 'I promised Mum I'd take care of him.'

Jamie glanced at the jetty; apparently in the last few minutes someone had finally begun supervising who was to be let aboard the hospital ship. The man was turning away anyone who didn't need immediate attention, which meant he would certainly be turned away, and so would the teary bloke, but not his brother. He needed a way to get on board and see Claire.

He stopped a pair of bearers. 'I need that stretcher.' The Indian men looked at him, dark-eyed and unsure. 'There are others up at the clearing station,' he assured. 'Nurse Nightingale insisted I get this man onto the hospital ship immediately.'

At the mention of her name the men's stance changed. The eldest of the two gestured that he could have their stretcher. 'Here, sir,' he said, politely.

Jamie had never been called sir in his life. He grinned. 'Thanks, mate. Here, what's your name?' he asked the distressed soldier.

'John Firle. This is my brother, Ronnie. I can't let him die. If I queue up back there, he'll be dead before they see us.'

'I know, I know, mate. Put him on here and we'll get him some help straightaway, all right?'

Firle looked at him as though he was a heavenly apparition but Jamie knew the real angel waited aboard the *Gascon*.

With Ronnie slipping out of consciousness and John begging him to hold on, Jamie led them to the gatekeeper. Before the man could even ask, Jamie took control, yelling above the bawl of the monocle-wearing Lieutenant Commander Edward Cater, who was on a loudspeaker directing operations of ships and barges from the pier.

'I was told to bring this man immediately on board.'

'But you're hit. Don't you want to get seen to at the clearing station?' The man frowned at the blood dripping from Jamie's fingers. He shifted his gaze to John Firle and the wound at his leg. 'So should he. You both look pretty bad.'

'That's the point. Me and Firle were told to get help at the hospital as well as this bloke.' He tipped his head towards the younger Firle but didn't name him or the supervisor might smell the lie. 'This way, if we're well enough to carry the badly injured, it doesn't tie up the stretcher-bearers who are needed back there urgently. The doctor wants to clear the dead to the cemetery – he just hasn't got enough help.'

The creases in the man's forehead deepened. 'And who gave you orders again?'

Jamie played his ace. 'Nurse Claire Nightingale insisted I do so immediately.'

The man's face relaxed. Even his tone changed. 'Righto. Go ahead, you blokes,' he said. 'You should just make the next barge leaving for the hospital. Once there it will be a queue of hours for someone like you who isn't urgent. Don't say you weren't warned.'

Jamie nodded his thanks and without saying a word moved the stretcher forward, holding his breath for fear of being stopped. He led the Firle brothers onto the flat-bottomed boat, laying Ronnie down on its base among the other stretcher cases, hoping none of the clinging mule dung he spied would infect the groaning youngster. Then he pushed the protesting John Firle to the front of the barge where the walking wounded seemed to be positioning themselves.

They were the last on. The barge pushed off from the cove just minutes later, towed away by a small steamboat whose fumes caught in his throat. Nevertheless the pungent smell was welcome for the invisible message it carried that they were moving away from hell.

4

Back onboard, Claire headed to theatre and attended to one helpless case after another. In four hours they had amputated one limb, patched up three serious head wounds, cleaned out shell fragments and sewn up holes on so many men she'd lost count. And through all the gruesome tasks it was the face of Jamie Wren that haunted her.

'. . . very quiet today, Nurse Nightingale,' the surgeon said.

She turned back from the medications shelf. 'Forgive me, doctor.'

'Doesn't do any good to go ashore,' he murmured. 'I did the same in my first week. All it achieved was make me question the purpose of my being here, our whole reason for bothering to patch these poor blighters up if the best we can do is send them home forever changed, or send them back out to be killed or maimed. War . . .?' He shook his head to say he had no answer for it.

'Big questions,' she said.

'Best not asked sometimes.'

Claire dug up a smile aimed at deflecting him; he was an older, avuncular man whom everyone respected. Nevertheless, Claire didn't want to tell him she wasn't exploring philosophical conundrums of the universe but instead was mooning around in her thoughts about the effect that a single soldier's sorrow had had on her psyche. Nor did she want to explain her newly developed anxiety for his safety, or her memory of the way his glance had tripped something in her heart.

As she returned to her task she wondered again whether Trooper Wren had got his wound seen to. Infection was rife on the ridges . . . it wouldn't take much – his grubby uniform alone after being buried in that putrid, germ-infested grime was sufficient to make him sicken within hours.

She cleared her throat. 'We're low on chloroform,' she said, realising she needed to get some air. She'd been cooped up in theatre for six hours without so much as a sip of water.

As if on cue, Matron glided into the theatre and cast her eye at the two assisting nurses.

'Both of you go and have a cup of tea, please, perhaps even some porridge. Changeover is arriving in moments. Nurse Nightingale, you look ready to drop. Sit on a deckchair for fifteen minutes away from all the patients. It will feel like a week. I need everyone at their stations and with high energy for the voyage tonight. The captain has advised that it won't be smooth sailing . . . and you know what that means.'

Claire did. It meant tying unconscious and even semi-conscious patients to their cots as a minimum precaution. If the cramped, smelly, irritable conditions felt impossible now, once the ship began heaving through high waves, it made even simple tasks such as changing a dressing feel impossible.

'Go,' Matron said to the nurses.

Claire nodded. 'Five minutes, Matron.'

'I said fifteen. And have some sweet tea.'

Claire pulled off her dirty theatre apron and stepped out into the corridor where a queue of men waited silently, some slumped on the floor, others leaning against the walls. There was nowhere else for them to wait.

'I'll be back in a jiffy,' she said to them as one. She skipped through and up a set of stairs to the next deck, her shoes squeaking on the iron. The air became immediately fresher and she moved straight to the supplies room where she found a clean apron and tied it on, adding to its pockets the necessary tools and bandages and dressings that were handy to have on her.

'Fancy a cuppa?' said a familiar voice. Rosie's sweet, smiling face appeared around the door, red curls still making a dash for freedom. 'I'm making one for some of the lads.'

'Oh, you're a treasure, Rosie. I'm just going to take some fresh air. Two minutes, I promise.'

Rosie grinned. 'Go. You look pale.'

Claire ascended to the deck where the small, intense world of Anzac Cove seemed unnaturally quiet. She moved away from the immediate loading area.

'What's going on?' she asked one of the doctors at the rail.

'They're telling us there's talk of an armistice.'

She looked back at him, perplexed. 'Really?'

'It's probably why there's not a lot of firing at the moment – everyone's waiting to see if it goes ahead.'

'Why now?'

'The Turks lost thousands of men the other day. Terrible scenes, apparently. All those corpses and this heat – it's a dangerous mix.'

'And what, they're going to call a truce so —?'

'So they can clear the dead, yes,' he said, dragging in a lungful of tobacco from the tiny stub of a cigarette he had left between his fingers. 'Strange to have it so quiet, isn't it?'

She blew out a short gust of despair. 'How ironic.'

'I know. Listen, Claire, when we get into Cairo next, are you due any leave?'

She lifted a shoulder. 'Yes, probably.' She looked away from him, knowing what was coming, and was already formulating an excuse.

'How about —' he began.

'Nurse Nightingale!'

They both turned at the voice.

Were the gods toying with her? 'Jamie,' she murmured and felt a ridiculous surge of pleasure and intense relief to see the smiling, bleeding Anzac waving to her from the other side of the deck.

The doctor turned back to her. 'You know him?'

She was sure she was grinning like a loon. 'Er . . . yes, our families know each other,' she said, hardly daring to believe such a whopping lie had slipped out with ease. 'I thought he'd died,' she added, hoping it explained her happiness. She moved away from the rail, crossing the deck towards Jamie before she could get herself in any deeper.

Wren approached, still smiling crookedly.

'You took my advice,' she said, beaming.

He nodded. 'Can't gallop a horse properly or bowl an off spin without my arm.'

'How's your hearing, by the way? You were obviously close to the explosion.'

'Bit dulled but I was lucky to be thrown clear. It will pass.'

She nodded. 'All right, then. Shall we see to your arm?'

He looked back over his shoulder at the line of shuffling men who were being gradually moved below deck.

'It's fine. Follow me.' She led Jamie down a different set of stairs and another two flights to a ward that was near enough silent. 'Most in here won't live out the voyage,' she whispered. Claire nodded at the nurse on duty. 'I can keep an eye on things here. Go have a breather.'

'Really?'

'Tell Rosie I don't mind cold tea. I'll pick it up in a few minutes. I'm just going to dress this man's wound.'

Her fellow nurse blinked in slight confusion but Claire was

counting on her being too weary to argue that this was not the normal way of things.

'This is Jamie Wren. Can't believe it – our families knew each other when we were children,' she said.

The nurse, as she presumed, was not interested and turned to leave. 'All quiet for now but fifth cot along, he's struggling. His name's Colin.'

They heard her footsteps retreat.

'Why did you lie?' he asked.

She needed a moment to work out why too. 'Sit down. Let's get that jacket off.' As she helped him, she explained. 'It was easier than admitting why I was breaking all the rules.'

'You didn't have to —'

'I know,' she said. 'I wanted to.' She cleared her throat. 'Right, I can't look at your face all filthy like that. Just let me gather up some stuff.'

She pulled a tray over towards her and moved around the supplies area, reaching for various items and pouring a tiny amount of water into a kidney bowl.

Rosie arrived unexpectedly, holding out a tin mug of tea. 'I knew you wouldn't go back and fetch it,' she said but her gaze cut to Claire's patient and her light green eyes glinted with mischief. 'Well, hello, handsome,' she said, turning on her most radiant smile. 'Aren't you the chosen one?'

'Our families —' Claire began.

'I heard.' Rosie smiled with intrigue. 'You'll have to tell me more later. Drink it, Claire,' she urged. 'Promise to look me up when the war's over,' she threw at Jamie before turning to leave.

'Thanks, Rosie,' Claire called, but as soon as her friend was halfway down the corridor, she pushed it at Jamie. 'Here, you drink it.' She watched him stare at it like she was holding out a tray of gold rather than a chipped enamel mug of muddy tea. 'I can make another one,' she insisted.

He took it, swallowed greedily and her heart broke a fraction more for him and all the parched men out there.

'It's got sugar,' he murmured with disbelief.

She wanted to ruffle his hair at his simple, boyish pleasure. Claire moistened a rag and began wiping away the mud on Jamie's oval face and watched as a golden-tanned complexion began to appear, with stubble that seemed neither dark nor blond around a right-angled jaw that led her to a neat chin; it hinted at a dimple, which had likely been more pronounced in childhood. She cleaned his cheeks and found a pair of intriguing creases running the length of each and she imagined how they deepened when he smiled. Claire continued, moving to the nose that was arrow-straight before she wiped away the grime from the two tiny furrows between his dark eyebrows. She worked on, cleaning away the dirt as best she could, following his hairline, which had grown over with flops of soft brown hair the colour of roasted chestnuts. And those eyes that watched her so intently were the same shade as the sweet nut's leaves. It prompted thoughts of the copse at the end of her English garden.

'I love English woodland,' she remarked, realising she had been holding her breath. He smiled to reveal even white teeth that emerged beneath widely defined lips. 'There, now I know who I'm talking to.'

'English woodland?'

She shrugged. 'Childhood memories. I spent my early years in Berkshire.'

'What happened next? I mean, after Berkshire?'

'My mother died young, then my father soldiered in Africa so I was sent to Sydney to stay with friends but only for just over a year. Dad joined me, met someone and we lived in Tasmania when they married.' Her expression clouded. 'I travelled back to England, turned eighteen on the ship, did my nurse's training, worked for a couple of years, ran away to war.' It sounded so dry and clinical.

'Didn't get on with the new wife?' Trooper Wren cut across.

She raised an eyebrow at his intuition. 'I was not mature enough, I suppose, to accept that my father could love anyone else but me. However, in my defence, she was equally one-eyed and I was clearly an encumbrance in her life. It was easier all round once he passed away.' She returned to brighter thoughts. 'Yes, your colouring reminds me of the woodland we used to enjoy wonderful picnics in when I was a child.'

'I'm glad. You sound like you were happy then.' He sipped from his mug. 'Almost as happy as I feel now, taking afternoon tea with you.'

Claire laughed. 'Let's have a look at this wound. I told you it's going to need sutures. But it's also going to hurt while I clean it out.'

He shrugged. 'Anything for Farina's First XI.'

'Farina?'

'South Australia's far mid-north. Grazing country. Have you heard of the Flinders Ranges?'

'Of course. Never seen them, though.'

'I'd like to show you one day.' He sighed at her surprised smile. 'In summer purple hills stretch over endlessly dry, copper-coloured earth, or golden plains of wheat so bright it hurts your eyes. But when the rains come, the world turns green overnight and wild-flowers shoot up at the first drench and paint the landscape with lilac and yellow, whole meadows of searing red.' His voice had taken on a faraway quality, and when he returned to the ward full of sleeping men where they sat, he shrugged. 'Makes you want to write about it.'

'You should,' she urged, delighted by his vivid description. 'You've made me want to see it for myself now. Are you a shearer?'

He grinned and she found his amusement disarming. It felt like each time he smiled, he stripped away another layer of her.

'My family are landowners in the region – it's a distant spot. There are four of us sons. Dad wouldn't let Hugh or Robert go to war – they're both needed on the farm. And my mother refused young John, even though he wanted to run away with me.'

'But they let you go?'

She saw the tightening around his generous mouth and the lines on his cheeks shifted. Those would deepen as he aged – and they would suit him, if he lived long enough. 'I'm twenty-seven. I guess you could say I'm the middle son. My father fought in the Boer War. He agreed that the Wrens should do their part in this one. But don't read them wrong. We're a close family in our own way. I reckon Mum will still be setting a table for six and demanding Dad check the mail for my letters even when she knows there won't be one.'

'Sounds like you all love each other,' she admitted, wishing she could wrap herself in a similar cocoon of affection even for a day or two. 'So, let's start cleaning this wound out. Tell me about them . . . your family. Tell me about your father.'

She watched his expression cloud slightly. 'He's a tricky person to explain because he's not easy to get to know.'

'You've been with him all your life.'

'Dad's a closed book. He refuses to be read.'

She smiled at that. 'My dad was the opposite – he was so affectionate and he'd get excited over the smallest stuff. I miss that in my life. I think I've become introverted because he's not around.' She nodded at the mug. 'Drink your tea. The sugar will help. I'm sure your father worries in his quiet hours about you over here. He's been to war, you say, so he knows what you're facing, understands the dangers.'

'Mum says his distant air is a product of his upbringing. He was an orphan, raised on hundreds of acres by mainly shearers, no other children, no women, and then thrown into Adelaide at seven to be watched over by maiden aunts who gave little love but plenty of criticism. Mum always reminds me that I should hold some pity for him because he really does do his best by us all.'

'She's right. Four sons. He must believe his job is to make men of you.'

'Have you and my mother been talking?' he asked with a cheeky wink and in that moment Claire was sure she could see the boy that Jamie must have been. 'The strange thing is that there's no doubting the love between him and Mum.'

In her daydreams Claire liked to imagine that her parents were inseparable when her mother was alive and that everyone around them could see they were deeply in love. 'Go on.' She found Jamie's husky voice irresistible with his fresh South Australian country accent.

'He's got this . . . er, well, this steely sort of gaze.' Jamie tried to mimic it. 'I swear he could herd sheep with his scary light-blue stare.'

Claire gusted with laughter.

'But you know, that hard look over the moustache that never seems to move, even when he talks, it just seems to soften whenever Mum's around.'

Claire stopped laughing and felt her heart melt. 'I think it's so special that you notice.'

He nodded. 'That's how I want it to be.'

'When you fall in love, you mean?'

He didn't meet her gaze, just shook his head slightly over an embarrassed shrug.

'Don't move your arm,' she warned gently. 'I'm getting to the tricky bit.' She took the empty mug, placed it down and he smiled his thanks. 'I'm guessing your mum has lovely brown eyes?' He nodded sadly and she didn't push. 'I envy you.'

He gave her a quizzical look.

'To be part of a big family and all that love.'

'Maybe that's what you need . . . to be part of a loving family.'

'Amen to that, Trooper Wren.' She caught him staring at her and realised how intimate their conversation had become. Matron may not approve but then Matron wouldn't approve of her being alone with him, showing such special favour. 'Well, I must say you are in the most romantic of all companies. I think the mounted troops are so dashing . . . even without your horses.'

Claire began to wash out the wound with syringes of water and antiseptic; knowing how it stung, she was impressed that the only clue to his discomfort was a frown.

She knew she shouldn't, but the words came anyway. 'Have you got a girl you miss?'

He nodded and she wasn't ready for how much his admission hurt, stinging perhaps as much as the disinfectant she was pouring over his wound. But she kept her expression even. 'Oh? What's her name?'

'Pip.'

'Pip? What's that short for?'

'Pipsqueak.'

'Pipsq—?' She stopped mid-word, seeing his eyes flash with amusement.

He laughed but winced at how it hurt. 'My dog. She's the best-looking border collie in Australia. Strong, brave, never gives up.'

'And is that what you look for in the girls you love?' Claire was surprised at herself for flirting. 'So . . . have you got a sweetheart?' she asked, regretting the words the moment they were out.

He shrugged awkwardly. 'I suppose.' Wren gave a sigh.

'Gosh, that sounds like true love.'

She had meant her remark to be light-hearted but he took it seriously. 'Because it isn't love.' He lowered his intense gaze.

'Maybe for Alice it was real, but not for me.'

'I'm sorry, I shouldn't pry. Where are you based? I mean, on the escarpment?'

He looked glad to shift topics. 'We're at a place called Walker's Ridge. Nothing to see, just scrubby valleys and spurs. Can't even see those or the beautiful sea, to be honest, because we walk through trenches most of the time. But, I guess, if you look to the east from the ship, that's where I am. Actually, if you know where the mules are mainly tethered – we call it Mule Gully – just follow the line up to Russell's Top and my ridge is like a knife edge that branches out, running to North Beach and leading down from a place called the Nek. I've been told there are sweeping views across the Suvla Plains but we just keep our heads down.'

As he finished explaining, a tiny piece of metal fell out of the wound and made a tinny, ringing sound in the kidney dish. They both stared at it glinting darkly in the bloodstained water.

'This is why it was a good idea to take my advice,' she said, full of relief. Another fragment dislodged and rang dully.

'It was a mortar bomb.'

'Well, some of its casing has found its way into you. We've had shrapnel the size of marbles topple out of face wounds but the tiniest fragments can create horrible problems.' She stared into the open wound, aware that he was staring at her.

'I don't know how you do it,' he said. 'You must see so much horror.'

'Even if we win this war, we're all going to lose.'

'Most of us don't even know why we're here, not in Europe.'

She remembered all those jovial boys back in Mudros Harbour who had been winking at the nurses from the decks of their troopships – yelling out promises of undying love and pledges to marry her once they'd seen off Johnny Turk. How many of those braves were now dead?

The Allies and the Germans had effectively ground each other to a standstill on the Western Front. Britain's inspiration to secure the Dardanelles and prevent Turkey from having any effect on opening up valuable military routes for the Central Powers had detoured many Australians into the eastern Mediterranean.

'Apparently we have to help take the pressure off the east, according to our First Lord of the Admiralty. I overheard one of the diplomats' wives while powdering her nose at Shepheard's Hotel. Churchill says he'll be damned before he lets the Germans run rampant through the Mediterranean.' She gave a long inward sigh, weary of wondering at decisions of the power brokers. 'I think that wound is clear of debris now.'

Was it how shattered she sounded in that moment? Or perhaps it was the way she happened to look up from tending his wound at the precise moment he raised his gaze to meet hers . . . Whatever it was and whichever forces had pushed them to meet this day, those same powers now propelled them forward. She presumed he felt a similar, uncontrolled need in that heartbeat because the gap between them closed helplessly, rapidly, as Jamie gently cupped his left hand around her neck and pulled Claire towards him. Their lips touched so briefly, so softly, she could probably later convince herself it hadn't happened, as vague guilt over his sweetheart snagged briefly in her thoughts but was then overlooked. Alice was the least of her problems; right now, notions of duty and responsibility clashed with yearning and desire. She was exquisitely aware of every rule being broken, while all her senses were enchanted by this Australian.

She stared at him in disbelief, her hands still clutching the bowl and syringe. 'Jamie . . .' she whispered.

He shook his head, his expression mortified. 'I'm sorry. I'm so sorry. Claire, I . . . forgive me.'

'Alice?' She felt lost for what to say next.

'It's over between us; I have no intention or desire to marry her,' he groaned. 'Even so, I . . . I'm sorry . . .'

It was as though someone else took control of her body in that moment; his vulnerable expression melted the core of her emotions that as a nurse she had worked so hard to defend. Suddenly all the barricades were lowered. Claire put the implements down, and after a quick glance along the corridor, she put a finger to his lips. 'Hush.' She leaned forward and kissed Jamie again tenderly, lingering just long enough so he knew she wasn't simply comforting him. She dare not be caught, though. This was far more punishable than to be found stealing a kiss with one of the naval officers on board.

Jamie stared at her in blank silence when they parted. Her message had been received but they both shared the feeling of how hopeless their situation suddenly was.

'Claire . . .' he began again, his voice thick as if a million words were clogged in his throat.

They both heard footsteps and she noticed he shifted his slouch hat more squarely across his lap. She was sure they were both furiously blushing.

'. . . and that now looks to be clean,' she said in her best matter-of-fact voice. 'We can get you sewn up, dressed and back to your . . . Oh, hello,' she said to the returning nurse. 'All good, not a sound from any of them.'

'Thanks, Claire. You're a brick. Oh, bet that hurts,' she said, eyeing Jamie's open wound. 'All cleared?'

Claire nodded. 'Yes indeed. All done.'

'Do you want me to stitch up? It's pretty quiet around here as all my patients are miraculously sleeping. It won't last, but I'm happy to help?'

Claire desperately wanted to remain exactly where she was: feeling the warmth of Jamie's body through her hands, which were still resting on his skin, still tasting his desire on her lips. She wanted to hold him and allay the anxiety she could read in his eyes that he had taken advantage of her.

'Claire?' her colleague prompted.

'Oh, sorry,' she gushed. 'I was miles away. Um, Jamie, remember me to your family when you write home. I'd better report back to theatre. We'll get you sewn up and back to your unit.'

'Thank you, Claire,' he said, not even glancing at the other nurse. 'Thank you for saving my arm . . . no, my life.'

'Stay safe out there, Jamie,' Claire replied. His gaze hadn't moved from hers. 'I don't want to see you back here,' she lied; she already wanted to see him again.

Claire turned away, hating to leave him and determined not to look around for a final glance his way. Untying her apron, she hurried to the stores area where she leaned back against the shelving and took some deep calming breaths. What was she thinking? Wren would, in all likelihood, not survive the next week, let alone the lifetime her suddenly love-struck mind was letting itself skip down. Love? She knew so little about it. Romantic love had never found her, nor had she looked for it. Yet kissing Jamie felt like the most natural, delicious healing sensation she had ever experienced in her lonely life. Claire blushed at the memory, recalling how a channel of pleasure had traced through her like an arc of lightning across the sky when he'd pulled her towards him.

Who would have thought she'd find romance in a battle zone? But now a new, far darker thought rode in to spoil her moment of awakening. Now she had a reason to live in real fear. She'd found Jamie. She couldn't possibly lose him.

———

The nurse inspected her stitching of Jamie's skin. She had to be a decade older than Claire, he guessed. 'I'll just dress it,' she said, reaching for the sterile pad of sphagnum moss.

Jamie nodded. 'Thanks. How well do you know Nurse Nightingale?'

The woman shrugged. 'There're so few of us on the wards, we get to know each other quite well.'

'Does she have a bloke?'

She gave him a quizzical look over her mask that felt like a reprimand.

'Sorry, it's none of my business, I know, but I didn't get a chance to ask her . . . I . . . er, thought I'd pass on the news to home that I'd seen her. Guess we don't know the next time we'll see each other . . . or even if we will.'

He saw her expression relent. 'You keep your head down, Trooper. I only like to patch my soldiers up once.' He grinned and was surprised how its effect made her gaze soften on him. 'Claire tends to keep her feelings to herself on most subjects,' she continued, 'but I sense she's a bit of a dreamer and doesn't let her defences down. She's enormously liked by the doctors and patients – all of us – but she's hard to get to know. Did you find that?'

'I really don't know her well. It's more our parents who know each other.' He winced inwardly.

The nurse tapped him gently on the non-injured shoulder as if to say he was all done. 'If she has a fellow, she doesn't speak about him.'

He was happy to hear that but kept his expression neutral. 'Well, as I don't plan to get blown up again or shot, I probably won't see anyone from this ship again. I'm grateful to you for this,' he said, testing his arm as he moved it. 'Feels all right.'

His polite manners worked. The older nurse gave him a beaming smile. 'Well, it will for now because I've put some local anaesthetic in the wound but it's going to be sore as it heals. Keep that dressing as dry as you can. Once it starts to itch, you can let it air. The casualty clearing station can take the stitches out.'

She showed him the way out and even though he remained vigilant, craning his neck to peep into every doorway they passed, he didn't catch sight of Claire again. His Claire. He *had* to see her again.

'Up that flight and you're on deck. Take one of the transports back to the shore. Bye, Trooper Wren. Stay safe.'

He followed the Indian bearer, surprised as he emerged onto the deck that there were no sounds of gunfire. Afternoon had slipped into dusk and his fellow troopers would be thinking about some bully beef; he imagined the raft of jokes Spud would normally be making about dinner or how curious it was that the smell from the latrines seemed to intensify at meal times. A new wave of sadness rolled over him and he felt he was being drowned again by the grief of his fallen mate and, of course, Swampy and Dickie. Jamie reached for the deck rail.

'Sir, are you all right?' Gupta asked.

'Just a bit light-headed.'

'Take a moment and rest. You must favour the wound for a day or two, sir.'

A soft evening breeze stirred his hair and sighing in with it was the question: was he imagining it, or had he fallen in love? This sensation of experiencing something so special and then having to walk away from it felt so different to leaving Alice Fairview. People spoke about the power of first love but he'd never grasped it because he accepted now that he'd never properly felt it before.

But as he clutched the ship's rail, he believed this new feeling of dizziness was not due to his wound but the result of kissing Claire Nightingale, that reckless kiss that had been returned. He'd been gripped by madness and yes, he was sure the pain of losing Spud was part of it, but most of the blame he laid at her feet. Those soulful grey eyes that revealed little and yet were balm to his pain. He imagined himself unpinning that sun-streaked hair he glimpsed beneath her veil and raking it gently between his fingers. He already loved the way her mouth moved in her heart-shaped face and how dimples creased either side of her mouth as though there was always secret amusement on her lips. They were strangers and yet they shared birds for a surname and Spud's death for a reminder that life can be taken so easily, and a kiss that told him love could be discovered instantly and without warning. He heard Gupta chuckle.

'What?'

'You just said, sir, that you loved her more in a single look than years of being with Alice.' He smiled at him.

'Did I?' he asked, embarrassed.

'I think you speak of Nurse Nightingale, sir. All the patients love her.'

There was no point in denying it. 'And the doctors too, I imagine.'

Gupta's bright smile from his dark complexion dazzled him. 'We all do, sir.'

Jamie nodded and felt a needle of jealousy sting him and knew how ridiculous that was. 'Mate, can you get a message to her from me?'

Gupta's smile narrowed.

'I know that's probably not the drill but Gupta, you know how it is out there. I could be dead tomorrow.'

'No, sir. I don't sense that about you at all.'

He smiled back. 'Can you read the future, Gupta?'

His companion waggled his head. 'My grandmother had the sight. They say I have inherited it.' He gave a little shrug. 'I don't see that for you. Not here,' he looked out across the beach.

'Then give her a message for me, just in case.'

'What is it?'

He reached for what was safe but cryptic to say. His eyes were drawn to the rough position of Walker's Ridge and where, he hoped, death wasn't beckoning.

'Can you bring her here and point like this. That's where I am, Gupta. She'll understand.'

'I can do that for you, sir.' The little man touched his forehead.

'I owe you, Gupta.'

'Repay me by staying alive, sir.'

'I have no intention of making a liar of your grandmother's gift,' he said and that made his new friend rumble with laughter.

'The next barge leaves shortly, sir. Good luck.'

Jamie stepped down onto the barge, waved to the Indian bearer and then he turned away to stare at the beach, so innocent-looking from this distance, like a fishing cove.

He had to be with Claire again. He thought about her all the way up the climb, keeping his head low, using all the familiar nooks and overhangs in the rough terrain to rest his shoulder and catch his breath while staying safe from sniper bullets. It took him more than twice as long to reach the summit, by which time the earth he was moving over had taken on an orange glow and he knew the sun was setting over his shoulder and that meant only one thing to Jamie.

He deliberately paused in a gully, pushing his back to the stone wall so he could face the sea, aware of all the scrabbling activity around him of men fetching and carrying. He raised a hand but not too high – just enough to acknowledge the men nearby who were dragging up some water. He recognised them.

'You all right, mate?'

'Yeah. Just taking a breather.'

'We heard about Primrose. Sorry he's gone.'

'He'll be missed.' He didn't want to linger on Spud; it was too painful. 'Not much gunfire,' he remarked.

'Yeah, real quiet this arvo. We're hearing about this ceasefire. Anyway, enjoy the brief peace.'

He nodded, looked away and closed his eyes. When he opened them, he was able to peer back down over the gnarled landscape he'd traversed. A series of sharp-topped ridges fell away, then rose steeply to The Sphinx, hiding the tiny beach where Spud had taken his final breath.

Jamie allowed his gaze to move beyond the rock formations to the now glimmer-grey of the sea at dusk. In the far distance, at the base of the islands Imroz and Samothrace a mist looked to have gathered, giving the overall scenery of the waters an ethereal ambience. And into that place beyond the fighting was a shimmering, golden stretch where the lowering sun cast its last light for this day. To Jamie in his sad mood it looked like a pathway to heaven, too bright to stare at for long. So intense in its golden light it had turned the water luminous white, gilded either side in a glittering halo of pinkish gold. He noted now that the hospital ship had already pulled anchor and was moving slowly, inexorably away.

'Don't fly away, Claire,' he whispered before he repeated her name in his mind. *Nightingale . . . Nightingale.* Jamie watched in a state of appalled sadness as the ship gradually slid into the molten gold and was swallowed into the fiery firmament until it was merely a shadow, and then a moment or so later not even that. It was as though the ship had melted. His angel had flown and although he could not remember before now the last time he had cried, Jamie felt tears sting for the second time today as he lost another person precious to him.

Now he believed he understood the pain of being in love. And just for a single beat of his aching heart he wished he had not met Nurse Nightingale, for now he was smitten, destined to be inwardly miserable until he could find her again.

He wiped his sleeve across the damp of his face and began the ascent of the final few feet to clamber over the ridge and into his trench.

'Keep yer head down, mate,' someone called.

'You too,' he choked out.

He would play his harmonica tonight, to farewell Spud and his fallen mates, but particularly to serenade the heart of Claire Nightingale in the hope she'd somehow hear him across their divided planes.

5

Shahin. His name meant hawk. He wiped a hand across his brow to scatter the flies sipping from the sweat. Açar Shahin possessed the keenest sight in his unit and with the hawk of his namesake for inspiration, he drew on that skill in the twilight murkiness to spot the enemy. However, he needed every motivation he could muster because pulling the trigger on his rifle and taking a man's life was a long way from the poet and storyteller he wished to be.

In his earliest memories he recalled how his serious-minded father had insisted he take up a profession, yet whenever Rifki Shahin was out of earshot his mother had urged him to be whatever his heart desired. By the time he turned twelve summers he was already showing leanings towards being reclusive; she was a year dead from a shaking fever, leaving him to live with a man whom he was convinced he was disappointing.

It was not until a married couple was killed in Sarajevo by a young Serbian conspirator that Açar Shahin felt the first stirrings of response to the politics his father murmured of constantly; suddenly they were both standing on the same side of the fence, united in interest as much as fear as to what the incident might provoke. He listened to his father's rational explanation that the murder of the Archduke Ferdinand would be the flame to the kindling of a fire that had been threatening to ignite within the major European powers at odds.

To the wistful Açar, who wrote poetry and composed music, there was something darkly romantic about his Serbian peer who had found the courage to cast aside fear and stand up for what he felt was right. As if the stars had deliberately conspired to align on his behalf, war had been declared and young able Turks were pressed to take up arms against the Western powers who threatened their independence, their religion, and their history of imperial power.

Açar had surprised his scholarly father with his fervour to join up even before the conscription order came through. Rifki Shahin had said little but Açar had sensed approval settle around his shoulders. It was as though for only the second time in his life he had impressed his father. The first was being born male.

Nevertheless, Rifki had made him wait until the neighbourhood's news carrier, Bekci Baba, had walked down their street in Istanbul, banging his stick and proclaiming that all men born between 1890 and 1895 must report for duty. Açar and his fellow soldiers had been loaded onto carriages bound for training grounds in the south. Not permitted access to him on the railway station, Açar's numerous aunts and female cousins had gathered at the side of the rail tracks like a small flock of silken birds in their dark robes, weeping and waving as the train rushed by. He'd glimpsed them, recognising first his father, who had escorted them. Rifki had stood slightly apart from his women, wearing traditional garments in sombre grey, but in his hand was a multi-coloured linen square that his son had sewn for him when he had been only seven, but hadn't realised until then that his father even recalled it. Had he misjudged his father through his teenage years? Had his mother inadvertently tarnished his attitude to the complex, often silent man who sired him? Big questions travelled on that train south with the 26-year-old soldier.

He joined the 5th Division, which had been stationed in Gelibolu since the previous year but was one of a stream of reinforcements brought in for the inevitable attack by the Allied forces, which had been softening up the region with bombardments for months. Açar found himself in the 57th Regiment attached to the 19th Infantry Division under the leadership of Lieutenant Colonel Mustafa Kemal.

Two months of intensive training had impressed upon Açar what the true meaning of discipline was. Elder soldiers with battle-hardened experience of the Balkan Wars had laughed at the 'boys' hoping to stand shoulder to shoulder with them. Nevertheless, he'd thrown himself at his training and he wondered what his father might make of him now with his newly acquired ability to march day and night without food, water or rest. Or his capability of breaking down a rifle and reassembling it in under two minutes, or the fact that he no longer felt he had a free-thinking mind – he simply responded to orders. His dead mother would sigh in her grave that he had stopped writing, stopped dreaming, and that he was being forced instead to imagine killing.

So far Açar had managed to avoid taking anyone's life; he had not had a clean shot at the enemy but he also fired his rifle deliberately off target. He was careful to join in the backslapping discussions of this shot or that, and disguised his fear with battle cries alongside his fellow Turks, inspired by ancient Ottoman history and a similar determination to defend their lands. He had wounded two men, he was sure, and had prayed both would survive.

He had begun to imagine a story of two young men, both in their third decade, from different backgrounds, cultures, and at war with each other but not really sure why. Neither wanted to kill. Neither had married yet. And in fact that's mainly what consumed their thoughts – being with a woman. He might write this story, if he survived the war.

His neighbour nudged him and Açar fired a shot to pretend he had been concentrating. He watched the bullet bounce uselessly off rock. He didn't think he'd survive the war and the truth was he'd felt a sense of melancholia creeping up ever since he'd heard the now famous tale that their commander had berated his men who had clapped eyes on the Allied fleet and wanted to flee. Mustafa Kemal had given the unnerved soldiers a stirring speech, the words of which burned in Açar's mind.

I don't order you to fight, I order you to die.

Açar fully expected to follow that order.

Kemal's troops had responded with limitless courage and fought with such determined ferocity that they were convinced the amphibious landings by the British with their Australian and New Zealand counterparts could only be marked down as disastrous. They had witnessed them face the unfamiliar and treacherous terrain, and become scattered, disoriented, and knew they were now crouching in hastily dug trenches or tiny ridges and overhangs, trapped like birds that dare not break cover.

He'd heard that the Australians had sunk headlong into four feet of water as they tumbled out of their boats because of the heavy kit each carried. Some were hit on the ten-yard rush to the foot of the hills. They soon cast aside all their equipment, and then like mountain goats had to find the agility to climb with only their rifles and fear for company, the soil crumbling beneath them.

Açar had liked hearing about the singing, though. Once there was no more need for stealth, the Australians had apparently begun to sing.

'*Australia will be there*,' one of his companions imitated and those listening laughed.

'*No! No! No! No! Australia will be there*,' his friends chorused.

He dared not admit feeling moved that his enemy sang in the face of death. He and his kind were manacled to the Germans, while the singing Australians were helplessly loyal to their Crown in Britain.

He felt another nudge from his comrade. Relieving soldiers had arrived. It was their turn now to drop back; he had high hopes that mail may have arrived from the surrounding villages. He slid on his belly into the trench, his back to the setting sun over the waters, and wondered what might distract him tonight from his dark thoughts of impending death.

In the camp the *saya* had recently arrived with a bundle of letters tied in cheesecloth. Açar heard the men grouped around him murmur a familiar phrase.

'*Cenneti-i Alâda*,' the friends of the fallen informed quietly.

'Truly? Mohammed is dead?' he queried Hasan, standing nearby.

The man shrugged. 'He is in paradise,' he said, repeating the familiar phrase.

Açar nodded sadly, believing too that Mohammed was in a better place, but he would miss the man's ready laugh and sense of fun. He watched the postman put Mohammed's letter back to return to his family. Is that how it would be when it was his turn to reach paradise? His father's letter would simply be returned, or would word be passed from village to village until it finally reached the city and all the way to his family home?

'Don't grieve for him, Açar. His family will be proud of him. I hope to make mine as proud.'

'By dying?'

'Dying while defending our country from invaders. Look how we have kept them confused, scattered . . .'

'And still they persist,' Açar said softly, as Hasan tugged his sleeve and nodded towards the postman.

'Your name is called. You have a parcel.' He raised a hand. 'Over here!'

It surprised him how thrilling it felt to see the men passing back the small package, his only link with those he loved. He took the parcel silently, his breath held, and moved slowly to a quiet spot where he could unwrap his prize. The British ships' guns were booming their rage, but he was well out of range and the noise seemed to fade when he ran his fingers across the neat writing on the front. He recognised his father's hand and tried to reach for a connection through the ink, tracing the letters of his name, imagining his father penning it, dipping his nib into the pot with that economy of movement he possessed. Açar sighed and carefully undid the string and opened the brown wrapping.

Inside he found a pair of thick socks, a small scarf and some lokum. He smiled, fingering the soft brown wool as the sight of the hard pink gel studded with purple and green pistachios from his favourite sweets shop and the nutty aroma reached him from the small pack of sesame halva. He knew he must resist eating it immediately and save it as a treat for after his meal, which he presumed would be chickpea soup and rice again. His belly growled at the thought of food but mostly because of the temptation of his aunt's halva. He knew the recipe, could almost taste its texture on his tongue . . . To stave off his hunger he reached into his pocket for the small thread of standard-issue rolled figs. Açar expertly bit one off, chewing slowly to savour the flesh for as long as he could. Then he finally slipped a finger beneath the envelope flap and opened his father's letter. He was aware of releasing his held breath through his nose as he chewed the final morsel of fig, trying not to notice his eyes misting slightly as the smell of his father's tobacco lifted from the tissue-thin page. That one sheet felt so precious he barely heard the sounds of his unit beginning to settle around him. The writing was tiny and he had to squint to make it out.

My dear Açar,

Thank you for your letter, which we were glad to receive and I shared it with the family over the evening meal of your aunt's chicken and rice. I don't know when this will find you – your letter took over six weeks to reach us – but I hope you are well and keeping up with your duties. It is hard to get much regular news from the south but we know you are in the midst of the fighting and we all pray that you remain safe.

Your aunt made the socks and cousin Amina wanted to knit a scarf to keep you warm through these cool spring nights but also for winter. I'm sure you'll thank them in due course for their endeavours. Your youngest cousin Demet misses you and says she will write as soon as her music exams are finished. We expect her to pass with honours.

We are fortunate to live in Galata. So many of the old-city dwellers have had to cross over the Golden Horn and find homes on this side of the waterway. They fear the invaders will want to control our ancient city first. Our big homes and gardens keep us protected, although these days even finding daily bread is a challenge. Formerly friendly neighbours openly fight over a small loaf.

Açar turned the sheet over, hungrily reading on.

I must share the sorry news that I have had to let Arzu and Fazil go. I know these servants are family to you but Fazil was called up in the second conscription and Arzu needed to help her family as its men have been called to duty. Ayfer remains – she's too old to start again or even live alone,

*she complains a great deal and now cooks for me . . . but
badly!*

*It remains stubbornly cool with a brisk wind cutting off
the Bosphorus but your mother's famous mulberry tree is
thickening with leaves again and we are expecting a big crop
of fruit this summer. Kashifa is planning to pound some of it
into pekmez and send that to you with her homemade sesame
paste to improve your morning meal. We were all disappointed
to learn from your last letter that eating for you was now
simply to stay alive – I thought the army would feed you all
much better, given that most of our country's food is grown or
reared for our soldiers. You can imagine what your admission
did to your aunt's state of mind. Anyway, I'm sure her
mulberry molasses will enliven you and remind you of home.*

*All is well here. Everyone keeps good health and we remember
you in our daily prayers. I am attending the Sultan Ahmed
Mosque whenever I can and it is certainly easier at the
moment because the university has moved to a new restricted
curriculum. So I have a lot more time to myself and in fact I
believe with the age limit now expanding to thirty-five years
and upwards I will soon be conscripted to work full-time with
the military in some capacity. I have offered again but they will
not permit me to join an active unit. It seems I am wanted in
Logistics in Istanbul.*

*I will send a larger food parcel next time. Remain diligent
in your prayers, son, and do not despair or question your role.
Allah alone decides. It is pleasing to know that you scribe letters for your fellow soldiers and keep their families informed
of their wellbeing.*

I expect it is warming up in the south but keep your new woollen garments safe for the winter. I will let you know where I am sent by the government once I know more.

Affectionately, your father

Açar stared at the dark ink on the page so neatly crafted into words, not a single smudge, clinically produced from that ordered mind of Rifki Shahin so incapable of expressing his real thoughts – his fears, his joys, his love. His father had never praised Açar for being made a platoon commander and while even he knew this was mainly because he could read orders and write messages, it was still an honour in one so young.

'I'm going to die here, Baba. You will never see me again,' he whispered to the page. *Never see me smile or hear my voice again. You'll never be able to chastise me again and unless you hurry you'll never be able to tell me that you do love me*, his inner voice continued. Açar accepted his fate wholly, somewhere deep where he no longer dreamed.

Hasan arrived to flop down next to him. 'Lucky you. Nothing for me. Everything good at home?'

'Yes . . . yes. Everyone is fine. They knitted me socks and a scarf,' he answered, digging up a smile.

Hasan nodded appreciatively. 'Any food?'

'You know there is. Lokum and homemade halva. I'll share it later.'

His friend grinned. 'Come on,' he said, standing. 'Let's go eat. There's a travelling finger puppet show on this evening for those of us off-duty.' Hasan slapped Açar's shoulder. 'That's us, brother. And there's a rumour that we may have potatoes and garlic tonight. I'm already drooling.'

Açar grinned. 'Nothing new,' he replied in a dry tone and took his friend's proffered hand, allowing himself to be hauled to his feet and to walk away from the sense of a bleak destiny.

'Hey, Açar, let's make a promise that tomorrow we do our best to shoot that Australian who plays the mouth organ,' Hasan joshed.

'Why would you want to? I like it – I wish I could meet him.'

'Ach, it's ugly to my hearing. You only like it because you play music but your kaval is far prettier in its sound.'

Açar sighed. 'The kaval is the sound of the shepherd, Hasan. It's in the Turkish soul. But we both make our music by simply blowing air through small holes.'

'Yes, but your pipe is of noble wood. His instrument is tinny.'

He shook his head. His kaval was made from the wood of the plum – nothing noble or important, but it was honest and its sound was indeed as sweet as the fruit it once bore. Nevertheless he secretly loved the music of the Australian in the trench not far from where he normally stood and it would be hard to explain that to Hasan. The soldier made gentle, sad music that spoke to Açar of dreams on the wind, carried on the wings of birds to families in faraway lands.

Fortunately the smell of frying garlic assaulted him and his whimsy about his opposing soldier was forgotten as Hasan dragged him faster towards food.

The guns had been quiet this afternoon, just the odd crack of sniper fire. It was a mild evening too and they'd even tasted something vaguely meaty in their food – hare, perhaps. *Salat* would be soon, he noted. As the sun was dipping beneath his sight, Açar reached to his pocket and touched the small, ancient prayer book of Islam – a gift from his mother's wealthy parents at his birth, crafted in Arabic. The mufti would wait until dusk to call the men to perform their ritual prayers. The enemy deliberately tried to find and kill the holy men, believing they could dim the determination of the Turks if they could kill their priests.

Açar smiled to himself. The enemy had a lot to learn about his faith. He caught the first gentle sound from the Australian trenches as his musical counterpart blew into the harmonica. His smile broadened to hear it.

'You are alive, my friend,' he murmured with gladness beneath his breath.

Hasan, never far away, nudged him. 'Play with him. Show him who is the better musician.'

Açar shook his head. 'No, I like to listen to him. He is wistful tonight.'

Leaning back, he let the music of the mouth organ reach hauntingly across the short distance of no-man's-land and the still night.

'He plays a song of the heart this evening,' Açar remarked. 'He's thinking of a woman.'

'To me it seems like the same ugly sound as always.'

Açar clicked his tongue. 'It's entirely different. Listen. Can't you hear how it's talking, telling her he loves her?'

Hasan shrugged and lit a cigarette. 'Well, you may get to meet him. They're calling a truce.'

Açar sat forward. 'Definitely?'

His friend took a long, slow suck on his tobacco. 'So I hear.'

He nodded. *Good*. Well, if it was the last thing he did on this earth, he wanted to meet the harmonica player from the opposing trench and thank him for the gentle music. Açar closed his eyes and let the breathy sound of the wind harp carry him away from the dirt tunnel and lift him on its notes to a place in his mind that was peaceful, without colour or texture. It was here from this pure position he felt no fear, no anxiety about pain or loss; in this place there was no past or future, for here he was not a worldly body – he was simply thought. It was serenity.

6

The waiter laid the golden tray on the table they flanked in wicker armchairs and gestured to them in invitation. Just the sight of the sherbets cooled Claire.

'*Mesdemoiselles, vos boissons*,' he murmured and got busy, putting out coasters and moving the drinks from tray to table.

The lingua franca in Egypt was English or French. Claire rather liked that he chose to speak French to two guests who clearly had English as a first language. It was a tiny defiance and she saw it glimmer in his eyes.

'*Merci, monsieur*,' she murmured politely, smiling briefly before leaning back to reflect on their day.

While the sleepier Alexandria was traditionally a world away in atmosphere from frenetic Cairo, war had turned it into a chaotically busy harbour. They had been given seven hours' leave and the two nurses had decided to flee the main port. Claire preferred Alexandria to Cairo – there was something more refined about its European influence evident throughout the city.

As they'd left the immediate port area eddies of dust flung fine grit into her throat and she'd flapped uselessly at the flies that constantly tormented them. Her mind rushed to a barren place – Walker's Ridge – but could only imagine. Where Gupta had pointed lived Jamie Wren in a hot, filthy trench. There flies plagued him, along with the threat of malaria, dysentery and a

85

host of other perils if the bullets and bombs didn't kill him.

She had forced herself to bend her thoughts away from Gallipoli and back to the press of the narrow streets they had wandered into, with crowded shops where sharp-eyed merchants had tried keenly to catch her and Rosie's attention. Far too experienced now, the nurses had remained in the middle of the alley, as best they could, and tried not to gaze left or right. They'd linked arms as they walked because the dusty road beneath was uneven, with potholes and ridges determined to trip them. She remembered now how she'd glanced up to see damp clouds that would give no rain but would keep the heat corralled below and send the humidity soaring.

They had moved past a row of shops and drifted level with a cavernous series of cafés, where men sucked on hookah pipes and hulked over games of backgammon while sulky-looking boys served them coffee that looked like tar in a glass. No women were present. The nurses had been searching for a welcoming hotel not too far from the port and knew just where to find it. It would have been easier to follow the waterfront but they'd both agreed they wanted to see some real life – people going about business that wasn't to do with war or killing.

They'd passed a stall selling cut fruit. Watermelons bled vivid juice the colour of blood to remind Claire she couldn't escape her imagination, while guavas were spliced with knives dipped in salt and spices, and the citrus of oranges overrode even the aroma of freshly boiled coffee and vaporised tobacco.

'Madam, madam!' the fruit seller had called but the nurses walked on, steadfastly refusing him eye contact. Claire knew that to even pause would mean all the merchants would begin to badger them, including the nearby corn seller with his luminous yellow cobs.

'The sun is bleaching your hair to the colour of that corn silk,' Rosie had noted and Claire had stolen a look at the roasting husks. Her friend was likely right; her hair had lost the buttery yellow it had been in England and had become a pale golden, not that it saw much sun these days. It was mostly hidden beneath her starched veil and only on days like today did she feel the freedom of loosening off some of the tight pinning so the soft waves escaped.

'Mmm, now I feel hungry,' Rosie had admitted.

Far more pressing than food for Claire had been her need to slake a thirst and wash away the grime of coal dust and sand blown in on the warm winds from the desert.

They'd veered once more towards the waterfront where the breeze off the sea found them again; normally fresh and salty, these days it tasted of fumes from the large fleet of ships that were taking on supplies or dropping off yet more soldiers. Trailing them had been a flock of small children with hands open and voices chattering demands.

'Come on, Claire, let's speed up or we're going to be mobbed.'

Giving a coin meant the begging only escalated and attracted a bigger crowd. She remembered how her gaze had fallen on an elderly man, looking like a pile of old rags, cross-legged and propped up in the full heat of the sun with only a piece of fabric wrapped around his head for protection. He had stumps for arms. When he looked up, drawn by the sound of the begging children, his rheumy gaze had connected with hers and the guilt he wanted her to feel had banged at the door of her chest like an unwelcome visitor. She'd hated herself for looking away and straight into the dark stare of two veiled women, shrouded in black from head to toe. Claire had envied them slightly in that moment; those women seemed to glide wraith-like through the maelstrom of children, street sellers, beggars, mules and carts, barely being noticed yet seeing everything through that slit in their veil. She wondered now what they thought of her, still in uniform, all crisply stiff in white and grey. Why did she care? War was hard enough without adding more pressure on her reserves by falling into this disconsolate mindset. It wasn't good for anyone – not her, not for the patients she tended, or the people she worked with . . . certainly not for the friend who stared at her now across the table from the cool verandah of the Windsor Palace Hotel with an expression that was a mix of enquiry and soft concern. Rosie Parsons loved a mystery and Claire knew she could sense one.

'Pomegranate and lime, or violet?' Rosie asked, reaching across the table for the gilded glass filled with a liquid the colour of a pink sunset. 'I think the violet suits your mood.'

Claire didn't argue. She took the green sherbet that Rose had ordered, made from pounded violet petals and boiled with sugar. Dainty, brilliantly purple fresh flowers floated on her drink and caressed her lips as she sipped; lips that could still remember the kiss that was the origin of this new and entirely unsettled frame of mind she was now in. Violet sherbet was an odd flavor, she decided as she swallowed; scented and subtle, it sounded so feminine but the floral taste wasn't refreshing enough for her.

'How is it?' Rosie sighed, pulling a rose petal from her tongue as politely as she could.

'I wish I'd gone for the pomegranate and lime now.'

'You certainly are in a contrary mood, Claire. What's wrong with you?'

'Oh, I don't know, the constant parade of death and destruction, maybe?'

Rosie's gaze narrowed at the sting of sarcasm. 'Are you going to share, or are you going to pretend this gloom is perfectly normal?'

Claire shrugged and put the violet sherbet down. It was making her feel queasy. She took a deep breath of air, clearer now that they were down on the Corniche, which ran for ten miles of the waterfront. In the distance, past the hush and tranquillity of the Windsor and its pampered guests, she could hear the squeal of the trains from the nearby Ramle Railway Station.

Rosie looked around, pretended to let it go, but Claire knew better. Her friend would find an oblique approach.

'I love this place. It feels like a palace,' Rosie gushed.

'I think it was built to give that impression. Those frescoes on the ceiling would have taken an army of painters and heaven knows how long to complete.'

'I think I could live in Alexandria,' Rosie sighed.

'Really? You wouldn't miss home?'

'I don't miss England. It's too wet and cold but I miss my family.'

'You said you ran away into nursing to get away from all those brothers and sisters.'

'I did. But war quickly has a way of making you realise what matters, doesn't it? Now I'd give anything to glare at my younger brothers for the tadpoles that grow into frogs and suddenly appear in my room, or to scold Lizzie for borrowing my cardigan, or to take the twins to the park to feed the ducks.' Rosie shook her head. 'I used to think my life was so boring but it was always full of laughter and love.' She gave a sad smile. 'Here's to laughter and love, Claire.' She raised her glass.

Claire did the same and sipped her odd-tasting cocktail again. 'I feel envious of your family and all that love.'

'And I envy you for living in Australia and travelling alone to England and now adventuring here . . . I'm sure you'll take off to new and exciting places when the war is done. I heard one of the doctors saying that he didn't think we'd be in Turkey for much longer.'

'Really?' She frowned.

'He was just guessing. I think I'd go back to England, maybe apply for one of the war hospitals on the coast. We could go together, maybe share digs. You can meet my family in Hove.'

Claire smiled softly. 'Sounds nice,' she murmured.

'Dad will like you because you're quiet. We're all chatterboxes. Mum's the worst of us.'

'How many of you are there?'

'Ten, if you include Gran. We're lucky we're given housing through Dad's job. It's a nice big house with a long garden and even an apple tree with a treehouse.' She laughed. 'I never thought I'd say it but I do miss them all and can't wait to see them again.'

A young African man, dressed in a richly adorned waistcoat and pantaloons, wearing a crimson fez that marked him as one of the porters, struggled with a small bag of golf clubs and two suitcases. Claire wondered who on this earth was thinking about golf in the middle of a war.

Rosie sat forward. 'Something's up. You don't seem yourself.' She frowned, considering Claire. 'Has one of the doctors made a pass?'

'No!' Then she realised maybe this was a way out. 'It's one of the patients I'm thinking about,' she admitted. 'I just felt sorry for him and I think his situation summed up this war for me. The whole push at Gallipoli feels hopeless.'

'We knew that from day one, didn't we?'

'Yes, but how many have to die to prove to the decision-makers it's hopeless?'

'What's his name?'

'Who?'

'Your soldier.'

'He's not mine,' she bristled.

'Really? I noticed you took special interest in one despicably handsome brave from the Light Horse. All that talk of knowing the families. I think you're sweet on him.'

She swallowed, feeling the colour rise to her cheeks.

'Claire! I was joking! But I'm right, aren't I?'

'Rosie,' she interrupted, as she signalled to the waiter with a raised hand, 'I had just held the hand of his closest friend who died while Jamie wept. I was on the shore, in the midst of all the despair and it caught me in an unguarded moment. Later I just happened to be on a break, insisted upon by Matron, when I saw Jamie arrive for treatment. Given what had recently occurred I thought I'd make it a little easier for him. I knew all he needed was a wound cleaned and some stitches. I left the stitches to —'

'I know, I heard. You've gone to some trouble to explain an inconsequence.'

'Because you're trying to make the inconsequential seem important,' she snapped.

Rosie chuckled, undeterred. 'Do you deny he's unspeakably attractive?'

'I deny that I noticed,' she lied. 'But yes, he's handsome enough. He was covered top to toe in mud and blood, incidentally.'

'Really? The fact that you call him Jamie while we call him Trooper Wren is a bit of a giveaway,' Rosie said, arching an eyebrow expertly as she sipped.

The waiter arrived and bought Claire precious moments; she wasn't ready to share Jamie with Rosie. What if he died? Then she'd have to put up with Rosie's pity but first there would be her friend's gushing enthusiasm for Claire's romance. No, Jamie was her secret for now. The man waited. 'Sorry, I wonder if I could order some lemonade instead, please?' She momentarily felt obliged to give an explanation but he would surely be used to the whims of the spoilt Westerners who frequented the hotel.

His expression barely flickered in response. 'Carbonated, madam?'

'Fresh, thank you.'

He removed himself and the violet sherbet, and having found the calm she needed, Claire returned her gaze to Rosie. 'Did you hear about the armistice?' she said.

'Yes. There's talk it will be underway by the time we get in tomorrow morning. It's too hot for the Nhouza Gardens after here.

Shall we look in on Davies Bryan? I need some hosiery and I like their fixed prices.'

Claire's lemonade arrived and she was instantly grateful for the sour, refreshing tang. She sighed her pleasure as it chased away the cloying floral sweetness of her previous drink. 'Yes, of course. I need to exchange some money anyway. Perhaps we can grab a meal at Walkers & Meimarachi before we go? We promised the owner we'd go next time we were in town.'

'Perfect. I wish we had time for the Alhambra. We could use some of the happy atmosphere and music of the club.'

Claire gave her a soft glance of reproach. 'I'm not in the mood.'

'Then, Claire Nightingale, something is definitely wrong with you. After where we've been you should be busting for some entertainment.'

Claire knew her friend was right.

'Claire?'

She let out a small breath. 'I was just thinking that perhaps the orchestra might be playing tonight at Walkers.' The name echoed through her thoughts. *Walker's Ridge where Jamie lives . . . or dies.*

'Oh, that's true. Wonderful. Something to look forward to. So, hurry up. I've finished,' Rosie said, draining her sherbet. 'I'm going to visit the lav, and then I'll find out how much it is to stay here. I think we should treat ourselves next visit. We could share a room – what do you think?'

Claire grinned her answer and waved her on as she sucked on the waxed paper straw in her lemonade. It would have been a relief to talk about Jamie but Rosie was a helpless chatterbox and she wouldn't have been able to keep Claire's secret between them. It made her feel guilty but as soon as Rosie had moved out of her line of sight her expression fell again and she pressed on her memories of two days ago like a bruise, wanting to feel the pain as though addicted to it.

He'd kissed her, apologised, and she could have left it like that – a moment's madness, an error. But she had pursued him, suffering her own heartbeat of insanity by encouraging him. By the time Matron had happened upon her in the stores room, Claire had accepted the truth that she'd been entranced by him from the first moment she'd seen him stagger towards her, wearing that agonised look of entreaty, which seemed directed only at her.

She'd thought about it far too often since and it now felt like a well-trodden pathway in her mind. So many unrelated incidents had conspired to bring them together on that beach of hell, within the same sun-drenched hour, and in that same moment of heartbreak. Claire had decided that they were two lone birds that had flown with the guidance of fate to this island. James Wren with his disarming smile and melancholy mood had trapped her, just like the tiny nightingale she was named after. And now, even though they were separated by many nautical miles, she was convinced he still held her heart captive.

Is this what it felt like – that most elusive of emotions? If love was meant to empower, why did she feel so suddenly and helplessly bound? Sitting here, fully dislocated from her life in either Britain or Australia, Claire wondered whether she was in love. How was it possible outside of novels to fall for a stranger so swiftly, so hard, in fact, that one's whole world seemed wrong unless that person were part of it? Her new grief stemmed from this pain of separation and the sudden relentless fear for Jamie's safety.

Rosie's voice gushed into her mind with a stream of words about the hotel and Claire dug up a grin for her friend and stopped pressing the bruise. Over the rim of her glass she saw an elderly woman watching her from another table. She was dressed in cream linens, far more suitable for the climate than her own starched uniform. They exchanged a polite smile.

'Ready?' Rosie said, gathering her bag, hat and cape – no veil at least. When in uniform Matron insisted they wear it proudly and properly. 'Wish we'd taken time to change now,' she grumbled, smoothing her uniform. 'I've paid, by the way.'

'Oh, thank you. Yes, ready, but now I need the lav. Why don't you go find us a horse and cab? My treat. I've got nothing else to spend it on.'

Rosie gasped. 'Oh, what fun. We'll make him take the long way to Cherif Pasha Street.'

Claire excused herself and went in search of the rest rooms, dawdling to peer into the elegant dining room and at the frescoes. A silent female attendant, dressed sumptuously in the hotel colours of deep crimson and ultramarine, stood guard to supervise the handing out of small towels and tiny scoops of soap paste. While Claire was washing her hands another guest arrived at her side to use the second basin.

Claire immediately recognised the elderly lady who had smiled at her from the verandah. 'Oh, good morning.' She glanced at the clock on the wall. 'Nearly good afternoon,' she grinned.

'Hello, my dear.' Her refined accent told Claire she was English. 'Are you from the Australian hospital?'

'I'm from the hospital ship, *Gascon*.'

'Oh, my word. You brave thing. Is it truly as terrible as the news we hear from the Dardanelles?'

'Worse,' Claire admitted with a sad smile.

The woman sighed. 'I've lived in Egypt for the last score years. I just can't seem to get any enthusiasm up to return to wet and windy Hertfordshire, although that's precisely what I'm doing, and while the news in Europe feels too incredible to counter, I still can't quite believe what's going on in our backyard here.'

'It's hopeless. That's the truth of it. We should pull out. Too many thousands already dead, or so badly maimed they probably wish they were.'

'War is a dreadful business. Women should run the world.'

Claire chuckled.

'Eugenie Lester,' she said, drying her hands before offering to shake Claire's. 'Do call me Eugenie.'

'I'm Claire Nightingale.'

'Oh, charming name – now there's a woman for whom I hold immense admiration; your inspiration, no doubt.'

Claire nodded. 'You're right.'

'You're wearing an Australian uniform, but you sound English.' Her eyes sparkled with interest.

Claire was used to this query. She kept her explanation brief, then concluded, 'I returned to England, did my nurse's training and . . . here I am in Egypt. I guess I straddle both countries, although I feel as mixed up as my nationality today.'

'Good gracious. But I sense you rather like the adventure of such a dangerous place. What's more, I doubt you'd take up nursing unless you enjoyed being valued?' The startling bright blue of her gaze searched Claire's and pinned her down as though she could see into all her private thoughts. 'I'll bet all your patients find a will to recover when treated by you, my dear. Don't underestimate the balm that a beautiful face, gentle manner and tender hands can be for a wounded man.'

The only one not surprised by Claire's sudden tears was Eugenie, who stretched her thin arms, tanned and wrinkled like tissue paper, around her. Claire instinctively bent into the embrace and wept. She couldn't remember the last time she'd cried. At the funeral of her father, perhaps, although those had been slow, silent tears, not this shaking outburst.

'Cry it out, my girl. I'm very glad we've met. I think we were meant to,' she soothed.

The attendant offered another towel and a shy, soft smile.

Claire sniffed and thanked her. '*Shokran*.'

'*Al'afw*,' she murmured, her dark eyes full of understanding.

She tapped her heart and nodded.

'I think she's right,' Eugenie probed. 'This is not about war, I suspect. This is about your heart.'

Claire swallowed back a small sob. 'I don't know what it is, but it hurts.'

'"It" surely has a name, my dear?'

'James Wren.' It was out before she could censor herself.

Eugenie didn't look surprised, and leaned harder on her walking cane. 'Ah. He's fighting, presumably?'

She nodded miserably. 'I'm good at my job, Eugenie. I wouldn't say I don't get involved because I feel touched by every man's wounds that we try and repair, but there's always the next in line and I've managed to keep a clear head and not get too lost or overwhelmed by it all.'

'Until this one, you mean?'

'Yes.' She told Eugenie about their two meetings on that fateful day. 'I'm not a girl with her head full of roses and romance. Part of this mood is my shock that I can't seem to think of anything else but him, filled with fear and dread. I barely know him, and —'

'Oh, you know him,' Eugenie assured. 'As Layla here can see, and so can I, you already love him; it happens. Accept. Love comes out of nowhere for the majority of us. And the best love is unexpected, while the least successful in love are those who plan it or force it. This young man has flown into your heart and made a nest.' She chuckled at her jest. 'Your very names make sense together.'

Claire dabbed at her tears with the towel and gave a watery smile. 'What if I lose him before I've even had the chance to tell him how this feels?'

'He knows.'

'But my whole life has suddenly changed. Now I spend every moment worrying. I never used to worry – not even about a bomb hitting the ship.'

'That's because, my dear, you've probably convinced yourself that you had no one to go home to, or give your love to. Now you do. Now there's every reason to fear not only for his life but for yours. Don't you see, this is precious? For whatever it's worth, I believe love is one of the greatest reasons for being alive.'

'What if he dies and —'

Now she folded Claire's damp fingers together and clasped them between her gnarled, slightly liver-spotted hands and fixed her with a pale stare that wasn't unlike her own. 'Claire, dear, you have no control over his fate in the same way that you had no control over fate bringing him into your life. But given what you've told me about him, I have a feeling that Jamie Wren, who was feeling just as adrift as you in this war when he met you, now has a reason to take great care and find you again.'

Claire blinked, relieved she'd shared her heartache with someone, though privately amazed that it was with this stranger.

'I feel certain that he wants to hold you and kiss you again and that will drive him to stay as safe as he can. You just have to believe in him.'

'But I don't even know how I'll ever see him again.'

'You will.' Eugenie said this with such confidence that Claire believed her and for the second time in a few minutes surprised herself by hugging her new friend.

'Thank you. Thank you for listening and making me feel better.'

'Keep him here,' Eugenie said, gently tapping above Claire's heart. 'Do you know the old German fable of the kinglet?' Claire shook her head. 'The birds of every land had a competition to see who could fly the highest in order to choose their king. The eagle outflew all and proclaimed himself their ruler until a tiny wren that had hidden in his plumage leapt higher still and claimed the crown.'

Claire laughed and Eugenie patted her arm.

'So, my dear, I think you should trust your wily young Mr

Wren. Come visit me when you find your way back to England. Radlett in Hertfordshire. Loom Lane is not far from the station. I'm returning early July, I suspect.'

'Thank you,' Claire said. 'I don't really know where Radlett is.'

'About fifteen miles north of London, very direct on the railways.'

Claire already felt cheered for knowing Eugenie.

'Anyway, promise me you'll visit?' She clasped Claire's hand. 'Loom Lane,' she reminded. 'I would love to see you again and offer you tea in my garden.'

'I promise.'

The elderly woman smiled and the lines around her eyes crinkled easily and deepened the kindness in her already gentle expression.

'Excellent. Now, in the meantime, stay busy. If you're always engaged in life, Claire, you won't have time to feel sad for yourself.'

Eugenie left and Claire, feeling much brighter for the illuminating chance meeting with the older woman, tucked some coin into the attendant's hand, thanking her again in her language.

She found Rosie impatiently waiting.

'Sorry, I got chatting with one of the guests.'

'Why are your eyes red?'

'I got some grit in an eye and, gosh, it hurt. She helped me get it out.'

Rosie seemed satisfied by the fib. 'Come on, our ride is waiting.'

They scrambled into the carriage and Claire sat back quietly to let her gaze drift absently over the passing scenes. It didn't need much more than the odd agreement or nod to keep Rosie happy and Claire was able to admire the elegance of this city that somehow blended its Arabic heritage with the tall European buildings of sandstone. Trams rumbled alongside and advertisements on hoardings promoted everything from suit outfitters to the Salonica

Cigarette Company. They overtook other carriages dropping off travellers and watched new arrivals wiping perspiration from weary brows as they finally arrived at their hotels.

Their horse clip-clopped into the familiar Cherif Pasha Street and passed Zivy Frères Jewellers and Horologists at number ten and onto Phillips & Lawrence, military and ladies' tailors at number fourteen, reminding Claire that she still had a dress fitting in this salon for a new frock.

The Welsh department store loomed and Rosie gave her a soft prod. 'Here we go. Have you got change?'

'Yes,' she said, digging into her bag for some of the Egyptian pounds and piastres she kept in a separate pocket. As they prepared to alight, Claire took a deep breath and Eugenie's advice to let go of her fear.

She now must trust that Jamie would somehow, amidst the carnage, find her again.

7

Jamie lay facing the wall of the trench, his left shoulder stiff from pressing down on that side for most of the night. Sleep had predictably eluded him but being left alone to meander through his grief was the best medicine right now. The rest of the blokes had lost three of their mates too. The sorrows were shared, but not having Spud at his side felt daunting – as though he'd been cut loose from the land and was now on an ocean, alone on a tiny raft. Claire Nightingale was the sea on which he found himself, dragging him further and further from the safety of the shore of his life.

He'd never felt more adrift than this moment, recalling her intimacy. She'd encouraged him, and he sensed she was no flirt. She had surged pure and without any warning or agenda and made him fall in love with her.

And that's what hurt the most: his guilt was the reason he had lain awake staring at the night-black wall, listening to sporadic gunfire and not caring about the ants or the itching lice. He should be grieving for Harry Primrose; instead he was yearning for the touch of Claire Nightingale.

He was no longer scared. He planned to outlive the Turkish bombs and bullets, the sickness and the sadness; he had a girl now whom he loved, and she was worth fighting to live for. He could picture her features in perfect detail: eyes that spoke of a sparkling winter's morning, clear and bright, skin he'd dared to touch so briefly, the colour of his pet hen's egg, with porcelain-like shells of golden tint as though recently burnished from the sun's warmth. That was Claire's skin, unblemished – save a tiny translucent silvery scar in the middle of her brow. Only she mattered. Seeing her again meant everything. He would stay alive just to see that smile of hers.

He felt someone shove him with a boot but not unkindly. 'Come on, Wrennie. You're on orderly duty.'

He pretended he was still asleep. 'What?'

'You and Smithy.'

'Where's Dag?' he groaned.

'As usual, busy as a one-legged bloke in an arse-kicking contest,' his companion muttered. 'He's on the crapper but I'll be giving him the hurry on too. The boys are looking for fried eggs, bacon, toast, butter, marmalade, tea with milk and sugar, and then a big slice of sponge cake with orange icing. All right, mate? Don't let us down.' The soldier chuckled dryly – they all knew their next meal would be only more bully beef and dry biscuits.

'It can't be my turn already,' Jamie grumbled, desperate to hang on to his private thoughts.

''Tis, cobber. Smithy's up. Come on, we're parched for a cuppa. Easy on the flies today.'

Jamie muttered beneath his breath, as odd cracks of gunfire were as determined as his grinning companion to make sure he knew another dawn had arrived. Mind you, cooking roster was more agreeable than being earmarked on the cookhouse fatigue for carrying up the water from the tanks in Shrapnel Gully, or searching for the wood to build the fires.

They all slept in their uniforms, so there was no need to do anything but swiftly visit the latrines, then make his way gingerly to the cookhouse under the shelter of some overhanging rock to get bully beef sizzling with a scarce supply of bacon. Eggs and toast were only in their daydreams, but he was alongside Smithy, one of those people who insisted on being disgustingly cheerful, whistling while he fried the food. He let Jamie make the tea in an old kerosene tin and get the hard biscuit sorted; Jamie knew his unit was taking it easy on him. There wasn't a man in the regiment who didn't know the stunned mindset of losing a close mate to a cruel death.

Jamie counted only eight flies in his dixie this morning and took it to be a good omen. Spud had once told him that one of the Chinese workers on his dad's farm had said eight was the luckiest of all numbers. Spud hadn't been able to back up that claim, but the notion had stuck. Jamie found himself counting off in eights. Eight steps, eight bullets, eight bombs, eight hours; his birthday date added up to eight, and he'd met Claire on the eighteenth, hadn't he?

He skimmed off the drowning insects as bullets zipped and popped, one piercing a sandbag that flung some of its contents into his face just as he sipped the horrible brew, grit adding to his first mouthful. He ignored the porridge he'd been given.

A drizzle had decided to become insistent, turning his surrounds into a steadily dampening swamp of mud and blood. His only consolation was that at least it wasn't cold. If they'd gone to the Western Front in Europe as originally planned, he couldn't imagine how much worse these war conditions might feel in freezing rain, waking up covered in frost. The flies suddenly seemed trivial.

'You all right, Wrennie?' someone asked. He looked up, glad that no one else called him by Spud's nickname. 'Eat it, man, before the flies do.'

They both glanced at the gluggy porridge.

'Do you want it, Jimmy?'

The older man, exceptionally tall, forever bending as a result in the trench, leaned in now. 'What's going on in here, lad?' he asked, tapping Jamie's head.

Jamie shook it. 'Nothing much.'

Jimmy's expression told Jamie he didn't believe that for a second. 'I think you think too much and too deep, son. Eat, drink, sleep, kill Abdul before he kills you. It's simple. We're here now. We can't change anything.'

'Thanks, Jimmy.'

'Good lad.' He looked to his right as they heard an odd eruption of voices too. Jimmy must have straightened a little too much because a shell exploded just outside the trench and some shrapnel caught him across one side of his head.

He dropped, his dixie of tea falling with him to spill into the trench.

'Strike me,' he moaned. 'Those fuckin' pipsqueaks.'

Jamie was at his side in a heartbeat. 'Jimmy? Where else are you hurt?' he urged, noting the head wound.

'Just here, mate.' He gestured to his head. 'I'll be right. My bloody tea!'

Jamie had to smile, felt a surge of pride at how most of the men managed to keep up the cheer for each other. He had no right to be mooching around.

'I'm sorry, Jimmy. That was my fault.'

'You didn't launch the seventy-seven, son. Bastard German weapons.' Blood was flowing freely, bright and glossy from the wound.

'You need to get that seen to,' Jamie cautioned, nodding at the pale flap of flesh that now hung from Jimmy's parting.

'My own fault not wearing a helmet. But my dear old mum insisted I take my hat off when I sat down at her table to eat.'

The comment pricked at Jamie's memories of his own mother: how she had grumbled at her sons to comb their hair and wash their hands before they sat down to their evening meal. 'No substitute for manners, boys,' she'd murmur to the hungry men scraping back chairs and reaching for her freshly baked bread cut into slices as thick as gravestones.

'Here, Jimmy, drink mine.' Jamie reached for his barely touched tea. 'I sneaked one back at the cookhouse,' he lied.

Jimmy's eyes widened with gratitude and he took the mug, swallowing it greedily.

'Do you want some help getting to the dressing station? That wound needs attention.'

Jimmy waved him away. 'Don't fuss. I'll go.'

A commotion seemed to be rippling through the trench and he sensed, rather than heard, its arrival as it passed from man to man. He noticed suddenly that all firing had stopped and Jimmy was handing back his dixie and sighing as he hauled himself to his feet. The man weaved his way between other men and the angles of the trench.

'What's going on?' Jamie asked Bert Johnson next to him.

'Something about the armistice.'

An officer lumbered into view and all the men began shooshing each other to hear what he had to say.

'Tell the blokes up front to send it down the line,' Jamie growled.

'They're looking for volunteers to help clear the dead in no-man's-land,' came the reply back via the men ahead of him.

He waited.

'Yeah, it's an armistice. Officially from seven-thirty this morning.'

He listened to some of the men around him complaining about not wanting to help Johnny Turk while others spoke of the airborne diseases from the corpses that could kill able men in the trenches. Discussions parried back and forth.

'I'll go,' Jamie offered in the spirit of his new decision. 'Anything to change the scenery,' he added and pushed forward.

'Watch your bloody boots, mate.'

'Can't help it if you've got feet like battleships, Jacko,' he replied and grinned even though he wasn't yet feeling nearly as chipper as he sounded.

'Come on then, handsome. Make room, boys. The movie star's coming through.'

Jamie loathed the constant references to his looks but had realised long ago, even as far back as school days, that he couldn't have it all ways. His looks had made him popular but they had made him various enemies too, especially blokes who weren't good around girls and loathed his easy manner with them.

'You're the one who has to make room, Richo. Your gut's too big.'

Richo rubbed his belly. 'Can't help the awning over the toyshop now, can I?' he said, grabbing his own crotch.

The men around guffawed and Jamie couldn't help but join in. Right now the teasing felt somehow reassuring.

'Bugger me, well done, Wrennie,' someone said and slapped him on the back as he passed. 'Here comes another one, sir,' the bloke called out.

The officer nodded at all the men volunteering, pointed them to one end of the trench. Finally, when he'd gathered a sufficient working group, he addressed them as one.

'Well done, you men. There will be no firing from either side guaranteed. The truce begins officially . . .' He checked his watch, flipping the leather case open and nodded. '. . . in about eight minutes.'

Jamie swallowed. It was a sign from Spud.

'What if they're really doing a reccy of our trenches, sir?' one of the men piped up.

'A fair point, Trooper. It's been considered and decided that a line is to be pegged out down the centre of no-man's-land. We'll be handing out some Red Cross flags for you to use to do that. The Turks will work on their side and our men on this side of it.' He raised a hand at the obvious question rushing to be asked. 'Any Turks found dead on our side are to be picked up and taken to the centre line. They will do the same for our boys. On other ridges, it's more complicated but that's not our problem today. Each of you is to wear one of these Red Cross armbands. Please ensure it's clearly visible. I have no idea how jumpy Johnny Turk might be today but let's not give them an excuse, all right, lads?'

'What about weapons, sir?'

'Good question. No one is to carry a weapon during the course of today's work in no-man's-land. Is that understood?' The men nodded. 'The Turks proposed this so we'll respectfully agree. Any rifles found on no-man's-land are to be gathered and placed on stretchers. Same pack drill. If they're foreign, you take them to the centre line after removing the bolts and return them to their owners. If they're ours, we collect them from the pegged line as well.'

The staff officer continued, speaking through his ingenious bullhorn fashioned from an old can. 'Sounds like the ceasefire has begun. Your job is to clear the dead as efficiently as you can. I'll warn you this is going to be an unpleasant and above all emotional task, so you need to keep your wits and stay strong, boys. Concentrate only on our brave fallen and get them swiftly back so we can bury them with the respect they've earned.'

Jamie nodded with his fellow soldiers.

'The Turks are estimated to have lost ten thousand men nine days ago, when they promised to drive us all back into the sea. They've got their work cut out for them and we may be moving some of our men into work groups at the worst areas to help the Turks. So we're handing out red armlets. You're to wear those so everyone can recognise why you're there and what your job is. Each unit will have a staff officer and medical officer to accompany it. I want you all to tie a strip of calico to the top of the stakes over there. You're to raise that as you go over the parapet so Johnny Turk understands.'

The officer glanced at his watch again. 'It's eight o'clock exactly.' Jamie blinked. 'Stand by for orders once the demarcation line is set up and readied. Finish your breakfasts and get your armlets on. I'll be back shortly.'

———

When the staff officer reappeared with the medical officer the men were told to move. Jamie estimated nearly a hundred of them were involved. Everyone else in the trenches was ordered to keep their heads down and not give away any positions, any clue to their numbers.

Jamie was one of the first to raise his head over the lip of the parapet. Weeks of keeping their heads low at all times made him feel tentative, but when no bullets came spitting back, he grew bolder and scrambled up the slippery wall until he stood at the edge of the trench that had been his home for more than a month now.

Red Cross flags marked out the centre line. Opposite, no more than a dozen strides away, stood the Turks in a variety of uniforms, from olive green through to one presumably important person wearing sapphire with gold braiding. They were short, stocky men by comparison to his compatriots – even Spud might have stood taller than most of them – but they stood proud, bearing red crescents on armbands, and made his contingent look positively scruffy in their shirtsleeves, some even stripped down to singlets. He sighed out the breath he'd been holding and without fully registering that he was doing so, he lifted a hand in salutation to one of them.

The man on the other side of the line who noticed smiled and followed suit. Other men scrambled up beside Jamie and also began hailing the opposing force like friends. The feeling was genuinely mutual despite the obvious air of suspicion. He heard a familiar sound of flute music, and turned keenly to see a young man in the distance. In delighted response, he slipped out his harmonica and played a brief riff. The young man turned instantly and they both waved, grinning helplessly.

Jamie's staff officer was now speaking through a cloth loud-hailer. 'Parties of stretcher-bearers will run our dead back. You boys work quickly. Concentrate on the men first. Weapons later. Remember, if you see any dog tags, ensure you place them in their pockets or reattach them if possible. Record every name anyway. This will be vital in getting the right information to the grieving families.'

Jamie looked around, noting that the Turks were as inquisitive about their enemy as he was of them. He noted a single man, standing apart, wearing a different uniform of charcoal grey with polished long black boots. German, he reckoned. The man stared back at their side of the white flags expressionlessly and made no move to join any of his comrades finally beginning to shift towards their dead.

Jamie pulled out his handkerchief and tied it around his face. Some men were now predictably retching but he had been around enough dead sheep to withstand the dense and hideously sweet smell of putrefaction. As he moved closer to the bodies strewn about the few hundred yards they'd all been fighting over, the smell intensified and became cloying, permeating their hair, their clothes, even their skin, to ensure they never forgot this sight or the sacrifice that had been made.

The sounds of men sickening escalated and the horror of their war settled with a great weight of collective sorrow in the pits of their bellies. The trails of dark stains behind some of the corpses were testimony to the efforts of the wounded men who had tried to crawl back to the safety of their trench before dying.

No one was observing the order for speed. It was as though some unspoken new instruction came through to not begin work immediately but to take a deep breath instead. Men began to reach for cigarettes and matches. A smoke would calm the nausea, help disperse the thick smell of death gathering in their throats and settle the daunting feeling of what was ahead. Jamie was not a regular smoker but he kept cigarettes on him because Spud ran out so fast. Now, though, he wanted to smell the tobacco and taste its bitter burn. He'd cough and feel light-headed but even that wouldn't matter if he could just chase the taste of death from his mouth.

'Hello, Aussie,' someone said and he turned to see a Turkish soldier inches from the demarcation line, pearly teeth glittering as his mouth stretched a bright smile across his swarthy complexion. He was the young musician Jamie had spotted earlier.

'Smoke?' Jamie offered, making the gesture of thumb and forefinger moving to and from his lips.

The young man laughed. 'I speak your English.'

'Really?'

'I also like your music.' He gestured playing a mouth organ. 'You make the wind harp talk. Last night I heard you play and I was sure your breath was speaking to a woman.'

He baulked, shocked by his companion's perceptiveness. 'I'm Jamie,' he said, pointing a finger to his chest.

'My name is Shahin.' He bowed his head slightly, hand on heart. 'It means hawk and I am proud to meet you.'

Jamie blinked at the disarming respect. He reached out a hand. 'G'day, Sher . . .?'

The Turk gripped his hand and as Jamie looked down he realised his skin had bronzed to a similar colour as his companion's. They could be brothers.

'Shahin,' his companion pronounced again, slowly this time. 'Açar Shahin.'

'Shahin,' Jamie repeated and his friend beamed, nodding. 'I'm

Jamie Wren. It means, er, wren.' He laughed at how ridiculous he sounded. 'You know, the bird.'

'I know bird. I even know wren. Hawks can kill wrens,' he teased.

'Not this one,' Jamie assured but he could tell his new friend had not meant to offend, especially as he bent and then arched his back in huge amusement. 'Smoke? They're good.'

The young man stared entranced at the small packet. 'I will keep your cigarette as a gift.'

'Then take two. Smoke one, keep one,' Jamie insisted.

Shahin's eyes widened. 'Thank you, James Wren. I knew I would like you from your music but I like you even more now.'

Jamie smiled at Shahin's formal manner. The momentousness of this hard-to-imagine truce after such cruel and vicious fighting began to tingle through his body as though forcing him to mark it. It would never come again, he was sure, and only the men experiencing this intimacy with the enemy would ever know this extraordinary sense of sharing and camaraderie. He presumed everyone else in his burial party was acknowledging a similar sense of the unreal as men leaned on shovels or shifted their weight to a relaxed stance and shared smokes and soft, sad laughter with their opposites. Some exchanged their gum-wounding hard biscuit for tough brown bread and tried on each other's hats. Language did not seem to be a barrier.

'Do they all speak English?' he asked Shahin with surprise.

The Turk shook his head. 'These are shepherds and farmers, all brave soldiers but uneducated. War needs no language. Neither does peace and friendship,' he said, echoing Jamie's thoughts as he likened this man's dark eyes to the black tourmaline he'd seen dug up and polished from the Flinders Ranges around where he had lived. *Had lived.* Would he see it again? Would he ever show Claire?

'Where do you come from?' he asked, keen to mask the needle

of pain which that thought had provoked.

'I come from Istanbul.'

'I've seen some photographs of the city.'

'Exotic for Aussies, yes?'

'Yeah, those . . .' and he began to draw the shape of a building in the air with his hands. 'I don't know what you call them.'

'They are mosques, James Wren. We call that shape you refer to as *minare*. *Minaret* in your language, I believe.'

'Is it a church?'

Shahin smiled again as he dragged back on his cigarette. 'A place of prayer and promise,' he qualified.

'And you do it all day long, I hear?'

He looked back at Jamie, amused. 'Just five times. It is not hard to do so.'

'In the trench?' Jamie asked, intrigued.

'Yes, in the trench. Allah does not stop listening just because we kneel below ground or because we are at war.'

'Why are we at war?'

This caught his companion's attention. He blinked, fixed Jamie with a dark stare, his Australian cigarette halfway to his mouth. 'I ask this question of myself each day. Because our countries have been coerced to support bigger, powerful countries that want to rule others, take their resources, enslave them . . .'

Jamie nodded. He didn't fully share that opinion but the sentiment felt right. 'I have no quarrel with you, mate.'

'Quarrel?' Shahin repeated, trying to work out the meaning.

Jamie balled two fists as though he was going to box but shook his head. 'I don't want to fight with you.'

'Ah! Quarrel. You have taught me a new word, James Wren. Now I must give you a gift.'

'It's just a word.'

'Words are powerful, my friend. Words are the most important aspect of being men. We start wars with them. We can end wars with them. Do you have a woman, James Wren?'

Jamie's breath caught. 'I do,' he replied and believed it for the first time.

'What is her name?'

'Claire Nightingale.' Just to say her name aloud made his spirits lift.

Shahin smiled with obvious pleasure. 'She too is one of our winged family. Do you love her?'

'With all of my heart,' Jamie said. It was now their secret. 'The memory of her is keeping me alive.' He realised he'd never said anything more truthful, emotional or private. 'I mean . . . I want to live to see her even just once more.'

'Have you told her this is how your heart feels?'

He shook his head and Shahin tutted. 'Imagine how she will feel when you do. I think I would give my life gladly if I was in love and loved by someone in return.' His smile faded and Jamie glanced over at the wintry gaze of the German, staring but not participating.

'He's German?'

Shahin nodded.

'Never seen one up close. Wish I had my rifle in my hand now.'

'Have you killed anyone, James Wren?'

Jamie puffed out his cheeks, then sighed it out. 'I don't know, to be honest.'

'I shall tell you this because we are now friends in here,' Shahin said, touching his heart again. 'I fire my rifle but I avoid killing with it. If my bullets have ever struck a man, it is without intent or malice and I hope he will forgive me.'

That came as a surprise. 'You'd better not share that with your men,' Jamie said. He could see the Australians drifting back to their ugly work.

'I would be dead if I did. I think I shall be killed anyway.'

Jamie's attention snapped back. 'Keep your head down, Hawk. We have to make music together again. Stay safe and when this is over we'll have a beer together . . . or whatever stuff you blokes drink.' He made the gesture of sipping from a glass and nodded. 'Promise?' He held out his hand to shake again.

Shahin's expression clouded with sorrow. 'I cannot promise that.' He reached into his pocket and pulled out a letter, stained brown. 'Will you keep this for me?'

Jamie frowned. 'Why?'

'It's to my father. Take it to him for me, James Wren.'

'You take it. You're going to see him.'

Shahin shook his head. 'I fear my father may be secretly glad if I died here. I don't want him to think I wasn't brave but I never want him to know I couldn't kill another man . . . my enemy. Let him look upon my enemy and see James Wren – maybe then he might understand in his heart.'

'Listen, Hawk —'

'Please. If I live, maybe I will have that conversation with him. If not, you show him. He must know what is in here and it carries my blood upon it – a small wound, nothing important, but he and I share that blood, so I didn't rub it off.'

Jamie began to speak but Shahin cut him off. 'I should give it to my own people, I know. But it is more meaningful if you deliver it. Live for me, James Wren . . . live for Açar Shahin and for Claire Nightingale.' He pressed the small folded letter into Jamie's fingers and covered both with his hands. 'We have unhappy work to perform, my brother.' Then he said something in Turkish before he grinned wide and bright as though they were saying cheers. 'I am bidding you farewell in my language and telling you to stay safe, James Wren. You bugger!'

Jamie wasn't ready for the expletive and despite the melancholy mood, erupted into delighted laughter. 'Where did you learn that?'

'Ah, we Turks hear you Aussies saying this regularly. We like this word. Is it a prayer?'

'It's an oath. Fair dinkum,' he replied in a wry tone.

Shahin didn't understand but it didn't matter. He reached into his pocket again. 'This is my prayer book. I want you to have it and think of me, for I no longer need it.'

'Why not? I thought you prayed five times a day.'

His companion looked back with a wistful expression. 'Because I am not long for this world but I am not scared either. I will be glad to be in Allah's care.'

Jamie was pleased he could respond in kind, digging into his breast pocket and pulling out his small Common Book of Prayer that his local reverend had pushed into his hands on the Sunday before he left Melrose for the Quorn Railway Station.

'Here's mine. I can't read yours but I can imagine it doesn't say much that is different.'

'And in spite of it we try and kill each other.'

'No bullet of mine will ever touch you, Shahin.'

Shahin tapped his head and then his heart. 'And should any Turkish bullet try and find you, my friend, let it pass over you like wind through the ravine.'

They smiled at each other and fell suddenly silent over the handshake before parting. There was nothing more to say. Jamie tucked the prayer book into his breast pocket over Shahin's letter and lifted a hand in farewell. He noticed that all the inquisitive Turks who were not part of the burial squads had either not been given the same orders or were defying them, because lines of darkly moustached men were lining their trenches' parapets, giving the ANZACs a clear view of their enemy's lines and the daunting number of men they were up against. He glanced over at one of the other troopers.

'Yeah, I see them, Wrennie. Deadset. Now we know. We can report back.'

'What about that bastard German watching like an overlord? I noticed he lifted a spade against one of the Turks, threatening him. Did you see?'

'Bloody oath! Wish I had my catapult. I could kill him like the strutting grey pigeon he is with a single shot.'

The gruesome task began again and for hours, favouring his wounded shoulder, Jamie lost himself in the deepest sorrow he had ever felt, or perhaps ever would again. So many of the fallen had lain on this ground since the day of the landings and in the heat had decayed so that the padre's blessings were murmured over near skeletons. It was a tragic day of heartbreak as Jamie lifted one man after another towards his final resting place and all he could think about were the women at home – mothers, sisters, girlfriends, wives and daughters who would weep – while their brothers and fathers, if not fighting as well, would punch walls, get drunk, be forever changed.

He touched his pocket where Shahin's letter was hiding and swore to keep a promise to a bright young man whom he would have liked to know better.

By just after three in the afternoon, with the dead finally cleared on both sides, the task of unbolting the strewn weapons became the paramount objective, but Jamie left that to another raft of men. He'd stood at the parapet and smoked, using it as an excuse to take every moment possible away from the trench. Looking down the hill he could see men, like tiny dolls, splashing in the water, taking a rare chance to bathe without the threat of a sniper's bullet. That's what he should do. He needed to wash away today's sorrows, rub salt into his skin and clean away the death. And perhaps spy Claire again – just a sighting of her, a raised hand over a distance, would be enough to sustain him.

He saw the staff officer look at his watch and begin taking

down the makeshift flagging. A new, tense silence had overtaken them that felt eerily dangerous and with it came the promise of more bloodshed, mocking the day's toil. He took out his father's watch and saw that it was now almost four-thirty but the Turks still lingered on the parapet, clearly unenthusiastic to go back into their trenches and resume the killing. And yet within minutes Jamie was back down in his trench with his mates, reluctant to share the experience of the day that felt as though he had communed with the spirits of the dead and released them.

A shell went off nearby and that set off a chain reaction that seemed to drag all the men from their curious stupor. Suddenly a volley of bullets was whizzing and spitting again but seemed to deliberately miss their mark. It was as though both sides were clearing their throats, warning of the end of their polite truce. The rifle fire only lasted a few heartbeats but it certainly signalled they were back to being enemies, locked once again in deathly combat.

Jamie thought of Shahin and felt a profound sadness grip him as he recalled the youngster's conviction that he would not survive the war. He reached for the letter through his uniform again, heard the paper crinkle, and as though that was a trigger he heard a shout ring out into the brief silence, and recognised the voice.

'Look at this silly bugger, will you?' his neighbour said. His name was Don but everyone called him Donkey.

Jamie turned at the sound of the yelling voice, hearing his own name.

'*Jamie Wren, keep your promise!*' came the cry.

'No!' Jamie howled in closed-eyed despair into the brief report of bullets.

'Stupid bugger,' Donkey sighed, lowering his makeshift periscope he'd fashioned from an old tin can of fruit. 'Some young Turk taking your name in vain there, Wrennie. What's that about?'

Jamie could barely swallow. He grabbed for Donkey's periscope to bear witness to Shahin's suicidal dash, but it was the last conscious action he made. The mortar landed as did the return fire and Jamie felt himself helplessly bent double before being flung by an invisible shove that tossed him aside with the strength of a thousand angry men.

Broken and unconscious, Jamie Wren landed, crumpled, in the neighbouring trench.

8

Claire was once again on the beach. Given the armistice, she had swiftly volunteered to help clear the backlog of men most desperately in need of nursing attention. She and another nurse had been given permission to accompany a doctor going ashore. Everyone on the *Gascon* was on full alert – without the fear of shelling, they planned to shift twice as many soldiers this evening towards the safety of Mudros and Egypt.

Claire closed her eyes momentarily as she alighted from the jetty to feel damp sand suck at her feet. She was now sharing the same land as Jamie. He wasn't even that far away, perhaps half a mile, and she cast a silent wish for the miracle that she might see him today. She shyly scanned the bathers, hoping that he may be one of the men laughing like schoolboys in the warm seawater. The playful atmosphere felt wrong given the awful work that was being carried out above them. Word was that the dead were so thick on the ground, so badly decomposed and mixed in with the Turkish corpses in some parts, that proper burial was going to be impossible. Some of the brave Allied soldiers would be left behind in Turkey, unidentified, but she couldn't dwell on that now; she had to focus on the living.

Ragged men were brought down from the dressing stations on high to the beach for hopeful removal away from their hell. She saw two Turks in among the wounded. One had his jaw shot away so badly she didn't spend much time examining him once she'd pulled away the dressing to see him hemorrhaging.

'We found him hiding in the scrub. A sniper. Can't imagine how many of our boys he's killed,' the accompanying soldier said. 'But he's still a bloke, probably with a family like me.' She'd squeezed the man's arm and thanked him for his compassion. The Turk had taken a final wheezing breath and died with a word on his lips she did not understand. It wasn't Allah, though. She could guess what it was.

'You did the right thing,' she assured the New Zealand soldier, who looked down at the dead Turk, hardly daring to believe he was gone.

'How bloody inconsiderate.'

She smiled sadly, knowing the dry humour helped the men to cope. 'We'll take care of it,' she said and the soldier sighed, nodded and moved on.

Claire shielded her eyes as she looked up the cliff face, once again searching for any sign of James Wren, feeling her desire to lay eyes on him again like an obsession. She noted a chaplain being helped to clamber over the scrubby landscape and imagined he would never have a busier day. Everything seemed to be happening at twice the normal speed as the ANZACs took full advantage of the ceasefire.

She refocused her attention on a man who cheerfully assured her he couldn't see anything and wondered if she might clean away what was blocking his sight. Claire couldn't bring herself to tell him that she didn't think his injury would ever permit him to see again.

'Let's get Lieutenant Shepperton moved down to the jetty for loading, please. He's to go on tonight's sailing.'

'Thank you, Nurse Claire,' Shepperton said. 'But if there's a man whose life might be saved in my place, please give him my spot.'

She squeezed his shoulder. 'Room for everyone tonight, Lieutenant,' she lied with a smile in her voice.

Claire couldn't hear a single rifle and after nearly a month of continuous shelling and gunfire, it felt unnerving. They'd all become so accustomed to the sound. The day wore on and the sun like a molten orb conspired with the drizzly morning to turn the atmosphere tropical. The stifling air was just how she remembered it in Sydney. Those Australian summers she recalled had made her feel like a fish suddenly dragged from the water, gasping to breathe. Her hair would stay dampish all day from her morning shower and her school dress would stick to her back while she waited for the train on a sunlit platform. She wouldn't describe those as happy days because she missed her father and worried for his life daily, but they were not unhappy, more an uneventful series of weeks connected by a railway line that took her either to school in eastern Sydney or back home on the North Shore. When the family she was staying with moved to Hunters Hill she enjoyed the ferry ride each morning and evening into the city, but she only had that pleasure for a short while before leaving again for the unknown of life in Tasmania.

However, she had taken control of that life as soon as she could and she promised herself now, on a small, crowded patch of beach in Turkey, that she would never permit other people's circumstances to crush her spirit as had nearly happened in Australia. And even though Jamie's situation was dire, she would not give up on him either. Somehow she would see him again and test whether their moment of madness on the ship had been real.

Right now she could feel teardrops of perspiration coursing down the shallow valley between her breasts, and a salty wetness stung her eyes. If the broken, damaged soldiers could remain cheerful, so could she.

It was nearing four-thirty when she diverted her attention to sip some water, without even looking up from her patient, and heard a hail of gunfire.

'The armistice is officially over,' Gupta confirmed.

Claire let out a slow breath of quiet despair. 'Well, I'm not leaving yet.'

Gupta gave her a soft look of silent reprimand as if to say there were already too many men destined for the sailing tonight but he said nothing . . . perhaps knew better.

'There we are, Maurie. Your broken bits are all immobile now. It will hurt a little but we'll get those bones set properly back on Mudros. You're off to sail the Greek Islands tonight.'

Maurie blew her a kiss with difficulty. 'Sounds romantic. Thanks to you, Nurse Nightingale.'

She stood and stretched out her aching back as Maurie from Gippsland was helped away between a couple of able men down the beach. Claire became aware that the sound of artillery had increased, a sobering reminder that no matter how many men she put through triage today, there would be dozens more taking their spots on the beach by tomorrow. It felt momentarily hopeless but a timely arrival of one of the doctors was just what she needed.

'Well done, Nightingale. The most seriously injured are now all accounted for and being loaded. Can you believe we're down to seeing men with non-life-threatening wounds now?'

She smiled. That did feel satisfying.

'That's truly something.' He beamed. 'After a month of feeling like I've been drowning, we've clawed our way to the surface because of one day of ceasefire.'

Claire wanted to say it would be so easy to have a ceasefire every day but the doctor suddenly frowned, looking past her, distracted.

'Spoke too soon, Nightingale. Looks like an urgent one. Come on.'

She dragged her hand across her forehead and then used her sleeve to dab away the drenched feeling on her face. Matron would not approve. Setting her shoulders, Claire trudged after the doctor through the sand, feeling the weariness of her long, hot day complaining through tired legs.

'Put him down,' she heard the doctor order and she saw the legs of a soldier on a stretcher appear. 'Right, we've got bleeding, Nightingale.'

She hurried around the doctor and knelt down, focused entirely on where the doctor was pointing. The soldier looked like any other, his features hidden by dirt and blood.

'Shears!' the doctor growled.

Claire began cutting away the uniform at the man's shoulder. He reeked of decay and she instinctively began looking for a gangrenous wound. She had to catch her breath, the stench was so powerful, and the doctor was pulling a similar expression. 'Heavens, that smell is far too strong – he should be dead.' Claire noticed a handkerchief was still tied around the injured man's face and pointed to it in query. 'What's this?'

'He was one of the burial party volunteers,' a stretcher-bearer nearby explained. 'You should smell it up there.'

The injured man's entire front seemed to be oozing blood. They couldn't guess where the main wound was located.

'How could this happen during armistice?' the doctor groaned, his happier mood of just minutes ago evaporated.

'It was the first shell of the day,' one of the men continued. 'Apparently Trooper Wren was one of the most stoic – he did the work of several men today.'

Claire gasped at the mention of his name.

'Right, let's make sure his airwaves are clear.'

She let out a tight squeal of anguish as the doctor pulled away the soldier's handkerchief.

'Found the wound?' the doctor asked, thinking that had prompted her surprise.

But Claire couldn't answer. She snatched the handkerchief, dipping it into the bowl of antiseptic and wiping away the dirt from Jamie's face. Her breath was coming hard and fast, sobs not far away. *Stay in control*, she urged herself.

'Nightingale?'

'I know him,' was all she could choke out. 'He's . . . a close friend.'

'Bugger!' the doctor said. 'You really shouldn't —'

'Don't!' she snapped, silencing him with a glare. 'Where's he hurt? We have to find the wound.' She ripped open his uniform frantically, slicing through his shirt with eager scissors, before letting out a groan of fear. They all seemed to share it. His shirt was soaked with fresh blood, wet, gleaming and eager to flow.

'Claire . . . this one looks —'

'No. No, please.' Helpless tears ran a line down both cheeks as she entreated her superior. 'We have to try.'

Claire could see as well as the doctor that James Wren would normally be given up as a certain death but today had been a special day of few bleeders. Maybe her luck would run as fast as her tears.

The doctor peered into the wound. 'Shrapnel. He's going to need immediate surgery if he's to last the next few hours. Go with him, Nightingale. But then hand him over.'

She sniffed, forcing down the uncharacteristic feeling of silent hysteria.

'Let's go! Follow me,' she ordered the stretcher-bearers and without even looking back to thank the doctor, she was pushing through the shoulders of others, marching down the beach, urging the stretcher-bearers on.

'Emergency!' she called to the man directing operations onto the craft.

One glance at Nurse Nightingale's distraught face made him call for instant action and in minutes she had supervised Jamie's loading onto the barge and they were being ferried towards the *Gascon*.

'Hold on, Jamie, hold on,' she murmured, feeling fresh tears sting, but she wouldn't let them fall as she pressed down on the hemorrhaging wound.

———————

It was a blur. She'd seen Jamie all the way into theatre before promising to return 'in a blink'.

Matron must have seen the sudden activity and after a glance at Claire's crumpled expression as she hurried into the nurses' station to scrub her hands, her superior's gaze settled to one of implacability. Claire got no further than untying her filthy apron.

Matron came up behind her. 'If you think, Nurse Nightingale, that I plan to allow you into theatre tonight, you are wrong.'

Claire swung around, but Matron's finger was already in the air. 'Absolutely not. Under no circumstances.'

'Matron —'

'No. Go change, get some food and a cup of tea, and sit tight. I have no idea why this soldier is so special to you but I shall see you soon enough and you can tell me then. Until I see you next, stay well away from theatre. That's not a suggestion, Nightingale. And for heaven's sake, change!'

Matron turned on her heel and Claire gulped back a dry sob that rose helplessly from her chest. If Matron was right about anything, she needed to pull her shattered mind together; she was no good to anyone, least of all Jamie, if she couldn't think straight.

'He's in the best hands,' Rosie murmured nearby, squeezing Claire's arm. 'Your favourite surgeon is clearing theatre for him.'

'Thanks,' Claire bleated.

'Wash your face, take a break, and get your mind back on the job. I wish I knew what this was all about.'

'Who's doing the anaesthetic?'

'Claire,' Rosie murmured with exasperation. 'Go.'

Her friend left her alone to stare at her hands, which were stained with blood – Jamie's blood. It could have belonged to others but she knew in her heart it was his life that had bled into her hands. She could feel the red-brown smudges burning, taunting her with the fragility of his life in the trenches and up on the ridges. *Live, Jamie, live*, she pleaded in the tilting, muggy silence of where she stood. *Live for me. And I will love you.*

She heard voices and turned away, but someone called her name.

'Claire! You're needed in theatre.'

She felt her heart give as her mind scattered to the possibilities. He'd died before they'd even had a chance to operate? No, he'd roused, was asking for her so she would share his dying words . . .

'I'm not supposed to —'

'Matron's orders.'

She ran back, ripping off her apron, scrubbing her hands and, flicking droplets of water, hurried into theatre.

Matron met her. 'Contrary to my best advice, our surgeon insists only you should apply the anaesthetic.'

Claire straightened, and the older woman forced her to return her gaze. 'Claire. It's not just one wound, it's several.'

She nodded, swallowing hard, and found the calm that her years of training had bestowed. The surgeon trusted only her. Jamie was depending on her.

'I'm fine, Matron,' she finally said, surprised her voice sounded so steady. In theatre she knew her role and already she felt more in charge of herself. 'I know what I have to do.'

Matron gave her a final warning but Claire saw beyond the stare to glimpse only sympathy.

'Nightingale!'

'Coming, sir.'

She finally approached the prone Jamie. His clothes were removed, his body stained with blood and his skin was slightly charred, but his face in repose looked relaxed and unmarked...vulnerable but desperately handsome. And hers. No one had belonged to her for years; now someone did. She wouldn't give him up.

Claire cleared her throat. 'Has he regained consciousness?'

'Briefly,' he answered crisply. 'Wondered about you, actually.' His face shifted briefly towards her, filled with enquiry.

She felt warmth spread from her churning belly and ascend to her throat in a surge of reassurance.

'Matron didn't want you to attend; obviously this soldier is known to you?' He looked up again from where he was staring at Jamie's abdomen – the old wound by his shoulder had reopened, there was a fresh wound at his arm, his other shoulder, and in his side. She nodded, saying nothing. 'Well, I can't be worried about that. If we're going to save his life, I need my best nurse working with me. Get him under.' She watched him pull off his gloves. 'These bloody things make me move around a man's insides like a bull in a china shop. I'll scrub with carbolic. Have him ready.'

It required all of her newly honed skill to calculate the amount of anaesthetic to use on a weakened man.

'I'm not going to use the Schimmelbusch alone,' she said, reaching for the wire-screened vaporiser. 'I'm going to try something.'

'This may not be the moment for experiments, Nightingale,' the surgeon warned.

'I've read about it. It's a gentler way of delivering the sedation.'

'He doesn't care,' he said, nodding at the tray of instruments on the trolley. She pulled them towards her.

'Its effect is lengthened but apparently with less impact on the patient. He's lost blood, he's weak.' She folded up a towel several times and placed the mesh over it. 'He'll need to be under for a while.' She dripped the chloroform onto the mask. 'He could wake up again if I don't give him enough.'

'Forget whoever this man is to you and just work with me now to save a soldier's life.'

Claire steadied herself with a slow deep breath and having finished with the chloroform, began administering the ether. The two drugs would work together to keep Jamie unconscious. 'He's ready.'

'Then let's begin.' The surgeon probed the ugly wound to the right side of Jamie's abdomen and Claire blinked at Rosie, who had arrived to assist, refusing to allow another tear to drop.

But despite their best intentions, before the doctor could so much as offer his thoughts, Jamie Wren's heart gave out.

'There's no pulse, doctor,' Rosie confirmed glumly. 'He's gone.'

Claire gasped and realised that the brief shriek echoing off all the hard surfaces was her own.

Even the surgeon had blanched above his mask at the suggestion that Claire had just put forth. 'Absolutely not. It's too risky.' He tore off his mask and pointed at Claire. 'I mean, for you. It's dangerous enough in sterile conditions and in a proper theatre of a proper hospital.' He shook his head. 'No, I don't wish to risk you or waste time trying to save the life of someone who is technically already dead,' he said as Claire pushed up and down on Jamie's chest, willing his heart to start again.

She looked over at Rosie, who had her fingers on the artery at his wrist. She nodded, her eyes lighting with excitement for Claire. 'I've got a pulse again.'

But the surgeon shook his head. 'His heart will stop once more, I assure you.' He didn't say it unkindly but he was firm.

Claire was hearing none of it. 'It's my decision to risk my life.

It's his only chance. Rosie, help me, please.'

Rosie looked unsure of defying the chain of command, glancing at Matron, who had arrived to hear the serious news, but with another glare from her friend, she hurried to help Claire get ready.

'Claire!' Matron breathed out in disbelief, all protocols apparently being dispensed with in the collective shock gripping the theatre. 'What exactly does this man mean to you? We've lost hundreds of others.'

'And he's already died once,' the surgeon added wearily. 'We've revived him but his blood pressure is failing again.'

'That's why we have to do this now!' Claire insisted, glaring at all of them. 'Let me give him my blood and give him a chance.' She searched the faces of those in charge, pleading with her gaze. 'I already know we're compatible from the blood testing in Australia,' she said, her final words wept rather than spoken.

Rosie chipped in, worried. 'Claire, this endangers your life. Don't you understand?'

'Of course I do! But his life is clearly over if we don't do this. And I don't want a life if Jamie's not in it.' There, it was out for everyone to examine. The shock of her words hit them all and slapped them from the stupor.

The doctor reacted fastest. 'Claire, listen to me now. The risks outweigh any potential chance he has.' He began to list them as Claire started rolling up her sleeve. 'Blood clots too fast, your arteries are too small for this sort of transfer, we have no way of knowing how much is being transfused, or —'

Claire crossed all the protocol boundaries when she clutched at the surprised doctor, her voice shaking as she snapped. 'Doctor, it's his only chance anyway . . . so any obstacles you suggest are purely academic. I'm going to do it, and for all the countless hours I've assisted you, do this just for me.'

The doctor looked vaguely helpless and then at Matron, who

shook her head, looking suddenly redundant. 'Matron?' he pressed. 'Please, she's in your charge.'

'No, I'm afraid Nurse Nightingale has a mind of her own,' Matron said in a hard voice but the look she cut Claire told her that she was impressed, proud even.

Claire would face any punishment later; right now Jamie's life was all that mattered. 'It's my decision, my risk. No one here is responsible for these actions except me. You've all heard it. Now, please . . . Rosie, can you do it for me?'

Rosie nodded with a soft smile and a glance at Matron, who acquiesced.

The doctor blew out his cheeks, giving up the fight. 'Right, well, we've only got minutes,' he said, looking suddenly flushed and excited. 'Let's get some space around them both. We need Claire lying down beside this soldier so their arms are together but we need her slightly elevated. Nurse Parsons, I want you to use the radial artery in her wrist.'

'Surely the median basilic?' Rosie wondered, gesturing towards Claire's elbow.

The surgeon glared over the top of his mask. 'Don't question me. This is hard enough as it is. We haven't performed a single transfusion on the ship. The radial is accessible – just do it!'

Within moments, Rosie had conquered her shaking hands and pressed the needle deftly into Claire's wrist, reaching the tiny artery. 'Thanks,' Claire whispered.

'You're definitely buying the drinks next time we hit Egypt,' Rosie warned.

The surgeon pushed past Rosie to wave a gloved finger in Claire's face. 'Right, we're going to move slowly on this. Claire, any tightness in your chest, difficulty breathing, if I sense you losing too much colour or getting dizzy, it's over, do you understand?'

She nodded.

'Right. Nurse Parsons, if you want your friend to survive this, you must scrutinise her colour. The first sign of paleness or nausea and you pull that needle out, all right?'

'Yes, doctor,' she replied in a meek tone. She turned back and winked at Claire. 'This is really going to cost you a big night out.'

Claire closed her eyes, and to stem her racing fear and to keep her blood flow calm, she disappeared into recollections of nursing school and the physiology of her blood vessels. She conjured the image from her textbook and then imagined tracing the path from her chest wall to under her arm and along to her wrist, where her strong heart that was full of love now pumped her lifeblood into Jamie's network of vessels.

'Well, thank heavens they insist on compulsory blood grouping before these boys leave Australia,' she heard Matron mutter, but Claire didn't open her eyes. She focused on the image of their bloods welcoming each other as happily as their lips had. They were compatible, they were in love and were both going to survive.

'His colour is improving,' the surgeon murmured into the tense quiet a short while later.

'Claire's isn't.'

'A minute more, then, and we'll call it,' he said. 'This will be the first and last direct transfusion I'll be performing.' Nevertheless, hiding beneath the bluster there was still a hint of excitement to have performed the difficult procedure.

Claire heard his voice close to her ear and yet somehow it seemed to be coming from a distance, as though she was drifting. 'You leave him to us now, Claire. You've done something very special and no doubt prolonged his life – I shall do everything in my power to save it now.'

She sensed him moving away.

'Now, get Claire out of here. She needs sugar – sweetened tea is the best way.'

9

Matron arrived by the cot where Claire sat in a bubble of silence. The patient she tended was tied to the bed for fear of him rolling off in the swell of the seas that carried them away from Gaba Tepe towards Mudros Harbour.

'Nightingale, what possible use to me are you if you're not going to rest, eat, drink or even stretch those limbs?'

Claire dropped her shoulders from the tensed, hunched position they'd adopted and she straightened, pulling them back with a soft sigh as her shoulderblade made a clicking sound. She checked the clock on the wall. It was nearly time for another flushing out.

'Well, he has good colour.' Claire cut her a smile. 'Who was in this bed before?' Matron continued, frowning at Jamie's slack face.

'A captain. I gave his disc to the chaplain.'

'Pity. I thought he might just make it.' Matron sounded genuinely anguished. 'They worked very hard on this young man too. How is he doing?'

'I can't tell yet. His colour suggests his blood pressure is well improved, and we seem to have his fever under control, but even I can't fight the shock that might potentially take him.'

'That was an extraordinary decision you made back there. Most nurses would never have even seen a direct transfusion performed.'

'I had a brilliant training, Matron, and I can't imagine you'd have done any less.'

'Are you going to tell me about him?'

'I know so little, there's not much to share,' she said. 'I barely know him at all, except . . . he's come to represent every soldier for me.'

'I thought he was a family friend?' Matron replied, her tone bewildered.

In the barely lit dullness of the ward, surrounded by mostly sleeping, hurting men, she told her senior an abridged version of events, leaving out the romance and her aching heart since.

'These are certainly extraordinary times and we're witnessing events not even encountered in our nightmares. It's understandable that you are feeling so unsettled.' Claire blushed, guilty that Matron didn't know the half of it.

'But you have to go deep within yourself and find extra strength, extra courage. If those men out there can, we must. Now, promise me you'll go up on deck and breathe something other than stale air.'

Claire nodded. 'I'll go up in ten minutes.'

'All right. How is that sweet young Francis doing?'

Claire glanced over to where a lad, just seventeen, lay in a cot, having lost both legs.

'I don't know whether to be pleased he's as strong as he is or to wish he never wakes up.'

'Don't be that honest with him when he does wake up, Nightingale.'

'Sorry.'

'Gather all that pain up and lock it away.'

'Matron? May I request a longer shore leave?'

'No, you may not.' It was not said unkindly.

'No one will care for this man's wounds as I will . . .'

'My, that's a low opinion you have of your fellow nurses.'

Claire's lips parted in shock as she struggled to find the right words. She couldn't. 'I . . . I didn't mean —'

'I know you didn't,' Matron replied. 'But that's how it sounds. You're no good to me on this hospital ship if your mind is going to be elsewhere.'

Claire put her hands up in appeal. 'Will you spare me a few moments, please, up on deck? I'll just tend to Trooper Wren's wound but I would appreciate your advice about something.' She watched Matron nod tiredly and was reminded that not only did her superior worry about the patients but she had the additional burden of worrying about the welfare of her nurses. Claire knew she was adding more weight to the woman's duties.

She began gathering up the equipment she needed to irrigate the deep shrapnel wound in Jamie's side.

As Matron left she said back over her shoulder, 'And only if you show our youngest nurse how to do this procedure properly; we must all share our skills.'

'Yes, of course,' Claire said, gesturing to the young nurse arriving on duty.

'Meet me on deck in fifteen minutes, Nightingale,' Matron said.

Claire nodded while she affixed the tube to the bottle of Dakin's solution. 'Like this,' she said to the nurse. 'You don't want to deepen the wound but you need just enough pressure for the liquid to flow freely. Back in Alexandria – in a decent hospital – I would prefer to do this manually with a syringe.'

'Why?' her student said, holding a lamp over the wound as Claire cut away the dressing.

'Because you can manipulate the application to precisely where it needs to go. The mixture is obviously caustic and can horribly irritate the patient's skin. Most are too ill to notice. We're flushing this out every hour.'

'That's a lot of work.'

Claire looked up from Jamie's body where his rib cage protruded in ghastly outline. It was no different to those of the other soldiers, but it was no easier to accept how thin he had become. 'This routine could save his life. It's worth the effort; you must always go the extra mile.'

The youngster was genuinely inquisitive. 'Does it hurt?'

'Yes, extremely painful. But this patient is still too concussed to worry about it.'

'Is it true he's your sweetheart?'

'Gosh! Where did that come from?'

The girl smiled. 'I don't know about Matron, but the rest of us think it's wonderful.'

Claire knew she had no business feeling indignant. 'I have to meet Matron now,' she said, checking the clock again. 'Are you all right to wait here for Rosie?'

'Of course. What could go wrong in a minute?' she replied breezily.

Everything, Claire thought silently. Kissing Trooper Wren had taken less time and her life had turned inside out since. She helplessly rested her hand against Jamie's arm, allaying her fears by touching his warmth, telling herself that as long as he was here within reach she could keep him safe.

———

Claire escaped the ward quickly, moving swiftly up the levels until she could drag salted air into her lungs. The *Gascon* lumbered slowly through the heaving waters, the captain mindful of its delicate cargo. Claire had found her sea legs quickly but even so, she could feel the lift and drop beneath her shoes as the ship groaned softly. There were sailors moving around their duties and she saw two doctors smoking quietly in a nook. Once the ship picked up more speed and the breeze stiffened, the deck would clear but for now the air was coolly welcoming with the capacity to blow away her confusion.

'You wanted to see me, Claire?'

She turned and smiled haltingly at Matron, only now realising she hadn't thought through what needed to be told.

'Thank you, yes,' she said, buying a little time.

Matron leaned against the deck rail and closed her eyes momentarily. 'Out in the dark silence, skimming across the deep, I can almost convince myself that no one knows we're here and the world is not at war.'

Claire was sure everyone aboard felt a similar sense of peace during the crossings.

'Matron, I want to tell you the truth.'

'Always a good plan.'

She spared no detail, admitted the slip in protocol was her fault alone and owned up to feeling besotted and unanchored ever since that moment of sheer madness.

Matron surprised her with a sad smile. 'There's no reprimand coming from me, if that's what you were dreading. Somehow I sense you are already suffering enough.'

Claire felt her eyes water and was glad the moon was not out to reflect their moistness.

'As long as he's breathing, there's hope, but let me just caution you about that heart of yours. It's easy to get one's emotions confused in these situations. Empathy is a powerful feeling.'

'I've never experienced anything like this before. There have been hours these last few days, even during the short leave in Alexandria, when I felt as though I haven't been able to breathe, when I've made a pact with anyone listening that I'd swap my life for just a few hours with him . . . and now he may die.'

'The universe in its wisdom has presented him to you twice injured. Keep faith.'

'I doubt they'll leave him in Mudros. He'll be sent on to AGH1. The Cairo wards are equipped for the care he requires.'

Matron waited to hear what Claire said next.

'He's Light Horse Brigade. These mounted regiments are precious. I suspect they'll want him receiving the best care we can provide so he can be well enough to ride into the next battle if the Dardanelles can be secured.' Her tone had turned miserable.

'You would be right,' said Matron.

'About sending him to Cairo?'

'About everything. Mounted troops are precious. And yes, he's destined for AGH1. You should go with him.'

Claire straightened, turning to face her superior. 'I thought you said —'

'I didn't have all the facts. Now I do. Two days, Claire. That's all. You know how much you're needed here.'

Her mood brightened instantly. 'I just need to see him wake and be sure his memory is intact.'

'And perhaps tell him something?'

She nodded, embarrassed, but her spirits lifted with excitement. 'I don't know how. I'm so used to holding my feelings in check. Now I'm overwhelmed; I think I'm scared to admit how this feels.'

'Don't be. I'm going to admit something to you now that no other nurse who works for me knows.' Matron sighed and uncharacteristically slumped her shoulders. 'I was one of the lucky few chosen to serve at a stationary hospital in the Boer War. You know nurses weren't exactly welcome at battlefields in the early years of this century. Not like you young braves today.'

Claire half smiled.

'I was based in Rhodesia. And there I met my dear husband, a lightly wounded but effortlessly cheerful officer in the British Army. I think I fell in love with him from the moment he first laughed, cracking a joke about getting in the way of a bayonet. He was tall, not especially handsome, but, oh, he had fine hands and a mellow voice that made my heart skip a beat and a laugh that could make a whole room light up with fun. His wound was ugly and infected but it wasn't life-threatening and he wanted no fuss. We cleaned him, sewed him up and sent him off again.'

Claire's mouth opened in surprise.

'He was in hospital for three days and somehow he persuaded me to marry him in those seventy-two hours.'

Now Claire gave a soft gasp and Matron laughed. 'It all happened so terribly fast but I was a spinster, not especially pretty, and I'd had no offers of marriage. I wasn't yet too old but I also wasn't young. My head was filled with the passion for my work that for the first time was challenged by the passion I suddenly felt for him. I had nothing to compare it to; it was pure instinct and I didn't care that he was a decade older. In fact, I was so eager to become Mr and Mrs that the chaplain married us in a makeshift church, beneath the clearing station's awning, and with my husband's arm in a sling.'

Matron sounded lost in her recollections, then she refocused abruptly. 'Sadly, Ernest died. Caught an unlucky gunshot through the heart two months later and I was informed that he was dead as he hit the ground. I've never remarried, although surprisingly I have received an offer or two. I'd known what love felt like and I have never wished to tarnish that by feigning a similar affection for anyone else.' She shrugged and smiled. 'If you feel it, Claire, trust it but be aware of how fragile life is right now.'

Claire couldn't find anything to say to follow such a touching story or heartfelt advice. She simply nodded. Matron turned away, satisfied, and Claire knew this conversation would not be referred to again.

She took a final deep gulp of the Mediterranean air and made a promise that if Jamie survived and admitted to loving her too, then she would not let anything or anyone ever get in their way.

10

Jamie's lids batted open and he looked around fearfully, trying to make sense of his surrounds. It was no longer a lice- and disease-ridden trench but a sunlit, draughty ward in the Australian General Hospital 1. Claire was officially off-duty but couldn't help herself. Dressed in civvies, she still lent a hand around the ward but now all of her focus snapped to the man who had brought her here.

'Jamie,' she murmured close to his ear where she bent. 'You're safe.'

His eyes searched wildly, then settled on her before disbelief crept into them. He croaked, trying to say her name. She nodded, thrilled by his recognition and smiling through her misted gaze. He said something unintelligible but she was already reaching for the cup of water nearby. She helped to raise him slightly so he could sip before his head fell back on the pillow.

'Let me talk,' she urged, 'until you get used to where you are and your throat isn't so dry.' She smiled and nodded, calming his thoughts that she was sure were racing to convince him this was a dream. 'We're in Cairo,' she assured and watched his eyes widen with surprise. 'Do you remember the armistice?'

He nodded.

'Well, at the end of it you managed to catch the rage of a shell. We gave you a direct blood transfusion, a procedure that's fraught with dangers, but everyone was so desperate to save you that we went ahead anyway.'

She hurried on, frightened by how his tender gaze made her feel so vulnerable. 'A sniper bullet hit your wrist and used your bones as a guide to rip up your arm and out through your shoulder. Pretty clever bullet, eh?'

She told herself to breathe as she paused. He was going to come through this.

'Luckily that German bullet didn't hit too much on the way through. You've opened up the older wound so that renders your other shoulder equally useless for the time being. Meanwhile you took some shrapnel to your rib cage and had us all baffled – two broken ribs and, impossibly, no organs hit. The angels are watching over you, Trooper Wren.'

His intense expression hadn't changed, pinning her with that depthless green gaze of his to where she perched on the side of his cot.

Being out of uniform was disconcerting too. Her professional, unflappable manner had fled with her chambray, exchanged now for a butter-coloured cotton walking suit, which left her slightly nervous and feeling naked without her armour of starched crispness. She took a hurried breath. 'The surgeon got the offending shrapnel that broke through your ribs and dug itself in deep. It was smooth enough, though, fortunately.' She reached into her pocket and pulled out a tiny piece of shell casing, a triangle of metal not much larger than a grain of rice. 'Here, I thought you might like it as a keepsake. It's smaller than the pieces we flushed out of your shoulder, I'm glad to say.'

His gaze finally released her, shifting to her palm where the shrapnel lay, but it soon found her eyes again. His scrutiny felt as though he could see behind her words, past her overly bright tone and to her hammering heart.

'And . . . er, there was also this,' she said, hoping she sounded triumphant as she retrieved a dull grey bullet tip. 'This, rather amazingly, was dug out from a small book of Arabic found in your uniform pocket. It seems the pages saved your life because that bullet was on a trajectory to claim your heart.'

'Too late,' he said, his voice gritty. 'My heart's already given.'

Claire had the breath knocked out of her. 'Well . . . er, that's a marvellous outcome then, isn't it. Your girl back home can —'

Jamie reached for her hand, wincing at the obvious shock of pain that surely ripped from his wound. 'There is no girl back home for me any more,' he rasped. 'I told you that before. There's only you. You have my heart.'

Claire's defences fluttered away like autumn leaves on a blustery day. The dull pain of anxiety for his safety since they'd met had blended with the new and unnerving feeling of profound despair to see him unconscious, bleeding, dying, which had turned her building fear into a soup of stress in her gut.

There had been no more histrionics after the transfusion, not even a tear: only relief and heartfelt thanks for his survival.

But Jamie's declaration undid her now and the pressure boiled and bubbled until it foamed like cinder toffee she'd watched being made in her childhood. The tremor came up from her toes and travelled like an incandescent path of lightning towards her crown. She couldn't smile, struggled to even breathe in that heartbeat of understanding of what he meant with the words *There's only you*.

'I thought you were going to die,' she murmured. 'It was the blood loss and the shock of concussion, plus —'

Somehow he found the strength to shift himself enough to squeeze her fingertips to cover the metal fragments that had tried so hard to take him from her. 'How could I die knowing that a single kiss from you was never going to be enough?'

Claire looked up. She bent to gently touch his hand to her lips. 'Thank you for living.'

Jamie continued to find reserves of strength that impressed her. This time he raised his hurting arm so he could stroke her hair, gently caress her face again. His voice was hoarse but he could talk freely now. 'You kept me alive. I've thought of nothing and no one else since we met. I thought I had imagined being kissed. By the time I was back in the trench, I'd convinced myself I'd made it up, but still I kept telling myself I had to find out if you could possibly feel the same —'

'I do!' She trampled his words with her own pledge.

He paused, as though making sure he understood her intent. 'Will you say that before a chaplain?'

Claire stared at him, speechless momentarily. 'You want to marry me?'

'Marry you, take care of you, live with you, cherish you . . . I will love you until my arms are too withered to hold you and my lips too shrivelled to kiss you.'

She laughed, defying her tears that sprang helplessly.

'Marry me, Claire. I know I sound like a lunatic and you probably don't want to rush into —'

'I do,' she said. 'The next time I say those words will be over a Bible and a vow with you next to me.'

He gave a lopsided grin. 'Am I on morphine?'

She beamed. 'Just a little.'

'Then I shall have to ask you again properly tomorrow.'

She felt dizzied by his promise and fell back on practicalities while she caught her breath. 'Well, then, you should know that they've closed the wound that we were irrigating on the ship. Your healing power is miraculous, I have to admit.'

'Just good country stock.' Jamie put the bullet back into her hand. 'I want *you* to keep this.'

'Don't want to show it off to your mates?' she asked.

'No. That bullet was meant for my heart, you say. Then you must have it, so you know you hold my heart in your hand. Now you know I'm invincible. Every time you look at that bullet you tell yourself that no matter where they send me, they can't kill me and I'm coming back to you.' He gazed intently at her. 'Understand?'

She let out an inaudible breath to slow her chaotic heartbeat. 'I want you to have this too,' he said, wincing as he reached to undo his identification tag.

'No, we're not allowed . . . Jamie, you need that.'

'I'll tell them I lost it. Quick, help me please, before anyone sees.' Reluctantly she aided him as he continued.

'Hold my name – that way it's yours already and the priest will only confirm it. I don't ever want it back from you.'

'I didn't think graziers were so romantic,' she said.

'Then you should read some bush poetry,' he grinned.

Claire could feel the warmth of the metal tag in her palm, his heat against hers. He seemed to sense what she was thinking.

'I'll feel you holding me until the war ends and then I will come and find you.'

She couldn't tell him this suddenly felt like a farewell.

'The last moment I can remember on Walker's Ridge was never feeling so sad in my whole life. Meeting you and not knowing if I'd ever see you again, losing Spud, then discovering friendship with a Turk who had a death wish. That's when I must have got caught by the sniper, because I reacted to his voice, and then the shell.'

She frowned.

'He called out my name, you see.'

'Who?' Claire asked.

'His name means hawk,' Jamie began and for the next few moments she listened silently as he told her about the young man he called Shahin, who played a flute and talked like a holy man.

'I've got friends back home that I don't feel as close to as I felt in those brief moments with him. We stood among our dead, feeling repulsed and yet bonded. We exchanged smokes and gave each other a gift and, I don't know, we sort of made a promise. It was like brother to brother. He was convinced he wouldn't outlive the war. I suppose in the emotion of the armistice he just decided to end it, rather than wait for death. He was shot by the men in my trench, just before the shell exploded around me.'

Claire waited but he said no more. Finally she spoke, her voice soft as a mother caressing her sleeping child. 'You're sure he's dead?'

He nodded. 'It was the periscope I stupidly grabbed to look at him that gave away my position. I saw his bullet-ridden body. Moments earlier we'd stood as family might and then as easily as flicking a switch, all the goodwill was gone and we were back to killing. My name was the last word he spoke.'

Claire stood to reach into the pocket of the jacket hanging on the end of his cot. 'I made sure we saved your belongings. The jacket has been repaired for you.' She held out the book she found. 'The Arabic book is his?'

He nodded. 'His book of prayer. I gave him mine. It didn't save his life, though.'

Claire offered him the book of hieroglyphics he would never be able to read, its middle pierced by the bullet it absorbed. She watched him regard it in soft awe. 'I found a letter as well. It's addressed to Shahin. I tucked it into the book.'

'Will you keep the book and letter please? It's to his father.' Jamie explained.

'I'm a stranger to your friend, though.'

'Claire, as soon as I heal they're going to send me back, whether it's Turkey or Europe. There's even talk of the mounted troops fighting new fronts across the desert. The letter is safest with you until I can get it to his father. It's something I have to do – I gave him my promise as I am giving you my promise that we will marry and have a farmhouse full of children.'

She laughed and it sounded like she didn't believe him.

'You said you envied my large family. We're going to make one of our own but in the meantime I'm going to take you to meet mine. We'll travel into the heartland and whisper our love to Australia's largest mountain range that holds ancient secrets. And I shall take you to where I come from because everyone will love you . . . except Alice, of course! And you can ride with me . . . oh, wait up, you do ride, don't you?'

She mocked an apologetic expression and shook her head.

'Well, as Mrs Wren you will surely be learning to ride and herd sheep.'

'Herd?' she squawked, making him laugh and wince at the pain. 'And where will we live?'

'Under a tree if we have to, but we won't have to. I'll be the first of the Wren boys married and Dad will give us our own farm. We can build a house or take over an existing one – there are plenty of cottages that just need a bit of elbow grease.'

'Oh, Jamie, I like this daydream.'

He turned earnest. 'It's not a daydream, Claire. You have to believe it. They'll send me away as soon as I'm well enough so we have to promise each other that we're going to do it.'

'I don't think I'll be much of a farmer's wife.'

'And I'd be a shocking nurse's husband if I didn't have animals to tend to and fences to mend. I . . . I'd be no good in a city, Claire. I belong in the outback.'

'I have no ties, so we go where you need to be, but what shall I do with myself? I don't want to be a burden.'

'What wouldn't we give to have a permanent nurse on hand, to patch us up after accidents or to help the midwife, and care for the anklebiters?'

Claire grinned; she hadn't heard that phrase for years and felt surprised how comfortable it sounded. Perhaps her years in Australia did count . . . maybe she could belong again.

'And how about taking care of the people of Farina?'

'You have no hospital?'

Jamie smiled. 'Well, there's a lot of bush medicine going on. We don't fuss much about minor injuries, you just wait for the next visit from the sisters. To have someone permanent would be a dream come true.'

'That sounds exciting,' she murmured truthfully.

'You could make such a difference to the town. You never were an apple eater, right?'

'Apple eater?'

He grinned crookedly. 'You don't have good memories of Tassie, so why not make my home your home?'

Why not indeed? 'Tell me about Farina. Such an odd name.'

'Yes, I think it means flour in Latin.'

'Why call it that?'

He shrugged. 'The mayor last century thought it would become an important wheat region but it never did. There's not enough water. It became more important as a railway hub. We were the end of the line for the Ghan, our railway that's named after the camel trains and their Afghan drivers.'

'You like your history, Jamie,' she remarked.

'It's more that I like my town. I thought I wanted to leave it . . . you know, go adventuring while doing the right thing for my country, but . . .'

She nodded. 'You don't have to explain. None of you brave boys knew what you were letting yourselves in for.' She held his hand, entwining her fingers with his.

'Everything I have or ever will have is yours now, Claire, including my hometown.' He smiled. 'Population three hundred but once we get there we can make it three hundred and ten.'

'Sounds as though I'll be permanently pregnant rather than permanent nurse.'

He raised both eyebrows suggestively and she giggled, barely believing the delight she was feeling. It was spreading through her like the first glow of dawn after a long, cold night. Yes, her life had been a long, cold night for too long and Jamie was the sunlight, warming her.

'Claire, I don't know how long I'll be here but I'm grateful to you for keeping that book and letter safe for me. It's the first thing I'm going to do when the war is finished . . . after kissing you, of course.'

'I don't want to talk about a dead Turk any more,' she admitted. 'I have only tomorrow until midday before I must report back for duty in Alexandria. We sail tomorrow night.'

They talked for another hour about inconsequential things, from Jamie's longing to taste a good South Australian beer again to Claire's admission of a new dress she'd bought on a whim during her last break in Alexandria, and her meeting with Eugenie Lester.

'I'd love you to meet her. She knows all about you. She's going back to England, though; she lives in a place called Radlett. I've promised to visit her sometime.' Claire's shoulders drooped. 'We're all making promises we can't be sure we'll keep.'

'I shall keep mine. You will marry me, won't you?'

She lifted her gaze from their hands: his large and battered – but warm and reassuring – encompassing hers and making her feel like a little girl again holding her father's strong hand, feeling safe. 'In a heartbeat. I love you, Jamie. I don't need a ring or any fuss . . . just your promise is enough.'

'I know everyone will think us mad.'

Claire laughed. 'Madly in love.'

'I know I am . . . but there's guilt as well in feeling this way in the midst of war.'

'Guilt is for those who have led us to war, not for those who are prepared to lay their lives down for it. Spud, Shahin, the men who fought beside you . . . these are the shameless innocents and they would celebrate your ability to survive, to find happiness in the darkness.'

'I've changed my mind. Why don't we just marry tomorrow?' he said suddenly. 'I can ask the hospital chaplain to perform a cere-mony,' he pressed.

She watched his eyes cloud at her hesitation. The summery woodland colour she loved turned to a night forest.

She kissed his hand. 'I do want to marry you more than any-thing in the world, but not tomorrow. I want to marry you in peacetime when I can hear birdsong rather than men weeping. I want you to stay focused on staying alive . . . not worrying about your wife. You could be back in Turkey or sent somewhere else with your regi-ment. It's very likely I could be sent into Europe any minute. Everything could change again in a blink.'

He nodded. 'All right, let's swear a different sort of oath to each other.'

She looked at him quizzically. 'What sort of oath?'

'A pact. When is your birthday?'

She frowned, amused. 'April the eighteenth.'

He grinned. 'Mine's March the seventeenth. So the midpoint between that is roughly . . . April the first. Agreed?'

'April Fool's Day!' she said.

'Righto, then. No matter where we're both posted, or where we end up, whatever happens, let's make this promise to each other – from the moment peace is declared, let's meet on the first day of April that follows. And on that day I'll ask you again to marry me.'

'Yes,' she whispered, feeling swept up in the romance of it. 'April Fool's Day, in peacetime.'

A nurse arrived pushing a trolley and Claire hastily sniffed back any threatening tears.

'Bath time, Trooper Wren,' the nurse said brightly.

He winked at the nurse and beamed her a smile that Claire imagined could win him any heart he wanted. 'My favourite time, nurse, is surely going to be with you and your sponge.'

'Oh, go on with you now, cheeky fellow.' She smiled at Claire and then frowned with dawning. 'Unless you'd like to do the honours, Nurse Nightingale?'

Claire cleared her throat. 'I'd be delighted to,' she said as she pulled the screen around them.

Claire rolled the trolley closer. 'So, let's get your nightshirt undone.' She moved Jamie to his back and undid the ties to lower the shift carefully over his shoulders and down to his waist.

He grinned for her to go right ahead. 'Guess you've done plenty of these before.'

'Hundreds,' she said, giggling.

'Come on now,' he insisted. 'Where's that strict nursey look?'

She was annoyed at herself for blushing at the sight of his exposed chest, the hollowed belly of starvation dipping beneath the sharply defined rib cage that now had thick dressings above it. Claire squeezed out the sponge. 'Let's start with your bare shoulder, shall we?'

'You start where you like, Nurse Nightingale. I'm going to close my eyes and enjoy myself.'

She began gently passing the sponge over his skin, and the normal distance she kept from a patient closed itself as the noises of the ward around her diminished and she could hear only her heartbeat. The smell of antiseptic was overridden by the soapsuds and the aroma of his skin, earthily male. Helpless desire now pounded inside as her knuckles grazed his stubbled jaw, and her hand followed the line of his prominent right clavicle across to his injured shoulder.

'That feels so good,' he admitted, eyes closed, which she was glad about because he would see her staring at his body in a state of building longing.

'I'm going to lift your arm. It'll hurt, but you'll feel better for it.'

'Do what you have to do, Nurse Claire. In your hands, I'm helpless.'

'Is that so?' she murmured dryly, gently easing his injured shoulder, trying not to tear sutures. 'What else did you do in Farina?'

'Oh, we played cricket, tennis, we even had a bowls team. There's a post office, couple of hotels, a bank. We even have our own bakery, built underground.'

'Are you teasing me?'

'No – the stove was put in around the time I was born. Works a treat. Fresh bread daily, if you can get there, although we're about ten miles out.'

She reached for the sponge again, and lathered up one hand.

He smiled tenderly. 'Tell me, where is your happy place?'

'Oh, that's easy,' she said, as she soaped and then sponged his neck. 'A village called Charvil near Twyford. That's in Berkshire, one of the southern counties of England. It was the house of my mother's closest friend, Anne – who I called Aunt – and whenever we visited, my father used to take me fishing at the ford at the end of the country lane behind. I wouldn't mind renting a place there sometime.'

'So we meet in southern England, then. And what was your happiest day ever?'

She laughed. 'Happiest moment? No doubt that would have to be the day Aunt Anne, father and I went to the Langham Hotel in London, at the top of Regent Street.'

'Means nothing to me,' he admitted, looking embarrassed.

'Well, let me tell you about it. The palatial hotel was built maybe six decades ago, famous for its elegance, and I've never forgotten being told that it had the first hydraulic lifts installed in all of England.'

'Did you ride in one?'

She shook her head. 'I was far too scared to. I was little. Anyway . . . it's terribly grand and I was dressed in my very best to travel to London with Aunt Anne, who was quite wealthy as I understand it now. She took my father and me for afternoon tea as a farewell before he went off to war and I sailed for Australia. She was bitterly upset that I couldn't be left behind with her.' She shook her head. 'I wanted to, but I wasn't allowed.'

'Is she still alive?'

'She died not long after I arrived back in England from Australia. It was heartbreaking but I suppose I was lucky to hug her again. I guess her loss was another reason I fled into nursing in London and not teaching in Winchester as I'd planned.'

'Tell me about that time at the Langham Hotel.'

'Aunt Anne chose the Palm Court for an afternoon tea – she called it "High Tea" because she was Scottish. I swear it took my breath away. It was the first time in Britain that a formal afternoon tea was served in a hotel, I was told. It's like you've stepped into a different world of hushed voices and silver salvers and cutlery, of exquisitely painted porcelain and dainty sandwiches and cakes.' She heard the brightness light in her voice at the memory. 'There are colours, Jamie, and flavours and smells that are so different from the ordinary world that you really could believe you've been transported to a magical realm. There was a small orchestra playing too . . .' Claire momentarily forgot herself, closing her eyes and travelling back to that happy afternoon of music and laughter. 'And I was allowed to meet the *Brigade de Cuisine*, as they called the kitchen staff, so I could tell the pastry chef just how much I enjoyed his team's amazing array of treats.'

Claire laughed, rinsing out the sponge again as he watched her intently. 'My aunt forbade us to dunk anything in our tea, and I was encouraged to eat very daintily. We had egg and cress sandwiches with the crusts cut off, and fluffy scones – still floured and warm – with black cherry jam and clotted cream so thick that my teaspoon actually stood up in the tiny pot on my plate. And the cakes! Oh, they were as gorgeous as precious gems – pink iced fancies, puffs of choux pastry with custard and draped in rich chocolate, soft jelly slices glistening in jewel colours, almond delicacies and coconut macaroons dipped in chocolate.' Claire nearly licked her lips in memory. 'Aunt Anne took her Darjeeling tea black with thin slivers of lemon that she elegantly stabbed with a special fork. Gosh . . . it was all so perfect and feminine. She taught me how to pick up the small sugar lumps gently with special tongs and stir in the milk without clinking against the side of the porcelain, and to sip as a lady must, like this,' she said, her little finger cocked expertly.

Jamie grinned.

'It was a wonderland.'

'Then that's where we're going to meet when the war ends: in that place of magic and wonder, on April Fool's Day.'

She stared at him, bemused. 'You're going to meet me at the Palm Court in the Langham Hotel in Portland Place on the first day of April whenever the war ends?'

He shrugged. 'I want to see you smiling like that again. And I guess I'll have to learn how to hold my little finger in the air.'

'I was wrong. I thought all Australian men – especially the farming boys – were rough and tumble, but Jamie, I do believe you're a diehard romantic.'

'Well, just don't tell everyone,' he grinned. 'Do we have a promise?'

She nodded.

'I'll be there, Claire, I promise you, even if I have to —' Claire placed her fingers over his mouth to prevent whatever next he was going to say.

'Yes, I will be there too, come what may, for afternoon tea at three o'clock. And I'm going to keep the memory of us making this promise to each other as the most important and lasting image in my mind of you.'

'You do that,' he said, kissing her fingers and sending a fresh thrill of arousal through her. 'I'll marry you that same day if you'll let me because then we'll be free of all this,' he said, gesturing around the ward.

Claire checked the curtain was fully drawn around his bed and kissed him, this time long and tenderly. She knew it surely hurt him but he lifted his arm so his fingers could sketch the outline of her ear, her jaw, her chin before sinking his fingers into her hair, and as he gently raked it she cast her normal caution aside and with a mind empty of anything but the taste of Jamie, she deepened her kiss, knowing she had never opened herself this way with anyone. It felt intoxicating to communicate silently through their lips, soft and comforting. This was love: a pure, bright ache that would streak through them no matter how far apart they were, and it would bond them as closely as their mouths joined now in perfect union.

'I have to go,' she finally said, pulling away and noting they were both breathing hard. 'You need to rest and I have to report back to our digs. They're quite strict and I have to pick up Rosie too.' She glanced at her watch and gave a horrified look. 'I'll be late meeting Rosie at the pyramids.'

'What about my pyramid?' he groaned, gesturing towards the sheet between his hips.

She exploded into delighted laughter.

He gave a soft groan of embarrassment. 'You're killing me.'

'No better way,' she whispered and her fingertips slid away from his.

'Tomorrow?'

She nodded. 'I've only got a couple of hours.'

'They're mine. I'll meet you on the verandah.'

Claire blew him a kiss and he caught it and mimed throwing it beneath the sheet, which sent her into a squeal of soft, rapturous laughter and then she was gone, hurrying from the hospital, hugging herself that maybe fate finally had a kinder plan for her.

11

It took a mighty effort and much as the doctor didn't approve, Jamie was determined to meet Claire the following morning in his wheelchair rather than from a hospital bed.

He knew she was staying in a small hotel in the city not far from the Heliopolis that had become the AGH1. One of the ambulance drivers had offered her a lift back to the pyramids to meet Rosie and Jamie had felt a pang of jealousy that another bloke would share Claire's company for a while.

He had woken from his drifting doze believing he had been flying. He preferred not to think of it as a memory of being flung by an explosion but more as hearts beating together like wings of their namesake birds, both of them small and unimportant in the great scheme of life, yet courageous and full of song. The notion of getting their marriage blessed again in the tiny Farina church in front of the townsfolk who'd watched him grow up made him smile as one of the nurses combed his hair. She'd shaved him this morning and even dampened his untidy mop, agreed to neaten it with a few well-chosen snips with her scissors too.

'There, you look smart now. I have to say you make a handsome pair of sweethearts,' Agnes admitted.

'Glad you approve.' He winked, ignoring the pain as she gently manoeuvred him into his uniform jacket. She'd kindly brushed it as clean of the dust and dirt as she could. He could see how hastily it had been mended.

'It's not perfect,' the nurse warned.

'But then neither am I,' he'd replied, making her laugh. His uniform jacket, its arms left empty and simply placed over his shoulders like a cape with a hospital shift beneath, looked comical, but he couldn't care a jot.

'She really fought for you,' Agnes continued. 'I've never heard of anything like it.'

Jamie looked up at her quizzically.

'Oh, hasn't she told you?' She made a tutting sound. 'She's too modest, that one. They were just about ready to give up on you in theatre – you were bleeding profusely and your pressure was dropping.'

'I did hear about a blood transfusion; pretty dangerous, I guess.'

'So daring, so romantic.' Agnes gave a small shrug of a smile. 'I can only imagine the complications at sea. It must have been so critical.'

'They made us all give blood before we left Australia to identify our type.'

'Very smart. I hear Claire was unstoppable but don't let Nurse Nightingale know I told you so.'

'Why?'

'Well, everyone was refusing the procedure but Nurse Nightingale just kept demanding until they let her lie down next to you.'

He frowned. 'What do you mean?'

'To give you her blood, of course.'

Jamie barely heard what Agnes said next as he digested the scope of her revelation.

'You see, Nurse Nightingale already knew she was group three and begged them to use her as the donor.'

'What? She risked her own life?'

She nodded with glee. 'That's what I mean,' she said, ensuring his hospital gown was straight and tied up neatly at the back. 'It's so romantic I'm breathless. Now the two of you are joined in blood.' She stood back and admired him, not grasping the impact of her chatter. 'She could have died, you know, but apparently she said not even the threat of death was going to cheat her of a life with you.'

Jamie was grateful in that moment that Agnes was called away by her matron.

'Thank you, Aggie . . . for everything.'

She nodded, left him seated painfully in the wicker wheelchair that was his choice. He was in a small back ward of the hospital that had been a guest room the previous year. Here seven other men were recovering from shocking shrapnel wounds and his injuries seemed minor by comparison. Each was either lost in an opiate haze or sleeping deeply to escape the pain.

If he were honest, he'd admit that his rib cage felt as though it were on fire while his right shoulder was screaming its own agony and his left protested with equal rage. It was what they called 'healing pain', and Jamie was surprising the medics by his rapid recovery. His body had decided that it could heal itself, especially now with Claire arriving shortly, appearing in the trembling heat like a cool, sweet drink for a thirsty man.

They were joined in blood. He shook his head. He now felt the urge to take a vow today and become man and wife, no matter the pressures of war or the cruelty of imminent certain distance.

Claire had told him about an ankle-length softly embroidered ivory dress that she'd bought only days ago. It would make an ideal wedding dress.

'I'll bet you look like a goddess in it,' he'd remarked.

She'd laughed. 'I don't pay much attention to all that.'

Jamie's instincts had already clued him that whether she was aware of how heart-stoppingly pretty she was, she displayed no outward show of vanity over it. She wore no jewellery, rouge or lipstick, not even perfume . . . nothing that enhanced her presence, but then in his opinion nothing was required to do so. He couldn't wait to see her smile, radiating warmth into the room as though she'd brought summer inside.

'I bought it last time I was in Alexandria simply to shut my friend Rosie up.' She'd lifted a shoulder self-consciously.

Jamie pictured her now in the pale cream cotton and lace as a bride, with her brightly golden hair caught up in soft tresses behind her head. He would live for the day when he could unlock that clasp and watch the waves fall to her shoulders, run his fingers without the hampering of bandages and pain through its pale strands that, even tied up, glinted as though each hair was individually polished to catch the light.

Agnes was back.

'Come on, then. Sorry I'm a few minutes late. I thought Nurse Nightingale might be here by now. I'm under very strict instructions that you remain in your wheelchair and be taken only as far as the verandah. And if you begin to bleed —'

'I won't, Aggie. To the verandah. Tally ho!' he pointed dramatically, ignoring the pain it cost him. Agnes giggled and wheeled him gently out of the ward and down the airy corridors onto the shade of one of the many breezeways surrounding the hospital. Patients dozed and men smoked quietly, staring out at the tall palms and the pure blue sky, unblemished by clouds, the sun still low enough for its light to reach beneath the eaves and make them squint.

'Should I find some flowers? There are carnations and even roses growing in the hospital gardens, as well as magnificent lotus lilies.'

'Would you?'

She nodded. 'Don't go anywhere,' she warned and grinned.

As Agnes left, a small dark man approached from below the verandah nodding at him. He was dressed in robes.

'Did you manage it?' Jamie asked.

'Yes, sir, yes,' he said, his lips splitting to reveal crooked teeth like old gravestones. He held out his palm and placed what had been a piece of shrapnel but was now a polished charm that had been drilled through its centre.

'Oh, good bloke, Bakari! Thank you. Did Agnes give you the money?'

'Yes, sir, yes,' he repeated.

Jamie admired it. He didn't have a ring to give Claire but he had thought about it after she'd left yesterday afternoon and now wanted to give her something meaningful and easily portable. He had nothing of his belongings other than the piece of shrapnel. She could wear it on a chain, perhaps. It would be a symbol of his love until he could give her a gold band they could bless in a church. He should write to his parents. What would his father say? His mother would cry. His brothers would shake their heads and tell him he was always the soppy one. But he'd be the first to fall in love with a girl and bring her into the Wren family. He sat beneath the shade, his pains forgotten, and let his thoughts drift to the garden he'd carve out of the hard earth of Farina for his bride. Roses grew well in South Australia, so did geraniums and —

His gaze had lazily followed the arrival of one of the ambulances as his thoughts had drifted. He watched absently as the driver alighted and walked around the front of the van, and the man's fearsomely red hair and sun-reddened complexion caught Jamie's unwitting attention. He knew the man's name: Bluey Wentworth. He'd heard Claire name him, had seen him come by to call her name the previous evening. Bluey had been the ambulance driver who'd offered her a lift back to her hotel.

Jamie whistled. It seemed polite to say hello. 'Hey, Bluey!' he called, and the man halted in his tracks looking for who had hailed him. He squinted in Jamie's direction. Then, as if Jamie was exactly the person he was searching for, he raised a hand and seemed to let out a breath of relief and pointed to the hospital steps to suggest he'd see him shortly.

In the meantime Agnes returned, clasping a sweet bunch of blushing flowers.

'They're beautiful, like you, Aggie. Thank you.'

'Oh, go on with you.'

'She'll be here any minute and I'm going to give her your flowers and this odd but meaningful piece of jewellery and ask her properly to be my fiancée,' Jamie assured, smoothing his hair. The importance of yesterday's decision moved from relief and effervescence to become somewhat daunting – how could he protect Claire when after today they were to be separated indefinitely? The thought had grown into a tight web of fear that had ensnarled him through his restless night.

At that moment Bluey emerged from the doorway.

'He seems to be looking for you,' Agnes said.

'Hello again,' Bluey said.

'Hello, mate. We weren't properly introduced yesterday.' Jamie shrugged and grinned. 'Neither arm's much good right now or I'd shake your hand.'

Bluey smiled, dimples folding the flesh of his round face. He looked at Agnes, and Jamie sensed he was feeling awkward. 'Lovely flowers.'

'They're for Nurse Nightingale. How is she getting here if not with you?' Agnes wondered.

Jamie blinked, finally registering Bluey's anxious expression and unshaven, dishevelled appearance. Words were tumbling from the newcomer. Something was wrong.

'Not coming?' he heard Agnes repeat.

As odd as it was, Jamie seemed to feel the alarms trilling through his three wounds, as if something of Claire remained with them and they too were responding to the news.

Bluey shook his head. 'She didn't even have time to write a note. Just begged me to promise I'd find you.' Jamie realised Bluey was speaking to him.

'What?'

Agnes answered. 'Jamie, she's been recalled to Alexandria in some haste.'

Bluey took over. 'The *Gascon* had to sail a day earlier than scheduled to outrun some weather, but there's also been a surge in casualties. They have to get them off that beach, mate, but heaven only knows where they're going to put 'em. Mudros is at capacity and they're already doing it tough enough on the island.' He must have realised that he was yet to make his point – the one Jamie and his companion were waiting to hear. 'The girls received an urgent telegram and we left the city after four yesterday afternoon, only just making it. There was chaos at the docks and with talk of huge numbers of wounded coming in on the next ship, you'd better expect things to get a bit mad here too.'

He stopped talking abruptly and a thick, uncomfortable silence settled.

Agnes spoke first. 'Jamie, I'm so sorry but it obviously can't be helped. Orders are orders. Seems like we're all deserting you.'

He frowned. 'What do you mean?'

'I haven't had a chance to tell you yet but I just got my fresh orders too . . . only moments ago. I'm going to be based in one of the Red Cross hospitals in Flanders.'

'Right at the coalface, eh?' Bluey said.

She nodded, blushing. 'Finally, I've got permission.'

Jamie knew he should congratulate her, although he couldn't find the words. 'You'll be missed,' was all he said, for he knew it was going to be a dark, potentially life-changing experience for the young, bubbly nurse.

'I'm sorry, Wren,' Bluey said.

'I'll put these in a jar by your cot,' Agnes offered, taking the flowers from his limp hands. 'They'll keep her close and they'll still be fresh for when she gets back, you'll see. And if not, you can ask one of the other nurses to cut some more,' she said, desperately feigning a brightness no one was feeling as she set off.

Control what you can. 'It's usually a three-day turnaround,' Jamie mused, swallowing his disappointment.

Bluey agreed. 'She said to shave again in a few days.'

'*You* need a shave, mate,' Jamie said, digging up his best cheerful voice. 'And a sleep. Thanks for coming.'

'I'll bring her back, I promise.'

Jamie nodded. 'Cheerio, then.'

Self-consciously they exchanged awkward glances as they cleared throats and said farewell.

Jamie didn't know if he'd somehow used mind over matter to keep it at bay, but the fever, which he'd felt gnawing at him through the previous night, seemed to sense his loss and with his defences momentarily shattered by the news, it now rushed to fill the void.

By the time Agnes came out to check on him an hour or so later, the malaise had him and the nurse found him drowsy and incommunicative. Trapped within his nightmarish dreamscape, Jamie believed he was in a trench, all of his mates hit by a direct shell, dead where they hid, gunfire snapping and spitting above, explosions all around while he revolved slowly, taking in the dire scene as a hawk flew overhead and he fretted about all the events he could no longer control.

12

Claire stood on the deck of the *Gascon*, her features carefully schooled but thoughts inwardly bubbling like the geyser she'd seen on holiday in New Zealand as a child with her father and step-mother, Doreen Turner.

Doreen's people were originally from Yorkshire in England but they'd settled on the other side of the world in New Zealand's Canterbury, to ride the sheep's back to prosperity. Doreen was one of six daughters, fourth born, largely ignored, from what Claire had gathered. The age difference between Doreen and her youngest sibling was a decade, with an elderly father who indulged his last daughter almost as a grandchild.

As Doreen had explained this to Jonathan Nightingale, twelve-year-old Claire had heard only a woman trawling for a husband and using her sob story and her dowry to attract one.

Claire blinked as she stared out to sea. Was it pure childish jealousy that had coloured her opinion and not allowed any room in her heart for Doreen? Couldn't it be true, now that she examined the memory objectively, that Doreen was actually good for her father? Had Doreen as a child not been trapped by the same sense of abandonment that Claire had felt? Did Claire look for elements in her stepmother to criticise – the downturned mouth, the heavy lips – because she was immature and believed she was stealing her father from her?

People around them had remarked on the genuine adoration between the two. Jonathan Nightingale was tall and wiry with a flop of light brown hair and eyes the colour of the ultramarine Claire had seen on precious Italian artworks in the British Museum. It was one of the last excursions she'd taken with her father before she was shipped off to Australia and he to war. She had held his hand and listened to his narration as they'd looked at everything from Egyptian metalwork to libraries full of leathered books in enormously tall chambers.

As a child she'd not sensed his longing for her mother – indeed for any other female company but hers – and she'd built a cocoon around herself that was her father's arms . . . his voice, his laugh, his nearness and protection. He had always managed to make her feel that she was the heart of his life. It wasn't until she was an older child that she saw him as damaged emotionally from the war in Africa, and that was the point at which she could tell a daughter's devotion wasn't enough. He had changed. That brightness in his eyes had dulled and his need to blot out his experiences was likely responsible for shifting that gaze from her to Doreen Turner, a friend visiting the cousins whom Claire lived with in Sydney.

Claire watched the clouds sketched across the sky reflecting the blue of the Aegean and relented, ashamed. Yes, now she could appreciate her father's distraction and could stand aside from her childhood pain of what felt like rejection and view it for what it was. Back then it had felt like the penultimate desertion of a father before he went all the way . . . and died.

Doreen had taken them on a holiday to New Zealand to persuade him to settle there. Her family offered land and opportunity but Jonathan wouldn't agree to it because it was too far from all that was familiar. He did, however, propose marriage to her on their holiday. And suddenly where they lived made no difference to Doreen – for she had won her prize but she convinced him not to return to England. They settled on Tasmania, which felt like halfway between Doreen's home and Jonathan's adopted one in New South Wales. As far as Claire had been concerned, nearing thirteen, they might as well have chosen to live on the moon.

It was in New Zealand, during their tour of Rotorua, that the couple had sat Claire down and explained their decision to move. She had had no say in it. She'd always convinced herself that it was a relief for Doreen as much as herself when she'd later fled Australia for Britain, but they'd all been in such shock over her father's death and she hadn't given Doreen a chance to get closer. Claire bit her lip in memory that it wasn't for lack of trying on her elder's part.

Her belly rolled with the lean of the ship into the waves and Claire was once again reminded of the steamy geysers at Rotorua and had been even more entranced by the slurry of mud pools that boiled and spluttered with their sulphurous smell. That's how it felt now – as though her insides were spluttering with that same volcanic action she could not calm. Instead of being dressed in her white lace and cotton, holding Jamie's hand and saying 'I will' to his promised question, here she was anchored off Anzac Cove, standing by for the next raft of broken, damaged and dying men.

'Nurse Nightingale?'

She turned. 'Yes, Matron.'

'There's an inordinate number of seriously wounded to be attended – hundreds. The first are being loaded in the next few minutes. They're bringing on board the shrapnel wounds first. I suspect you'll be in theatre all day – the doctors predictably want you on the anaesthetic.'

She nodded, relieved to have something else to focus on. 'Shall I head down now?'

'Please. It's going to be an ugly day. Oh, and we're doing another swift turnaround. I've just told the others there will be no shore leave granted in Egypt.'

Claire blinked. 'Of course.'

'I'm sorry, I haven't even asked – how is your young man?'

'He's recovering fast and in the best place,' she admitted, not trusting herself to say any more. She hadn't even told Rosie yet about Jamie's proposal. It still felt too fresh and private. So, it could be another week or even longer before she was in Alexandria and could think of getting a ride to Cairo. 'Thank you again. It was wonderful to see him open his eyes and smile at me.'

Matron gave her a sympathetic nod. 'Who knows, he may even pop the question next time, although if he did, you'd likely be sent home or at best to a safe hospital – England, maybe – for the rest of the war.'

'Pardon?'

'They don't like married woman anywhere near the danger zones, my dear.'

Maybe a power mightier even than her own will had decided to intervene and prevent her marrying Jamie in Cairo. Claire knew she was needed; men hadn't stopped falling from injuries simply because she'd fallen in love.

The thought of being needed comforted her as she hurried once more into the bowels of the ship to help save more lives. She took some comfort in the knowledge that none of those who may succumb today on the ship would be Jamie.

13

Jamie woke groggy and disoriented, blinking at the translucent glow from the ceiling that oddly reminded him of custard. But the hospital ceiling he remembered had been white, and the ward had dark timber beams and greyish floorboards. Familiar groans and the smell of antiseptic told him he was still under hospital care but he couldn't work out where. It wasn't even a building. He coughed, tasting dust.

'Hello, there,' said an officious but bright voice. He focused on an older woman. 'I'm Sister Louise. I run this ward. How are you feeling?'

He cleared his throat. 'Er, thirsty . . . um, and confused.'

'That's to be expected. You've been in and out of your fever for a few days but it's broken now, which is excellent news. Here, let me get you a sip of water.' She helped him to drink and as he gulped he took a moment to stare around him.

'Where am I?' he croaked, able to focus more now on the tented ward that covered a desert floor and shallow, makeshift cots.

'You were moved. I know it's disconcerting but there was a sudden influx of very badly injured men who needed beds and intensive care. We moved you less seriously wounded here, to an auxiliary hospital in Abbassia.'

He frowned, none the wiser.

'Outside Cairo.'

'How long have I been here?'

'More than a week.'

'What's the date?' he groaned.

'June the first. You've made a pretty remarkable recovery, though, I might add. Your wounds are clean and dry and there's no infection . . . you fought off whatever was attacking you. We think you were essentially terribly weakened from the blood loss.'

He recalled. 'Yes. From Nurse Nightingale.' Saying her name aloud helped to anchor him because he felt his thoughts lifting off and scattering like a flock of startled birds. He could tell she didn't know any of the details.

'I'm going to hand you over to Nurse Jenkins now. She'll be looking after you.'

A short, plumpish woman arrived. 'Trooper Wren?' she said, matter-of-factly.

He nodded.

'Nice to see you awake.'

He tried to smile but it wouldn't come.

'Nothing to worry about. It's a tent but we run a dash good medical service here. We'll have you up and about in no time and, I hope, back with your regiment. In fact, I think you're going to be relocated again. We were just waiting for you to wake up.' She urged him to keep drinking.

He came up for air, having swallowed the entire contents of the cup, eager to please. 'Did Agnes leave any message for me?'

'Agnes?'

'The nurse from Cairo.'

She shook her head, took his pulse and put a finger to her lips. 'I'm sorry, I have no idea who that is. It all had to happen very fast that day. There was no official handover. We only had some hastily scribbled notes pinned to your uniform. You don't even seem to have an ID tag.' He remembered giving it to Claire, but didn't bother explaining. If they didn't know Agnes, they certainly weren't going to know a nurse from a hospital ship based out of Alexandria.

'Anyway,' she rushed on. 'They needed your cot and have probably turned it over several times already to different men. You have nothing to worry about; you seem to be making an enviable recovery.' She stuck a thermometer into his mouth. 'I don't get to say that to as many soldiers as I'd like to.'

Nurse Jenkins busied herself around him, checking his dressings and making encouraging noises. 'That's all looking very nice indeed. We might get you exercising that left arm. Stitches can come out soon. The right shoulder needs a few more days.' She reached for the thermometer and concentrated on it momentarily before looking back at him. 'Perfect,' she said, flicking the mercury back down before putting it into a jar of antiseptic. 'I'll be back.' She smiled and left him staring at dozens of other men on the floor in rows.

He wanted to ask for pen and paper but then realised with his injuries he couldn't write and all the nurses seemed understandably too preoccupied to scribe for him. Claire would understand. He would pen something as soon as his right arm was well enough and he began to construct a letter in his mind.

Dear Claire . . .

No, he started again.

My darling Claire,

I don't know when or how this will reach you, but the nurse in a tented hospital at somewhere called Abassa, which I do not know how to spell but I am told is outside Cairo, seems happy with my progress. They are going to move me again

but I do not know where yet. There is talk of sending me
back to the regiment, which I would be glad about because
I will not feel as far away from you as I do now and might
even catch a glance at the hospital ship while I carry water
rations up to the ridge . . .

Sister Louise was back and he came out of his thoughts. 'I've just been told that the Light Horse soldiers here will be returned to barracks in Cairo. Apparently you have new orders.'

He blinked. 'Where are we being sent?'

'I'm sorry, I have no idea.' She smiled. 'You just worry about getting well. I doubt you're headed back to that hellhole at Gallipoli.'

Jamie nodded but felt a sense of anxiety creeping into his thoughts now. Claire wouldn't know where he was and he couldn't tell her yet. His mind helplessly returned to the letter he had begun constructing.

I will never change my mind regarding how I feel about you.
I love you, darling Claire, and you are the reason I will promise
to stay alive and try not to catch another bomb or bullet.
Wherever they send me – I've just heard it's probably unlikely
to be Gallipoli – I won't die because I have to see you again
before I let that happen.

And when this war is done I will keep my two promises.
The first is to meet you in London at your happy place as
we agreed on the first day of April and ask you to marry
me again, if you will have me. And then I shall take you
home to Australia and on the way we can stop in Istanbul
and return the prayer book of the Turkish soldier I think
of as my friend. His father sounds a little like mine but I do

not believe for a minute that Shahin's father does not care about him. I shall make sure he knows that his son died thinking about him. I can do that much for a friend.

Jamie imagined himself drawing a little stick man with a big grin on his face next to his cryptic admission.

I love you and the pain of injury is nothing in comparison to the pain of not being with you. Do not worry about me. I am in good hands, which I wish were yours, but we shall be in each other's arms some time soon. I shall hold that thought close until I next see you.

Yes, he would write it exactly like that. Just as soon as he was well enough . . .

———

It was nearly a month before Claire could get a pass for one day's leave and together with Rosie they cadged a lift into Cairo. It was a dusty ride of monotonous level plains of sand in searing heat. The road was filled with potholes that the jeep crunched and bumped over to jar Claire's teeth. She bit her tongue once so fiercely it made her eyes water. The Arabs had it right, she thought, glad she'd taken their lead by wearing a long voile scarf as a veil that she'd wound around her head and mouth to keep the sand out.

The landscape trembled in the distance, punctuated rarely by a glimpse of a camel train of the brightly garbed Bedouin folk, moving so slowly it looked as if they were a still-life image, only shifting because of the heat thermals that distorted her vision of them. She wondered absently how the war affected their primitive lives and whether in fact they were the clever ones with their unchanging and isolated lifestyle that moved to the rhythm of the desert and its seasons and watering holes.

'You look gorgeous, Claire. I told you that dress is a winner. I'm going to have to borrow it sometime.'

She smiled. 'I feel like a bride in it,' she admitted, as excitement gathered in the pit of her belly.

'Why didn't you tell me you were so hooked on this bloke?'

She shrugged. 'I don't know, Rosie. Don't take this the wrong way, but it felt as though if I shared it, I might spoil it.'

'I'd be screaming it from the top of the pyramids. I want to be in love. I envy you.'

'Don't.' Claire sighed. 'All I do is worry.'

'You're really going to marry him?'

Claire knew Rosie was right to advocate caution – there was nothing sensible about her decision. She had to rely on her primitive responses when it came to something as untried as love. She had to trust that the tumult of emotion she now lived with and the way even thinking about Jamie's touch could provoke such a strong yearning meant that this was indeed the real thing.

She smiled confidently. 'I am, dear Rosie, but I think we should wait until there's peace.'

Rosie frowned. 'As I live and breathe, Claire, you could be waiting forever! Who knows how long this hateful war will last?' She waved a hand at the empty landscape. 'And over what? Owning this . . . nothing but sand that just goes on forever.'

Claire sighed. She too asked this big question repeatedly but came up wanting. She changed topics and the mood in the car by leaning forward to speak to their driver. 'How far now, Bill?' she asked an orderly who was driving them.

'You should be able to see the pyramids in about fifteen minutes.'

She turned back to the window to wait it out and Rosie seemed to fall into a similar quiet mindset, only breaking into the sound of the rhythmic rumble of the van to ask about the strange hive-shaped structures in the distance.

'Are they barns?' Rosie asked.

'Correct, but you'll never guess what's kept in there,' the driver replied, raising an eyebrow.

'Grain!' Rosie jumped in.

'Animals?' Claire suggested.

'Well, you're getting closer. It's birds.'

'Birds?' Claire queried, astonished.

'Homing pigeons for the war?' Rosie tried.

The driver coughed and laughed, flicked his cigarette out of the window. 'No. They are full of small birds, a bit like canaries.' He mimed putting food in his mouth.

Both girls looked instantly repulsed. 'Oh, no!' Claire gasped, stricken.

'Local delicacy out here.'

'Oh, you've upset her now,' Rosie warned. 'She feels an affinity for any feathered friends. She's even going to marry one.'

By the time they reached the hospital Claire's cool cotton dress was sticking to her flesh unpleasantly. 'This is hotter than Australia in summer.'

Rosie laughed. 'This is hotter than Hades, my girl. Listen, I know you want time alone so I'll just say hello and goodbye and then leave you to it. Where are we meeting up later?'

Claire pointed to one of the hospital buildings. 'He was over there last time.' She led the way. 'I'll find a lift back. We can have a cool drink at Shepheard's, maybe, and Bill said he'd pick us up outside at five.'

'Perfect,' Rosie replied.

They both sighed at the visceral pleasure that the cool of the corridor provoked after the ferocity of their seemingly endlessly long journey.

'You go first,' Rosie offered. 'Because I'll admit I'm happy to lie on the floor right here,' she sighed, leaning against the wall and dragging out a handkerchief to dab her face.

Claire smiled. 'Back in a moment.'

She entered the familiar ward and looked for Jamie, all the heat and tiring drive forgotten, even the past month of frustration and desperately ill men put aside in her anticipation of seeing him again. But she immediately noticed that it was a different man in his cot, his entire head bandaged while he sipped water through a tube.

She stopped a passing nurse and introduced herself. 'I'm looking for a patient who was brought into Alexandria off the *Gascon*.'

'One of yours?'

Claire smiled. 'You could say. His name is James Wren.' In her pocket she could feel the outline of his name on the ID tag she carried habitually.

The nurse frowned. 'There's no one of that name on this ward.'

'Oh, perhaps he's been moved?' Claire pulled out the long, slender pin to release her hat as she watched the nurse consider before shaking her head.

'No, not in this wing. I work all the wards. What's his injury?'

Claire explained.

'Abigail is due back on the ward any moment. She will probably know. Wren, you say?'

Claire nodded and swallowed slowly. As if on cue, a strapping nurse entered the ward, along with Rosie.

'Abby, do you know of a patient who was on the ward in the last few weeks?' She pointed at the cot in question. 'He was here. His name is —'

Abby nodded, cutting across her colleague's words. 'It was a bird, or something like that, wasn't it?'

'Yes.' Claire laughed in relief. 'Jamie Wren.'

'Jamie?' Her brow knitted and then relaxed as she smiled. 'Ah yes, James does sound a bell. I didn't work the ward a few weeks back. Agnes knew all the patients on this ward very well but she left for the Western Front on the same evening that we had a sudden influx, and a lot of the men under her care were moved immediately. It was a frantic time, with no chance for a formal handover. We barely knew their names, and beds were turning over so fast.' She shook her head in memory.

Claire and Rosie nodded in agreement. 'One minute we've cleared Anzac Cove and by the time the ship returns, the beach is full of seriously wounded men again,' Claire said. 'So, can you point me in the direction of where Trooper Wren is now? I don't have very long in Cairo.'

'Oh.' Abby's expression darkened. 'Er, I'm sorry – how well was he known to you?'

Was?

Rosie ran out of patience. 'Claire's engaged to marry him!'

Claire wished her friend hadn't spoken. Even so, she could see that this nugget of information only made it worse and she watched the nurse's complexion blanch. 'What's wrong? Did he have a relapse? Has he been moved from Cairo? What?'

Abby shared an uncomfortable glance with her colleague. 'He died, I'm afraid. I'm so sorry to be the one to tell you . . .'

'No!' Claire gasped, a hand up in defence before Abby could say more. 'That's not right. It can't be. He was showing almost miraculous healing. He was propped up in bed and talking to me . . . we planned . . . promised . . . no!'

She felt Rosie clutching her tightly. 'Claire —'

The other two nurses were apologising with their eyes, their hands reaching shyly, words tumbling from their mouths. Claire felt as though the walls she'd built around Jamie and her were suddenly a house of cards falling down.

'He was going to be fine, I tell you . . .'

Rosie pulled her out into the corridor, Abby following, concerned. She spoke to Rosie now.

'I was there,' she murmured. 'It had to be three weeks ago at least. He was feverish and died of infection. I can't properly remember – malaria probably, rather than his wounds.'

'Describe him,' Claire said.

Abby shook her head. 'I don't think I can. It's just the notion of the bird that triggers the memory and I think he was called James. We were inundated – there was no time to linger with anyone. To be honest, we knew them more by their wounds than their names or even features. Oh, actually I do know he didn't have any ID tag on.'

Claire gasped again and was convinced she could feel the treacherous tag like a scald through her pocket now.

Abby looked over her shoulder. 'I'm so sorry. I have to go . . . will you be —'

'I'll take care of her,' Rosie assured. Claire was staring at the floorboards.

'Claire?' Rosie's voice was tender, unsure.

She couldn't help it. The grief hurt so deeply she felt dizzy. It didn't pay to love. If you don't give up your heart, it can't be broken. But even as she thought this she hated herself for so quickly hating his memory, and despair came out in a low moan of anguish as she slipped down the wall to squat on the floor, hat and hatpin discarded carelessly nearby. It was unseemly and certainly unbefitting of her role but she was not in uniform and in this moment didn't care about anything but how unhinged she suddenly felt.

'Come on, now.' She could feel Rosie holding her, rubbing her hands. She thought absently that her friend must have pulled off her gloves or she wouldn't feel Rosie's skin against hers. Where were her gloves? Did she care?

She was aware of the world around her and yet felt trapped

within a cage of dismay and indecision. She could hear concerned voices echoing down the corridor and Rosie assuring them. She could smell the disinfectant from the floor and feel the ceiling fan stir the strands of her hair that had escaped her loose chignon. But inside she could feel nothing but helplessness. Claire absently became aware of being pulled to her feet and guided away. She didn't care where they were going. Early summer gleefully welcomed them back into its warmth and the sun registered on her skin, as she squinted into its sharp light and noticed how suddenly dry her throat felt.

'Claire. Just sit down here,' Rosie said. 'I'm going to see if I can learn some more and get you some water. Don't move.'

Claire needed more than placations. She knew how to cope with loss. And it wasn't loneliness that scared her. But she needed reassurance that this feeling of spinning helplessly on the foaming angry current of her emotions without a rudder would pass and that she would find calm. She stood, rubbed her palms dry of their nervousness on her dress and straightened the cotton fabric. Out of habit she touched her hair to make sure it was still intact and picked up her wide-brimmed straw hat and pale suede gloves that Rosie had placed on the hospital's verandah table. She affixed the hat to her head with the pin, put on her gloves to protect her hands from the burn of the sun, and none the wiser to the fact that Jamie had sat in this precise spot awaiting her several weeks previous, she left the shadows.

Hurrying away, she paused only to speak to a soldier with one side of his head bandaged and an empty shirtsleeve dangling beside him.

When Rosie returned, the one-armed soldier introduced himself and duly passed on the information he'd been asked to.

'What do you mean? Where's she gone?' Rosie queried.

'That's all she said, luv, I'm sorry. She'll see you on the ship as scheduled. She said you knew what that meant. And if you feel like going dancing, I've still got my legs.'

Rosie smiled sadly at him. 'Sorry, I have to find my friend.'

'Next time, then.' He winked.

Claire had glanced briefly at the rows of tents and huts that the ANZAC and British troops had erected along the Corniche but her mind was set to one mission and she hurried on, arriving slightly breathless onto the verandah of the five-storied Windsor Palace Hotel. Curiously the flavour of violets hit her senses as she walked beneath the cool awning and recalled her disastrous sherbert of her previous visit with Rosie. She scanned the clientele reclining in chairs reading newspapers or talking quietly in pairs over pots of tea. She looked anxiously until her gaze fell with intense relief on the familiar face of Eugenie Lester, taking tea alone. Her silvered hair was swept up into a neat chignon to take her sun hat and Claire could see the wide-brimmed hat cast aside on the chair next to her, whose striped ribbon matched perfectly with the soft pebble grey of her cotton dress, which was inlaid with panels of ivory open-work lace. She sat straight-backed and still, a picture of elegance.

The older woman sensed her arrival before Claire could speak and she looked up and beamed her a smile of such absolute delight that Claire instantly felt stronger for the sight of her wise friend.

'I wondered if I'd see you again before I left. Good heavens, girl, you look exhausted.'

Claire blinked, struggling to find the words, but in spite of her internal battle, she felt her control returning now in this woman's calm presence. She couldn't be bothered explaining that she'd been hurrying between Alexandria and Cairo and back again for most of this day. 'May I join you?'

'Of course, my dear, how delightful for me.' She signalled to the waiter for another cup and saucer. 'I take a strong brew at this time with lemon, dear, is that suitable for you?' Eugenie gestured for her to seat herself.

Claire was reminded of Aunt Anne and afternoon tea in the Palm Court. 'Yes, thank you.'

'Fearsome temperature today,' Eugenie continued as though they had been mid-conversation. 'But I warn you it shall only get worse before it gets easier.'

Claire nodded, not sure if they were still talking about the weather.

'In spite of your obvious fatigue, you look exquisite, Claire; I suspect you don't bother to get out of uniform too often and can only imagine you have done so for your soldier sweetheart.' She sighed and fixed Claire with a familiar unblinking stare. 'Are you going to tell me why you're here and not with him?'

The waiter returned and set down the tea things. Eugenie silently dismissed him with a nodding smile as she reached to pour for Claire.

Every part of her willed itself not to succumb to tears; every fibre needed to stay strong through this test. She fought it and won but its cost was the difficult silence that Eugenie allowed to stretch. Finally, Eugenie nodded. 'I see. Well —'

'The nurses in the Cairo hospital told me he's dead. I don't believe it.'

'Good. Why not?' Eugenie handed the cup and saucer to her. It was a strong brew but the lemon scent rose on the steam and its citrus fragrance enlivened her.

She sipped and sighed. 'I would feel it, wouldn't I? Shouldn't my heart somehow know . . . my rationality accept, even if the emotional side of me refuses to?'

Eugenie gave a smile of such tender empathy that Claire had to start fighting her tears all over again. 'Indeed. Why don't you tell me what has occurred?'

It came out as a torrent: all of it, down to the decision not to marry until the war was over and the pact to meet on the first April Fool's Day as soon as peace was declared.

Finally, when Claire took a breath, Eugenie gestured towards the dainty china cup of tea for her to keep drinking. Claire picked up cup and saucer again and inhaled the scent of the lemon zest heated and perfuming the air.

'I wouldn't give up hope, my dear. Not at all.'

Claire's hopes flared. 'Really?' she breathed and the tea felt soothing to sip.

'Well, from what you tell me, no one is at all certain about anything. I suggest you banish the anguish and hold tight to hope, my dear. I wouldn't be at all surprised if many names got muddled – all that would have mattered in those hours was saving lives. Even the most diligent of document keepers would have been challenged.'

'I have nothing to go on.'

'Of course you do!' Eugenie admonished. 'You have a man's word that he will meet you on a given day. You have his promise that he wants to marry you and no other. You have his oath that he will not die, not under any circumstances.' She smiled gently. 'He's a wren, remember? Wily, smart, knows how to remain invisible and cautious.'

Impossible though it seemed, Claire realised she had found a small curl of a smile.

'There we go. Hold that feeling, child. It's called hope. And when you have hope, you have everything.'

'What if it's an empty hope?'

Eugenie gave a tutting sound. 'There is always hope and it comes with no qualification. When it exists in your mind, you will remain strong. Now, while you say you have no proof of your young man's survival, the truth is that you actually have no proof of his demise. Not even that nurse who seemed to have some recollection of him could unequivocally confirm that the soldier she was thinking of was your soldier.'

Claire sighed. 'There were coincidences, though, Eugenie . . . the bird name, the regiment, the lack of ID tag . . .'

'I knew a man called Starling once. It isn't the same as Wren, but do you imagine the two might be confused in extraordinary circumstances?'

Claire stared at her, hardly daring to breathe now.

'And a regiment is a lot of men, my dear. Many thousands, presumably.'

Claire opened her mouth to say something but Eugenie spoke on. 'I admit to knowing four people called James. No, make that five. And those are just the ones here in Alexandria. If I bothered to sit down and count up how many men called James I've known in my life, it is probably double that number. Perhaps you might counter that these two men with similar surnames might also both be called James.'

'That's a lot of coincidence,' Claire muttered.

'Coincidence by its very nature is odd but coincidences happen every day to every one of us – it's just that a lot of the time we barely notice them. How many women are wearing a broad-brimmed straw hat in this very hotel?'

Claire dutifully glanced around. 'Dozens. That's not a coincidence, though, is it, Eugenie? Just practicality, surely?'

'With a cream silk ribbon?' Eugenie pressed.

'Well, that's just fashion.'

Eugenie's wrinkles shifted as her smile shone from her face. 'No, dear girl. It's about perspective. And your perspective is skewed right now because you're frightened. I'm not suggesting you have no reason to be concerned, but a series of unrelated facts do not necessarily make up the full account. Leave some room for oddities because life, I have found, is rarely neat. Drink your tea. It has magical properties to make every shock feel less dramatic.' Eugenie's indulgent smile deepened. 'I'm glad you came.'

'I couldn't breathe. I deserted my friend in Cairo. I didn't have a single straight thought all the way here other than I needed to find you because I knew you'd help me make sense of it.'

'And have I?'

'You've made me feel a lot better than I did when I arrived. Thank you.'

'Don't mention it. I meant to give you this last time but didn't have one on me.' She dipped into a small lace purse that hung from her wrist. 'My address in Hertfordshire, just in case – you are most welcome to stay any time. The invitation stands. I'd like to hear more about your trip to Turkey to return the prayer book too.'

Hope genuinely found its wings in her heart now. 'Do you think I'll ever get to do that with him?'

'Oh, you must, even if you do it alone. There's a father grieving somewhere and it matters not which side his son fights for.'

Claire glanced at her watch and a spark of panic trilled through her. 'I must go, Eugenie. My friend Rosie is going to be frantic as it is, but I have to report back shortly at the ship.'

'Of course, my dear. Now you must promise me that you will keep faith with the vow you gave James Wren. We can only imagine that wherever he is, he is clinging to that to keep himself safe.'

Claire instinctively reached for the name tag, wrapping her fingers around it in her pocket to keep him close as she had promised him she would. She kissed Eugenie Lester farewell on both cheeks and then hugged her.

'Thank you for making me feel strong in here again,' she said, tapping her temple.

Eugenie touched her heart. '*Al'afw*,' she murmured, and they shared an affectionate smile in memory of their first meeting.

Claire arrived back at the dock's meeting point where the face of her friend who greeted her looked frightened rather than angry, as she'd expected Rosie to be.

'The man who died was a light horseman, Claire, I'm so, so sorry.' Her voice wobbled but she checked herself and took a breath. 'I made sure. One of the other nurses had seen his uniform, remembered it because it stood out from the everyday soldiers' garb. He was from the 9th, she recalled, because he kept repeating that he had to get back to his brigade. The 9th was Jamie's brigade, wasn't it, 3rd Regiment, you said?' The words were tumbling out in a warble.

'Stop it, Rosie,' she pleaded, her throat husky from the emotion she was struggling to keep under control.

Her friend's complexion normally matched her name, but Rosie's cheeks were pale and her usually ready smile was failing her today. 'I lie to patients all the time, Claire . . . tell them that we'll have them back on their feet in a jiffy, that they'll be swimming in the surf off the Sydney beaches or watching the footy again in Melbourne soon – avoiding telling them that they're probably going to be buried in the Mediterranean. I can lie to them effortlessly because it's my job to reassure a patient who is dying, but I can't lie to you. You're my friend and you're a nurse who knows better. You'd see through my lies straightaway and hate me for them. I have to tell you what I know or what kind of a friend am I?'

'There's no proof!' she growled. It had become her mantra.

Rosie shook her head. 'You're precious to me so I have to be honest with you and admit there's more proof of his death than there is of his survival. I'm so sorry.'

She reached for Claire, who finally surrendered to the river that had tried all day to flood her, and she wept with low, shuddering sobs. And in that moment of heartbreak as Rosie hugged her, Claire decided that without Jamie, there was no more hope – especially not in a world at war with men dying by the thousands daily. Was he one of them? Had this war killed him? It seemed it may have – others certainly believed so. The thought struck her that she should remove herself, get away from everything that might be familiar and prompt her to think of him, especially Egypt . . . and Turkey. Running away from pain was something she was good at. Claire knew that time alone would soothe her pain. Fate had brought her together with Jamie and if it now wanted to break her by taking him away, then she'd go where fate had the opportunity to throw everything it had at her. She would apply for the Western Front . . . immediately.

Jamie watched as the nursing team was pushed well beyond its limit and still it dug deeper and found more hours, more speed, more determination to heal wounded men. The letter he wanted to have written to Claire just didn't feel important enough as he watched the committed women move through their duties on far too little sleep or food or down time. He'd asked once, mentioned it again later; they knew he needed a letter scribed but days had passed and suddenly he was being moved again into a different, tented ward.

Days drifted by, feeling was coming back into his shoulder and soon he would write that letter for himself.

Finally he was well enough to leave nursing care and was thrilled to be reunited with the horses at the old Cairo camp at Mena. He was issued with his new regimental colour patch of black over white so he could be distinguished as belonging to the 3rd Light Horse Regiment. Here, just ten miles from the Cairo hospital where he had last seen Claire, Jamie underwent fresh training and integration into the regrouped mounted corps as more survivors of Gallipoli trickled in. There was talk of pulling out of the Dardanelles, which he was glad to hear, but for now he was content to look after the horses and spend the weeks coaxing his body back to full strength. His right arm still wouldn't work properly for him – not enough to write a letter, and he couldn't write with his left but he began to put out enquiries with everyone he could, hoping the army grapevine might help him find Claire. This morning he'd persuaded one of the other blokes to scribe a letter of brief enquiry via Claire's Alexandria base. He anticipated a couple of weeks before he may be lucky enough to hear back.

It was late afternoon and the worst of the day's heat had passed. He was walking alongside one of the horses he was gently leading up Artillery Road to stretch out a sore leg the animal was nursing and he marvelled at the small town that had grown up in the desert with its canvas tents. Soldiers boiled billies in the sand with a vast pyramid to their backs that they barely noticed any more. Jamie paused to check his horse's leg when a bloke he had come to know well drew level with him.

'Hey, Wrennie?'

'Johnno, where have you been?'

'I had a dose of the trots. I'm fine now.'

'Good. How's that kangaroo mascot of yours doing? I haven't seen it in days,' he said, impressed at how well he'd learned to use his other arm for rubbing down the animals. His right side was still healing, the arm in a sling to prevent him becoming too enthusiastic.

'I had to give Banjo to the Cairo Zoo while I was sick. Miss him, actually. I guess they won't be giving him back anytime soon. Best for Banjo I s'pose.' Jamie grinned and waited. 'Anyway, that friend of yours, the nurse you were looking for?'

He swung around. He hadn't told Johnno anything more about her other than that he'd met her a couple of times during his time at Gallipoli and that she was good to the men. 'Claire Nightingale? Have you heard something?'

Johnno shrugged. He was a good sort and Jamie liked that he worked hard, loved the horses and had not complained about being left behind in Cairo, even before the horror stories of Gallipoli had begun to filter back. They'd become friends, looked out for each other; he couldn't replace Spud but having someone to rely on, drink with, joke with, helped ease the loneliness.

'She's gone.'

'Gone? What do you mean?'

His companion shrugged again, bigger this time. 'I don't know what I mean, mate, but that's what I was told through a bloke who works on the docks.'

'Which bloke?' Jamie demanded.

'Wentworth. Bluey, he's known as. I did a pick-up today in Cairo and he helped me load some stuff. As he drives an ambo for our mob I thought it was worth asking at least.'

Jamie's insides churned with worry as he nodded. 'Go on.'

'According to Bluey, she's gone from the hospital ship. He seemed to know her but says she hasn't been in Alexandria for a few weeks now.'

'Where's she gone?'

'Not sure exactly. But Bluey seemed to think she's left for the Western Front.'

All the optimism that he'd worked hard to breathe into his mind began to deflate. The demons pressed closer, their voices louder. *She's going to get killed in a field hospital.*

'Sorry, mate,' Johnno offered. 'He said a few of the nurses he'd got to know and liked had moved on into Europe.' He shrugged, frowning. 'You weren't sweet on her, were you?'

Jamie didn't want to explain. 'She's a lovely girl. Everyone liked her.' The horse he was grooming butted him gently as it swished its tail against the flies. 'Anyway, I'd best get this lovely girl back for a feed.' He wanted to run into the desert and scream his despair but instead, he touched his slouch hat in farewell.

'By the way, our orders have come through,' Johnno called to his back.

'What are they?' he said, distracted with thoughts of Claire in a Red Cross tent near the frontline.

'We're off to somewhere called Jordan. Any idea where that is, mate?'

Jamie shook his head. He no longer cared where they were sent. All that mattered now was getting through this war and coming out alive so he could find Claire.

PART TWO

14

JANUARY 1919

The war had been officially over for two months but it was now approaching four years since she had last kissed Jamie Wren and felt the warmth of life. For all she knew he could be in a cold grave, but until she did know, she clung to hope and a date in less than twelve weeks when they'd promised to meet.

The passenger seated next to her on the bus had a floral scarf tied under her chin and had clearly been bursting to chatter, casting sidelong glimpses at Claire as they'd rumbled down Oxford Street crowded with people and the traffic of motor vehicles and horse-drawn ones. The woman with small dark eyes who Claire suspected noticed everything finally popped her question. 'Not wearing a mask, luv?' she said, pointing at her own.

Claire shook her head as though the answer wasn't obvious enough. 'I think I'm immune,' she added, forcing a smile, while inwardly wishing the Spanish flu that was rampantly killing across Britain and Europe would find her – it might solve a lot of problems.

'I'm not sure anyone is, luv. I heard yesterday that the wife of a friend's friend had woken with the shivers. She put it down to it being winter and the fire burning too low.' Over the top of the triple-layered muslin mask, Claire watched her companion's eyes widen. 'Well, within three hours she'd turned a nasty purple – just like the colour of spring violets. She couldn't speak for the sore throat. And then the shivers turned to sweats – her sheets drenched and she retched herself to death in the early hours of the following morning.' She gave a huge, sighing shrug.

Claire's horror at the tale didn't change her expression. She'd heard similar tales of despair. People were dying by the hundreds up and down the country. It was worse in the cities but the country-dwellers were not spared. Claire knew there were myriad ways to contract the flu. And no one could say she wasn't trying her damn-dest to find it.

'Poor dear,' her companion continued. 'I blame all the celebra-tions in London. They've said it doesn't take much to catch it. All those people cheering and coughing. So easy to spread.'

Claire nodded, said nothing.

'Do you live in London, luv?'

'No. A village in Berkshire.'

'Then you should stay there. Must be safer. I wish I could leave London. But my son, bless him, he came home but left a leg behind in France somewhere.' She chuckled at her grim jest. Claire didn't. 'He needs a lot of help, you see.'

'He's fortunate to have his family around,' she offered.

'I do my best for him. So, why d'you think you're immune, then?'

Claire didn't, in truth, but she had to say something now to back up the claim. 'Well, I nursed at the Front,' then instantly regretted sharing so much.

'Ohhh . . . Where?'

'Belgium.'

'My son was at Ypres.'

She nodded. 'Does he talk about it?'

'No. Won't even talk about the day he got blown up . . .' She shrugged again.

'I understand. I don't like to talk about it either.' She smiled.

'Oh, here's my stop. Excuse me,' she said, standing and easing past the woman's large knees.

'You look after yourself, luv.'

'You too.' She hurried off the bus. It wasn't her stop and she'd had no intention of getting off in Regent Street. She had just wanted to ride the bus and forget herself and her sorrows for a while. Claire had discovered that, as curious as it was, travelling with a busload of strangers who ignored her was quieter than being at home . . . for her mind, anyway. At home her thoughts spoke too loudly and crowded her head with images of men dying as she tended them, listening to their final words. Nothing had changed from Gallipoli to Flanders. They still died bravely and horribly. They still cried for their mothers and wives.

She was neither, though.

No soldier would die with her name on his lips . . . or maybe he already had. She prayed this was not the truth and that Trooper Jamie Wren remained alive somewhere in the world. Was he back in Australia by now, or was he buried in the sands near Palestine or Egypt? Maybe he had travelled with mounted troops into Western Europe, or he'd transferred regiments, if that were possible, and died at Ypres, or the Somme, or any one of the number of romantic-sounding but horrific killing fields. The voices in her mind were loud and persistent. That's why she needed the bus and the distraction of others – their coughs, their conversations, their chattering children and whispering elders. And she needed London passing by, feeling the push and pull of the groaning bus – it all soothed the inner voice and allowed her to escape the fetters of her imagination and live in the moment that had no memory. There were also times, like now, when Claire wondered if she rode the buses around London simply to reassure herself that she was still alive, still connected to life . . . even if it was other people's lives.

'Watch out, darlin',' a rag-and-bone man said, leading a horse and trailing a cart laden with oddities. She stepped back, realised she was lost in thought and watched him move on into the distance, wondering why he might be in such a busy district of central London. She scanned absently to get a fix on where precisely she was. And it was only in that moment that her breath caught to realise where she was standing.

She was at the juncture of Portland Place and Regent Street, and towering in front of her stood a grand, honey-grey brick building of fussy late-Victorian design. She recognised it instantly from childhood and in the gloom of a winter afternoon the lights that glowed from behind the arched windows looked like eyes staring out at her. Were they mocking her? She walked around to face the classically shaped portico that proudly displayed Union Jack flags flying from its balcony balustrade and she remembered walking up the short flight of stairs beneath that portico, holding hands with her father and her aunt to enter the foyer of the Langham Hotel.

Coincidence?

The soft chuckle of a woman she hadn't thought about in three years echoed through her mind. She'd been surprised and delighted only yesterday to receive a letter from Eugenie Lester. Eugenie had somehow tracked her down as simply Claire Nightingale, care of Twyford Post Office. No doubt her sharp mind recalled Claire mentioning living in the village of Charvil. Her note was brief, yet Claire felt the familiar affection reaching out from the few words like a soothing hug.

Dearest Claire,

I've been thinking about you, wondering how you are.
Do visit – the address is on this card. Just come . . . anytime,
my dear, but make it soon. Yours, Eugenie.

They had once shared a discussion on coincidence and she was sure that Eugenie would scoff that Claire standing outside the Langham was anything but divinely crafted. On the two occasions they'd met, the older woman had found just the right words to set Claire back on sturdy track when she'd felt so lost. And here was a letter from her out of the blue. Perhaps Claire should see it as a sign that Eugenie might guide her wisely again?

Maybe it was Eugenie's age that gave her such perspective, but Claire now wondered how to find balance in a world gone mad. Millions were already dead from the war, and now a new killer was on the rampage, as effective as bullets or mortar but it rode the explosion of a sneeze or a cough, a laugh or a splutter. It attacked through something as tender as a kiss and didn't restrict itself to killing enemies. Family member infected family member, friend infected friend, stranger infected stranger as they passed in the street. Perhaps she *was* immune . . . immune to everything, though, including the invitations she'd received from men, eager to get on with their lives and back to normality.

She'd not demobbed to Australia. It had felt easier to get lost in Britain, but she couldn't outrun the demons that hunted her. Where was he? She'd written two letters since the end of the war. All she had was an acknowledgement of her first enquiry that she'd made just before Christmas 1918 when she'd come out of the nursing corps at the Front. It had been easier through the years at the Casualty Clearing station in Belgium to get lost in the war and its bloody work. There were more staff, less time to get involved with the patients who seemed to pass by her care on a steadily moving queue – in one day for intensive treatment, gone the next.

Nevertheless, although other medics admitted that every wounded soldier began to look the same, Claire endlessly searched the slack-jawed faces of her patients, always looking for him, clinging to the hope that one day he would come back into her life. If he was broken, she would mend him. If he was bleeding, she would staunch him. If he was dying, she would save him.

Claire reached into the pocket of her drop-waisted jacket and felt for her touchstone, his identity tag, clutched it to warm it through her gloves and to remind her why she was feeling so rudderless. She kept the bullet tip at home, took it out from time to time to rekindle his promise that he wouldn't be killed.

She had to stay busy, distracted, until April. It felt like a lifetime ahead of her but it had been more than three years since they'd kissed, so what was nine weeks more?

She moved back to the bus stop and waited. The fierce wind turned the area where she stood into a cauldron of bright, thrashing cold and she pulled her velvet cloche hat closer to her turned-up collar, and as she shivered she was reminded of how they used to complain of the heat in Turkey and Egypt. Oh, for a little of that sun now . . . just a few minutes so she could warm her bones. But Claire knew it was her soul that needed warming.

She looked up, tried to imagine the warmth of the Middle East and, curiously, instead of seeing herself laughing on the verandah of Shepheard's Hotel in Cairo, she saw herself on a different hotel verandah: it was Alexandria and she was sipping tea and smiling with Eugenie Lester. As her bus heaved towards her, one that would take her to Paddington Station where she would leave the city and take the Reading line for Twyford, she thought about Eugenie's invitation and pondered whether there was a hidden message in that line that she should visit soon. She'd read it three times and couldn't shake the notion that the underlying prompt was cryptic.

Without dithering further, instead of boarding the bus she marched in the direction of Oxford Circus Tube Station. Descending into the stale air of the Underground, she was grateful for the warmth and press of people and moved with the swarm onto the platform to board the next train that would hurtle through the catacomb of tunnels and deliver her to London St Pancras and a train to Radlett and some more of Eugenie's wise perspective.

———

Claire stood on Watling Street, which the stationmaster assured her cut a direct path south to Marble Arch in London or north all the way to York. Radlett was a hamlet, barely a speck on the English map, and only relevant because it sat on the ancient highway from the capital to the northern cities where travellers would blink and pass it on their way to the abbey town of St Albans.

From what Claire could tell on first sight, Radlett – despite its proximity to London – was located among a thickly wooded area, even now boasting little more than its railway station, a couple of pubs, a church, village hall and the usual array of shops – butcher, fruiterer, grocer, bakery, post office. Claire watched her breath steam and dissipate, feeling oddly comfortable in this small settlement. At this moment on the edge of winter, it looked vaguely dislocated and lonely, and that suited her. She moved towards the railway inn for directions.

When she reached Loom Lane she knew instinctively which house she sought as she stood among the colourful fallen leaves beneath the giant overhang of a beech tree and its cousins. She imagined herself as dwarfed by the tall but well-clipped hedgerow on either side in the narrow country path and stared at the gabled house made of the distinctive local flint, dressed with a rich red brick at its edges and topped by the dark, smoky-coloured slate tiled roof. The windows were painted a creamy white with numerous small panes that gleamed at her, attesting to regular cleaning. It was too large to be called a cottage by her standards. She shivered, accepting that it was probably dry and cold enough to snow. She couldn't stand out here much longer without losing touch with her toes and fingers, or perhaps without drawing attention.

Claire stepped beneath the elaborately wrought arbour arching over the small iron gate and marvelled at the thickly gnarled branches of old roses that had twisted themselves sinuously and blended with a hedge of fearsome holly. The bare rose bush looked forbidding and yet she imagined in summer the blooms of heavily perfumed roses would soften the appearance of this entrance and welcome all-comers to walk through a heavenly scent.

Claire walked up the neat, brick pathway and sensed a wide garden stretching away on both sides of her and curling around the house like a meadow. She stepped up onto the porch and took a breath of hesitation before she pulled on the bell. From behind the door she heard movement and a few seconds later it was opened. A woman who looked to be in her early forties greeted her, dressed in an old-fashioned uniform more reminiscent of the Edwardian era that Britain was shaking off since the war.

'Yes? Can I help you?'

'I'm looking for Eugenie Lester. This is her house, isn't it?'

'It is.'

She explained their history briefly. 'I do have a letter from her asking me to visit.' She began digging into her bag for the card.

'Mrs Lester is unwell . . . um, this may not —'

'Oh, please, Miss . . .'

'I'm her housekeeper, Miss Chambers.'

Claire gave her best smile, imagining now who was behind the fastidious cleanliness of the windowpanes and the clipped precision of the lawn. 'I've travelled a long way today to keep a promise to visit. I should have written ahead, I realise that, and I'm very sorry to hear she's unwell, but if I could just see her for a few moments please, I would love to pay her my respects.'

The housekeeper's expression softened slightly. 'I shall ask but make no promise. Please come in.'

'Thank you. It's extremely cold today.'

'You can wait in the reception room. I'm afraid there's no fire. We weren't expecting anyone,' Miss Chambers said, slightly pursed-lipped.

Elegant furnishings of a bygone era greeted her and Claire imagined that Eugenie must have decorated the house from before she left for her desert home as it was a testimony to an affluent Victorian era. She tiptoed across the darkly polished boards onto a carpet of faded former grandeur reflecting the generally ruby colour of the room, to the cast-iron fireplace that was made up but remained unlit as warned. She hugged herself, rubbed some warmth back into her arms through her jacket and admired the richly painted and gilded porcelain urns that flanked either end of the mantelpiece. Claire didn't want to sit on any of the crowd of plump armchair cushions, or risk disturbing anything in the room for fear of Miss Chambers' disdain.

The housekeeper returned silently to stand at the entrance of the room and Claire let out a breath of relief she hadn't been caught touching anything.

'Mrs Lester will see you now. Follow me, please.'

She was led into the hall and quietly ascended the flight of stairs that curved onto a landing where a stained-glass window drenched a vase of creatively arranged rosehips with soft winter light. They rounded the landing and continued up a short five steps that groaned pleasingly for Claire, who recalled a creaky staircase in her parents' cottage where she'd been born and had lived for those early happy years.

'In here,' Miss Chambers gestured. She opened the door and Claire entered first to see the eager, affectionate smile of someone she barely knew and yet was perhaps her most intimate friend.

'Eugenie,' she whispered and didn't wait for permission but hurried to her side and hugged the elderly woman.

'Oh my dear, my dear,' her old friend replied, in no rush to let Claire go from her embrace. 'I've so wished for this moment to know you're safe and hoped you'd not forgotten me. You received my note, yes?'

'A couple of days ago. I'm sorry I haven't been —'

Eugenie made a gentle sound of disdain, waving away Claire's apology. 'You're here, child. You've brightened my existence just by arriving. Thank you for coming.'

Claire drew back to regard Eugenie in her postered bed with silk awnings that were tied back with gold tassels. She was propped up on fine damask and lace pillows but for all the finery, her friend appeared withered and half the size Claire recalled.

'Let's have some tea, Chambers, shall we?'

'Yes, Mrs Lester, right away.'

'All the trimmings, please. This is a special friend of mine.'

The woman acquiesced with a nod of her head and withdrew.

'Scary, isn't she?'

Claire laughed. 'A little bit, yes.'

'She puts the fear of, well, I don't know quite what, into most of my visitors, especially the rector. But you've probably worked out that she has my best interests at heart.'

'Is she family?'

Eugenie shook her head. 'But might as well be. She treats me like a giddy old aunt. She's the daughter of the woman who used to run this place for my parents. So she feels rather proprietorial at times.'

'So I've noticed. But you were gone for so long.'

'Yes, I think it's why she's punishing me. All those years of being in service to other people when all she wanted was to be here.'

'I'm glad you're reunited,' Claire said. 'I didn't know you'd be here, of course. I came on a whim. I'm so pleased you are.'

Eugenie nodded. 'I came home to die, my dear, and before you make placations, I *am* dying and I decided that as much as I loved Egypt, it wasn't fair to leave my body behind there for strangers to care for. Makes it so difficult and we Brits hate to fuss, don't you know?' Claire's shoulders drooped in a private sorrow. Now she understood the cryptic quality of Eugenie's request for the visit. 'Besides,' Eugenie continued breezily, 'I got it into my head that I wanted to be buried near my parents and Edward.'

'Edward?'

'My husband.'

Claire gasped. 'When Miss Chambers called you Mrs Lester, I realised I barely knew anything about you, and yet you know almost everything about me. Why did I assume you were not married?'

Eugenie shrugged. 'Perfectly reasonable. I gave no clue that I was. Besides, there's nothing that needs knowing, my dear. My life was drawing to its close when we met, whereas yours was essentially only beginning. I was far more interested in your life than mine anyway, for I came from wealth and never needed anything. I was a loved child, a beloved wife, I knew no adversity and when Edward died in Africa on one of his exploration expeditions that young men seem to think equates to heroism, I ran away in search of a bit of adventure myself, or certainly somewhere to escape everything that reminded me of him. I loved him so much that curiously I didn't want a single bit of him near me, not even his grave. The heart is strange.' Eugenie suddenly paused, looking down at her hands, which now bore a wedding ring that Claire had not seen her friend wear previously. It seemed she was ready to have everything that reminded her of Edward kept near as she drew closer to death and joining him again. 'Anyway, Egypt is the past and soon I'll be past but you've made me so incredibly happy that you kept a promise to visit.'

Chambers arrived and set all the tea paraphernalia down on a table by the window.

'I've brought some parkin cake left over from bonfire night.' She stared at Claire.

'Er, parkin cake?' Claire wondered aloud, before she could censor herself.

Chambers blinked in irritation but Eugenie chuckled. 'Treacle and oats. A favourite of northerners and this is a good one, deliciously sticky.'

The housekeeper pointed at the biscuits she'd also brought. 'I hope you like ginger stem?'

'Oh, I do,' Claire nodded, would not have dared say otherwise.

'Mrs Lester likes the tea to brew for four minutes, or would you prefer I wait and pour?'

Claire stood, affected a breezier voice and smiled gently. 'No, I can do it, thank you, Miss Chambers. I'd like to,' she said and began slowly walking around the room, gazing at all of its fascinating *objets d'art* as if Miss Chambers was already forgotten.

It was an eclectic mix of Eugenie's travels and she was pleased to see much of her friend's Egyptian influences had found their way into this, her most intimate living space. And so the colours were brilliantly rich like precious jewels, which somehow didn't seem to clash with the self-patterned emerald wallpaper depicting peacocks or the massive gilded planter with its overflowing fern.

She realised the housekeeper was watching her.

'Thank you, Joy,' Eugenie said as a soft dismissal. As the door closed, she added, 'She doesn't suit her name but she's had an unhappy life and there's nothing I can do to draw her from her sorrows. She lost her father and three brothers in the war.'

'Oh,' Claire said. 'That explains plenty.'

'Indeed. But it was the death of her fiancé that finished dear Joy off. She had finally found someone as she entered her fifth decade, and I'm afraid he didn't come home either. Died at Amiens just a few months before the Armistice.'

Claire's heart opened with sympathy. 'I was serving on the Western Front.'

'I suspected you might, after we heard about the evacuation from the Dardanelles. But I was sorry to lose track of you so suddenly. I won't ask how it was because it's obvious.'

Claire gave a sad smile and gestured at the tray. 'I'll pour, shall I?'

'We took tea together the last time we met.'

'But I see you take milk now,' Claire teased, removing the tea cosy.

'I'm in England, dear. And it's winter. And you'd better nibble a biscuit whether you want to or not.'

Claire brought the cup and saucer over. 'Can you manage?'

'Dying I may be, but I'm not a complete invalid. Not yet, anyway.'

She frowned. 'What ails you?'

'Oh, old age, I'm sure. But they say my heart is giving out. I guess you know the feeling.'

Claire hesitated. 'Does it show?'

Her elder nodded. 'In every part of you, child. Your eyes see but they don't seem to search hard enough; there's no curiosity in them. Tell me you haven't stopped looking.'

Claire's emotions stirred at the remark. She allowed her gaze to roam beyond the glass of the window into the garden. She looked past the gate, even over the hedgerow to the spire of the parish church nearby. And still her gaze searched: beyond to the peaceful patchwork of Hertfordshire's countryside to where sheep grazed on thin pickings and fallow fields waited patiently through the winter. No snow today, a steady drizzle had begun and tiny rivulets of moisture striped the glass in the window and it seemed to mirror her tears.

'Claire? Come and sit.'

She dabbed at her eyes with a napkin and joined Eugenie with her tea. 'Forgive me. Truly, that's the first time I've dropped a tear in years. I've seen so much ugliness and despair that I feared I've become immune. At least it proves I still have a heart,' she said in a dry tone, trying to lighten the mood. She sipped her tea that was deliciously strong.

But Eugenie was clearly not having it. 'I take it you haven't heard from Mr Wren?'

Claire shook her head, sipped again and swallowed her emotional outburst with her tea.

'Fill me in on what happened since we last met.'

Claire gave a potted version of her life, from hugging Eugenie goodbye at the hotel to this morning's conversation with the stranger on the bus and finding herself outside the Langham Hotel.

'So you have tried to find him through the official means?'

'Yes. It's a waiting game, I'm afraid. I'm one of the many women growing older and sadder, hoping for news. I looked for him on every stretcher, in every tented ward, even on the few days off in local towns in the hope I might glimpse him. I sent letters to AGH1 but there was no news.'

'What about his family?'

She shrugged. 'Now that we are in peacetime I have to use the channels set up to find a soldier because I don't know his people, and even if they are aware of my existence, I'm a perfect stranger. However, we all love him, all want him back safely. Anyway, I have written, but I'm likely many weeks away from hearing back. Mail is so slow. Besides, so many soldiers are yet to demob that his family may not yet have reliable information.' She shrugged. 'It could take a year or more to see him, even if he is alive.'

'He could have been posted.'

'And he could have died at Gallipoli, for all I know, or been that same soldier who died in Cairo.' She shrugged. 'Or died in Palestine, Egypt, Jordan. He could have been sent to France or Belgium, or —' The warning look from Eugenie halted her.

'There's still the promise.'

Claire gave a small, wry smile. 'Nothing wrong with your memory.'

'It's all that remains sharp about me, my dear. You will keep the rendezvous, won't you?'

'Yes. That promise was precious.'

'So, with that to aim for and with the war behind us, can you not find a reason to look forward?'

'Well, I reached that decision this morning, actually, and part of it was to reconnect myself with others – hence my visit. I've been moving around in a bubble of my own pity for too long.'

'And the other part?' Eugenie asked, leaning forward.

'Well, that part's harder but I know what I need is a purpose: something that will keep me occupied and distracted until April, but something that is meaningful.'

Eugenie gave a triumphant sound. 'Good for you, my girl. That is indeed the spirit. May I point out that your body could use some fattening up,' Eugenie nodded at the parkin cake, 'and to find some curves again. Your mouth – smile more often; force it if you have to.' Claire was reminded of Doreen's mouth. 'Your eyes . . . light them up, they've seen more than their fair share of death and that winter of war is behind us now – look to spring peacetime. Your clothes . . . dress them up, and your hair . . . oh, my dear, for heaven's sake, cut it!' Claire giggled. Eugenie had always managed to amuse her. 'So what is it to be, this fresh purpose – a new job?'

She shook her head. 'Not yet. I don't feel like nursing again straightaway but you're right, I know I need a purpose. So firstly I'm going to find a friend of mine from my time in the Mediterranean. We were in Gallipoli together.'

'Go on.' Eugenie's gaze sparkled over the rim of her tea.

'Do you remember the Arabic prayer book?'

'Of course I do.'

'I'm hoping she has it.'

'Why would she have it?'

Claire gave an embarrassed wince. 'I came hurtling to you that day after the nurses in Cairo told me Jamie had died from his injuries.'

'And I was perfectly sure that we'd set that aside on the basis that there are many Jameses in the world and the bird surname could have been mixed up in the chaos.'

Claire lifted a shoulder in resignation. 'Except when I came back to the dock that day Rosie looked so downhearted I knew she had more bad news. She said the nurses recalled that it was definitely a light horseman called James, with the bird surname, who had died.'

Eugenie made the connection. 'And that's what sent you off to the Western Front.'

Claire nodded.

'I see.'

'I was in such a state, in here,' Claire admitted, touching above her heart. 'I was so angry at the world that I just wanted to get what felt like the inevitable over with. I couldn't wait for orders to come through so I could —'

'Jump the queue?' Eugenie offered with soft sympathy. They both knew they were talking about death.

'Yes, I suppose I was extremely eager to put myself in direct danger as a way of shaking my fist at fate.'

'Tell me about the prayer book?'

Claire shook her head. 'It was in Alexandria with the rest of my belongings but I left in such a hurry and I didn't want to take anything so precious. At least in the Middle East our lives had a sense of routine on the hospital ship. We had places to store our belongings and so on.' She frowned, only now thinking it through properly as she nibbled on a biscuit that was delicious with its hum of ginger warming her tongue. 'I'm going to find Rosie Parsons – I know she would have been given the task of packing up my stuff and storing it for me. I'll have to start with her family because I've no idea where she ended up. Actually you may recall she was at the hotel with me the day you and I met.'

Eugenie shook her head. 'I don't recall her clearly but do you mean to say you haven't been in touch with her during the war?'

'I'm ashamed to admit that I haven't, but even you can see that I ran away from the Middle East. I was convinced by others and what felt like overwhelming circumstantial evidence that Jamie had died and I needed to leave everything that reminded me of him behind.'

Her friend sighed. 'I understand.' Claire smiled at the wan, birdlike woman who now sat against the pillows with hands that trembled when she held her cup and saucer, and her still neatly coiffed hair was now so white against the linen it seemed transparent. 'Here, take this, dear, before I spill it.' She handed the crockery to Claire and drew her exquisitely embroidered shawl closer around her shoulders. 'So this Rosie and the prayer book is your first step to what?'

'I'm not sure yet, but it feels as though they are pieces to the jigsaw of my life.' Claire shrugged. 'Sorry, I know that sounds dramatic.'

'Not at all. I think it's as valid as it is a wise plan. It's important to reconnect with anything familiar – places, people, things. They make us feel safe. They also give confidence. It will help you to believe in Jamie Wren.'

Claire gave a firm nod. 'Until April first comes, I will not give up on him.'

15

Claire strolled from Hove Station munching on a Fry's Turkish Delight Bar, which she'd seen advertised beside the young boy selling newspapers. In a whimsical mood she'd allowed herself to believe the universe had its spiritual hands firmly against her back, encouraging her in this mission to find the Arabic prayer book.

The flowery taste of Roses of Otto and the scent of rosewater that overtook her senses as she bit through the paper-thin covering of chocolate to the pleasantly chewy pink gel beneath it took her instantly back to her days in the Middle East, sipping floral-flavoured sherbets with the very friend she was hunting. Claire recalled that the Ottomans were famous for using the extracted oil from rose petals to flavour drinks, bathwater, even food, and especially their sweet treats. She smiled as she let the floral taste engulf her senses while she focused on remembering the directions from one of the railway staff for how to find Wilbury Crescent.

'Take you about ten minutes, miss, maybe fifteen if you dilly-dally. But it's a beautiful morning so a gorgeous girl like you might as well take your time and enjoy some rare sun. Lots of daffodils and tulips about.' He lifted his cap to her.

Claire was now imagining three years of news to catch up on with Rosie. Guilt slightly soured the sweetness of chocolate as she acknowledged how poor it was that she had taken this long to make contact again with the woman who had worn a smile for her throughout those tireless working hours. Rosie had always managed to find something to look forward to amidst all the horror, even if it was as simple as a proper bath.

She set her shoulders and began to look forward to hugging her friend again. Claire checked the street signs. She'd been walking down a long, wide avenue called The Drive for ages, it felt, but now she was mercifully faced with a choice: left or right down Eaton Road.

An old woman was passing with an equally elderly dog. Claire interrupted them to ask for help.

'It's that way, dear,' the woman said, pointing left. 'Follow this side of the parish church and once you see the vicarage, I think you turn left.'

'Thank you,' she called to the woman's back, but only the dog glanced around, panting. Claire looked up at the grand, imposing sandstone building and followed the southern walls down Eaton Road. The church filled the block and right enough she saw Wilbury Crescent to her left. With a fresh skip in her step she passed the vicarage and began looking for the house number of Rosie's family home. She remembered it from the countless letters she posted on behalf of Rosie to her family.

Finally she stood in front of the right sandstone brick Victorian villa with its large bay window. She saw the net curtains part and a woman's face peep out at her and she lifted a hand in salutation but the curtains snapped back into place. Claire hesitated only momentarily before she walked up the short flight of stairs to tap gently with the doorknocker.

'Yes?' the woman who opened it asked. She looked nervous, her eyes not fully making contact with Claire's gaze.

'Hello, are you Mrs Parsons?'

'Yes.' The woman threw a quick glance behind her. 'Can I help you?'

'I'm Claire Nightingale.'

'Yes?'

She smiled, embarrassed. 'I'm sorry to just arrive like this. Let me start again. I'm Claire and I'm an old friend of Rosie's . . . this is the home of Rosie Parsons, am I right?'

'Yes.'

Claire wondered if she would ever get more than a single syllable from the small, mousy woman who had still not opened the door much beyond a crack where a narrow column of her face and a glimpse of her floral pinny could be seen.

'Um, Rosie and I used to nurse together. We were, well, close when we worked together in the Mediterranean on a hospital ship.' She shrugged, not really wanting to explain all of this on a front doorstep. 'I rather hoped she might be home.'

A couple of young faces with masses of sweet red ringlets suddenly pushed the door open more and poked around Mrs Parsons' shoulders.

'Oh, this must be the beautiful twins! Rosie told me all about you. Now, which of you is Meggie?'

One girl gave a shy gasp.

'So you,' she pointed, 'must be the older twin by one minute – Sally, right?'

Sally nodded but her expression was more cautious than her sister's. 'Who is it, Mum?'

'Rosie's dead,' the woman said flatly, ignoring her daughter and fixing Claire with a dull-eyed stare. It felt like an accusation.

'Dead?' She began to hear a ringing sound in her ears like the howl of a lonely animal. 'Rosie's dead?' she repeated, as if by saying it again she could change what the words meant.

A man had arrived. 'Who's this then, luv?'

'Er, Mr P-Parsons?' she stammered in shock.

'That's me. Can I help you?'

Claire explained again. 'Your wife has just told me that Rosie died.'

He nodded grimly. 'You knew our girl, did you?'

'Yes, we were good friends.'

'Odd that we haven't seen you, then,' he remarked and the truth bit hard. 'You remember her mentioning a girl called Claire, don't you, luv?'

Mrs Parsons barely blinked.

He returned his attention to Claire. 'Lost our lovely Rosie last year. Go on, you kids. Let the lady be.'

The youngsters disappeared into the shadows and she was left with Rosie's parents, and the Roses of Otto tasted only of guilt now.

———————

Claire was propped, straight-backed and glum in the dark sitting room, as Bill Parsons told her the full story. She didn't want the tea that was clutched in her lap but she also didn't want to appear rude; plus it gave her something to do with her hands. She couldn't cry, couldn't talk, could barely breathe as his trembling voice told of their loss, but she could hear the pulse of her heart-beat in her head and with each beat it echoed her internal scream of shame.

'. . . just one of those things, I guess. The bomb landed right on the hospital tent where our Rosie was. About fifteen others were killed outright too, we heard through the Red Cross. No suffering, the second letter said – that one was from a nice doctor who knew her and wrote to us of his sadness. He was first on the scene and assures us it was instant; he believes the blast flung her against an iron cot and she, um . . .' He glanced at his wife, who stared into the distance expressionless. 'Well, it was her neck. Broken.' He found a sad smile. 'I think he was a bit sweet on her, wasn't he, Nell?' He touched his wife's hand gently.

Nell Parsons nodded silently. Claire smelled cabbage cooking, powerfully overriding the sweet aroma of wax polish that made all the dark wood surfaces gleam around her, and could hear the twins' muffled voices coming from somewhere upstairs.

'Anyway,' Bill continued, clearing his throat, 'she loved her work, that girl, and she made us proud. We've got all her letters and I do remember your name coming up fondly.'

'We were separated when I suddenly went to Belgium and obviously Rosie moved on to France.'

'Yes, and she knew the dangers. But what can you do? I could name a dozen families right now who've all lost someone close. We're no different,' he said, taking Nell's hand into his lap and squeezing it. 'But we do miss her. She was special – our first child and always such a sunny girl.'

Claire looked away and stared past the net curtains and the sash windows to the street, where the sound of parish bells were echoing.

'They practise at this time,' Mr Parsons said, reading her thoughts.

She nodded, smiling sadly, and looked back towards him. 'How is the rest of the family?'

'Oh, you know, trying to get back to normal. Robbie survived and without any serious injury so we have to be grateful. Danny and Charlie were too young to go and they're both blessed enough to be working. Lizzie . . .' He looked down. 'Our Lizzie's been changed by the war. She did her bit on the home front, worked hard, but she took Rosie's death badly. She's got a nice young man now, though; returned soldier who walks with a stick, and he'll do all right, that boy. I'm hopeful that Dennis can bring Lizzie back to that happy-go-lucky girl she used to be. They'll be married next year so we have that to look forward to.' He patted his wife's hand again. 'Grandchildren and all that. Lizzie said if she has a daughter, she'll call her Rose.' He cleared his throat and fell silent. His wife gave no eye contact, no clue even that she was still following their conversation.

Claire drew a silent breath. 'Do you mind me asking if you received any of Rosie's personal effects?'

'All of it, I think, luv, didn't we?'

'Yes,' his wife answered, surprising Claire. She stood and started clearing away the cups and saucers. Claire hurriedly swallowed the tepid tea and thanked Nell with a nod when she handed hers onto the tray. The woman left the room with silent footsteps.

'I'm afraid my wife has taken Rosie's death deeply to heart. You'll have to forgive her.'

'I do,' she murmured.

'They were great friends, she and Rosie. It's been a year but the way Nell behaves you'd think the telegram arrived yesterday. My wife's nephew died on his way home this month too, can you believe? Spanish flu, we think.'

'Oh, Mr Parsons, I'm so, so sorry.'

He sighed. 'I'm sorry you've come all this way for nothing.'

'Do you mind me asking if you recall a prayer book in Rosie's stuff . . . it was written in Arabic? I know that sounds terribly strange for her to have such a thing but there is good reason for it.'

He shook his head, frowning. 'Nell?' he called. Then called again. She finally returned. 'Did Rosie have a prayer book in that box?'

'In Arabic,' Claire reinforced gently.

'Yes.'

Her heart leapt. 'Um, forgive me, but that book belonged to me . . . well, actually not me, but to my fiancé.' It was easier to fib at this point. 'I was hoping I might have it returned. He's gone missing and I have nothing of his except that. I've convinced myself that if I can find the prayer book, I might be able to find him.'

'Your fiancé's an Arab?' Mr Parsons asked, incredulous.

'Oh, no, no, not at all. He's Australian. From the Light Horse.' She felt the pride rising at the mention of these facts, glad to note that she was speaking in the present tense. Already he was beginning to feel alive again for her. 'No, he . . . um, that prayer book was a gift from someone special,' she said, skirting the truth. 'I promised I would look after it but I had to leave in a hurry from Egypt and I was hopeful that Rosie would keep it with her things and now I know she did.' She shrugged.

Rosie's father looked unimpressed. 'The soldiers you cared for were fighting the Arabs out there, weren't they?' The fresh accusation in his voice punched through his kind, gentle demeanour.

She forgave him, though. Everyone wanted to blame someone for losing loved ones and it didn't matter that it was the German army that lobbed the bomb in France with Rosie's name on it. 'Um, no, the men we cared for in Gallipoli were fighting Turks.'

'Same thing,' Mrs Parsons said, finally speaking up.

'Not really, no, but that's academic now,' she said, her embarrassment at correcting them colouring her cheeks. 'I mean, we all just want peace and to patch up our lives, don't we?' she appealed.

Neither of them answered.

'James Wren – he's my fiancé – asked me to take care of this prayer book and I simply want to find it. It's no good to anyone else.'

'Well, we don't want any book like that in our house, do we, luv?'

'No. It's why I got rid of it.'

Claire's throat felt suddenly as dry as the faded rose petal potpourri in a dish in front of the fireplace. Had she heard right? 'Did you say it's not here, Mrs Parsons?'

'I didn't like it,' she remarked. 'It was all damaged and you couldn't read anything anyway. I couldn't imagine why our Rosie would have such a horrible thing. I thought they'd made a mistake when they sent it.'

'Oh, gosh – please tell me you know where it is?'

They both looked back at her unmoved. Mrs Parsons shrugged. 'It went out with the jumble.'

The air suddenly felt too thick to breathe. 'To a jumble sale?'

'No, I did take it to our church jumble sale but someone took an interest in it before the event. Seemed to know what it was all about. Gave me half a crown for it. I was happy. Helped towards the memorial plaque for Rosie in the park gardens.'

Claire lifted her hand to her mouth to stop her letting out the sound of soft despair. She gathered herself. 'Er, do you know how I might reach him?'

'Oh, I remember that fellow,' Mr Parsons chipped in as his wife began a slow lift of one shoulder. 'He was a collector, wasn't he, luv?'

'I don't recall.'

'Yes, I'm sure he told me that while you were talking to Eleanor. He was with his "friend".' He coughed meaningfully and Claire blinked, not understanding the innuendo. This time he didn't wait for Mrs Parsons to offer her anticipated careless shrug. 'Yes, he told me he keeps a place in the Lanes of Brighton, if I'm not mistaken.'

Claire felt her hopes rise. 'Where? Would you know?'

'I don't, but if you ask around he couldn't be too hard to find. Um, I think his name was Fotheringham.'

Claire repeated the name silently: *Fotheringham*. 'I'll go straightaway. I'm presuming it's not too far?'

'No.' He snorted softly. 'Fifteen minutes on the bus from Church Road. Just follow our street down towards the sea. You'll know it. Main road that takes you from Hove into Brighton.'

'Thank you both,' she said in the politest tone she could muster above the pounding of her pulse. 'For the tea and for your help. I'm deeply sorry about Rosie.'

Mrs Parsons looked relieved to show her the door.

'There's no grave, I'm presuming?' Claire wondered as they walked into the hall.

'No, she's buried with the others in France,' Bill replied for his wife. 'Well, farewell, Miss Nightingale. I hope you find your book and that your young man returns to you.'

She smiled. 'Thank you again.' She shook his hand and followed his wife to the front door. 'Um, please say goodbye to the girls for me. I'm sorry I didn't bring them anything, but I shall send something.'

'No need, Miss Nightingale,' Rosie's mother said, her voice as leaden as it had been since their eyes first met.

16

Claire had ambled through the warren of narrow streets that centuries earlier had been the alleyways of fishermen and smugglers in the old town of Brighton. The crowded lanes later developed as cheap housing for workers servicing the gentry of Brighton in their fashionable villas by the seaside. More recently the myriad alleyways had become popular with antiquarians who gobbled up the creaking, shabby houses and shopfronts to give them a new lease of life and value.

Nevertheless, in parts it felt intriguingly medieval to Claire as she began asking in various shops and eating houses about Leo Fotheringham; she was rapidly losing hope when an extremely elderly man in a dusty gold and silver exchange shop frowned for a long time and said he vaguely knew Fotheringham but hadn't seen him in a while and the place to find him was likely the Sussex Arms where he drank with his friend. Again the word sounded loaded but Claire was not interested in Fotheringham, only in what she hoped he still had in his possession.

She found the pub and while it might not be seemly for a young woman to enter alone, she didn't give herself a second's hesitation. She gazed around the dim interior where dust motes hung lazily in the thin shafts of light from small windows, feeling deeply self-conscious as men leaning against the wide bar, or huddled over tables sharing a mumbling pint, regarded her.

The man behind the bar looked up from where he was lifting a large glass, overflowing with froth, onto his counter. He glanced her way. 'Looking for someone, luv?'

'A Mr Fotheringham,' she murmured.

His friendly expression gloomed over and she watched his gaze shift to where a man with a sweep of silver hair sat alone and hunched at a table over a glass of amber.

'Bernard?' he called.

'What? Can't you see I'm drowning my sorrows?'

'Er, there's a young lady asking after Fotheringham.'

She leaned further into the pub from the doorway where she stood so that Bernard, whoever he was, could see her and she noticed silver eyebrows meet in the middle of his frown. 'Do I know you?'

She shook her head and then glanced around, further embarrassed to be drawing attention. 'May I speak with you a moment?'

He stood. 'No. I'm busy.'

'Mind your manners around the lady, Bernard,' the barman warned. He nodded at Claire with encouragement.

She approached the man. 'I'm Claire Nightingale.' She held out a gloved hand.

'*Enchanté*,' he growled with a flawless French accent that was loaded with sourness.

'I'm very sorry to interrupt you,' she said, noting his half-drunk whisky.

'Then do me a fine favour and leave me alone.' He lifted the glass but didn't drink from it, instead banging it down on the table.

'I just want to ask a question, um, Mr Fotheringham.'

'You've got the wrong person, Miss Nightingale.'

She looked over at the publican.

'Bernard Jenkins, don't make me come around and shake you. That'll be your last drink if you don't act politely.'

Claire was confused. 'I'm sorry, um . . .'

He looked up from red-rimmed eyes. He wasn't drunk, not yet, but she sensed he was planning to be. 'Ask your wretched question and leave me to another Scotch, will you?'

'Do you recall the Parsons family from Hove?'

He considered her question, downing the rest of his nip of liquor as he did so. 'If I do, I can't bring them to mind. Now, excuse me,' he said, standing, adjusting his cravat before reaching for his hat and pushing past Claire. 'See you later, Don.'

She was so surprised at his rudeness that she watched him until the pub door closed behind him and it was only the sound of its slam that stung her into action. She rushed out after Jenkins.

'Mr Jenkins!' she called, soon catching up. He used a cane to walk but swung it in an affected way, clicking it down every third step on the pavement. 'Forgive me,' she began again.

'No, I won't. Stop following me. Just leave me and Leo alone.'

She halted, unsure of what next to do, watched him cross the narrow street and head down another alleyway.

If you let him go, you let Jamie go, breathed a voice loud in her mind, silent to the world.

'Wait!' She hurried after him and caught up, panting and pulling at his arm.

He shook her hand away. 'Oh, for pity's sake, leave me to my grief, you wretched woman!'

Grief. She thought she could swallow the rising anger but it beat her, quickly finding its way out. 'Mr Jenkins, I too am grieving. The world is grieving!' He turned. 'I am not here to interfere with your life but I believe you have something that belongs to me and I would like to get it back, please. I will trouble you no further once I have.'

He looked at her from those slightly glazed, red eyes, which she now understood appeared sore from weeping. 'What the hell are you blathering about?'

'Well, if you'd pause long enough to let me explain, perhaps I'll stop bothering you.'

'Damn it! Not here!' He stomped off. Then turned around. 'Well, come on, then. This is your idea.'

She ran to catch up again, following him at a hurried walk as he strode, ignoring her, down one street and another until Claire had lost her sense of direction and her vision had narrowed to following the polished heels of tan brogues peeping from beneath brazen, caramel-coloured trousers. It only struck her now that she thought about it that Jenkins was a dapper dresser, flamboyant, even, given the tweed jacket and matching waistcoat that was far more colourful than most men chose to wear.

Suddenly the brogues crossed into a garden-like setting and she was following him into a sweetly scented courtyard of bright freesia. She hadn't expected anything so pretty but didn't let her gaze linger. He unlocked the door, stomped across the threshold and up some stairs. Claire quietly followed, disconcerted and embarrassed, but she was on her mission now and refused to leave empty-handed. She closed the door and tiptoed up the flight where he met her at the landing.

'Right!' he growled, swinging around. 'You've pushed your way into my house. Whatever this is about, let's get it over with.' He marched to the cabinet and pulled down a decanter.

'Mr Jenkins, let me quickly say this and then you can return to your, er . . . day,' she said, glancing at the fiery liquid being sloshed into a crystal glass.

He turned back and swallowed the contents defiantly while watching her. Claire breathed in through her nose, adopting her serious nurse's expression.

'Say it, then,' he demanded. 'I'm already bored of you.'

'Why are you being so rude?'

'Because I hate you for being here and talking to me because it means I'm alive and having to get through yet another bloody day.' His voice had escalated to a shout.

'Be quiet!' she snapped. Stunned initially, Jenkins then began laughing to himself. He tottered deeper into the house. Claire looked around her and was treated to a sumptuous and tastefully furnished sitting room. The colours were bold with a rich yellow and green palette. She'd not seen anything like it. Jewelled colours reminiscent of Egypt. She stared at the chuckling man and knew she needed to rescue the situation before he really did drink too much to make sense.

'I . . . I admire your art, Mr Jenkins,' she said, glancing around at the post-Impressionist landscapes.

He blinked, clearly not ready for the compliment. 'Thank you. I've been acquiring them for nearly ten years. A French artist, and I suspect he will be "highly desirable", as we say in the trade. We used to spend whole nights discussing them.'

She looked around. 'We?'

'Leo and I,' he said in a dull tone. 'We were lovers, Miss Nightingale, does that shock you?'

She paused. 'I know you want it to,' Claire admitted. 'Look, I told you, I just want to claim back something that belongs to me. As I understand it, it was wrongfully sold to Mr Fotheringham by a Mrs Parsons.' She briefly recapped the situation.

His mouth twitched with a heartless grimace. 'This is not my problem, Miss Nightingale.'

'Do you have the prayer book?'

He sighed. 'I do.'

She closed her eyes briefly against the instant watering of relief that welled. She reached for a chair back, leaned against it as she aimed for a steady voice and forthright tone. 'May I see it, please?' she asked, achieving neither. Claire cleared her throat of the gathering emotion.

He lurched to an elegant writing bureau near the window and pulled back the desk door, reaching inside to retrieve the familiar book. He held it up and Claire felt a moment of dizzied desperation to wrestle it from him. The book felt like a talisman winking at her when the sunlight caught the golden gilding.

She rapidly calculated what it might cost to persuade him to return it. 'Mr Jenkins, how about —?'

'This belongs to me,' he said. 'It was a gift from Leo . . . the last thing he gave me. I loved him, Miss Nightingale, and I don't expect you to understand that or be anything but repulsed by it, but he was everything to me and when he gave me this book he was perfectly well, filled with laughter at having escaped married life in Hampshire to live six glorious, secretive weeks in Brighton with me. Within two days, Miss Nightingale, the only person I've ever loved was dying in my arms. I had to deliver him to a hospital so he could die there alone, frightened, but at least his family and their name was protected from scandal. All I have now of darling Leo, apart from memories, is the faint smell of his pomade on my pillows, some clothes hanging lifelessly in my wardrobe and this Arabic prayer book. He knows my interest in the Levant.' He gave a mirthless grin. 'No word of a lie. The world of the Arab and the Muslim faith is thoroughly intriguing to me.' His voice returned to its cut-glass sharpness. 'Leo lived off his wife's inheritance, Miss Nightingale, and he lived off me. I didn't care. He made me feel alive in a way I haven't since a happy childhood in Berkshire.'

Claire blanched. 'You could be describing me, Mr Jenkins. I was born in Berkshire as well and I recall being very happy. And then, perhaps like you, I simply was no longer happy, not for many years, until I met someone called James Wren. And I feel about Jamie as you clearly do about Leo: that Jamie has no equal. And my world has been dismantled since I lost sight of him in a Cairo hospital.' She said that deliberately to pique his interest and saw a flame light in his gaze at mention of the Eygptian capital. She continued, pretending she hadn't noticed. 'I'm a nurse. He was gravely wounded, even died once in a hospital ship's theatre en route to Egypt, but both times we managed to revive him. This was the man I loved but now I have no idea where he is or even if he is still alive. Just as you do, I have some short-lived memories and a couple of curiosities, one of them that prayer book that he gave to me.' She didn't believe Jenkins needed to learn the truth.

'How do I even know it's yours?'

'Look!' she said, holding up a hand to stop him saying another word before dipping into her pocket and retrieving the bullet tip she carried habitually. 'May I?' she asked, gesturing towards the prayer book.

Jenkins stared at her suspiciously initially and then relented, handing it to her. She stepped closer and showed him. 'See how this bullet tip fits into that depression?'

He let out his breath in a sigh of wonder; his expression briefly allowed a flash of a smile. 'I have been trying to imagine what occurred.' He surprised her with a small chuckle as he rubbed his finger across the depression. 'That's exciting.'

'I can give you more,' Claire pressed. 'I can give you the provenance of that prayer book.' She'd pinpointed his weakness and waited only a heartbeat to see the glimmer in his gaze at the suggestion. 'This prayer book belonged to a young man called Açar Shahin, a Turk from Istanbul, fighting in the German allied forces in the Dardanelles. From what I learned, Shahin was an ascetic, a poet, a dreamer, Mr Jenkins. He played music, he wrote stories, refused to kill any of the enemy deliberately. I gather from someone who knew him briefly that Mr Shahin wanted to follow the ways of the mystics, but he believed wholly in some manner of his own heightened awareness that he would not survive the war. During a day-long armistice he met Jamie and he gave him this book,' she said, loading her voice with as much gravity as she could muster, 'and Jamie responded in kind.' Yes, she would tell the truth, she decided in the tense moments as he watched her, and Claire didn't pause to consider this decision any longer. After she'd told him, Claire ended with a shake of her head. 'It is a journey of forgiveness,' she breathed, suddenly understanding Shahin's gesture, and her voice warbled slightly in that moment of dawning. 'Shahin called Jamie his friend . . . no, brother. And Jamie admitted to me he felt closer to this Turk during that bright, brief, heartbreaking time of the silenced guns and the thousands of dead than to many people he'd known all of his life. These two men have come to represent for me all the suffering innocents who were bearing the burden of other people's greed, desire, anger and power.'

She watched Jenkins swallow his anger.

'And what do you wish to do with my book?'

'It is not about whether this is your book, my book, Jamie's book. This is about honour, Mr Jenkins. You honoured Leo's family at the last, even when you were at the height of your suffering. I am suffering now and I wish to honour the dead too. Shahin wanted Jamie to have this book.'

Her words had guided him to a place of peace, it seemed, for he regarded her now with what felt like respect; it was grudging but he straightened.

'That's not entirely correct, Miss Nightingale.' She blinked in annoyance. 'The Turk did not wish your friend to have this book. He wished his father to have his book returned. There's a difference.'

'Yes, but —'

'I will give you this book on one condition.'

'Go on.'

'That you return it to the Turkish family.'

She opened her mouth but couldn't think of anything to say initially. They stared at one another awkwardly. It had not occurred to her to take on such an adventure alone . . . was it her place? But even as she thought this, the answer came back that it didn't matter who returned the book, so long as it was given back to Açar Shahin's family.

'I mean it. If you really want to honour the dead as you claim, then honour your nursing friend who kept it safe for you, honour your fiancé who promised to be caretaker of this book for its owner,' he said, waving it before her, 'and honour unreservedly the dead owner's wishes for this book. Nobility takes deeds. I took action that hurt me deeply but prevented pain for others. So take the book back to Turkey or don't take it from me at all. If it's going to gather dust among your lace underwear, it might as well gather dust in my desk.' Bernard's eyes blazed with the fervour of his challenge.

'You may not keep it, Bernard,' she said in what sounded just short of a growl. Claire took a breath and said in a milder tone, 'I know Leo gave it to you but Jamie gave it to me first. It's my only connection to him.'

He glared at her.

'But I will return it. I shall go to Istanbul.' She was giving voice to a promise that her mind could barely keep up with, but her heart took over – the pact was made between Jamie and Shahin and she and Bernard and even Leo were irrelevant to that equation. She aired this thought.

'Nonsense! All that matters is that the book is returned. Your Turk will lie easy in his grave and your fiancé, if he's alive, will surely admire your pluck. Are you plucky, Miss Nightingale, or just clucky?'

Claire felt her lids narrow and she was sure she was giving Jenkins a look of pure scorn.

'Ah, I feel your rage like a scald, Miss Nightingale,' he mocked. 'Can I get you a cooling drink? I know I need one.' He walked over to the cabinet and poured himself another small tot.

'A water, please,' she said and could hear the strain in her voice.

He poured her a small glass of water from the jug he kept near the whisky to dilute it. He returned and handed her the glass. 'Shall we or shall we not drink to Istanbul?'

Istanbul! Was she mad, agreeing to such a dare? Claire's acceptance of the challenge blazed back through her eyes like mica glittering from the hard countenance of bedrock. '*Serefe!*' she growled.

'Indeed, cheers, Miss Nightingale,' he said clinking his squat, crystal glass against her thin beaker. It made a dull sound of celebration as he held out the prayer book to her. 'Take it.'

Claire stared at it for several seconds. Finally she took it, privately rejoicing at the feel of the vellum once more against her skin. 'Thank you, Mr Jenkins.'

Relief, like an explosion of radiant light, pulsed through her. She was back on course, one step closer to her purpose. Another obstacle to Jamie felt as though it had been conquered and as daring as it was, she couldn't deny that the hum of fresh energy was not all anger or even relief but a new sense of purpose, of adventure, even.

She was surprised at being able to dig up a smile.

'When will you go?' Bernard asked.

She finished her water, handed him back the glass. 'As fast as I can. I might have mentioned that I have a date in April to keep.'

'Oh, what a cunning girl you are. Bravo, Miss Nightingale, bravo. I hope you will write and tell me how it all turns out. I have a vested interest in this prayer book, after all.'

'I will. When were you last in Egypt?'

'As a young man. Too long ago. Would you like to see the house, Miss Nightingale?'

She nodded. 'I have a few minutes before I must leave for my train. But only if you'll call me Claire.'

'Then please call me Bernard,' he replied and for the first time since they'd met, his expression cleared. 'Oh, and by the way, can you enlighten me as to who those people are in the photo? They don't look a bit Turkish.'

'What photo?' she frowned.

'May I?' She handed him the prayer book and he opened the back flyleaf from where a tiny photograph fell out into his hand.

Claire gasped. 'I had no idea that was there!'

He stared at her quizzically. 'Surely you looked at the book when it was given to you?'

'Not really,' she admitted. 'We were on the ward in Cairo, Jamie was finally conscious and I didn't want to even think about the wretched book then. All I cared about was making the most of our hours together. I put it in my bag, haven't really thought about it properly again until two days ago when it suddenly became important again.' They'd both been staring at the tiny photo as she spoke and now her voice shook slightly. 'This is Jamie's family,' she said with certainty, regarding the tall, striking woman leaning against a verandah post. The house itself was lost as the camera had tried to capture the people in close up but the image was grainy nonetheless. The woman was laughing, dark head tilted, caught in a moment of delight. Claire touched the woman. 'His mother,' she whispered, in awe of seeing his family captured in the surrounds that she suspected Jamie loved as much as he loved her; not that she could see much but it was as though she could suddenly feel the dry heat of the desert winds and taste the eucalypt on the air. A boy sat cross-legged on the steps with a grin that was heartbreakingly reminiscent of Jamie. Features were smudged on the two other men, presumably his elder brothers, who leaned over the railing near their mother, and she sensed that their relaxed poses in white collarless shirts with their sleeves rolled up included big smiles.

But it was to the serious expression of the older man in the photograph that her attention was called. He was formally attired in a dark three-piece suit, a small terrier at one side and a black-and-white sheepdog by his feet, looking up at the man rather than the camera. The man stood straight-backed, arms crossed, a bushy moustache covering his mouth, looking solemnly at the lens. He was tall, angular but although features were lost again there was a mesmerising quality to his grave expression. She remembered how Jamie had spoken almost reverently about his father.

Bernard flipped the photo over and Claire felt her heart speed to see an inscription in spindly script of dark ink.

Son . . . we miss you, especially your beautiful mother. Be safe.

Claire began to cry silently. Now she knew exactly what her pathway was.

A hand squeezed her shoulder gently in comfort and she was touched by the show of affection from a person who minutes earlier had felt like an enemy. 'Do you know them?'

She shook her head. 'No, but I wrote recently to his parents care of a place called Farina in South Australia where Jamie comes from. The postmaster can hardly not know a family of Wrens, and even if they've never heard of me I don't care, we have Jamie in common.' She returned the photo to the back of the book, convinced that Jamie had to be alive and April couldn't come quickly enough.

17

'Yourself? All the way to *Constantinople*?' Eugenie exclaimed. Claire was back from Brighton and wheeling her friend around the pathways of her beloved garden. 'Is travel to Turkey possible yet?'

'It is possible. We call it Istanbul, by the way.'

'Oh, I prefer the romance of the name the Roman imperialists gave it. So tell me how you've made this happen.'

'The British hospital in the capital is seeking nursing staff. Not many people want to be on the move yet – most of the nurses are only now just getting demobbed. I was fortunate to get repatriated so quickly.'

'Yes, I meant to ask how that came about.'

She shrugged. 'I put my hand up to escort some soldiers home, all of them blind, several needing round-the-clock nursing. The bonus was that I got back to Britain sooner than most. Anyway, I suspect the hospital in Istanbul will be happy to take me on for a short period . . . a month, six weeks, perhaps.'

'That's quite an adventure you have planned there. And you think Jamie will approve? I mean, he won't mind you carrying out that task alone?'

Claire explained about Bernard's coercion. 'I wouldn't have Shahin's book if I didn't agree, so I don't have a choice. Jamie will have to understand that I was put on the spot and had to make a decision. I need to believe he'll be gladdened to know the prayer book is delivered and that the promise to his friend fulfilled.'

'Will you contact the Turk's family?'

'I'll write to them immediately. The young man died in May 1915 and, given how I feel about Jamie, I know they will likely want to learn every scrap of information about their boy.'

'Plus it's warmer than here,' Eugenie remarked with a grin. 'It is a gallant act, Claire. You honour Jamie and the Turkish family through it. Nobody loses, everyone gains, especially you.'

'Now I just have to make sure I have the means to —'

'Claire dear, I have all the means in the world but just not the strength or I'd come with you!' At Claire's instant shaking of her head, Eugenie's expression became dismissive. 'What else can an old woman like me do with her money? I have no family left and I could never have children. I'm already near enough blackmailing a grumbling family solicitor who clearly feels uncomfortable that I plan to bequeath much of my wealth to charitable pursuits. Might as well do some good for others,' she said, with a birdlike wave of a hand that had become so thin it was clawlike. 'I've led a selfishly indulgent life. And in death I plan to share it.'

'That's wonderful, Eugenie.'

'Staring at death sharpens one's grasp of reality and there are a lot of homeless, helpless people after the war. I have no use for it. I'm going to fund an orphanage and I hope to fund a new clinic too but it's a beginning. And I have lots of cottages that sprawl across the land and I'd like to make those available to women and children whose men haven't come home.'

Claire shook her head. 'You make me feel useless.'

'Good! Then agree to run the clinic for me.'

'What? No, I can't do that. Jamie and I are planning a life in Australia!'

Her friend hid it well but Claire saw the disappointment flash in Eugenie's eyes before she blinked it away. 'All right, but you can help get it set up, perhaps work out how to structure the clinic, think about how to staff it . . .' Claire stared at her with a slightly incredulous expression. 'I am serious, Claire. Now that you've walked back into my life, I shan't let you go without winning your word that you'll help continue something that's important. Radlett is an affluent area mainly owned by a handful of rich families but there are places just beyond here that are surely desperately crying out for medical and nursing assistance.' Again, she didn't wait for Claire's response. 'You need not answer yet because if you would, I'd be most grateful if you'd consider staying close long enough to see me through to the end.'

Claire baulked. 'Let me think on this,' she appealed.

Eugenie smiled. 'Of course. So, what about the travel into Constantinople?'

'I read only yesterday that there are warships gathering again in the waters as the Allies plan to occupy the city.'

'Well, we shall know soon enough with the Paris Peace Conference only days away. Anyway, you can take the train from Paris all the way through and with my money you can make plans immediately. Out of the war something good can come and enemies need not remain enemies if people like you make these gracious acts. Say yes. I can call my tour agent today and make arrangements, and as you agree, also say yes to the other business. Don't let them drag me off to die in a hospital, Claire. I promise to be swift and off your hands and conscience before midsummer – how's that? I want to die here, surrounded by Egypt and knowing Edward is waiting for me. Now, lose that expression and agree to give me a good send-off with affection and laughter.'

Claire took a deep breath, suddenly deeply aware of a sense of excitement and purpose. 'Yes to everything, including nursing you,' she replied. 'I cannot refuse.'

18

3 FEBRUARY 1919

Reveille sounded and the walking wounded, awaiting repatriation, began the amble to the mess hall.

'Can't wait for my first cuppa on Australian soil again, Matron,' a fellow on crutches remarked, arriving to deliver her a written message. 'My lieutenant asked me to bring this to you. I can't believe we've finally got orders.'

'Thank you. Well, I will certainly miss your cheerful smile, Frank.' The stout woman in crisp whites grinned at him from a dimpled face.

'You know we all love you, Matron. You're not at all like the other starchy heads of wards I've come across before. You've been very kind to all of us, so I don't want you to take it the wrong way when I ask if you have any idea of when we'll be on our way?'

She handed him a small jar of bright yellow flowers. 'The new date is second half of March. Not long now. Six weeks, maybe. Give those to Hugo Pickford, would you? I picked them for him this morning. I thought they might cheer him while he gets used to losing his eye. Tell him they're called Coltfoot.'

'You see, no one like you, Matron.' Frank winked but then grew more serious as his gaze slid to a man in a wheelchair near the window. 'What about blokes like him?' he said, nodding towards the staring patient, his gaze unfocused, features slackened.

'We're still hoping for news of who he is. He seemed to get separated from his unit. I'm glad to say I've got my way to repatriate him through England because he needs surgery.'

'No, send the lad home for it. Every bloke wants to get back.'

'We could, of course. But I happen to know the long journey back to Australia might add unnecessary risk. That arm is severely damaged, one leg badly crushed. Horse and camel, as I understood it, fell on him as he was trying to pull a fellow soldier to safety. The information is sketchy at best. And he has no identification tags. We know he belongs to the 3rd Regiment so we're making all enquiries but everything is very slow at present. I think he'll be gone from here in the next day or two, though, before word gets through.'

'Has he spoken?'

She shook her head. 'Not yet. A close explosion can do that, though. We call it neurasthenia, or shellshock – although around here that seems to apply to everything from being stunned by an explosion and losing hearing and so on to malingering. The impact can put men into a stupor for weeks until their minds clear the fog. They can't hear properly and the disorientation lingers. He'll get there with the right care and understanding. Anyway, thanks for delivering this, Frank.'

'How's your leg, Matron? I forget you got injured too.'

'Oh, I'm fine. It gets a bit stiff but nothing that a good rubdown with liniment can't improve.' His expression told her he suspected she was fibbing. 'You go off and get yourself fed.'

'Righto, Matron,' he said, whistling as he turned.

She spared a few moments to limp over to the injured fellow. 'Afternoon, Trooper.'

He registered her arrival with nothing more than a blink.

'I know it's all confusing in your mind right now but it will clear. You'll be going to Dartford Hospital in England the day after tomorrow. They'll provide the post-op care you're going to need on

that arm. But I'd love it if you could smile for me before you go.'
Matron beamed him a smile, searching his green-eyed stare that
was hunting memories elsewhere, she suspected, as she uncurled his
fingers to reveal a shiny piece of metal. 'Still holding that, eh? That's
good. It connects you to where you belong, I'm sure. Keep holding
it, Trooper, and come back to us soon.'

She sighed, squeezed his uninjured shoulder and hoped with
all her heart that someone was looking for this handsome young
Australian . . . or at least waiting for him.

———

It was mid-February before Claire left London bound for the Taksim Hospital in Istanbul, which the British had taken over. It was
clearly difficult for the former German hospital to find nursing staff
willing to be on the move again so soon after the horrors of the war,
so her offer to work for a month was quickly taken up. Nevertheless, she was determined to travel independently of the military and
once her train ticket was booked it suddenly felt right to be on this
journey and she felt glad to be focused on nursing again.

She had visited Eugenie once more before leaving so that she
could thank her again for this opportunity and promised to telegram
as soon as she had arrived. They'd agreed she would offer the cottage that her aunt bequeathed her for rental soon after her return
and Claire would move into Eugenie's house at Radlett. 'For as long
as required,' Eugenie had said, with a knowing twinkle in her eye.

And now here Claire sat on the newly reinstated Orient Express
train bound for the exotic city of Constantinople, stopping in
Vienna, Budapest and Bucharest. She smiled at the older man seated
opposite, whom she was sharing a table with for dining. They'd sat
in a companionable silence over breakfast while he read the paper
and she again scanned the letter she had received back from Turkey
a week ago. In it, Rifki Shahin had expressed his surprise at hearing

from her and especially regarding her visit to Istanbul, as he called it. Without referring to his son's death, or much else from her letter, he agreed to meet with her in the French military occupied zone: *You might find it easier than I to move freely between the occupied zones*. He had added that the university where he taught was in the old city known as Sultanahmet, where the palace and playground of the famed Ottoman royals had been.

It was polite but terse with no indication of his grief or any glimpse into his life. Eugenie had been right: this felt like an adventure and for all the right reasons. Preparing for this brief posting meant she had barely dwelt on Jamie Wren and her preoccupation suddenly prompted a strange pang of guilt.

She blinked. 'Pardon me?' Had her dining companion spoken? Beyond good manners of a cursory salutation, their gazes had barely met. In fact they'd both read their respective books over the first night's dinner and avoided any threat of conversation.

His perfectly trimmed white moustache twitched. 'I said that I recognised that stationery.' He nodded at the letter in her hand. 'Forgive me, I'm not prying,' he coughed. 'Are you visiting the university too?'

She smiled. 'Er, no, actually I'm on a brief posting to the British hospital. I'm a nurse. But someone I am hoping to meet is a tutor there.'

'Oh? I'm travelling there to give a lecture in physics.'

She shrugged. 'He doesn't tell me which campus he works from.'

'I'm guessing you've not been to Constantinople before.'

'You guess right, Mr . . .?'

'Professor Leavers.'

'Claire Nightingale,' she said, holding out a hand in proper greeting.

'Rather lovely name you have. Most appropriate for a nurse,

although I'm sure that's not the first time you've heard that jest?'

She grinned and shook her head. 'Should I be calling it Istanbul or Constantinople? It's all rather confusing.'

'Not nearly as confusing as it will be once we get there and encounter a city being supervised by three nations. Can't wait for everyone to leave it and let life return to normal. The Turkish prefer Istanbul – many just call it the old way of Stamboul, but I think we British, never ones to let go of tradition, keep to the old city of Constantine. Is your friend a modernist?'

'I have no idea, Professor Leavers.' At his quizzical expression she gave him an abridged version of her mission.

'Well, I admire your pluck. I lost a son in the Dardanelles campaign but I bear the Turkish no malice. They lost twice as many of their young braves. It was a hopeless, ill-conceived plan and the more people like you and me try and mend broken threads, the faster everyone's lives can resume.'

The food arrived. Even on rations the dining carriage was managing to serve up exemplary dishes.

'Dover sole in lemon butter: I dare admit this looks better than back home in my memories.' He chuckled. '*Bon appetit*.'

'*Merci*,' she said, smiling.

'Are you not sharing your compartment with someone?'

'I was expecting to, but whoever had booked hasn't turned up.'

'Good grief, the whole sleeper to yourself, eh? That's a stroke of luck. I'm sharing with a dreadful snorer and someone who likes to talk a great deal. Forgive me, I pretended I knew you and used you as an excuse to sit here.'

She laughed. 'You're forgiven. How did you know I would not become a terrible burden of small talk for you?'

'It crossed my mind, but you carried a book and I had to trust that you were more interested in reading than chatting up an old codger.'

'I've barely read a word of my book, to tell the truth.'

He told her about the various stops they'd make and how long they'd linger at each, apologising for potentially boring her, which she denied vehemently.

'Are you staying long in Constantinople?' she enquired. 'Actually, I think I'm going to stick with Istanbul and be modern.' She grinned.

He shook his head as he ate. 'A few days. The university provides lodgings. Does the hospital look after you?'

She nodded. 'I've no idea but after the Western Front, nothing much intimidates me.'

'My word, you're a brave one.'

She shrugged.

'Well, do explore the old city if you're permitted. The Byzantine architecture is breathtaking. Stay veiled, though your uniform should take care of that.' He pointed to his head. 'It's all about the hair and shoulders.'

She nodded, understanding.

'Turkey may be relatively liberal but Western women are rarely seen out and about without close escort. I have no doubt you'll be able to move freely around the various Allied supervised zones, and from what I hear life in the old city hasn't changed much. If you need any help, you can contact me at the university.'

'That's extremely kind of you, Professor.'

'What's your tutor's name, by the way?'

She glanced at the letter, making sure she got the pronunciation correct. 'Shahin.'

He gave a small shake of his head. 'Rings no bells but perhaps our paths might cross. Well,' he said, dabbing his mouth with great care to clean his moustache. 'Forgive me for deserting you, but I'm preparing for my lectures and I must steal my quiet time while I can.'

'Of course,' she nodded, as she put her silver cutlery together on the plate. 'Your company has been delightful, thank you.'

'My son wouldn't have been a whole lot older than you when he joined up. He wasn't married either,' he said, glancing at her left hand. 'If he had been, I'd like to think it would have been to a young woman as wholly independent yet as feminine and lovely as yourself.'

Claire felt sure she blushed brightly.

'You'll enjoy the romantic alpine scenery, particularly through the forests and Carpathian mountains after passing through Transylvania. And if that doesn't capture your imagination, then I suspect crossing the mighty Danube and moving through the lush valleys of Bulgaria surely will. Certainly better than if you were sailing back to Turkey, I'm sure.'

She nodded, not really wanting to remember all those crossings between Greece, Egypt and Anzac Cove, but knowing her heart was never going to let her forget them because somewhere in that triangle was Jamie Wren.

The matron welcomed her warmly onto the ward that was full of light from the tall, wide chamber and abundance of windows. Despite the exotic plants she could see beyond the glass and the welcome, soft breeze. Like every other hospital she'd ever worked in the smell of antiseptic was overwhelming – even reassuring – but more comforting was the discovery that her patients were not hovering between life and death. There were no screams of pain, or tears of misery.

'No shrapnel to dig out, no bullet wounds to suture, no limbs to amputate, but there is Spanish flu here,' Matron added, her smile faltering. 'All the usual precautions are necessary. Beyond that it's the common or garden array of ailments, from sore throats and fevers to gonorrhea.'

Claire lifted an eyebrow and grinned, certain she already liked this towering, bespectacled matron with a no-nonsense, direct way about her. 'Thank you for my room. It's lovely and airy.'

'Good. I appreciate any nurse prepared to leave home again so soon. You're happy doing the morning shift?'

'Whatever suits the team, Matron.'

'Excellent. Well, you're on at six and from one you're free. You understand how the city is being policed by Britain, France and Italy?'

Claire nodded.

'Just carry your ID papers and you're free to move around the three zones.'

'Thank you. I am hoping to meet one of the professors at the university.'

'Oh? That's fast work,' she remarked.

'I met him on the train coming over. Promised we'd take tea together.'

Matron regarded her with interest.

'He's old enough to be my grandfather!'

'Good for you. Well, the university is in the Fatih area, near the very grand and beautiful Blue Mosque in Sultanahmet – you can't miss it and it's an easy walk, especially at this time of the year. You can take the ferry across from Taksim and walk up from the harbour. You'll enjoy it but while our women enjoy certain freedoms, Claire, just bear in mind that Turkish women do not. I have given all my girls the same talk – please respect the Turkish ways.'

'I understand. I've no intention of being abroad alone very often, Matron.'

'Good. And if you are alone, I want you in uniform and veiled at all times. I also suggest you carry your cape that covers your arms, and keep your hands crossed within as best you can.'

Claire knew the drill from her war days but accepted the advice with a gracious smile.

———————

It took six days of her routine before Claire was able to place a call to the university and another four days before she received a call back; one of the other nurses found her in her room to say there was a gentleman asking for her on the communal phone. She wondered if it was Professor Leavers but hoped it was Açar's father as she hurried down the two flights of narrow stairs in the stone building at the back of the hospital where her lodgings were. They were sparse and functional but she was grateful for running water and a relatively reliable electricity supply. After the deprivations of war, every normality from soap to sugar felt like a luxury to be grateful for.

'Hello, this is Claire Nightingale,' she answered.

There was a tense pause and she imagined how confronting it must feel to have a stranger wanting to discuss your dead child.

She heard him clear his throat gently. 'I am Rifki Shahin,' he finally said and his mellow voice brought her an unexpected sense of relief. She hadn't realised how much this call meant to her.

'Oh, Mr Shahin, thank you for returning my letter and message.'

'You said you have something for me that belonged to my son.'

She was surprised at his directness. 'I do, sir.'

'Perhaps you could leave it for me to collect from the hospital?'

'Oh,' she said, regret taking her unawares. 'I rather thought we might meet.'

Again came the pause. 'I do not wish to be rude, Miss Nightingale, but I wonder what it is that we might have in common.'

She took a slow breath to cover flashes of disappointment pricking through her like a thousand needles. 'Well, we do have your son in common.'

'You knew my son?'

'No.' She sighed. 'Forgive me. I don't mean to sound presumptuous but I've travelled a long way to return your son's prayer book, Mr Shahin, and in doing so hope to fulfill a promise I made to someone I care about very much. And he did know your son.'

'I see. A promise once spoken should never be broken.' She gave a smile at his poetic words that resonated, seemed to sum up her present life that was connected through promises . . . to Açar Shahin, to Jamie, to Eugenie, even to Bernard Jenkins. But she waited, would not press any further. 'In that case, Miss Nightingale, let us meet in the gardens of Gülhane Park. Do you know the old city?'

'No, but I desperately want to see it so you are giving me a wonderful excuse to explore. I am holding my breath in anticipation of seeing one of the wonders of the world, your Blue Mosque.'

'We call it Sultan Ahmet. The area surrounding it is rather calming and it is also an appropriate place for strangers such as us to meet. Are you free tomorrow at all?'

'In the afternoon I am.'

'Shall we say three o'clock?'

'Perfect. Er, how shall I know you?'

'I shall likely know you, Miss Nightingale, in your nursing uniform and carrying an Arabic prayer book. However, I shall meet you by the Column of the Goths. Would that be suitable? It is quiet and scenic. You will enjoy its aspect and view across the Bosphorus.'

'That sounds delightful. Thank you. Until tomorrow, then, Mr Shahin.' He said no more and she put the receiver back on the hook, realising she was trembling slightly. She laughed at herself for how uncertain he had made her feel. She was not prone to a show of nerves and put it down to not wanting to be late for her shift. They persisted, though, throughout her shift and on into a restless night and a new day that couldn't come quickly enough.

19

Claire was woken by the first wail of the muezzin calling his faithful flock to their morning prayers. Hauntingly alien, the sound rode the clear, chilled twilight air from the top of a mosque's minaret into the winter darkness of morning's earliest moments and urged her to rise. While most of her colleagues, especially those not on the early shift, were irritated by morning prayers, breaking into their sleep with a mesmeric howl in a language they didn't understand, Claire found the recitations comforting and a perfectly reliable wake-up alarm. For someone who was used to the Muslim culture from her time in Egypt, she found it an easier adjustment than a couple of her colleagues had, when some of the locals who helped out or provided services to the hospital would disappear frequently for prayers.

She enjoyed waking to the scent of bread baking, which wafted up from the streets reaching high into her room, through the shutters, and the accompanying unfamiliar spicy fragrances that drifted in from the hawkers and eateries nearby.

She pulled back the sheet and dropped her legs to the cool floor, always a slight shock as her mind anticipated carpet. Claire remained seated as she yawned and arched her back to stretch out her spine. She shared this room with another nurse but as they were on opposing shifts they rarely saw one another and hardly knew each other except through their belongings. Claire was aware, for instance, that her roommate had big feet and that she was most likely vain – if the variety of lipsticks and two small mirrors, pots of creams and rouge were any indication. She didn't dare wonder what Nanette Baines made of her.

Claire had quickly got used to the odd way of bathing with a pail and tin mug. She'd found soap in the local souk that was perfumed with attar of roses, yet was nothing like the overpowering 'old lady' rose fragrance of the soap at home. This thick, hard, low-foaming soap smelled to her of memory. It was heady blooms gently scenting a summer's evening in Cairo or a sherbet in Alexandria; it was the drift of perfume as one walked past a hedge of rose bushes in Wahroonga on Sydney's North Shore; and how she imagined it would be stirring the fragranced air beneath the arbour of blushing tea roses in Radlett.

She'd been careful not to wet her hair, having washed it yesterday. Indulging in some of her roommate's vanity, she stared at her reflection in her colleague's mirror and was pleased to see that her hair had lost its freshly washed frizz and had settled into its shape. Claire had taken Eugenie's advice and finally cut her hair. Now it hung in a neat waved bob-cut, just long enough for her to pin back for her duties but for the first time in her life she could wear her hair without any ties or stays on her time off. She pinched some colour into her cheeks but noted her complexion possessed a glow that had been lacking in London. Eugenie would be pleased, she thought. She should write again and made a promise to do so this afternoon after her meeting with Mr Shahin.

The work hours passed so quickly she had to check her watch twice when the relieving team of nurses came for changeover. It hadn't been particularly busy; the usual raft of odd accidents and stomach upsets. There had been one fellow who'd ended up below an upturned cart that had been carrying heavy goods, so bones had needed to be reset but that was about as dramatic as the day had got. And yet it had ticked by her with the speed of the war-time when days and nights blurred and no one kept track of shifts, and there were always dozens of emergencies presenting at once.

'Got something planned for today?' Matron asked.

'I thought I'd stroll through the gardens in the old city,' she replied, deliberately vague.

'Ah, perfect day for it. Are you going alone?' she frowned.

Claire shook her head. 'I'm meeting that friend working at the university.' She knew it was fine to leave it at that and yet she added a fabrication. 'You remember the old gentleman I told you about . . . the lecturer?' *Why the lie?* She didn't know. But Claire had promised herself she would move on instinct between now and April first. She would not analyse her motives, consider her position, second-guess any situation. She was falling free of encumbrances both physical and mental, likening it to how it might feel to jump from a plane into the clouds. This adventure of hers to return the prayer book was like the parachute Leonardo da Vinci and various other dreamers of flight had been developing for centuries. Now it seemed from a recent radio report that the safe jump and landing with a parachute was believed ready for trial later this year. It was exciting and she could only imagine what trusting one's life to some-thing as ethereal as silk must feel like. A lot like trusting one's heart and its lovesick state. Istanbul and the prayer book were her para-chute; it would keep her safe through the flight of the next six weeks of not knowing whether Jamie would turn up at the Langham.

'Have a lovely afternoon,' Matron said.

Claire swallowed her shame. 'I will, thank you.'

By a quarter past two she was walking beneath the thick Roman portico that allowed access into the royal gardens of the old walled city. She imagined how in its heyday of Constantine, chariot races had screamed around the cobbled hippodrome but now it was a far quieter place, mostly for reflection. A toffee seller expertly twisted melted butter and sugar around sticks from his confectioner trolley, while a man with a large tray on his head, balancing pyramids of his wares, called out his freshly made simit, the delicious chewy, circular bread that she knew was dipped in molasses and covered with toasted sesame seeds, similar to the bread called koulouri that they'd eaten during the early days of the war on Mudros Island.

She wandered on into what looked to be a main avenue for strollers that led her beneath a canopy of tall trees, passing exotic and beautiful multi-faced marble fountains with a bowl and spout on each side, where the dutiful could quickly attend to their ablutions before prayers.

She continued walking steadily before she spotted the Roman victory column on its incline, standing cracked and weather-beaten but still proud after centuries since its erection in front of the walls of the Topkapi Palace. Now it was kept company by a family of crows who eyed her with suspicion but gave no other outward sign that her presence disturbed them. One watched her from on high at the top of the Corinthian capitol that crowned the soaring victory pillar of marble.

She sat down on a wooden bench nearby. Claire checked her watch, thinking she was likely half an hour early for her appointment but she'd obviously taken a slower stroll than she'd imagined. Only ten minutes early. Shahin was right; it was a quiet, exquisitely pretty spot where the breeze of the Bosphorus whispered against her face and she could see its sparkling waters from her position. Shahin had also been right about finding her; she could see now that he would easily pick her out. She was highly conspicuous but it wasn't so much her narrow, barrel-skirted cream and grey outfit as the fact she was a woman. The two local women she had encountered on the way to this place had been garbed head to toe in their dark robes, walking a pace or two behind their men, one leading two dark-eyed children. She regretted not taking Matron's advice to stay in uniform but she'd wanted to appear less intimidating than her uniform allowed. However, Claire was very glad for the silk shawl she'd thought to bring and self-consciously had used it to cover her golden hair since leaving the hospital grounds.

She looked into her lap where her gloved hands rested; it was easier that way to avoid the glances of other people strolling the gardens and she instead focused on the small book she'd brought. She ran a finger over the Arabic script and touched the fragile gold leafing bordering each page that looked like a cartouche. The delicately painted headpieces on the tissue-like leaves depicted flowers. She knew each of its few pages well and yet she never failed to appreciate the beauty, despite the blot in its centre. The minutes passed quickly, it seemed; then a man with a long, fluid stride approached her.

'Miss Nightingale?'

She recognised the voice and shielded her eyes from the winter sun as she looked up.

'Yes,' she stood as if scalded and she had to keep looking up for he was tall. 'Hello.' She held out a gloved hand and realised instantly she should have known better.

He regarded it for a heartbeat before taking it and she felt only the barest pressure as she stared into greyish eyes, filled with curiosity, that appeared to reflect the silvering in his close beard. There was none yet in his hair, which he wore short. She hadn't known what to expect – an old man in robes and a fez, probably. Yet here stood a disarmingly attractive, forty-something, olive-skinned gentleman in a tailored suit and tie with a neatly clipped beard and a question in his pale stare. He cleared his throat to snap her out of the silence surrounding them that was mercifully pierced when Professor Leavers suddenly arrived, hurrying up to them, huffing and puffing. 'Oh, I'm so sorry, I was stopped by two of my students.'

'Professor Leavers!' she said and it sounded like an accusation. 'I thought you were only here for a few days.'

'I was, my dear, but an opportunity arose to stay on, and . . . oh, suffice to say I'm here for another week or so and damned pleased about it too. So you've met?'

Claire returned her attention to Shahin, who had not, she realised, switched his attention from her and it felt as though that grey stare could see beneath her dove-coloured linen jacket and long-sleeved cream silk shirt right to the place where she harboured her innermost feelings. 'Forgive me,' she began before he could speak. 'Have I put you in a difficult position?'

In his eyes she saw amusement register but he didn't let it touch his mouth. 'I have, as you say, broad shoulders but Professor Leavers was kind enough to accompany me to prevent any awkwardness.'

She smiled polite gratitude at Leavers before she said to Shahin, 'That's why you preferred to pick up Açar's book.' She felt instantly stupid for being so slow at appreciating the customs of this region. 'I forgot myself. Is it just easier if I hand you this and walk away?'

Now the amusement did reach his mouth, which curved slow and slight just for a second.

'Nonsense!' Leavers said. 'I am your chaperone, Miss Nightingale, and most pleased to take the air with you both.'

Shahin's eyelids shrouded his gaze momentarily before he turned, gesturing carefully ahead. 'Shall we?'

'Yes, thank you,' she replied with a self-conscious sigh of relief and fell in step but deliberately left a careful distance between her and her Turkish companion.

'I don't know if you've already visited but I thought you may enjoy a brief stroll around our famous mosque, Miss Nightingale.'

'That would be delightful, thank you.'

They made small talk as they strolled until they reached the vast and magnificent forecourt paved with a striped grey marble that matched Rifki Shahin's colouring. She looked up, helplessly awed by the vaulted ceilings of perfect lines of the arcade that encircled the courtyard, decorated with the deep henna-red stones. Everything about this exterior was about size and the visitor achieving an impression of majesty. She must have said this aloud for Shahin answered, his tone eager.

'Indeed, that was the whole point. You see that chain hanging there?'

She nodded.

'Only the Sultan could enter through that doorway on the western side and the hanging chain forced him to bow his head to pass beneath.'

'So that even the Sultan was humble?'

He smiled. 'Yes, so that he knew he was in the presence of the Divine.'

'And the fountains are exquisite,' she continued, delighted by such practical use of the beautiful marble.

'Muslims must come to their prayers clean of body and mind,' he said softly and she cast him a glance but said nothing. He looked away.

'Why is it called the Blue Mosque?' she asked him.

Leavers nodded. 'I've always wondered that too. Nothing terribly blue about all this,' he said, waving a hand. 'Is it to do with the reflection of the sea against its pale walls?'

Claire watched Shahin nod, impressed.

'On a summery moonlit night it does look very pale, but I suspect it has earned that name because of the many thousands of blue iznik tiles that line its walls.'

'Iznik?' she repeated.

'Nicea. South of here. It was famous for its distinctive porcelain favoured by the sultans.'

'Ah, thank you. The mosque is so very beautiful. I was up on the hospital roof marvelling at the six minarets.'

'And nine domes,' he continued. 'It's not dissimilar to the Hagia Sophia,' he said, pointing towards the great Roman Catholic church in the distance, 'in terms of the Byzantine elements, but it does show off its classical Ottoman influences. Are you interested in history, Miss Nightingale?'

'Yes, as a matter of fact, classical history of this whole region has intrigued me since school days. It's all so very . . .' He looked back at her quizzically as she searched for the right word and she liked the eagerness in that expression. It struck her that Shahin was genuinely interested in her responses. She wanted to say 'biblical', but instantly thought perhaps that might offend and finally the right word erupted. 'Epic,' Claire finished, and this drew a brief gust of laughter from him that she sensed was a rare show of his thoughts.

'Have you been inside, Miss Nightingale?' Leavers enquired.

'Not yet.'

'Another time, perhaps,' Shahin said, glancing at his watch. 'Forgive me, but I have a lecture at four. You would need to sit in the women's gallery, of course.'

'Of course,' she said, surprised to feel indignant at the mention of segregation. It was another culture, another custom, but still she felt vaguely affronted.

'I thought we might take some tea. Would that be agreeable?' he asked. 'There's time.'

'Absolutely, old chap,' Leavers answered for them both. 'At nearing three-fifteen, every Englishman and woman is thinking tea, what?'

Claire smiled faintly at Shahin and nodded. She followed the men, happy to hang back slightly as they strolled, retracing their footsteps to the victory column and on to the portico that would lead down to the harbour. Here, a row of small, stepped canopied areas served as tiny tea gardens and she was relieved to see several European women were also taking their afternoon beverage.

Shahin gestured towards a table beneath the tall trees. Claire seated herself, making soft kissing sounds to the mother cat and two kittens curled up in a tiny hollow near their table. The tabby cat meowed at her and yawned; her babies stretched and resettled themselves, too warm and comfy to even open their eyes.

'Hello, lady,' the man in charge rushed up to say to Claire in his pale suit and fez. She smiled back, stroked the cat once and sat down in the chair that Shahin offered.

Meanwhile Leavers raised a hand and began laughing as he spotted someone in a small crowd of people. 'Good heavens! It's Lacey. Haven't seen him in donkeys. Will you excuse me briefly? Er, don't wait. Do order.'

They watched him approach another grinning man of about the same age and pump his hand before finally Claire and Shahin felt obliged to return their attention to each other.

———

Rifki Shahin had not looked forward to this meeting. Good manners prevented him from avoiding it. What's more, he was busy. He would have been late if it hadn't been for his new acquaintance, Professor Leavers, who said it would be extremely 'poor form' to keep the young woman waiting. He'd muttered in soft despair that in Istanbul everyone ran late for everything and no one made a fuss. As it was, he'd had to ask Leavers to accompany him.

Even so, he was not ready for the person who awaited him. For no obvious reason, he had anticipated a stout, dour-looking woman in thick stockings and a starched white uniform with hair piled behind her head. Instead here was a nymph-like creature, with skin the colour of blushing almond blossom, and he was sure beneath that shawl was defiantly short hair bouncing near the sweet line of her jaw that shone like rose gold beneath the winter sun. And her smile! The horrifying result was that this slim, angular English nurse was making him feel like a moonstruck youth. He was nervous. And he abhorred it!

'What would you care for?' Shahin asked, clearing his throat.

'Um . . . what would you recommend?'

'Well, normally coffee,' he said in a slightly arched tone that made her chuckle and he wanted to hear that sound again. He hadn't even tried to be amusing. 'But that has been impossibly expensive during and since the war. So I would suggest çay.'

'Chai?' she repeated.

He smiled helplessly at her gentle manner. 'Yes, it's a simple black tea that we grow on the eastern coast of the Black Sea. Of course there is any number of floral or herbal teas that Turkey is known for.'

'Like apple?'

'I sometimes think that's all we Turks will ever be known for. Yes, apple of course, or pomegranate, sage, linden, lime, rose hip . . . our teas are endlessly varied.'

She grinned. 'Sage sounds lovely.'

'It is, although strictly speaking it is more of a . . . how you say, tisane? A herbal infusion.'

Claire nodded, understanding. 'Why would a Turk drink it?'

'Calming. Cleansing. I doubt you need help in either area, Miss Nightingale. You look entirely calm and may I say extremely clean.' He wanted to say 'beautiful' but bit back on that last one, which would have been an error to mention, even though to him it was simply the truth. She giggled again.

'Oh, have I trespassed?'

She shook her head and her eyes sparkled at him with delight. 'Well, a bit of calming, cleansing infusion couldn't hurt. Besides, clean is every nurse's mantra. So no, Mr Shahin, you have not offended but instead given me a fine compliment.'

'You should try the wild sage, then.' He signalled a waiter and ordered briskly in his own language. 'Would you like simit, or gözleme?'

'I don't think I need any more delicious bread or pastry today, thank you. Tea is perfect.'

He nodded at the waiter and muttered a few more words before turning back to her.

'Your English is excellent,' she remarked.

He shrugged. 'It is the language of the world.'

'Thank you for coming today.'

He looked into the pale, rain-puddle blue of her eyes and for a moment was completely mesmerised. The pause made her uneasy; he saw her hesitation.

'Is something wrong?' she asked.

Rifki shook his head slowly. 'No, I was just thinking that the porcelain painters of Nicea would like the colour of your eyes.'

She blushed. And he felt more helplessly charmed by that furious, instant show of her self-consciousness than any of the dozen or more women who had tried to lure him into their lives since the death of his wife, save the one woman who had not.

He banished her name from his mind. 'I suspect it is my turn to seek an apology. I did not mean to make you feel uncomfortable.'

She shook her head, and he could see her relief when the tray of tulip-shaped glasses arrived and were set down together with the double pot of sage tea and the other plain tea. A small coloured square of cloth was expertly tied around the metal of the handle to prevent a burn.

'*Te ekkür ederim,*' she murmured and Rifki nodded, impressed.

'Very good, Miss Nightingale. Perfect pronunciation too.'

'The hospital orderlies are teaching me,' she admitted, smiling at his praise. 'So how does this contraption work?' she wondered, regarding the double pot.

'One has the steeping tea, the other is extra water. I like mine strong.'

Claire poured her and Leavers' glasses and gestured at the lumps of brown beet sugar. 'Do I?'

'Yes, if you wish. It's nice with the sage.'

Leavers' tulip of dark tea steamed untouched and Rifki was suddenly glad that the nurse's chaperone was distracted and his chatter was not peppering their tense silence, which seemed to thrum with an excitement that was novel for him. He poured his own glass and pretended to search for the smallest lump of sugar, all the while watching the neat fingers of his companion hold the spoon delicately and stir her tea. He watched the sugar in her glass disintegrate and cloud the brew momentarily before dissipating into its invisible sweetness.

'Can you hear that, Miss Nightingale?'

She frowned at him.

'This sound of metal against glass is like a symphony through Istanbul – everyone stirring their tea. It's how to find a nearby tea garden, even in unfamiliar surrounds.'

She smiled, looking pleased with the notion.

'Except you. You stir silently; so carefully, I note, that your spoon does not touch the glass.'

'Ah, now, there's a reason for that.'

He listened to her tale of taking an afternoon tea in an English upper-class establishment with all of its pomp and finery. He smiled as she spoke and he sipped, allowing the pleasant bitterness to warm his tongue, waiting for her to sample her tisane. Rifki watched her lips finally close gently around the glass, blowing first, then tasting her wild sage tea. He blinked, as deeply embarrassed as he was aware of how sensual her mouth had looked to him. Suddenly it felt as though he was sipping from a forbidden cup in that heartbeat. It must stop.

He put his glass down and feigned the polite smile. 'You have something for me?'

He saw her nod, replace her glass in its saucer and reach into a small cloth bag.

'I know I've already said so in my letter but again, Mr Shahin, I am so terribly sorry for your loss.' With her gaze dipped, he took in the soft fall of the silken blouse against her breasts, desperately wanting to look away but his treacherous eyes refused.

She drew the familiar book from her bag. Since her letter had arrived he hadn't so much as considered that the sight of Açar's prayer book would make him feel like someone had just punched as hard as they could into his exposed belly.

He stared at it, unable to breathe.

————————

Claire was glad to get onto the business at hand as she was finding her tea companion helplessly disarming. While Shahin deliberately kept a physical distance, that unnerving glance of his had an intimate quality she felt neither equipped nor prepared for. He was hardly a chatterbox, clearly a person who chose his words with care, but even so she was taken aback by his sudden stillness and silence at the sight of the book.

'Mr Shahin?' she finally said after an uncomfortable half a minute or so. Claire glanced over to Leavers, who was still in the thick of exchanging news and memories with his friend. He wasn't even looking her way. She swallowed. 'They say that tea is very good for shock. As a nurse, I can attest to that.'

He lifted his eyes to her and she saw in that moment of pain that all of this man's defences were lowered and she glimpsed deep anguish. He reached for the book but appeared suddenly frightened to touch it.

'Tell me about your friend,' he finally murmured. 'The one who knew my son.'

Claire put the book down between them, letting go of her penultimate connection to Jamie, deliberately withdrawing her hands in a motion that to her felt like her job was done. She had kept Jamie's promise to Açar Shahin at risk of losing one of the final fragile threads that bonded her to the man she loved. It was triumphant but at the same time the parachute had just slipped off her. She was now falling alone, no umbrella of silk to slow her descent, just a rushing sense of fear.

'Please, Mr Shahin, drink your tea while I talk.'

He sipped obediently, silently, showing nothing in his expression. She noticed that he did not watch her eyes but her mouth, as if he preferred to read her lips rather than hear. Was it less painful that way, she wondered? Shahin, she decided, appeared determined to fix every nuance of the words she was choosing as carefully as she could to explain what she understood about the death of his son. She gave him the details concisely, taking care not to embellish, and yet she felt each word was like a fresh blow, striking at an old wound.

―――――――

He had received the news four years ago of his son's death together with Açar's musical pipe and few belongings; he'd noticed then that his son's prized Sufi prayer book was not in the small parcel. His intense grief had buried the thought until the letter from Claire Nightingale had explained the mystery.

Death had brought profound pain and he wished he could travel back in time and say much more to his son that he had unwisely left unsaid. He thought time had created sufficient distance between him and his loss but he realised now as this stranger spoke in her tone like a cooling flannel to a fever that he had inflated a fragile vacuum around himself. With each word she punctured that vacuum, deflating it, until Açar was alive again in his mind but bleeding on the soil of the south and he was helpless to save him.

'. . . strong sense of kinship between them,' she said. 'And so this journey felt important to honour your son's wishes.'

He watched her lips stop and wished they would go on moving for eternity. As long as she kept talking he could keep the pain at bay but now all he had to stare at was the bow of her lips that he had already spent far too much time contemplating. It occurred to him that finally he understood; at last here was the incarnation of what poets referred to as Cupid's Bow. It was true that the double curve of her upper lip resembled the exaggerated shape of the bow supposedly used by the Roman god of erotic love. He liked the way her lips, even in repose, turned up ever so slightly at their edge. It spoke of invitation.

'Are you feeling unwell, Mr Shahin? How can I help?'

He shook his head and they both seemed to reach for the book in the same second. She got there first and so his hand covered hers for the barest moment and it felt to him as though he'd received a jolt, like the time he'd participated in an electricity demonstration at the university. On that occasion the static shock had disconcertingly warbled through him for an hour or more and every muscle of his body had felt on fast twitch, as though his entire nervous system was sparking while fighting to calm itself.

It was wrong on every level for him to have touched her bare skin – culturally, socially, spiritually . . . As he sharply lifted his hand to disconnect he looked around to make sure no one had spied the indiscretion. He heard her apology, was sure he shook his head as though it was nothing to be sorry for, but he laid his right hand in his lap and curled his fingers into his palm. He tried to pretend it was a way of ridding himself of the slip in protocol but he instinctively followed his true desire, which was to close his fist around that feel of Claire Nightingale and imprison it as something precious that belonged only to him.

———

Claire didn't know whether to be horrified or to make light of the way their hands had met and then how they'd both overreacted. In England or Australia it would have been set aside through a simple burst of laughter and apology but here in Turkey she realised it was a serious indiscretion, potentially a sin. She quickly tried to defuse it.

'I was going to explain to you what that hole in the book is.' She carefully pushed the book towards him and withdrew her hand to her lap. She watched his long fingers, with their neatly trimmed nails, emerge from beneath the table to touch his son's prayer book tentatively.

He cleared his throat lightly. 'This is a Sufi prayer book. Do you know what Sufism is?'

She shook her head and watched him search for the right explanation. 'It is a dimension of the Islamic belief . . . a mysticism. This comes from Persia; to say it is old is to understate it. Sufism promotes total dedication and a complete disregard for possessions, or the pursuit of pleasure and wealth. I believe my son wanted to follow the path of an ascetic but was torn by his youthful needs, his desire to keep our family name strong. He viewed life differently to most and searched for enlightenment through his prayers, as though ever reaching for the perfect truth, the perfect understanding of his own spiritualism. Does that make any sense to you?'

'The way that Jamie described your son's behaviour that day attests to those beliefs. He made the ultimate sacrifice so that he wouldn't have to kill anyone, but also so that he was no longer answerable to a world at war.' She swallowed. 'I admire him.'

His bruised glance held her. 'I encouraged him to go . . . I ignored his leanings and —'

'Here I am. Oh, do forgive me,' gushed Leavers, arriving to explode the tender and intimate atmosphere. Claire looked at Shahin and felt their exchange of a private, silent apology and within it she sensed a longing from him, as Leavers explained how he and his friend had known each other from schooldays.

Shahin took his chance while their white-haired companion sipped his tea. 'Miss Nightingale was explaining the significance of this damage to my dead son's prayer book.'

That silenced Leavers. 'Oh, I say, how intriguing.'

'I've said enough,' Claire murmured with a polite smile. She, Jamie, Rifki and Açar were inextricably linked through that book and its bullet hole. It was not necessary for Leavers to learn of it, and she had no desire to hear his take on it. She glanced at her watch. 'Well, look at that. I suppose I should go and let you get back to your lecture. I have taken up more than enough of your time, Mr Shahin.'

'Please, we have taken tea together now. Call me Rifki, as my friends do.'

She smiled. 'Thank you. But then I insist you refer to me as Claire.'

He bowed his head politely as he stood. 'It was a pleasure to meet you, Claire.'

'I am a convert,' she replied, gesturing at the near-empty tulip glass. 'Wild sage tea may well be my new poison.'

'"Ada çay" is how you order it,' he said, as they lingered over pleasantries as a way of somehow holding on to each other's company for a few moments longer.

'I'll remember that.' She beamed. 'Professor Leavers, it was so kind of you to come along.'

'Oh, my dear Miss Nightingale —'

'Claire,' she corrected, throwing a glance at Shahin. She had been wrong. His eyes weren't grey. Now they looked charcoal, like his short hair and dark suit. She blinked, realising poor old Leavers was answering her.

'. . . anytime at all.'

'Thank you. I'm here for a couple more weeks at least and

could use a chaperone to explore more of the cultural spots of the city. I hear there is a remarkable cistern worth viewing.' She grinned, deliberately addressing Leavers. 'Although the truth is I'm perhaps more interested in the culture of the region. I wish I could meet more Turkish folk, learn further about their lives.'

'What is it you wish to discover, Miss . . . Claire?'

She looked back at Shahin and lifted a shoulder slightly. 'Everyday life,' she said, noncommittally.

'I was about to invite Charles to experience the hammam – do you know what that is?'

She nodded. 'The public baths.'

'I'm surprised.'

'We have Turkish baths in Charing Cross, I gather,' she said, remembering a snippet from the newspaper. 'There's a separate bath for the ladies, of course.'

He looked surprised and nodded, impressed.

'Gentlemen enter from Northumberland Avenue, as I understand it, while the women have a special entrance in the Northumberland Passage . . . off Craven Street, The Strand.'

'That's extraordinary,' he said, genuinely delighted.

'Yes, I read an article about it. I think it cost something in the order of thirty thousand pounds to build and there is a suite of bathrooms and cooling rooms beneath a dome.'

'The dome has a purpose, of course, to circulate air and achieve excellent ventilation.'

'I have to admit, I've never seen the inside of those baths.'

'Well, while I cannot extend an identical invitation to you that I have to your friend Charles, our visit will coincide with a family celebration for the birth of my sister's first grandson. She and the women of our family and her husband's family will be attending the hammam and later there will be a gathering of both families at my sister's house in Istanbul. She lives not too far from your hospital in

Taksim. You are more than welcome to accompany the women to the bathing ritual and perhaps you and Charles may like to join us at the festivities afterwards?'

She knew she hesitated. Was it right to accept this man's invitation? And was she hesitating out of cultural respect, or because he was an attractive man and it felt as though she was betraying Jamie to even acknowledge that?

'Please don't feel obliged, of course. It is simply a way for you to share some typical local family rituals. My sisters and the women of our family would be intrigued to meet you.'

There, she told herself, it was an innocent invitation and would be a fascinating insight. She too would love to talk at length to the women of Shahin's family. 'I'd be delighted to,' she said.

'Absolutely, old chap,' Leavers said. 'Sounds exciting.'

'Next Friday it is,' he said, looking pleased. 'I will get details to you at the hospital.'

'Perfect. Well, until next week, thank you both again. Enjoy your afternoon.' Claire turned and could feel his gaze on her back as she walked away, her thoughts racing to reassure her that he was simply interested in the connection to his son rather than her.

20

It was several days before Claire was once again called to the telephone, this time in the nurses' station.

'It's a Professor Shahin from the University of Istanbul's Mathematics Department for you,' Matron said, arriving beside where Claire was giving a patient a shave.

She looked back at Matron, trying not to reflect the pleasure that rushed to follow her private delight at the mention of his name. 'Ah, how kind of him. Professor Shahin is a colleague of Professor Leavers whom I met recently and he has some information for me.' She turned to her patient and squeezed his shoulder because he was a fraction deaf. 'Will you excuse me, Mr Wilkes?'

'Anythin' for you, darlin',' he said.

'Thank you, Matron, I won't be a moment,' she promised and wiped her hands as she walked quickly to the phone. 'Hello, Mr Shahin?'

'Rifki,' he reminded her and she smiled, liking his mild tone, finding it hard to imagine him ever raising his voice.

'How are you?' she continued.

'I am feeling very good, thank you for asking. I have made arrangements as I promised. My sister will send some women to collect you on Friday.'

'Why do I suddenly feel nervous?'

'You will enjoy it, Claire. My sister has assured you are welcome and afterwards in her home.'

'That's most generous. I am looking forward to it.'

'Perhaps I shall see you tomorrow evening then at the celebration.' He paused as if he wanted to say more. She waited. 'Good afternoon.'

'Yes, good afternoon.' As she put the phone back on the hook, one of the Turkish orderlies walked by and she hailed him, glad he was one of the youngsters who spoke reasonable English. 'Ali . . . I'm going to a Turkish house to celebrate the birth of a baby. What should I take?'

He laughed. 'Only gold will do, Nurse Nightingale. It is the custom. A small gold coin.'

Gold! Well, she couldn't risk being embarrassed by taking the wrong sort of celebratory present and she persuaded one of the doctors, whom she'd become friendly with, to accompany her to the nearby souk that evening to find a jeweller.

'We can't find a jeweller in Taksim?' she asked as Edward helped her to step up to the ferry at Karacöy. The craft was shifting slowly atop the Bosphorus as though slumbering, awaiting its next load, which seemed to be filling surprisingly quickly.

Edward shook his head. 'I know a reliable jeweller, but he's at the back end of the Grand Bazaar and down an alley. We can rely on him to give you excellent quality and price. In fact, I might find my sister something there. It's her birthday soon.'

'I saw her yesterday, I think. Dark-haired, Liverpool accent?'

He grinned. 'That's my Janet. We seem to be ships that cross in the night at the moment – our shifts are all out of kilter but she loves nursing as much as I love being a doctor.'

'It must be wonderful to be able to work overseas together.'

'Well, after what we both saw during the war, we're enjoying being family again and neither of us wants to be separated if we can help it – not with both our parents dead.'

Claire understood all too well.

'Have you visited the Bazaar yet?'

She nodded, leaning on the rail, and memories of the *Gascon* flooded back, except this time she was staring across beautiful blue waters to an ancient city. 'I've never experienced anything like it but it can be overwhelming.'

'I loathe it, frankly,' he admitted, taking off his glasses to polish them with a pocket square he drew from his pale linen jacket. 'But it's more to do with my lack of trust for crowds and tinkers.'

She laughed. 'They're hardly tinkers, Ed. Everything I saw was a work of art . . . even the food.'

The signal was given and the ferry groaned and heaved lazily away from the jetty, gulls circling them with keen eyes.

He put his glasses back on and it immediately aged him, given that his hair was also thinning. 'You're right, and I do enjoy experiencing another culture. I tend to think that medicine is a frontier, isn't it?' he said. 'So much of the human body, human condition, human psyche is unknown. There is no map – we're discovering it. So pursuing your calling to medicine is throwing yourself straight into the unknown.'

She smiled and squeezed his arm. 'You're an adventurer, Ed, without knowing it. And thank you for being so gracious about accompanying me.'

He grinned. 'It wasn't a hard decision, Claire. I'm sure I don't have to tell you that every red-blooded doctor in the hospital is hoping to have your pale gaze fall upon him.'

She inhaled silently. 'I'm spoken for, Ed.'

'I know. We all think he's a thoroughly lucky fellow too.'

'You're sweet, thank you.'

'Sweet is what my last girlfriend called me right before she called our engagement off.'

Claire threw him a look of sympathy that she hoped also told him she didn't really want to discuss romance.

'Anyway, my Lady Claire, we don't need to walk in through the main entrance of the Grand Bazaar – we can skirt it and move straight to the area of the gold souk where the haggling will begin.'

'Do you know how?' she teased.

'Of course.' He grinned. 'I don't like bargaining but unfortunately I'm wretchedly good at it. You see, it's a game . . .'

They walked in a relaxed, jolly haze of chatter in neutral Red Cross uniform to show they were not part of the military or the politics that had split up the city. Her companion knew his way and she tagged along, happy to follow down the twisting lanes that got busier the closer they reached the main building, which had reputedly been trading since the middle of the fifteenth century.

'We need the southern side,' Edward said and Claire became entranced by the labyrinthine feel of the souk with tiny alleyways running off streets to dark, intriguing places she couldn't fathom. Robed locals moved in a river of purposeful activity and haggling voices were all she could hear as the sounds of the city were drowned.

She soaked up the sights of the brightly coloured fabrics of carpets and shawls, of tins and jars of products she could neither read nor fathom their contents. Strange smells leaked towards them.

'Toasting pistachios for lokum,' Charles explained. 'They say lokum is what the gods would eat on Mount Olympus.'

Claire nodded. 'I'll eat Turkish delight in all of its incarnations. It's exquisite.'

He pointed to small, bronze-coloured lumps piled up in a basket. 'Ever chewed Arabic gum?'

She shook her head. 'What does it taste like?'

'Well . . . a bit like how cedar wood smells. Bit bitter but then gets better the more you chew. Aids digestion, apparently.'

'I'm sure we have a lot to learn from this part of the world,' she remarked, remembering how little she understood of the medicinal products sold in Alexandria and Cairo and yet the locals who worked alongside her swore they had magical healing properties . . . from argan oil to combat skin diseases to the biblical frankincense for aiding arthritis.

She was glad the awkward moment of romance had passed and she could now follow her companion, chatting amiably, into a wide, much quieter street where gold glinted with alluring intensity in the lamplight and men lurked in shadowed doorways watching purchases being made by Istanbul locals crouched in the street as the seller weighed gold. Money exchanged hands in both directions – some merchants were selling, others were buying.

He dropped in on her thoughts and spoke quietly, close to her ear. 'We see gold almost entirely for its beauty and then its value. But here, in this street, it is about wealth.'

'How do you mean?'

'Well, people don't drive cars or live in fancy houses such as Mayfair. They wear their wealth. And silver but especially gold is their currency. It's the measure of their financial worth . . . like a bank.'

'So, help me find a gift of gold coin for a friend's newborn.'

'Ah, they have coins for everything . . . births, weddings. And the greater your friend, the bigger the coin.'

'I don't know these people personally.'

'A small one, then. Come on, just down here.'

Inside the dark shop, which looked like a shanty that may fall down at any moment, Claire saw an old man wearing wire-rimmed glasses standing quietly behind a counter.

'Not busy tonight, Mr Hakan?' Edward enquired.

The shopkeeper nodded. 'As you see, sir. You are my first customer so you bring me luck.'

Edward gave Claire a wink. 'They all say that,' he muttered.

'We're looking for a gold coin for a new child.'

Hakan pointed to a dilapidated case before him. 'I have some attached to white silk bows.'

Claire leaned forward to get a better view of the glinting coins, which sat in soft depressions of the velvet within the case.

'The small coin is fine,' she said, pointing. 'And thank you, the one with the white ribbon looks perfect.'

Claire watched as Hakan retrieved the coin. He held it up and she nodded, enjoying the ritual of him polishing it carefully and retying the bow it was attached to. He showed her and she smiled.

'Perfect, thank you.'

Mr Hakan took his time weighing it against tiny spheres. When he looked up, Edward grinned. 'Let the haggling begin,' he murmured.

Claire had already handed him the maximum she was prepared to pay so she drifted away to the entrance to watch the street in its constant motion until the deal was done. Edward soon arrived beside her and held out a tiny package, wrapped in brown paper and folded expertly. 'Here you go and it wasn't as much as you were prepared to pay, first sale of the day and all that. What a fib!'

She looked over her shoulder. 'Thank you, Mr Hakan.' He nodded at her. 'You keep what was saved,' she offered to Edward.

'Oh, don't be daft,' Edward said in mock horror. 'Share a pot of tea sometime with me.' Claire smiled but his wink as he spoke gave her pause. She had no intention of encouraging another man into her life. As it was, the mention of tea, which should have only brought images of Jamie, suddenly made her think of the scent of warmed sage and the tentative smile of Rifki Shahin.

———

Friday eased around and Claire hadn't realised how much she'd been anticipating the opportunity to glimpse 'behind the veil' with the women of the Shahin family. Even so, she approached with mixed feelings about walking into the unknown world of the hammam. None of the other nurses had experienced it but several made remarks.

'Are you really happy to walk around naked with a bunch of strangers? Let a strange person wash you?'

Claire had shrugged. 'Well, I give bed baths all the time to people I've never met before. They don't seem to mind and neither do I.'

'I've heard their massages hurt.'

'Oh, I can't imagine that. This is to be a celebration.'

'It's dirty, Claire.'

'No! Cleanliness is spiritual to Muslims. The bathing rituals are part of their faith, so water has a powerful religious significance.'

She had dressed with great care after coming off her shift, choosing a new dress she'd had copied from a magazine by a tailor close to the hospital. She'd been amazed that from his daughter taking her measurements to his wife handing her the finished garment, it had taken only a day. She'd ensured the design deliberately covered her shoulders and arms and had used an enormous and exquisitely woven shawl she'd bought on her second day in the city. It was so delicate it was near transparent, so beneath it she wore a simple iron-grey shift. From afar it shimmered, as part of it was woven with tiny silver plates. She wore no other adornment and when she arrived to stand at the hospital entrance, carrying a cloth bag with the newborn's gift and a neatly wrapped package of lokum for the celebration at the baths, she saw two women approaching in black robes. She'd chosen a mix of mastic and rosewater gels presented in small mouthful-sized cubes dusted with cream of tartar and touched with glinting gold leaf; and the same amount again of less perfectly shaped mouthfuls of a harder, chewier gel of pistachio and date with silver leaf. And yet despite all of her prudence, which she'd convinced herself was all about respect for her hosts, Claire heard the small voice within mocking her that all of this was only to impress him.

No! she argued back, alarmed by such a notion. The only man in her thoughts was Jamie, she reassured herself, reminding that she was simply being polite and doing her best to engage with the culture.

'Miss Nightingale?' one of the robed women enquired as they neared, seeming to float beneath the dark, voluminous fabric. Big, dark eyes of ebony smiled above the veil.

'Yes. Are you Amina?' she asked, relieved she could speak to this young woman in English.

'I am.'

They all regarded each other hesitantly for a moment and then Claire stepped forward and kissed them on each cheek. 'Thank you so much for coming for me.'

Amina's eyes crinkled more as her smile widened. 'I am Rifki Shahin's niece. This is my cousin, Jehan.' Claire nodded at the other girl, guessing she was not fluent in the language being spoken.

'Rifki has a lot of nieces,' she remarked.

Amina laughed. 'I think six. But I'm the only one with good English,' she confirmed. 'Please forgive.'

'Nothing to forgive. I wish with all my heart I could speak Turkish.'

'My uncle did not tell me you were so beautiful.'

Claire smiled. 'Well, shame on him.'

Amina laughed. 'Did you have your dress made here, Miss Nightingale?'

'Please call me Claire. Yes, I did.'

'I recognise that work.' Amina said a word that Claire didn't catch. 'It is a very old tradition and very clever for you to turn it into a dress.'

'Thank you, I'm glad you approve. Amina, I'm nervous about the hammam.'

Amina looked sideways at her. 'Why?'

'I have no idea what to expect.'

'There is nothing to fear. It is a special outing for the women to be together. You will find it joyful. It is not far now.' She noted the girls were walking briskly and presumed it had to be because they were not normally out during the day without a male family member to escort them; special privileges had obviously been given on her behalf for these girls to be here. Instead of feeling reassured, Claire felt a fresh tension knot itself within.

———

In a country where females were required to cover themselves head to toe in dark robes, which included shielding their hands with extra-long billowy sleeves, Claire didn't know whether to feel exhilarated or shocked to be in a room full of women who were near naked. To add to her confusion, she was convinced that her paleness must appear comical among the sensuously toffee-coloured skin of the local women. Nevertheless they gave her smiles, nods and mutterings of '*Merhaba*' in welcome that were as warm as the temperature of the marbled tiled chamber she stood in. She again checked that the knotted fringe of the pestemal was securely tucked in beneath her left shoulder. The pale straw-coloured linen was flat woven and seemed too thin to be useful as a towel, but was her only covering between modesty and nudity.

As daring as she had sounded to her colleague, when the moment came to slip out of her clothes and underwear, she had felt a rush of clammy terror arrive. This experience was so alien, so completely opposed to all things British. And yet as unnerving as it all suddenly felt, there was also a small voice of adventure calling to her to try it. A new experience, a new awakening to a culture not her own; she wanted this and without giving herself another moment's hesitation, Claire stepped out of the small cubicle wearing only the whisper-thin linen.

She'd had a notion that the baths would be filled with steam but the truth was that the air was clear of vapour and simply felt moist. Her hair protested immediately, however, and began to curl unpleasantly around her ears.

A woman, taller than her and of Rubenesque stature, glided lightly over the tiled floor that was laid in a geometric pattern of pale green, blushing pink and white marble with striations of grey. Her long untied hair had clearly once been coal-black but was now feathered with silver at her foreline. Large, smoke-black eyes regarded her with intense interest and held Claire's gaze away from her large, bared breasts, which to Claire's initial glance, were surely full enough to make any man feel weak. She was certain her own covered pair appeared as inconsequential mounds by comparison and she had to fight the inclination to adjust her pestemal even higher. The wooden clogs she balanced on felt strange and she was sure she was going to topple over and embarrass herself.

'You are Claire, no?'

'Yes,' she strangled out, glad once again for the single common bond of English. 'Thank you for having me. I feel as though I've entered a whole new world of curious discovery.'

The woman gave a lazy, throaty laugh, rich with amusement and generosity. 'My name is Kashifa. I am one of Rifki's sisters.'

'How many of you are there? He didn't mention.'

An eyebrow lifted slightly with practised speed. 'He has six of us. Like my daughter, I'm the only one of our peers to speak English fluently.'

'Six sisters? He must have been spoilt.'

'He was my mother's little prince. We're all proud of him.' She kissed Claire on both cheeks and as she did so, Claire felt the touch of Kashifa's warm, smoothly skinned body against her own. It felt oddly comforting.

'You are very welcome among us. Rifki speaks highly of you.'

Claire blushed. 'I barely know him.'

Something in her companion's gaze denied her statement. 'You know him,' she said, touching her heart, and Claire blinked, unsure of how to understand the comment. Kashifa looked unaware of Claire's discomfort.

'You and Amina really do have such good language skills – I'm embarrassed at how useless I am.'

Kashifa nodded once. 'Thank you. I am the sister closest to Rifki. He taught me from quite young,' she said. 'I think it is important to understand the world around us even though we must stay in our homes. The world is changing. I don't know what my daughters will face.' She sighed and smiled at the cacophony of women's voices echoing off the hard surfaces. 'Hammam is the only place we can gather and gossip.' She lifted an eyebrow again in a suggestion of wickedness and Claire laughed. 'Come and meet my grandson and the reason for all this fuss.'

She took Claire's hand and led her through the main public bathing space to where more than three dozen women, in all shapes and sizes and ages, were excitedly chatting.

'Are you thirsty?' Kashifa wondered.

'A little.' Claire shrugged and watched her companion move expertly on the wooden pattens to a small pool where bottles cooled. She returned with two earthen beakers with a clear, lightly fizzing liquid. 'This is gazoz.'

Claire looked back at her quizzically.

'It is how you say um, slightly . . .?' Kashifa began.

'Effervescent?' Claire offered and Kashifa looked back at her with a frown to make Claire laugh. 'Um . . . bubbly,' she tried again. 'Fizzy?'

'Ah yes, fizzy, I have heard this word and it describes gazoz well.'

'In England we call this soda water.'

'Each region produces its own gazoz, so the flavours depending on where you are in my country are unique.'

'How lovely,' Claire said and sipped. 'This is delicious. Slightly fruity, is it?'

Kashifa laughed. 'Then it's not local to Istanbul.'

They walked on and Claire noticed that some women reclined on the various divans and lazily listened with an air of superiority, as though detached from the general activity. Kashifa led her to a quieter, more private area that could be screened off.

'I decided to treat my daughter to her own special washing chamber, where she can receive her guests and gifts,' Kashifa explained.

She saw a woman resembling Kashifa, whom Claire aged at possibly nineteen, clutching a tiny suckling infant. She wasn't ready for how her body instinctively responded to this most natural act, which Claire in all of her nursing days had not witnessed. She felt it first like a single pound of a door in her chest before her nipples stiffened and a curious glow suffused her as she became aware of her carefully guarded expression relaxing . . . melting, in fact, at the gentle sounds of the happy baby.

'He is beautiful,' she said tenderly, deeply touched by the sight of the naked, gurgling infant. 'Will you tell your daughter congratulations from me?' She offered the tiny coin that she'd unwrapped and held in her hand since arriving.

Rifki's niece beamed, thanking her traditionally in Turkish.

'*Rica ederim*,' Claire replied.

Kashifa laughed. 'Not bad. We like very much that you try.'

'That's almost all I have. My Arabic has a few more words.'

'Ah . . . you have spent time there?'

She nodded. 'A little, during the war.'

'We lost the only boy in the family we had to that war . . . until now.'

'Açar is why I'm in Istanbul.'

Her friend nodded. 'Rifki told me you travelled from London to keep a promise to my nephew. We admire you and wish to give you a family thank you. Come, let us begin your education into the hammam. Here is a copper basin for you. It needs to be filled from the central fountain but the water is very hot; be warned.'

'I'm sorry I make so much noise as I walk.'

'Your takunyas look large for you. Here, try mine.' She slipped off hers and Claire, not wishing to offend, obliged. 'Those look better.'

Claire took a couple of steps and grinned. 'Much. I have control of my feet again.'

Kashifa stepped into her new clogs and expertly glided on, making half the clatter that Claire had.

They came to a narrow canal that had been cut into the floor to carry away the dirty water.

'Claire, I think you will be amused by our custom but you may wish to follow me and spit three times into this used water.'

'Did you say spit?'

Kashifa gave her smoky laugh again. She nodded and, still chuckling, added: 'And you must say "*destur bismillah*" each time you spit.'

'For good luck with bathing?' she asked, confused.

This brought a louder laugh from her host. 'No, my girl, we are warding off the evil spirits in the dirty water where they inhabit. This incantation is being polite to them. If we acknowledge them, then we are respecting their presence even though our words are about banishment.'

'I see.' She didn't fully understand but it was a harmless enough ritual and so she followed Kashifa's lead and made a soft '*tisoo, tisoo*' sound, feigning spitting into the channel of water, and said the rote words three times. Claire felt ridiculous but she was keen to be respectful of not just the spirits but also the kindness of her hosts.

'Now we can cross.' Kashifa beamed. 'We are safe from their touch.'

She knew she was being watched but a rare sense of freedom had overcome her. Claire could swear she had stepped out of her body and was watching herself from the other side of the room. She could feel the warmth of the floor through her toes as she followed Kashifa into the main bathing chamber where it all became quieter and she was reminded momentarily of a chapel. Its peaceful sounds, soft voices and splashing of water gave her a sense of worship, the reassuring sound of its trickle made her feel secure, important to the continuation of life. The drier heat of the large, atrium-like main bathing chamber boosted the fragrance of jasmine and sandalwood that she was able to pick out immediately on entering. She imagined gazing at her reflection as she walked to the spout and it was true her flesh stood out as paler than her companions but it was young, unblemished and clung firmly to her skeleton, which moved straight-backed. Her belly was still taut, unlike the majority of the women beginning their ablutions, and she knew none of the dimpling of their buttocks or flabbiness of their thighs appeared on her. She still lived in the realm of youth and her breasts, though small, had a pleasing rounded shape, she decided, now that she considered so many others on display. She could see the individual bones of her rib cage delineated through the all-too-thin covering of her skin and it made her realise just how badly she had been taking care of herself after the war, for she lacked the enviable fecund appearance of the younger, exotic women around her. The temperature in this chamber was perfect – neither cold nor overly warm – and she no longer had an excuse. Claire found the courage to cast away the linen that covered her; she was a foreigner in a foreign land.

She knew they all noticed her still-emaciated frame, testimony to the deprivations of the Western Front and her arduous hours spent over broken men with no regard for her own nourishment or sustenance. The memory made her think of Jamie and a surge of sadness gripped her.

'Claire,' Kashifa said, covering her hand. 'Are you not —'

'I am well,' she replied with a reassuring smile. 'Sorry, I became lost in a memory.'

Kashifa nodded. 'You have seen many things, I think. The hammam is a place for relaxation . . . to forget those memories and to ruthlessly gossip.'

Claire laughed. 'Is that why you come here?'

'Of course, otherwise I am surrounded by the walls of my house. Hammam is the escape.'

'What does your husband think of your escape?'

'My husband is dead.' She didn't say it with any severity in her voice, or with any sort of admonition. Claire was glad that Kashifa required no answer either and continued as though in conversation. 'He died in the war, along with so many of the husbands, brothers and sons of the women in this room. It is why the birth of Arin is so important. He is the beginning. He is pure, is not a part of the war, or a remnant of it. He was conceived in peace and in love. And he brings new life to our family, which has known too much death.'

'Then I feel privileged to share this with all of you.'

'It's a pity you cannot share our gossip.'

'Is there a common theme?' Her friend frowned as though she didn't understand. 'I mean, what is everyone mainly gossiping about?'

'Each other,' Kashifa quickly replied, and they both laughed. 'But mainly the suitability of the young women.'

It was Claire's turn to frown. 'Suitability?'

'One of the important reasons for a girl on the verge of womanhood to be seen at the hammam – and especially a woman who has bled – is to catch the eye of the mothers with sons.'

Claire opened her mouth in surprise.

'Yes,' Kashifa continued. 'How else can you show that you are a good choice? This is why you will see a lot of the youngsters strutting around making sure their fine bodies are shown off to their best.'

Claire nodded to where a woman reclined, looking uninterested in everything around her. 'I'll bet that's a mother of a son.'

Kashifa's eyes sparkled with amusement. 'Oh, yes. Two of her sons are now available so all these mothers of daughters will be desperately trying to engage her in conversation because the family is wealthy.'

Claire shook her head with soft awe, delighted by this education. 'The truth is, Kashifa, it's no different in our culture. We've just got our clothes on when it's happening!'

They both chuckled in easy companionship. 'Sons are currency in our culture,' Kashifa continued. 'It's why Rifki was so precious to my parents, why Açar's loss was devastating to our family and why my new grandson is the most valuable gift from the heavens I could wish for.'

'Do you as a woman ever feel bitter that sons are revered while daughters have far less status?'

Her companion cast a shrewd smile. 'That's only on the outside, Claire. Women have plenty of power; they just have to be clever about where and when it is at its height, and how best to wield that power. A man is a simple creature – she must rely on her subtlety to get the most out of her life and her man.'

Claire sighed. 'You are so knowledgeable.'

'I grew up among a harem of many women and female servants so I had to learn fast how to get what I want. Now I have daughters and so I must teach them how to achieve their desires in the home and how to retain their power.' She gestured with her chin. 'You see that girl over there?'

Claire followed Kashifa's line of sight. 'Yes.' The youngster looked well developed; she guessed maybe fifteen, even sixteen.

'That conversation between her mother and the other woman will undoubtedly result in marriage. The girl is thirteen and she is mature in body and undeniably beautiful so she has her own special form of currency that her mother can wield.'

'Married,' Claire repeated, incredulous. 'At thirteen?'

'Oh, yes. Perfect age. She can start bearing children from fourteen summers and keep bearing them for years if they choose.'

'How old is the boy?'

'Fifteen, I think.'

Claire made a soft whistling sound.

'Rifki was married at fifteen, his bride fourteen. I married my lovely husband at that age and he had just turned sixteen. It's our way. It was your way too once.'

Claire was shown towards the small marble cubicles where she followed suit, lay her pestemal down and let warm water flow over her from the spout, as hot as she could bear, as bid by Kashifa. It felt deliciously indulgent and she was reminded of how precious water had been during the war at Gallipoli, how parched the men had been. She banished these unhelpful memories and let her mind wander into a blank space where there were only the soft murmurings of others, the scent of rose, jasmine and perfumed oils of sandalwood, rosemary and agar, and the refreshing sound of water. The truth is that Claire had never felt more alive. The afternoon's soft light filtered through the intriguing circular holes punched into the domed ceiling and it felt to her as though heaven was leaking into this place where cleanliness was being worshipped.

Her host returned. 'Come, Claire; now it's time.'

'For what?' Claire reached for the corner of her thin towel to dab her perspiring face.

Kashifa gave another low gust of amusement. 'Your bath. You are our special guest. Your natir awaits.' She gestured to an older, paunchy woman dressed only in a pestemal around her waist, who bowed once. 'She is your bathing attendant.'

Claire followed them into another room, much hotter and more humid, where she copied Rifki's sister in lying down on a large, raised marble slab which was punctured with small holes that warm water bubbled through freely.

'You'll feel like you can't breathe once your natir starts pouring water over you.'

The water pouring began.

'I can't,' she spluttered.

Kashifa laughed. 'Just relax and let your body get used to it.' She spoke in rapid Turkish to the two female attendants. 'I asked your natir to go gently on you. Very rich women bring their own slaves to wash and massage them. But I have hired this woman for you and I know her to be very good.'

A moment later the natir began oiling Claire. It was deep – painful at times – but she trusted Kashifa, who whispered encouraging words.

'You will feel loose and like you are walking on air later,' she chuckled. 'You'll thank me for it.'

At this moment, however, it felt as though the natir's fingers were claws with a pincer-like action that could get into any muscle she pleased with shocking accuracy. Claire groaned a complaint and at the sound of women's laughter she realised she had an audience and decided it was simply easier to close her eyes and bear up as her patients so often had. Later she was led to a more private nook in the chamber where a sharp blade appeared in the hand of the attendant and Claire, feeling stultified momentarily, allowed her hands to be raised and for the razor to glide swiftly and expertly over her underarms, then legs. The woman gestured between her legs and Claire, her eyes widening in fright, shook her head. The woman bowed again and gestured back to the central marble slab.

'Claire?'

'Yes,' she answered, relieved to hear Kashifa's call.

'You'll enjoy the rest.'

At first her limbs were stiff with inner tension and her self-consciousness of being soaped up by her attendant. But she gave herself over to the experience and soon became lost in the rhythmic washing and the intriguing way that the woman was able to manipulate her over the marble, spinning her without using much strength, but instead the slipperiness of the suds and the water bubbling from beneath. The soap was perfumed with a heady mix of floral and woody bouquets while the mint content added a refreshing note and felt as though it cooled her in this suddenly intense heat.

Her arms were tapped gently and she was encouraged to raise them above her head again as gritty soap was applied to cleanse; then she received another tap to signify she was to roll over or move a limb. She got used to it, began to anticipate what the washing woman required of her before a rough cloth was rubbed all over to smooth her skin until it tingled in response. She could imagine her body shining from being polished so expertly.

Gallons of increasingly tepid water were poured over her in the process of the washing and she suffered only momentary panic – during the final dousing from a height and over her head. She gasped through it as the gush of water finally eased.

Amina arrived and Claire appreciated how her eyes peering

over her veil had only hinted at how darkly pretty she was once free of that shroud. 'Everyone is impressed – we don't see many Western women in the hammams.'

Claire smiled as she used the pestemal to again dab her face, which now felt aglow. 'I'm not at all surprised you don't. But I've seen more naked men than you can imagine.' This began the afternoon's hilarity as Amina quickly translated and the women started to chortle and conversations branched out, which Claire assumed by the laughter concerned their men and how they looked naked. 'We're all the same, aren't we?' she added.

Kashifa nodded, also freshly glowing. 'That's a woman talking. We are all the same and still our men lead our nations into war and we are no better off for it . . . only worse. I wish dear Açar had never been sent.'

Claire followed her host in drying herself. 'He volunteered, did he not?'

Kashifa shook her head and led Claire to a stone bench where she expected to feel the shock of cold as she leaned back but felt the singular pleasure of the tiles at a perfect blood-warmth temperature. 'Ahhh,' she groaned, thinking privately *This is what so many of our recovering soldiers in England could use.*

Her host began to reminisce. 'I can remember that terrible day – evening, actually – when Bekci Baba began calling for the men.'

'Bekci Baba?'

'He was the local peacekeeper and eyes and ears of the neighbourhood. He would announce government messages, patrol the streets, act as guardian, you could say. He walked the laneways, a drummer beside him tolling his mournful noise to rouse households. Bekci Baba proclaimed that wintry night in 1914 that men born between the years of 1890 and 1895 were to report to the recruitment offices or face prosecution. Just like that, men were torn from their families, their businesses, their lives, and made fodder for the German war machine.'

Claire sighed. 'Well, my experience, and everything I've heard while at war, was that the Turkish soldiers were courageous, fearless and mightily respected by the Allies; certainly the Australian and New Zealand force rather liked the Turkish.'

Kashifa smiled sadly. 'And still we tried to kill one another.'

Claire nodded in equal sorrow.

'What you say is likely true, my friend, but few of those courageous men had a choice. Some were already doing their military service but those who were at home barely had a couple of days before they were pulled from their families and sent – with no uniforms, and whatever food we could push into their packs. They had to become gun-wielding killers overnight. Poor Açar, he was a poet, not a soldier.' She waved a hand in a motion of deep despair. 'Rifki will not speak about it.'

Claire blinked. 'I'm so sorry, I didn't realise . . .'

'My brother now keeps it all tightly here,' Kashifa said, placing a fist at her chest. 'Sometimes I think he will simply break in half but he has no one to blame but himself for not sharing with his son how much he loved him.'

So that explained Shahin's awkwardness. 'Perhaps my coming back to Turkey was not a good idea.'

Kashifa raised a finger. 'No, it will make him face it. He has never shed a tear for that boy but it is not that he doesn't weep inside for him each day. Rifki loved his son so deeply I think it terrified him.'

Claire took a deep breath of the dry, warmed air. 'What do you mean?'

Her companion sighed, letting her head fall back against the warm tiles and closed her eyes. 'His marriage was arranged by our parents and anyone could see it was loveless. She was a difficult child who grew into an even more difficult woman and died when Açar was nine. Rifki raised him.' Her lids opened and she regarded Claire. 'Rifki was raised by a hard man but he had a tender mother to balance life out. Açar did not have that same . . . how you say, um . . . luxury. His mother died so young.'

'You're saying Rifki is hard?'

'He's hard to be with, but he is not a cold man . . . not to his sisters or nieces. He is a proud man, however, and that can be mis-interpreted. He is an only son. His job was to look after all of us even though he is the youngest. He takes his role seriously. Since my husband died, Rifki takes care of me, provides money for me and my children. He will now be like a grandfather to my grandson. Rifki is a mathematician; he likes order and struggles to show the chaos of feelings that go on inside here,' she said, again touching a hand to her chest. 'And yet once . . .'

'Once what?'

Kashifa took a slow breath. 'I can remember a time when Rifki was so in love it was enchanting. I don't think any of my sisters or even my married daughter are loved by their men the way he loved Sehr. Her name means sunrise, and that was what she was to my brother . . . his sunrise, his reason for waking.'

'Why couldn't —'

'Her parents didn't believe him suitable. They wanted their daughter to marry a doctor or a lawyer . . . someone professional. Rifki was considered too much of a, how you say, dreamer.'

'Your brother . . . a dreamer?'

'In his youth he was a deeply romantic soul. He wrote poetry. I don't know if Açar knew that. My parents insisted he marry very young, produce a boy. He did both because he is dutiful but their choice of his wife and the responsibility of a child crushed the sun from his days.' She smiled sadly. 'Oh, how he loved Sehr and she him. They both had to marry who their parents chose, though, and so my brother changed and began dreaming a different way.'

'In what way?'

Her companion shrugged. 'He became determined, passionate . . .'

'What was suddenly driving him?'

'He was driven by revenge, I think, to show Sehr's family that they made a wrong decision. Rifki was a father by sixteen, but he studied at night and worked in our family's business by day. He was good at numbers and now as well as growing the family's enterprise successfully, he is at university teaching others.'

'And would Sehr's parents think him good enough now?'

'Oh, yes. Professors are highly regarded and of course Rifki manages his business and his money with cunning, so he is wealthy and continues to be so.'

'Did Sehr marry?'

Kashifa frowned. 'Yes, no children, though. I'm sure I heard somewhere that her husband died in the early days of the war.'

'How sad for both Rifki and Sehr.'

A fresh linen towel was wrapped around her and she was led to yet another chamber; this one was full of steam and Claire couldn't imagine she would last more than a minute or two in this one. Women sat around chatting animatedly as the steam billowed around them.

Later in the cooling chamber Claire found a quiet spot where her attendant left her and she closed her eyes and forgot about the former oppressive heat, and even the sounds of women as they now feasted on stuffed vine leaves or rich, sticky pastries.

And whether it was the ache from the massage or the sensual relaxation that was overtaking her, she convinced herself the tears that swelled and dropped down her cheeks were perspiration and not at all connected with missing Jamie and wishing her mission to Turkey had brought peace to Rifki Shahin.

21

Later, in a tall wooden house not far from the hammam where Kashifa lived with her unmarried daughter and another sister and her family, the celebrations began. It didn't matter that the women had enjoyed a splendid array of sweet treats and drinks at the bathhouse; now it seemed the real feasting began and Claire was astonished to see the amount of colourful food on offer. None of it looked familiar but it was plentiful and the spicy smells of stews and freshly baked bread were irresistible.

Claire enjoyed helping out in the back of the house, which the women referred to as the harem.

'Do you feel imprisoned?' she finally asked.

Kashifa laughed. 'No! Claire, my girl, I imagine you have many freedoms we Turkish women do not but you should never believe we are prisoners or slaves. This house runs to *my* rules. I am the eldest sister, the head woman. My brother may own it, my brother-in-law may sit at its front and welcome his friends and be served by his wife and daughters, but no man dares tell any woman how to run this house.' She waved a hand. 'Outside is their domain. In here, they answer to me.'

Claire laughed. 'All powerful?' she added.

Kashifa tilted her head back and tasted some of the meat she had been shaving off a haunch of roasted goat. 'This is true. In my domain, I am all powerful.'

Lanterns were lit, music struck up and dancing began in the courtyard that was overlooked by a magnificent and huge mulberry tree. After what she considered a polite period Claire decided it must be time to leave the family to their celebration and hoped someone would guide her back to the hospital before night fell. She went looking for Kashifa upstairs, but found Rifki staring out of the window of one of the rooms.

'Oh, forgive me,' she said, stepping back into the narrow hall.

He swung around and she saw sorrow etched on his face.

'Ah, Miss Claire. Did you enjoy your bathing rituals?'

She floundered momentarily. 'Yes, indeed. It was enlightening . . .' She moved her shoulders. 'Mostly painful.'

In the lowering light she caught a soft smile, its amusement dancing in his eyes.

'I . . . I didn't see you,' she continued. 'I didn't think you had come to the gathering.'

'I was with the men next door while the women bathed, but I took my time returning to the house and entered via a side entrance. I'm not much fun at parties.'

'Really? Just parties?' The question had slipped out before she could censor herself.

Rifki let out a sigh of a laugh and shrugged. 'As you may say in Britain, fun is not my middle name.'

She grinned and looked around. 'I'm sorry, are we allowed to talk . . . ?'

'It is permitted,' he murmured, although Claire wondered if this were true and whether he was being polite and she was trespassing.

'I really like seeing you in your traditional dress,' she said to fill the pause. The dove-grey caftan seemed to lighten the colour of his eyes today and its length made him seem more slender, even taller.

He looked down at himself. 'It is a traditional day for our family.'

'Well.' She smiled awkwardly. 'It was certainly a marvellous day of celebration. Thank you again. I was looking for Kashifa to say farewell as I was just leaving.'

'So soon?'

'I'm on shift early tomorrow morning.'

He nodded and she felt an even more uncomfortable pause arrive.

'You never did tell me about the damage to the book.'

'You're right,' she admitted, glad to have something to fill the blank yet tense space that stretched between them. 'Let me tell you now. Where should we —?'

He gestured to a small balcony and Claire moved onto it and looked down into the courtyard where the rest of the revellers enjoyed the celebrations, including Kashifa, she noted. She realised he was ensuring they were seen.

'Do you all live on this side of the Golden Horn?'

He sighed. 'Our grand family home was once not far from the Blue Mosque, near the water, with beautiful gardens and sprawling fig trees for shade. But when war threatened I suggested we move to Beyoğlu as a precaution. It seemed to me that the Europeans – whether they were our German allies or our British and French enemies – would want to overrun the old city. I think every Turk in Istanbul privately agreed that his family would be safer on this side. Most fled Beyazit and surrounds – it's a pity, for we lived in style. I don't even know where all our faithful old servants are.'

Claire sensed his sorrows crowding in as much as his physical presence. 'Well, where to begin?' she said, feeling conscious of his height as much as his attractive manner within the confined space. She was suddenly acutely aware of not permitting his charisma to crowd out Jamie. This whole trip was about Jamie, she reminded herself, as she dipped into her pocket and gratefully pulled out her talisman, the bullet shell she still habitually carried. 'This is what fits into the hole of Açar's prayer book. The book saved the life of the man I love because it took the force of this bullet and stopped it embedding itself in his heart.' She felt her inner tension subsiding at the relief of being able to explain to Rifki slowly and quietly about Jamie: how they'd met and fallen in love within the most chaotic and fearful situations. She went over again how Jamie and Açar had come to know each other – avoiding mentioning his son's death – but explaining how Jamie had been badly wounded that same day when the armistice ended, the rush to Egypt, the rash pledge made to each other. To Claire it was cathartic to relive that time, to speak it aloud and remind herself this is why she got up each morning and continued to breathe, why she forced herself to go through the motions of the day.

'Because each night I mentally tick off another day closer to April the first,' she finished.

———

The pitch of her voice soothed him. He wondered if her hospital training had taught her how to use it to make men feel safe. Again he watched the bow-shape of her lips move, sometimes anxiously when she referred to the man she was smitten with, more easily when she spoke of his son. He sensed she chose her words with care around Açar and as she moved her neat hands, unadorned by jewellery, the air became scented by the oil of roses that she had bathed with.

He was finding it intoxicating; the helpless desire he had begun feeling for this Western woman the week before had now escalated and intensified, knowing how much her heart ached for another man. He couldn't explain it to himself why that added the extra dimension but he wanted to understand, accepting that mathematicians needed their problems to add up and present neat answers. But there was no solution for him, other than doubt and despair after all these years of withdrawing deeper into himself, that a woman – not even one from his own culture – might unlock a formerly closed door.

'If not for your son, I would now have no hope,' she finished.

He blinked as she stopped talking, flustered by his increasing sense of weakness. When he said nothing, she looked uneasy and clearly felt required to fill the blankness between them.

'Er . . . Kashifa told me about your wife.'

'Kash talks too much,' he said, not wishing his dead wife's presence to intrude. He shrugged. 'I should never have taught her English.'

He saw she liked his soft jest and watched her smile broaden and lighten her expression.

'And will you ever allow another man into your heart, Miss Claire?'

'I'm like you. There is only one person for me.'

'Ah, but I'm sure my sister's busy mouth told you I did not love my wife. She never was the one. She was only ever Açar's mother and she had my respect and my care because of it.'

She nodded, holding his gaze seriously. 'You were dutiful,' she said.

'Duty is important.'

'Important enough to lose your son for it?' Her words wounded him and she knew it. Suddenly she reached for him, laid her hand on his sleeve. 'Oh, Rifki, I am so sorry. I have no right to —' He felt her grip of apology like a burn and he flinched. She immediately pulled her hand away, looking horrified for the second time in as many heartbeats for her actions. 'Forgive me . . .'

If only she knew how he truly felt – he had not experienced this sense of being out of control since his early teens but his voice did not betray him. 'Please, Claire. There is nothing to feel such despair over. What you say is true. I have asked myself this question over and again. Many fathers probably feel the same on both sides of the war. We must live with that knowledge and die with its despair in our hearts.'

She sighed and turned back to the party. 'We're pitiful, aren't we? Both not living our lives fully.'

'I possess a much better excuse than you,' he replied.

'I have to believe he will come.'

'And if he does not?'

She shrugged. 'I don't know. I refuse to think beyond then.' She saw Kashifa glance up and notice them. Claire lifted a hand to wave. 'Your sister is very fond of you.'

'I love all of my sisters, but Kashifa is my favourite . . . despite her mouth.'

Claire smiled. 'You are fortunate to have family.'

'But I have no one to love the way you love James Wren.' He wanted someone's eyes to mist that way when they thought or spoke about him. He lied. He wanted Claire Nightingale's eyes to soften like that just for him. He cleared his throat softly as he knew he habitually did when he was self-conscious and looked away. 'Ignore me,' he said, hating that he'd revealed such closely guarded sentiment.

'Well . . . I must go.' She sounded shyly uncomfortable.

Had she sensed his yearning was directed at her? He prayed not, could wish, in fact, that she had never brought the prayer book to upset his neat world where he had locked his hurts away.

'Of course you must. I've kept you long enough. Claire, it's been an honour to meet you,' he said, nodding a polite bow.

'Thank you for today – it's an experience I shall cherish.' He heard the slight strain in her voice, was sure he wasn't imagining it. 'Especially, I suspect, when I'm back to being naked and bathing in my freezing bathroom in England – oh!' She must have regretted referring to herself so brazenly and painting such a picture for him. Her expression was one of chagrin. 'You must forgive my clumsiness.'

He waited until she looked him fully in the eye. 'I forgive you everything except the pain you leave behind.'

She swallowed. 'Pain?'

'The memory of my son,' he quickly said, covering the treachery of that inner voice again. 'But even as I say that I will be eternally grateful that you brought me something of him that he considered most precious. And when I touch that bullet hole, I will think of you and hope you are blissfully happy with the man whose life it saved.'

She held out her hand, clearly unsure of the protocol.

Later he would analyse his response but right now he reacted purely on instinct. It was a dangerous decision but Rifki closed his hand around hers and pulled her into the shadows where he knew they would not be seen. He kissed her cheek gently and fleetingly before twisting his head to her left side and, just for a heartbeat, lingering next to her soft skin, inhaling the soap's scent of roses and everything that was Claire Nightingale. They were apart almost as soon as he had brought her close. 'I wish you happiness,' he murmured and stepped back fully into the darkness of the hallway.

Jamie Wren was resurfacing. His thoughts had felt like they were pushing through dark treacle. It was a strange sensation of limbo; he could see people but not properly work out their features; these seemed to shift and slide from their faces. He could hear them talking but their voices seemed to be coming from the bottom of the sea – distant, gulpy, words indecipherable. Smiles turned to grimaces, hands reaching out seemed to turn into rifles and bayonets.

'Scrambled egg, James Wren,' his mother used to accuse when he was a teenager and would forget a simple instruction moments after it was given.

Yes, that's how it seemed, but he was emerging. He could feel things now. He could certainly experience pain again, which up until now had been numbed or distant. His head felt as though it was bleeding inside. Maybe it was . . .

How long had he been lost in this murky place of his mind? How long since he'd had a drink, more to the point? He was parched. He turned his head sideways and saw the beaker and jug. He thought he reached for it but his arm barely moved and the pain was like bright light in his mind even though it was dark wherever he was.

'Ooh, wait up there,' a smiling voice said in an accent he loved. An Aussie woman, much older than him and in a nurse's uniform hovered into view with a lamp. *Claire!* Not Claire. Claire sounded English.

'Welcome back!' the woman said, delighted. 'I'm Jane.'

He tried to talk, but croaked. She was already reaching for the water and he swallowed greedily as she held the beaker for him. He tried again. 'Where am I?'

She smiled beatifically. 'You're in Dartford Hospital in England.'

'England,' he murmured, but his spirits lifted like a spring butterfly flapping off joyfully. 'That's good.'

'Oh, I'm glad. Most of our lads headed the other way . . . back to Australia.'

'I'm sorry, I feel so useless.' He tried to push the unruly hair from his eyes but nothing happened. He looked down at his arm and realised although he could feel it, his sleeve appeared empty. He regarded Nurse Jane with a comical expression. 'Where have you put it?'

It really was a joke – he'd get it moving in a moment – but she wasn't smiling any more.

'What's your name, Trooper?'

'James Wren.'

She sighed and he saw relief flash in her gaze. 'Oh, well done. That's so good to learn. Um, listen, James. You were badly wounded in the Middle East. I gather you were part of a major repulse attack in Jordan towards the end of the war.'

'End of the war? What, you mean it's over?'

He saw her eyes glaze with a sheen of water. 'Yes, sweetheart. Peace has finally arrived. But it cost you.' He nodded, sensing something dark shrouding him. 'We had to amputate your arm, James. It was really badly smashed up and you'd already injured it prevously. It was a mess. The matron from the hospital you were last at argued for your dispatch to this Australian Auxiliary Hospital in Dartford because – well, because you were a bit lost for a while – but we also needed to decide on the best treatment for your arm. The decision wasn't reached lightly.'

He stared down at the empty sleeve. It really was empty this time, not like that day when he got out of his hospital cot in Cairo to marry Claire.

Claire! He frowned. 'What's the date?'

She looked perplexed by his question. 'It's March the twenty-second.' Her patient went to rise. 'Wait, James! You can't go anywhere yet. Your leg.'

He toppled over, yelping with the pain shooting through his body.

———

Claire fled, her emotions on edge and thoughts scrambling with confusion. She was grateful to be distracted by the rounds of farewells from the women, who took turns to embrace her, and she began to feel she should never wonder if she had family. It felt as though she belonged with Açar's kin, although his closest relative she dared not look at again. There was something intensively dangerous about the way Rifki's presence unnerved her. The way he looked at her, behaved around her . . . even his mellow voice put each follicle of hair on alert. If she described this to a stranger she knew they would likely suggest she didn't like this man, but Claire suspected the opposite: everything about him was unhelpfully attractive to her. They had only formally been within the same few feet of each other twice but to her dismay Claire believed she could close her eyes and describe everything from the way his hair curled behind his ears and the spare symmetry of features, with eyelashes so dark she could swear his sisters had got to him with the kohl, to the bony shape of the knuckles on his long fingers and even the modulated pitch of his voice. What made this frighteningly vivid recall so disturbing for her was that she didn't believe she could describe Jamie's characteristics with the same clarity. And so she needed to get away. Be alone in her thoughts to find Jamie's face and voice, his hair, his smile. To remember his kiss and his promise but all she could hear was her acclamation and Rifki's careful words in response.

I have to believe he will come.

And if he does not?

'My eldest sister and her husband will accompany you back to the hospital,' Kashifa intruded on her rising panic. 'Neither speaks English so don't be embarrassed.' She smiled. 'Promise me we shall see you before you leave Istanbul.'

Claire couldn't make that promise but gave Rifki's sister a final hug before she turned and smiled at the couple waiting for her. At the sound of a dull shriek coming from the house, their trio paused.

It was Amina who appeared at the doorway, her expression showing relief that they hadn't yet disappeared. 'Claire, I'm sorry to stop you but can you help, please? It's Uncle Rifki.'

'Rifki? What's happened?' She pushed back through the house and into the courtyard where she saw people clustered around and recognised the grey of Rifki's robe in their midst. Claire had no idea what Rifki was saying but even in the lowering light of dusk she could see droplets of blood splattered where he stood. 'What's happened?' she said crisply and Kashifa appeared beside her, her expression concerned.

'Look at him!'

People parted and Claire saw him holding his hand, with linen wrapped around it. He looked up at her in irritation mixed with despair. 'This is nothing,' he tried.

'Let me see.'

'It's just a cut.'

She didn't stop to consider the many customs she was trampling on as she pushed him to sit down and unwrapped the fabric that he'd wrapped several times around his hand to hide the severity of the wound. Those standing closest sucked in a collective breath at the sight of the gash and Claire gave a sheepish, lopsided smile.

'Just a cut, eh?'

Rifki lifted a shoulder slightly. 'As you see.'

'How did it happen?'

He blinked. 'An edge on the iron railing.' He nodded towards where they had been standing.

'This wound has to be stitched.' He started to pull away, making sounds of disdain, but she didn't let his arm go. 'And washed out properly with antiseptic.'

'Claire, please.'

'Rifki, this is deep and made by something rusty so the chances of tetanus infection are high.'

'Tetanus?' his sister repeated.

'It usually begins here,' she said, defying social acceptance and reaching toward his jaw, his surprisingly soft beard lightly grazing her careful fingertips. 'You could suffer spasms. We call it lockjaw and those muscle contractions can quickly spread to your neck, your shoulders, your spine, until you will lose control completely.'

'Claire,' he muttered.

She knew only a few others understood her words. 'Have I

painted a vivid enough picture?'

'What is to be done?' Kashifa demanded.

Claire sighed. 'The blood flow is not yielding to pressure. Rifki must accompany me back to the hospital.'

'You will go with Claire,' Kashifa instructed and her tone to her brother and the implacable expression she directed his way brooked no defiance.

The hospital wasn't far away but it was up a steep hill and Claire apologised to the elderly couple as best she could before she used the eighteenth-century Camondo Stairs to climb the hill.

'Tell them to take their time,' she urged him to repeat. 'I have to get that blood staunched.'

Claire barely waited for his translation before she began harrying her patient to climb the famous hexagonal-shaped steps.

'Thank heavens for the Jewish banker who donated these stairs,' she remarked.

'Do you know why he built them?'

'Is it important?'

Rifki laughed. 'No, but it helps pass the time as we climb.'

'Tell me then,' she said, wanting to shove him along faster from behind, 'but keep moving.'

'The banker lived near the Galata Tower – you know this is the financial district of the Ottomans?'

'I didn't, but go on.'

'Camondo's children went to school nearby and it cut the time immeasurably if they could access the way down the hill via these steps, but he designed them in such a way that should any child fall, they would not topple a dangerously long way but simply roll down only a couple of shallow stairs. Hence the odd but pleasing shape.'

'Lovely story. Where is your house, by the way?'

'In the neighbourhood at the top of the stairs and not far from the Galata Tower.'

Claire knew them to be expensive and fashionable. 'So even the rich and famous could use the stairs to nip down to do their banking?'

'Or to the docks, yes.' He was puffing.

'Are you all right?'

He called back over his shoulder in Turkish. 'I was just telling my family members to come slowly.'

'I can send a hospital porter for them.'

'No. They'll be fine.' He breathed out loudly as they reached the top of the steps.

'I can see you don't use the stairs that often,' she quipped.

'I will from now on. No more ponies and carriages!'

Claire moved him quickly through the narrow street that led to the Galata Tower and made for the hospital that looked like a monastery, peaceful in its quiet grey stone in this whisper-quiet part of Istanbul. Together they leaned into each other as they moved beneath the stone arch and up four shallow half crescents of marble stairs to reach the pretty mosaic path of grey and black pebbles. The double doors at the entrance were illuminated by flickering lamps that hung off scrolled iron cressets and these cast a ghostly light across the lower balconies that overlooked the small gardens filled with citrus and mulberry.

There were four floors, which covered an entire square. The hospital had become a central part of this community, attracting vendors and street sellers around its perimeter and in fact a lemon and aubergine seller was still packing up. Once inside the main doors, she sat Rifki in a chair.

'Wait here, please. I shall find a male member of staff. Keep the pressure on the wound.'

Rifki gave her a sad half smile, said nothing and by the time she returned alone his family had arrived.

'The only staff I can find working tonight are female and I realise that your culture would require a male to attend to you.'

She watched Rifki mumble to his eldest sister and husband.

'Did you explain?'

'I said we could have gone to a local healer.'

'Yes, you could have but I'm relieved you listened to me. I want to be absolutely certain that someone I trust is in charge of cleaning it thoroughly. Give me one more minute,' she promised and skipped off again.

Claire searched all the main wards but there was no surgeon available. It might as well be her, she decided; Rifki was not going to let another nurse that close, and besides, she had the fastest, deftest touch when it came to stitching. How best to handle this delicate situation, though, without giving offence to Rifki's people?

Claire returned to the waiting area. 'I've found the right person.' She beamed and as Rifki stood and his elders followed suit, she held a hand up. 'Forgive me. Can you ask your relatives to wait here, please?'

Rifki frowned.

'It's hospital rules. Only the patient. They can come in shortly and in fact you shouldn't be too long. I shall send out a coffee for them. We have some here.' He spoke in rapid Turkish. She smiled to reassure them while he explained. 'Come with me please, Rifki.'

He followed obediently, keeping the pressure on his wound as she'd instructed. Claire led him to one of the day clinic rooms. They would have privacy here, although she wished the hospital wasn't as quiet as it was this evening. A few more Turkish orderlies scurrying around, or some brightly chatting nurses would have made her feel more comfortable than she did at this moment to be found alone with a Turkish man – and of all Turks, this one who made her feel the stirring of interest for another man, which she hadn't felt possible. She had no intention of exploring that awakening – not until she was sure that Jamie wasn't coming back for her.

'Have a seat,' she gestured, dragging a tray trolley on its casters next to him.

'Where's the doctor?'

She took a breath and regarded him. 'I lied, I'm afraid.' She nodded in the direction of his relatives. 'They don't have to know but we do have to get that seen to.'

'So you are going to take care of me?' he asked.

'Yes.' She didn't meet his gaze. 'There are no men available. Now, I have to scrub my hands. Don't move. Keep the pressure on.'

When she returned she felt more in control because she was back in her familiar domain, its smells and equipment, and busied herself assembling her tools and dressings.

'Are you going to tell me how that really happened?' she wondered aloud.

'No.'

'Why?'

'Because I don't want you to feel responsible.'

Claire saw that his chameleon-like eyes reflected the shiny metallic surfaces of where they sat. Flinty and troubled, they regarded her far too tenderly.

'It was a rusted nail,' he finally answered. 'I banged my fist down in anger at myself when you left.'

She seated herself alongside him and placed his arm so it rested on the towel she had laid on the small rolling table between them. Claire gently pushed up the loose sleeve of his robe and as she did so her fingertips unwittingly traced against the soft hairs on his long, slender arm.

To cover that forbidden touch, she deflected his attention. 'What is it you want?'

His shoulders drooped at her question and he let go of the pressure on his wound. Fresh blood oozed through the linen and Claire immediately began to unwrap his hand. 'You,' he said, sounding miserable.

'Rifki,' she murmured, reaching for the syringe of Dakin's fluid like a lifeline. When she worked, she was strong, calm, in control. It was like the war again, having to flush a wound. She noticed he didn't wince despite the hefty sting of the antiseptic and spoke to distract him from it. 'This is a highly emotional time for you. You have a new boy in the family and I've arrived to stir up all your memories and perhaps regrets. It is possible even —'

'Please . . . do not —' He paused. 'It cannot be neatly rational-ised into a comfortable explanation. It is irrational and thus chaotic. My feelings towards you bear no relation to my son, or my family. They belong to me alone. My chaos. In maths terminology we call this ergodic theory.'

'You've lost me.'

'It is connected with a point – let's call it X – possessing a sensi-tivity to initial or present conditions with potential for a different trajectory depending on those conditions.'

She fixed him with a smile. 'You are X, I take it.'

'Yes, and you present the condition I am sensitive to and my future is thus uncertain.'

Claire took a silent breath. 'Do you reduce everything to mathematics?'

'If I can, yes; I appreciate its reliable simplicity, for to under-stand is to have control.'

'Yes, but people can't be controlled like numbers, Rifki. One day we behave this way, tomorrow another. The heart can act in complete opposition to the mind, too . . .'

'Indeed,' he agreed. 'And that's where chaos occurs. But as I say, the chaos is mine . . . and does not belong to anyone else.'

She blinked at his abstract view and cursed herself inwardly for finding his curious and naive approach to life helplessly attrac-tive. She could almost feel the bullet tip burning in her pocket, though, reminding her who her heart was waiting for, impressing that Rifki's attention was flattering but not to be acted upon. 'Is this hurting?' she asked, knowing the answer but wanting to change the topic. Her face was close enough to smell the clove on his breath from the spiced celebration pastries they'd all eaten, and suddenly she could taste the spice, as though they'd kissed, and with that notion arrived a discomfiting warmth of shame.

'Pain is a strange feeling,' he admitted.

She gave him a still slightly blushing, sideways glance of puzzlement.

'Why do we press bruises or let our tongues search out the aching tooth? It alerts us that something is wrong, yes?'

She nodded.

'But it can also divert us, and when you stop hurting me with your instruments I know I shall feel relief that it is over but it would have distracted me from the original injury with a capacity to hurt a great deal more. Plus, I shall be stitched and healing.'

'That definitely confirms it for me – your mind is odd.'

He laughed, and she hadn't seen such a spontaneous, unguarded moment in him. It was momentarily intoxicating, like smelling a beautiful bloom or tasting an exquisite treat . . . or kissing Jamie.

'I mean, you speak about simplicity through your numbers but you actually think in such a complex way.'

'I'm a mathematician.'

'I pity you. Life doesn't need to be so complicated,' she whispered.

'Mine is, though, Claire,' and he shocked her by reaching with his hand to touch her hair, feeling its curl between his fingers with an expression of wonder. 'So soft. I've wanted to do that since I saw you seated on the bench in the gardens. Your hair shone as though it was gilded with the golden paint of angels.'

His whimsical words helped her to move on from the shock of his action. 'A poet as well as a mathematician?'

He smiled, dropped his hand. 'You have made turbulent what was a straightforward, routine life.'

'Right, I think that's as disinfected as we're going to get it,' she said, dabbing at the wound, still oozing.

'I'm glad the stinging is done,' he admitted.

'Ah, well, the best bit is yet to come,' she said, pointing to her needle and catgut. 'I can give you an injection for some local numbing if you wish?'

———

He shook his head in answer. The bright pain as her needle worked kept him in contact with her. If she'd numbed the area he wouldn't be able to feel her ministrations and he wanted to experience every moment of Claire Nightingale's touch, even if it hurt to do so.

'Tell me. How does a man – a near stranger – hold on to a woman's heart when she hasn't seen him in nearly five years?'

'Why don't you ask yourself that?' Claire replied, drawing the thread taut and expertly knotting and snipping its end. He had been absently wondering, as he watched her stitch, why they called it catgut when he knew her thread was made of sheep's intestine.

'What makes you say that?' he replied, puzzled.

She fixed him with a stare and he knew she had attempted to speak with surety but her eyes betrayed her and he knew if he was ever going to kiss her it was now. He desperately wanted to taste her . . . even if it was just once . . . even if she pushed him away. And it was as though she knew he was poised on the threshold of doing something that defied the neat rules of his life – and culture – or following instinct like the dreamer he had once been.

Claire decided for him. 'I want you to accept that maybe now you and Sehr can be together.'

Sehr. He closed his eyes. Now, that truly was unbearable pain. Kashifa's mouth had certainly been busy.

'It's none of my business, but —'

'No, Sehr is not your business,' he muttered, feeling windows in his mind opening that he had thought he'd barred shut.

'Rifki?' She shocked him by moving around from the side and bending to cup his face in her cool, healing hands. 'Do you remember how it felt to be in love with her?'

She was determined to make his sutured wound feel shallow by comparison to the deep cut of her words.

'You don't forget how love feels,' he groaned.

'That is how I feel about Jamie.'

He watched Claire's expression soften from earnest to compassionate. She reached for a chair nearby and pulled it over so she could sit close enough that their knees touched. Whether she was aware of that innocent yet forbidden kiss of flesh beneath clothes he couldn't be certain but he felt it within himself like a candlewick flaring into life.

'Rifki, you represent a dangerous precipice.'

He grinned. 'Good.'

'No, not good for me. The promise Jamie and I gave to each other has evolved and become something spiritual for me. When I was at the Front, personally witnessing men die by the dozens each hour, I think all my innocence was torn into hundreds of pieces and rode the winds in all directions. Meanwhile my dreams rushed inward and coagulated into a hard lump of despair. There was nothing of me any more, Rifki. I was like a doll: immaculately groomed, with a permanent soft smile of encouragement painted on my face but inside was the void. I was hollow – no anger, just dutiful, but empty. It was as though the universe had decided to strip me of all hope and the harder I worked to save lives, the faster they slipped from me. Within a few months of seeing so much death

I was lifeless myself, except for one tiny flickering flame in the corner of my battered mind. The flame was all I had . . . my warmth, my light, my hope. And the flame was the promise that Jamie made to me and it transcended a naive pledge between new lovers and became religion. As long as I trusted it, as long as I stayed faithful to it, there was hope for me in a world that felt hopeless. And the reason I came here to honour your son was to stay busy, have purpose, hold the faith that was Jamie . . .' She clasped his good hand, sending fresh sparkles of sweet agony through him. 'And now here you are, threatening to disrupt my spiritual wellbeing.'

'So we were simply an excuse for you?'

She gave a disappointed sigh. 'No. Your family was my lifeline. Açar's book was a symbol of hope – if I kept the promise, I hoped the gods would smile favourably on me . . . on Jamie.'

'How do you feel about me, Claire? The truth.'

She risked stroking the wiry, close cut of his pepper-and-salt beard, not appearing guilted by it. 'In a different world, Rifki – and if I had known you before the war – I would be helpless in your presence and I'd defy your culture and your age to be with you. But I met Jamie first and he has my heart. This is my world . . . and it revolves around James Wren. So I'm asking you not to risk me unbalancing on the dangerous precipice that you are. Fate guided me to Jamie; it chose for us to meet but it was nothing so ethereal between you and me. Jamie guided me to you for a specific reason.'

'You truly believe him alive even though there has been no word in nearly five years?'

'I know this is going to sound very strange, but I hope you can grasp this. I've made a spiritual pact that if I don't move from the path of remaining faithful to his love, then Jamie will come back to me. In less than two weeks I will know if my private religion has been misguided. But it kept me alive when bombs were exploding around me and killing others. It inflicted terrible sights and experiences upon me and now it's testing me with you to see if I am true. I cannot and will not betray that religion.'

He nodded, experiencing a river of admiration swell for her and wishing he were on the receiving end of that kind of faith in love. Twice now he had fallen deeply for a woman and both were unattainable.

'Are you finished?' he said, glancing at his hand and the ugly black pattern of eight stitches running down the meaty flesh at the base of his thumb.

'I'm finished when I say so,' she instructed.

'You are quite frightening, Claire, for someone nearly half my age.'

She began daubing a bright orange solution on his wound. 'Are you angry with me?' she asked, sounding hesitant.

'Yes.'

'It's Sehr you long for, not me. It's the memory of that yearning that I've likely reignited. Others got in the way of you and her. You don't love me, because you barely know me. You *want* me. There's a whole world of difference between the two. But you loved Sehr; you knew everything about her. Perhaps she's waiting for the day she'll see you again. And don't say she's married because I happen to know her husband has been dead for years.'

'I shall punish Kashifa for this.'

'You'll do no such thing, or I will never forgive you. We are kindred spirits, Rifki. We both have lost loves. I don't know if mine will come back to me but you're a coward if you don't remind Sehr of how you felt . . . possibly still do.'

The truth of her words slipped through his defences as easily as her needle had punctured his skin and the pain was just as bright and sharp.

'You'll never know unless you stop making the numbers add up neatly, Rifki. Love is messy. Be untidy for once – take a risk.'

'I thought I was.'

She smiled sadly at him. 'Yes, but with the wrong woman. The right one is Turkish, lives in Istanbul, shares your faith, your culture. The wrong one has silly short hair that goes frizzy in the damp, likes the miserable cold and rain of London and is hoping a fairy-tale is going to come true.'

'I love your hair,' he admitted.

'And I love your expressive eyes.'

'So you do love something about me?'

She nodded. 'There is plenty to love about you. That's what makes you dangerous.'

'You said in a different life . . .'

'Yes, Rifki, I would say yes. But in this life, it's no.'

———

She had worked in silence, dressing his hand, and when she'd split the bandage and tied it off neatly, she once again ignored protocol and bent forward to softly touch his cheek with her own before laying a tender kiss of farewell.

'I couldn't do that out there in front of your family so I thought I would say goodbye properly to you here.'

He touched his cheek, looking surprised and moved by her gesture. He stood, waited a heartbeat or two to test that he wasn't dizzy. She smiled at him and he nodded. 'Goodbye, Claire. I hope Jamie finds you.'

'And I hope you will go in search of the happiness that might still be yours if you take the real risk.'

'Total chaos?' He grinned.

'What's to be lost?'

'Thank you for this,' he said, raising his wounded hand.

'It's going to start throbbing soon.'

'It already has.'

'Those stitches can come out in about ten days. I'm sorry I won't be here to remove them for you.'

'It's probably for the best.'

She nodded. 'I'll see you out.' Rather brazenly, she linked her arm through his good one and he didn't protest. Rifki was starved of affection and she needed him to go in search of it again. She dropped her arm as they rounded the corner and emerged into the waiting area.

His sister and husband helped each other to their feet and pointed at his hand, laughing nervously. He exchanged some Turkish with them.

'I told them it looks worse than it is.'

Claire kissed Rifki's sister and said goodbye in her modest Turkish. The sister stroked her cheek.

'She says you are beautiful,' Rifki translated. 'And for once I agree with my eldest sister.'

Claire blushed, shook hands with his brother-in-law. 'I'd like to hug him too.'

'I'm sure he'd like it but best not to.'

'And now I want to hug you but I am forced by your tradition to do this,' she said, holding out her hand. 'Remember all we've said. Think of me when you hold Açar's prayer book.'

'I shall kiss it perhaps and pretend.'

Claire swallowed. He was not going to make it easy for her. She nodded and smiled as though she was simply saying a goodbye.

He clasped her hand, his warmth transferring as a frisson of energy up her arm.

'And I shall often think about that alternative world you spoke of and imagine what it might be like. Most of all I shall try very hard not to think of you naked in your tin bath at home.'

She laughed, half embarrassed, half delighted. 'Don't translate that.'

'Laughter like that needs no translation.'

The elder couple turned away, began lightly arguing with each other over something, and Rifki turned back to her with feigned despair in his expression. Claire laughed gently but realised she was also crying, her eyes damp and threatening to spill tears. He nodded, understanding, and this time when he led his quarrelling relatives out of the main door he did not look back and she did not follow . . . and soon he was nothing more than a deepening shadow in a moonlit Turkish night.

22

27 MARCH 1919

The taxi dropped Claire outside the gate of Eugenie Lester's home and as the cold March wind welcomed her back it carried with it the scent of freesia and lilacs to remind her that spring had arrived.

The housekeeper met her with her usual suspicious countenance. 'You're back already.'

'Hello, Joy . . . er, may I call you Joy?'

'It's my name,' the woman replied, taking Claire's umbrella, hat and gloves. 'No luggage?'

She shook her head. 'I went back to Berkshire first. I still have to pack everything up there. But I couldn't bear not to visit immediately.'

'Well, she'll be thrilled to see you, Miss Nightingale.'

'Do call me Claire.'

'She's having a good day. She's on the patio, expecting you. I'll serve some coffee shortly.'

'Thank you. I'll see myself there.'

She followed her nose out through French windows onto the patio to where Eugenie huddled, rugged up in a wicker outdoor armchair; she didn't turn but chuckled softly. 'I sensed your arrival at the train station. I've been counting the minutes.'

Claire was crouched at her side in a heartbeat, hugging her friend. 'Are you a seer?' she asked as she kissed Eugenie's cheek with deep affection.

'No, my dear, just attuned to you.' She beamed. 'My, my, I'm amazed at what a few weeks in a warm climate can do. You're glowing.'

Claire could not say the same for Eugenie. She blinked. 'Am I? I'm sure I worked for most of those weeks.'

'You look wonderful, my dear, and so I can only assume it was a happy time for you.'

She couldn't lie. 'Yes . . . yes, it was and I met some marvellous local people.'

'You returned the prayer book?'

Claire nodded. 'His father is . . .' She hesitated.

'Is what?'

She shook her head with a small smile. 'I think most would call him a cold fish.'

'But you didn't?'

'Not at all.' She cleared her throat as Eugenie's regard intensified. 'He's charming and was delighted to have his son's precious book.'

Her elder raised a thinly fleshed hand and Claire was struck by how much weight her friend had lost in the short time she'd been in Turkey. 'No need to explain any more, my dear. I think I understand. And you look so bright.'

Claire turned away, hating that she felt so guilty. 'Oh, it's good to be back in England, though,' she gushed, hoping to cover the sudden memory of Rifki that came with the scent of sandalwood oil that he had bathed with on that day of celebration.

'Well, it's lovely to see you so happy and no doubt filled with anticipation.'

'To bursting point. He's going to be there, Eugenie, I know he is.'

Joy cleared her throat from the French windows and brought out the coffee tray, taking her time laying out the accoutrements.

'Thank you, Joy,' Eugenie murmured and dismissed her with an endearing smile. 'I don't know what I'd do without you.'

Joy's lips pursed slightly and Claire wondered as she watched the housekeeper leave why Joy couldn't simply smile.

She turned back to Eugenie. 'I'm still waiting to hear from his parents,' Claire remarked. She shrugged. 'I guess I'll know soon enough.'

Eugenie gestured. 'I thought you'd like to pour.'

'Of course,' Claire replied, moving to the small table, her expression entirely back under her control.

'And while you do, perhaps you'll explain why you need to fib to me.'

Claire put the coffee pot down on the tray with a sheepish expression. 'That obvious?'

'I'm afraid so. You'd never win at cards.'

Claire gusted a sad laugh, relieved to be able to talk about it. 'I nearly lost my head in Turkey.'

'I'm presuming you mean that figuratively?'

She grinned and nodded, began pouring the coffee.

'Actually, you don't have to tell me, my dear. Secrets are rather nice so long as they do no damage and can nourish us.'

Claire tonged a sugar lump which made a soft gulping sound as she plopped it into the coffee and warmed milk.

'When did you get to be so wise, Eugenie?' she said, placing the cup and saucer into wrinkled hands.

'It's just age, dear, and years of experience that teach that one cannot control the universe, or who walks into your life.'

Their eyes met. There was nothing rheumy about her friend's gaze; Claire saw only alert interest.

'It felt scary,' she admitted, glad to let it out.

Eugenie nodded, sipped. Waited.

She wasn't sure why she felt the urge to speak of it but having lived her life off instincts, she knew this was no moment to break faith with them. 'I had a moment of desperate need. I can't lie about that. He was sad, damaged, soulful . . . I could have changed his life and he mine.'

'I didn't hear the word love, Claire.'

She lifted a shoulder. 'We barely said more than a few dozen words to each other.'

'It was the same with Jamie, as I recall, and yet you knew you loved him.'

Claire sucked in a slow breath of enlightenment. 'You're right.'

'And the Turk was different?'

'Yes,' Claire said, letting out a sigh of relief. 'So different.'

'Obviously you made the right decision.'

Claire sat down and sipped her coffee, sighing inwardly at the tarry, licorice flavour, mellowed by the steaming milk and rounded off with the smallest lump of sugar she could find in the bowl. Her spine curved as her shoulders relaxed. 'Did I? What if Jamie doesn't come?'

'Keep faith with him, Claire, we'll know soon enough. What are your immediate plans now that you're home?'

'"Home". I like the sound of that. Well, I refuse to mooch around. I still need distraction and packing up the house in Berkshire will take a couple of days. I also want to get a new dress.'

'Perfect!' She glanced up. 'Yes, Joy?'

'Forgive me, Mrs Lester. I meant to mention this to Miss Nightingale on her arrival and her comment reminded me. My apologies for being remiss.'

Both of them frowned. 'What is it?' Claire asked.

Joy slipped her hand into the pocket of her black long-sleeved, drop-waisted dress over an embroidered white camisole. She wore it as a uniform; Claire had never seen her wear anything else but she'd not noticed the pockets before. She gasped softly as Joy withdrew an envelope, recognising the stamp immediately as one from Australia. And then she noticed the spindly writing in black ink.

'Jamie's father . . .' she whispered, unable to say anything more.

The housekeeper held it out to her, looking immediately uncertain as Claire's hands remained steadfastly by her sides.

Claire suddenly had no desire to take that envelope. It was larger than average, and clearly containing more than a polite response. She could tell by the bulge. Had Jamie's luck run out? The sinking feeling turned dangerous. Claire felt she was drowning. She began to swallow.

'You didn't mention that letter,' Eugenie said in a tone with a scolding edge to it.

'Mrs Lester, it was delivered only this morning,' Joy said in bleating defence. 'The postman said it was redirected from Berkshire.'

'Claire, dear?' Eugenie said with an edge of concern.

She rallied her courage and nodded. 'I asked for my post to be sent on to this address,' she murmured, still not reaching for it.

They all stared at the envelope from Australia.

'It's not going to open itself, darling girl.'

Claire cut Eugenie a misty glance. 'I don't think I want to read what's inside,' she admitted in a small voice, backing away from Joy.

They watched the housekeeper place the letter on the table between them. She stepped away. 'Maybe it's good news,' she offered, her features suddenly and uncharacteristically softened.

Claire was reminded of how many loved ones this woman had lost to the war and guilt danced across her fear for one person's life. Joy nodded encouragingly and Claire felt her heart give a little for the woman. 'Let me get a fresh pot,' the housekeeper murmured and turned away.

Now it was just the two of them staring at the envelope that looked scuffed for all of its travels. It lay harmlessly next to the tray, but Claire felt it carried within it the power to breathe life into her world or to snuff it out, like a candle starved of its oxygen. She realised she was holding her breath.

'Open it, Claire. Whatever it says won't change for the waiting. Whatever it contains we shall face together.'

Claire became acutely aware of her breathing as well as the pound of her heart. She could hear Rifki's gentle voice querying her commitment to a daydream.

'Would you like me to open it?' Eugenie's voice reached her from what felt like a much farther distance than she knew to be true.

She shook her head slowly and picked up the letter. The stock felt furry, almost gritty, from its journeying and she imagined all the different strangers who had handled it on its voyage to find her. She knew she was putting off the inevitable and so did Eugenie but her friend remained silent.

Miss C. Nightingale was looped in a small but bold spindly script and beneath it her address in Charvil, the forwarding note scrawled above.

She finally turned the envelope over and realised she had no letter opener but the flap yielded beneath the barest of pressure, and the glue released easily.

Claire inhaled softly and deeply. This was it.

Birds trilled happily in the garden and she heard the drone of a single bumblebee nearby, exploring the spring daisies that had flowered in pots on the patio. Claire felt an immediate kinship – they were both searching to start their life – and she slid the letter and its accompanying contents from the envelope.

With tears gathering, she opened up Jamie's father's letter with a rustle of crisp paper.

Dear Claire,

We were glad to hear from you. I hope, even though we have not met, that you are not offended by my familiarity. We share a common love and now a common grief, so suddenly etiquette seems irrelevant.

Claire gasped aloud, felt as though she were struggling for breath, eyes watering to blur the words, but hurriedly she read on, unable to stop herself now.

I am enclosing the originals of the letters we have received from the Light Horse. I think you will find them self-explanatory. Please return them at your convenience to our address at the top of this letter when you have finished with them. Frankly, my wife, Laura, wanted to burn them. I am at a loss for how to console her in her grief.

She stopped, dizzy and suddenly nauseous.

'Claire?' Eugenie asked softly.

'It's not good news,' she choked out, now presuming the worst as she forced herself to read on.

Jamie is – was – her favourite. I know that's unfair to our three other sons but . . . well, I feel sure I do not have to explain why to you and I am also sure her secret is safe.

I am deeply sorry to deliver this grave news contained in the accompanying letters and I wish we were closer so that we could meet you and offer comfort. We are strangers but loving Jamie has made you family to us. To find a perfect love as you describe is likely impossible for most people. I was lucky and it seems my son was blessed with the same lucky streak to have found you, dear Claire, in the most dire and bleak of situations. We will keep you in our thoughts and prayers as we grieve either side of the world for a fine young man who by all accounts carried out his duty to King and country with courage.

I regret with all of my heart that I failed to tell him just how proud I was of him and I regret that it has taken his death for me to be able to write with such affection about a child I loved but never told. I am glad you did.

Sincerely,

William Wren

All other sounds had been swallowed by a single long buzzing in her head like the drone of a machine; she could no longer hear, speak. Even colour had drained from her vision so her world had turned down its tones to blue-grey and narrowed to the manila package from William Wren. Without wanting to, yet inexorably drawn to the enclosure, Claire put Wren's letter behind the bundle and confronted the second envelope.

It too was buff and grimy from plenty of handling. She ran her fingertips over the navy-coloured stamp, absently flattening out a tiny triangle of its rouletted corner, then drew out the pages to confront her deepest fear. The first had an address at Victoria Street, London SW, and was typed.

Dear Sir,

I enclose details of witness accounts of Wren Tpr J W 799 that we have been able to compile. As you can see these are –

Claire lost patience and slipped the introduction to the back of the sheaves and hungrily scanned the next, which was headed up

Australian List A.I.F. Ist A.L.H. It was from Egypt. Her gaze was drawn to the title *Unoff.M. Oct 1917 W.&.M.* but before she could fully grasp the meaning her desperate need for detail pushed her headlong into the main body copy.

> *Witness said he believed:*
> *Trooper Wren may have been killed in a charge in the Jordan*
> *Valley during the escalating battles to liberate Jerusalem.*

Hope withered but still she needed to read more. Claire ripped another sheet out and sound returned to her senses as an anguished mewl escaped her tightening throat as she scanned. Her gaze tripped across the blotchy font of the typewriter as the queen bee merrily buzzed on, tripping from petal to petal. Except for Claire there was no golden pollen to be gathered but only cold, harsh, black words that bounced against her heart like pebbles stoning it.

> *. . . body not recovered. Ref:- F.D.Grant. Desert Mounted Div.*
> *Ward 19, Harefield. Note: Informant seems a quiet man who*
> *knows what he is talking about.*

Claire helplessly read another page.

> *Witnesses thought that Smithson (division) of the ANZAC*
> *mounted division was out all the day that Wren was lost, not*
> *coming in till the following morning, and that he might know*
> *something about him. Smithson is 4th or 5th reinforcement.*
> *Witness Smithson thought Wren was felled during the Es Salt*
> *raid. Described him as a handsome fellow from South Australia.*
>
> *Reference Trooper T W Smithson 1 A.L.H. Squad B.*

Montazah Hospital Alexandria

E.M. Foster

6.12.17

She read the first line of the final page through her helpless tears and then could not read on.

He was one of my mates. I saw him shot.

Claire watched her hand shake as she placed the sheaf of papers onto the tray, heedless of how the pages landed across the small sugar basin and milk jug. Although she considered folding herself into the empty chair conveniently nearby, she turned and walked away from Eugenie's anguished glance and stepped down from the patio. The sun was bright but its fragile warmth of early spring couldn't touch the chilling pain that was wracking Claire's body. Talons of bleak, aching fury grappled their way through the blur of disbelief until the weight of her sorrow felt so burdensome it forced her knees to bend and Claire sank in a slow, collapsing motion to the damp lawn.

Jolly birdsong cruelly continued and she was eye to eye with a dancing white daisy that seemed to throw all the brightness and hope of a new spring back in her face. She could hear Eugenie calling to her but she needed a few moments to gather up the pain, turn it all back neatly like a well-folded sheet that nurses were so adept at achieving with sharp creases and perfect lines. She needed to pack the hurt away and accept that she'd been building a future on make-believe. Rifki had been right. Jamie's and her ridiculous promise was always a dream, nothing more. She'd seen what war could wreak and she'd been involved daily in what bullets and shrapnel, bombs and firepower could do to flesh. Dear, sweet, affectionate Jamie. Forces more powerful than their pact had pushed them apart, kept them apart and now shattered their chance to come together again.

'Hopeless . . . helpless . . . hapless,' she murmured beneath her breath, echoing an alliteration game she used to play with her father.

Let's see who runs out of words first, he'd laugh. *All the words have to begin with the same letter and relate to the original situation.* She had never beaten him until the last time they'd played on the way to the hospital in Hobart before he died. He hadn't run out of words. He'd run out of hope. This is how she felt now and just as she wanted to fold in on herself, Claire felt strong arms embrace her and she smelled the curiously spiced fragrance that she had come to associate with Eugenie's housekeeper.

'Let me help you. You'll catch your death in this damp grass.'

'Maybe catching my death is a good thing, Joy.' She was surprised she could talk.

Joy's voice broke into her musing. 'Nonsense! Come along now, help me and push up.' Claire obeyed. 'There you go.' She was back on her feet but a tremor began, she didn't know from where; it seemed to radiate from her core and soon her entire body was trembling. 'This is shock, Claire. You of all people know it. And for shock you need quiet, warmth, and I've always believed tea works wonders but I've never known why.'

'It's the sugar,' Claire replied, feeling entirely disconnected as Joy supported her. 'What is that smell?'

Joy seemed to know precisely to what she referred. 'It's tincture of benzoin, sometimes called Friar's Balsam.'

'Ah, they're different, of course.'

'Yes and this one has rosewater.'

Of course it does. Attar of roses. It was haunting her. 'Are you using it as a styptic?' Claire found it easier not to confront the envelope or its contents, or her pain. It was far easier to discuss Joy's ailment.

'No, my hands react poorly to soap. I'm using it on chapping to prevent blisters,' Joy said, making small talk as she guided Claire back to the patio step.

'They say you learn something new each day.'

'So they do.' The housekeeper soothed.

'And I've learned today that the man I want to marry is dead,' she replied in a tone to match her final word. She gently shook off Joy's hands.

'Claire Nightingale, if I had the strength I would wash out your mouth with my highly scented lavender soap,' Eugenie threatened from her chair. In her hands she waved the leaves of the letters. 'Nothing in here *confirms* he's dead.'

Eugenie's look of disgust dragged her from the self-pity she so badly wanted to lay down in. 'Did we read the same pages, Eugenie?' Claire gasped as she arrived back onto the patio, shoulders slumped and the trembling more intense.

'Unless I'm blind, we did. But clearly I have perspective that you lack. You're presuming more than what is given here,' Eugenie continued. 'These are unofficial accounts. They have no body, no proof, just statements of war-weary men more than capable of confusing one trooper for another.'

'Tell me how you read it differently,' Claire whispered.

'I will, but first let's go inside. I can't watch you shiver like that a moment longer. Joy?'

'Leave everything,' the housekeeper replied. 'Claire needs tea.'

Claire. Since when had Joy started calling her by her first name? It sounded pleasant, comforting even, as though suddenly she had family pressing around her. She let them fuss, Eugenie giving directions while Joy settled them both into the sitting room and lit a gas fire. The sunshine had fooled them.

'Claire, listen to me.' She raised her gaze at Joy's voice. 'I don't know what is in those pages, but I've experienced enough pain of this nature in my time to assure you that unless the Red Cross or the military clearly confirms in writing the sighting of your young man's body and can confidently identify him, then don't give up hope.' She nodded before turning. 'I'll get a pot of tea,' she announced softly and left the room.

'I hope what Joy just said is getting through to you because all I'm reading here are accounts.'

'His family accepts them. They're witness accounts,' Claire groaned.

'And where does it say anyone witnessed the death of Trooper James Wren?'

'The last —'

'Unless I can't read English the last one says he was seen *shot*. It doesn't say killed.'

'You're reading into the words, Eugenie.'

'And I could argue that you are also! We're reading them differently, though.'

'What would you have me do?'

'Anything but give up, dear Claire. Now, unless I'm mistaken, today is 27 March, yes?'

She nodded miserably. It was only her sense of good manners that was keeping her pinned to the armchair. She wanted to run from the room; she was convinced now that this episode of her life was not meant to end happily ever after. The heavens had conspired to allow her to glimpse a potential life but the universe had already clued Claire to its intentions during her teen years. It had moulded her to expect a bleak future and had first taught her how to cope with death and loneliness and sorrow; then it had trained her as a nurse and sent her to war so she faced nothing but death and despair. It had teased her with Jamie, tested her with Rifki, and now it was showing her how cruel it could be in taking both from her.

'. . . organise a car for you,' Eugenie muttered.

She blinked. 'Pardon?'

'To London.'

'London?' Joy arrived with the tea tray and Claire no longer minded that the housekeeper shared her conversations.

'The Langham, Claire!' Eugenie said with a tone of admonishment.

'And punish myself just a fraction more?'

Eugenie held up a warning finger as Joy seemed to hesitate between pouring and remaining statue-still between the two women. 'He made a promise.'

'Oh, Eugenie, aren't these letters and all the anguished waiting sufficient torture?' she wept, finally breaking down. 'It's enough!'

'There's nothing final about what those letters say. Even the Red Cross explains that nothing is official.'

'Witness accounts,' Claire growled through her tears.

'I don't blame the Wren family for reading it as final. Heaven knows my heart breaks for them. But witnesses can be wrong in war. Fatigued, hungry, parched, fearful soldiers are disoriented, memories get muddled, facts distorted . . .'

'Or maybe it *was* Jamie,' she challenged, her voice dull, eyes cast downwards. She sniffed. 'And you're not prepared to accept it.'

Eugenie sighed with obvious disappointment. 'No, I am not at all prepared to accept it. I say you give that young man who loves you the benefit of the doubt and you make sure you keep that date with him. For all you know it's the promise of seeing you again and holding you again that has kept him alive through all the terrifying situations he's encountered.'

No one said anything and Joy remained still. The clock on the mantelpiece monotonously ticked away the seconds of her life as Claire considered the potential for yet more pain if she kept the meeting. The fire guttered as though there was a break in the gas supply, and she heard Eugenie clear her throat gently as the silence lengthened. 'Why give up on him now?'

She closed her eyes and cast her mind towards Jamie, reaching to see his handsome features against his tanned complexion and his slightly crooked smile. Amazing that now in the presence of his death she could see him clearly in her mind's eye. But then Jamie's vision dissolved and she was left with Rifki Shahin's face, which was neither smiling nor sad.

Eugenie had lost patience with her, it seemed. She was waving away all the tea paraphernalia. 'Joy, please call Bertie Cartwright and tell him to get out his Daimler. And please fetch my wheelchair.'

'Mrs Lester, I —'

'Do as I bid, please, Joy. Claire, I know you've only recently arrived and I suspect you need to lie down and gather your wits, but so help me I need to jolt you out of this morbid mindset. Minutes ago you arrived here so rejuvenated and happy, so come with me; let me show you something.'

Claire sat in astonishment as she bounced along in a superbly glamorous car, whose bright-red paint – polished to a high gloss – reflected Radlett's thin, winter sunlight off mirrors and brass, making her wince. Joy had walked ahead with the wheelchair, complaining that this cold air was not at all good for Mrs Lester. Meanwhile Eugenie seemed perky and fresh, wrapped up from head to toe in voluminous shawls and rugs so that she looked like a child in a papoose.

Bertie Cartwright was a ruddy-faced, genteel fellow who clearly had more money than notion for what to do with it and Claire liked him immediately for his ability to keep up a non-stop stream of apologies for everything from why he hadn't gone to war to why his passengers might be 'smelling a bit of oil in the back'. Claire was perched in what Bertie called the dickie seat.

'Just over twenty-two horsepower this beauty is, Miss Nightingale.'

'That sounds like it can go fast, Mr Cartwright,' she replied, pulling her scarf tighter, knowing it was what he wanted to hear.

'Well,' he chortled, 'enough to make that gorgeous golden hair of yours blow in this wind. I say, do call me Bertie, by the way,' he added over his shoulder, lifting a hand covered in a glove that came halfway up his arm to protect his tweed jacket and voluminous driving overcoat.

She found a smile for his sweetness and he stole a shy glance returning a grin from pudgy cheeks below his oversized driving goggles that sat below a huge tweed flat cap. He looked vaguely ridiculous but helplessly endearing.

'Eugenie,' she yelled over the sound of the car. 'Where are we going, exactly?'

'You'll see. It's barely another minute away but I think it's important.'

Claire sat back, sighing to herself, and while the distraction had been welcome for this last half hour, she now reconfronted the despair of the letter that she'd read. It was back with all of its black vengeance of pain. She deliberately forced her mind to wander down another pathway as Bertie expertly cornered away from Watling Street and up the hill towards woodland, to wonder what Eugenie could possibly think was important here.

'Now, if you don't mind waiting back with Bertie and his car, Joy, I do believe Claire can take me from here,' Eugenie said, settling in comfortably to her wheelchair.

Joy stomped away back through fallen leaves on the tiny path a few feet away to where Bertie had managed to negotiate his vehicle. Claire bent down. 'Really, Eugenie, what are you up to?'

'Straight ahead, dearest.' She pointed.

'To where?' Claire could see only trees.

'That lovely big old beech. Push hard or I'm quite likely to get stuck in these leaves.'

It took effort to push Eugenie's wheelchair deeper into the woodland and by the time they arrived at where she directed Claire was breathing hard and happy for the release of the tension, both physically and emotionally.

'Here?' she asked breathlessly.

'Yes, darling, now get me up.'

The wood smelled of damp earth and slowly rotting leaf-fall. It wasn't disagreeable. To Claire it smelled of peace and the cycle of life. She looked over at the sound of a rustle and saw a bright-eyed red squirrel dash away, seemingly oblivious to their presence, and she recognised the loud song of finches. These were pleasant thoughts but they were disrupted by Eugenie's struggling.

'Eugenie, please —'

'Don't patronise me, Claire dear, I am not long for this world, and I didn't think I'd have a chance to see this again. I'm unbearably happy to share this moment with you of all people, so indulge me and help me to walk, will you, or shall I do it myself?' She waved at Claire impatiently. 'I will never be strong enough, or my body willing enough, to attempt this again.'

Claire, with the practised motion of a nurse, eased Eugenie out of the wheelchair, realising sadly that her greatest friend felt bird-like in her arms, weighing far too little. 'All right, we'll take this slow. How far?'

'Just there, darling. It's this one,' Eugenie held a wavering finger towards the tree. 'It hasn't changed a bit,' she continued, and Claire heard the tremor in her voice. She wasn't sure if it was from exertion or emotion. They took four unsteady steps to the tree. 'There,' Eugenie said again, proudly.

Claire looked to where a curious arch-shaped gnarl appeared on the tree. It was a smooth patch where the bark had fallen away. It was grey and weathered, and she could see that a heart had been carved into its centre. An arrow bisected the heart, alongside the initials *EL* and *EL*.

She sighed at the romantic symbol. 'You and Edward?'

Her friend nodded and Claire saw with surprise that her elder was weeping softly but smiling.

'He brought me here for a picnic. It was the day Eddie first kissed me and then told me he loved me and couldn't imagine he could spend another day without knowing I shared his initials.'

Claire smiled in spite of her mood. 'He asked you to marry him here?'

'On bended knee when this whole area was a meadow of buttercups,' Eugenie admitted, waving an arm expansively, even though the action cost her a wince. 'I was even dressed in yellow, I seem to recall. We toasted ourselves with beakers of my home-made lemonade and swore we'd never be parted except in death. We kept that promise.' Eugenie touched her gloved fingers to her lips and with difficulty she bent to place her fingertips on the centre of the heart. 'Now it's your turn, Claire.'

She frowned. 'I don't understand.'

'Well . . .' Eugenie motioned towards the chair and Claire helped her back to it, assisting her friend to be seated comfortably again. 'Do you see that the gnarl of that tree is arched?'

Claire looked back and nodded.

'Eddie said to me that's the fairy door. *It is a secret opening into another kingdom*, I recall were his exact words.'

Claire smiled at the whimsy of this notion. She loved Eugenie for bringing her here; already she was feeling a fraction more optimistic.

'The fairy kingdom?' she said.

'Yes, Claire,' Eugenie continued, proceeding with a more droll tone. 'If you were a pretty little five-year-old, you'd be quite excited to hear this but because you are a beautiful 25-year-old, I'm going to have to rely on you to accept the idea based purely on the romanticism of this notion.'

'I will,' she promised, surprised she could feel even as vaguely lighthearted as she did in this moment.

'Good. We all know that it's the fairy world that grants us our wishes, agreed?'

'Agreed.'

'So, Claire, as Eddie made me, now you must knock on that door and after you do so, make a wish. Eddie said the fairies would be listening on the other side and if they like you they will grant you your wish. They granted me mine, which was to convince my parents to let me marry Edward Lester. I wish I'd thought to include in that wish that he might live as long as I.' She smiled sadly. 'Go knock and make your wish. You'll be surprised who is listening.' Claire stared at Eugenie for a moment. 'Do it, Claire,' she whispered. 'If you say it and cast out that wish, then you'll believe in it as I did; hold his memory close, bring him home.'

Claire felt moved by these words, but they were soft, plump tears of swelling joy rather than despair this time. 'Thank you,' she mouthed to her friend before she turned to the tree.

Claire bent and, with all of her heart open, she tapped gently on the fairy door and prayed they were there and paying attention to her.

'If you're listening, fairies,' she began, 'please bring Jamie Wren safely back to me on April Fool's Day. I don't want to believe he is dead. Just make him safe. Bring him to me – even if he's hurt – and I will heal him . . . I will believe in you forever and help set up Eugenie's clinic to help heal others as my namesake did so faithfully.' She touched her fingers to her lips, and as Eugenie had done, she placed her fingertips to the centre of the carved heart.

Claire turned. 'There . . . satisfied?' she said, affecting a tone far drier than she felt.

'Completely,' Eugenie admitted. 'Thank you for coming here with me.'

'It's a very special spot,' she agreed. 'So beautiful. I think I could live here beneath this canopy of beech trees forever.'

Eugenie smiled. 'First you have a date to keep, yes?'

Claire nodded. Eugenie was right. *Why would I give up on him now?* 'Every time we've met you've had to remind me to keep faith with Jamie. Maybe you're the fairy, Eugenie.'

Her friend snorted a laugh.

'I think I shall head back to Charvil – I need a couple of days to navigate through the shock and I'll go to London from there.'

'Let me organise a car for you so that you don't get rained upon or blown about and so you look your picture-perfect best for Mr Wren.'

She didn't think it would matter to Jamie how she looked. 'Thank you, Eugenie, but I think I'd prefer to find my own way; it's good thinking time on the bus.'

'Well, at least let me send someone to pick up your belongings from Berkshire and bring them here.'

Claire nodded. 'All right, thank you. My belongings will be ready in a couple of days.'

Eugenie cast a glance backwards. 'Best we don't keep the others waiting much longer. Plus I don't believe I can feel my nose any more.'

Claire grinned. 'Just for a while, in fairyland, it was easy to forget the cold, wasn't it?'

'Keep your wish close in your thoughts, Claire. It will keep you warm these next couple of days.'

23

Thin sunshine peeped through the morning drizzle of the twenty tall, small-paned windows of the ward and lit all corners softly. Anything that was white seemed to be bathed in a special glow of starched, spring purity. It was cold enough to snow, though, and the heating in these long draughty wards at Dartford was struggling.

It was a kind team here, mainly involved in nursing neurotic soldiers returned in a state of anxiety and suffering more from stress than from their injuries. It was slightly different for him; his wounds were so blatantly obvious but he was mostly here to recover from the shock of an explosion that at the same time as wounding his arm had bounced him up into the air and flung him beneath two huge animals. He'd heard later that he'd been fortunately dragged out immediately, or perhaps he would have perished on Arab soil beneath his beloved horses.

All was relatively quiet on the ward save the irregular thump of his wooden crutch on the long, light-coloured floorboards. Mornings were easy here. The men with the broken minds seemed to find peace enough to sleep from the early hours through to full daylight. It was the dark hours that were nightmarish, when all the demons would be at play; he understood, but he was free of those nightmares now and if not for the wails and shrieks from his fellow soldiers, he was sure he might heal even faster. Instead he lay awake a lot of the night to the sounds of his comrades' mental anguish and felt guilty for conquering his trauma, and returning from the stupor.

Nurse Jane rustled in her crisp white uniform and gave a sigh of approval. 'You are doing so well, James. You really shouldn't be here but I haven't got the heart to move you to Southall Hospital, where you should be now, and give you all that upheaval again.'

'I'm happy here.' When he nodded he was aware of droplets of perspiration flicking off his face, landing on the newly dusted fronds of the palms in pots. 'I'm sorry.'

'Don't be. That's a clear sign of the effort you're putting in and it's being rewarded. Look at you. Already up on your feet. It's a marvel.'

'I need to go faster.' He shifted the single crutch and pushed off again, negotiating his way down the straight corridor formed between the neat row of equally spaced black enamelled iron cots.

She caught up, gave him a look of caution, and he paused again, sweat running like an opened tap down his back and dampening his shirt. 'Listen to me now. I was at the 3rd Auxiliary Hospital in Cairo when it opened at the sporting club in June 1915, also when it closed just over a year later, and I was right here the day we reopened 3AAH in October of 1916. I have seen a steady stream of wounded, broken soldiers, some men with almost identical injuries, James, not once or twice, but repeatedly. And I can assure you that I have not seen anyone make the kind of rapid recovery that you have made.' She helped him to sit down in a wheelchair. 'You cannot push too hard or there'll be a price. You could relapse, or you could damage something else. There's no race.'

'There is for me, Nurse Jane.'

Her lips narrowed in a sympathetic gesture. 'I know. Claire Nightingale.'

'Have you heard anything of her whereabouts?'

She shook her head. 'I would have told you. I would have run in here and screamed it at you.'

He gave a sad grin.

'But I don't want to bring it up for fear of sending you into a bleak mood when you're doing so well. When you arrived here you couldn't speak a word; you seemed altogether lost in your mind from the trauma. Now look at you. We're all so impressed. Have you written to home?'

He nodded. 'One of the nurses scribed it for me. She posted it yesterday but it will probably take an age to reach South Australia. They probably think I'm dead,' he joked.

'Well, you'll be out of here soon.'

'I'm leaving on the first of April,' he promised.

She gave him another gentle smile. 'The most recent information I can offer is that she was repatriated with a group of invalid soldiers in September 1918.'

'So she's given up nursing?'

'I wouldn't be at all surprised, would you? But no, it doesn't mean that at all. She could be in Australia looking for you right now for all we know. Why don't you have an address for her?'

'I never had an address for her,' he said. 'It was such a strange, unreal sort of period in Gallipoli and then in Egypt – me in hospital . . . we just thought there was time for all that. But all I have of her now is April Fool's Day.'

'So you're determined to go?'

He nodded. 'Too right. I'm determined to arrive at the Palm Court Lounge of the Langham Hotel at three o'clock.'

'Have you thought that she may feel differently now . . . I mean, the war plays havoc with our hearts and minds, doesn't it?'

'This date and the promise we made is all that has kept me going. I nearly lost my life in the August offensive at Gallipoli, and then all the battles in the desert campaign. Gaza, Es Salt; they were lucky escapes but I was injured at both. And each time I forced myself to be well because Claire would be waiting for me.'

'I know. I understand.'

'As for someone else . . .' He tried to shrug but couldn't. 'How? When?'

'Oh, doctors, officers . . . she's been in Europe, after all.'

He shook his dark head with confidence. 'Not my Claire. We're in love, we're going to marry. Besides, I can't think like that or I might as well give up.'

'Well, you're an inspiration, Trooper Wren. I hope your dream comes true. I'll see what I can do about getting you a lift to the station in a couple of days but you'll be on your own from then.'

———————

The previous week had been wet and miserable in Berkshire but today, March thirtieth, snow was predicted. Packing up at Charvil had kept Claire occupied, but only briefly, and had been far easier than she'd imagined. In her mind as she'd hugged Eugenie farewell it had felt as though she was facing a mountain to climb in starting to pack up her life.

However, the reality was that her life was now summarised by a few trinkets, some photos, some books and two suitcases of clothes. Standing in the small hallway of the tiny two-bedroom cottage, she looked at the luggage and the three fruit boxes of belongings and felt instantly embarrassed that this was all she could muster to speak for her quarter of a century on this earth. The old adage that a rolling stone gathers no moss rang loud in her thoughts. She had been on the move, skittering from place to place and deliberately not staying long enough to gather possessions, friends or even many happy memories. Her aunt had left her this cottage and yet it felt unlived in, unloved. She couldn't sell it but she didn't feel she belonged here either.

There were few people she could say she loved. And of the one she had loved the longest, her father, she had only his shaving kit left, the single physical memento his second wife had permitted her. No, Claire corrected herself – the shaving brush that was made of badger hair was the only memento she had chosen to take with her. The watch she had admired as a small child – the one she would have loved to own of his – Doreen had kept. And she could understand that now.

Claire reached for 'badger' now, touching it against her cheek the way her father had used to when she'd watched him lathering up for his morning shave. She caressed the white-tipped hairs of the brush and remembered the smell of the suds, her father's wide grin from beneath the lather and their shared laughter, which had stopped with the arrival of Doreen.

Claire realised now that she'd been running away from the lonely, often mirthless life she'd imposed on herself ever since. She baulked as the horror of this truth washed through her mind. Running away to England from Australia, then running away to war from her non-life in England. After losing Jamie she had fled from Egypt straight to the battlefront in Europe, taking more and more risks. Then she'd deliberately exposed herself to Spanish flu in a bid to run from the reality that there was no more war and only a lonely existence here in Charvil. And then there was Istanbul and its temptation. Had she failed the test? Somewhere in the back of her mind she'd almost convinced herself that the recent news was punishment for her emotional entanglement in Turkey.

And now she was running away again from Charvil in the hope that she could reinvent herself alongside Eugenie . . .

'But Eugenie is dying,' she murmured to the boxes in the hallway. 'Then what?' Claire asked into the silence of her loneliness. She pushed her hand into her pocket and found his identification tag. *J. W. Wren* its letters challenged. She raised the metal to her lips and kissed his name. 'Stop me running, Jamie. Come back to me.' As she made this plea snow began to flutter past her windows and paint her world white.

She took it to be a sign. A fresh start? Virgin white. Definitely a new life. And if she was going to keep her date in London, then she needed a new outfit; she would wear it like armour.

_____

Claire caught the bus into Reading the following morning with the vision of treating herself to an entire outfit, from new silk underwear to hat and gloves. It had been far too long since she'd splashed out and it wasn't as though she didn't have money. Claire was well aware that stepping into this calibre of salon would likely cost her a small fortune; she'd barely spent anything of her savings in years and it felt exciting and just a fraction wicked. Perhaps more than anything this was all part of turning the page and starting the new chapter she had promised.

'Good morning,' the woman said, approaching. She had to be fifty, Claire decided from the skin at her neck, but she looked amazing for those decades: so svelte, and of course her day dress was dazzling in its simplicity. 'Welcome, I am Jemima Dove, owner of the salon.'

Another bird name. Another sign. Claire grinned, extending a hand. 'Claire Nightingale.'

'Ah, what a beautiful name you have, but then I'm biased.' She smiled. Her make-up was immaculate, hair coiffed in perfect waves to her chin in the most up-to-date style, even though it was graphite grey. Claire felt positively dowdy standing before the elegant woman. 'What are you looking for today, Miss Nightingale?'

'Well, I'm looking for something special. I don't really know what it is yet, but I'll know it as soon as I see it.'

The woman smiled evenly and it crinkled the corners of her

eyes with amusement. 'Is it for an occasion?'

'Not really.' Claire fingered a silken gown in the window. 'Oh, this is beautiful.'

'To make an impression?'

Claire shook her head, moved on to the next outfit that was standing on a mannequin. It was a suit, appropriate for a day in the city.

'For someone special?'

She turned, let out a breath. 'Yes.'

'A man, I am presuming.'

'I haven't seen him for years.'

The woman shrugged. 'This is not so unusual. No need to be nervous – I suspect this gentleman would like you in a bed sheet.' It was meant as a compliment but the unintended innuendo made them both blush. 'Oh, do forgive me – that came out entirely wrong.'

'Call me Claire,' she said, 'and why don't you tell me what you would suggest?'

'First, over a cup of tea, you will tell me about this young man.'

Tea was briskly served by an assistant and while that occurred, Claire began to pour out her heart to a stranger she felt instantly at ease with, speaking about Jamie as though he were alive. It helped her mood immeasurably.

'. . . you see, look at you, it's so effortless,' she said, waving at the women's chic attire.

Jemima Dove's gaze narrowed. 'It looks that way, yes,' she said in a wry tone to make Claire smile. She put down her cup and saucer. 'Claire, this is a man you see yourself marrying, so I like the idea of you wearing a colour that reflects this, especially given the romantic nature of your reunion. Wait here. Let me show you a dress but be prepared to fall instantly for it. It will fit you too, so you won't have any excuse, I'm afraid.'

She whispered to her assistant standing nearby, who

disappeared and returned with a long muslin bag on a hanger. Jemima pointed to a railing and the woman hung the bag there and withdrew.

'Now,' she said, unbuttoning the bag. 'I defy you to say no.'

Claire gave a low gasp as a creamy-coloured dress emerged.

'We call this buttermilk,' Jemima explained, 'it's a play on ivory so there's that slightly bridal undertone to it, but it's definitely not white and it's too warm to be pure ivory.'

'It's magnificent. How much is —?'

'Do not talk about the cost yet. Try it on.' She gestured to the assistant. 'I have stockings and shoes to go with this. Just trust me.'

Within minutes Claire was staring at her reflection in the long mirror, barely recognising her glamorous self. The colour reminded her of the pale cornsilk she'd seen poking out from the husked cobs roasting on open fires in Alexandria on the day she and Rosie Parsons had gone in search of a chilled drink on a cool verandah, the same day she had met Eugenie. The dress whispered towards the most pastel of yellows and yet somehow remained firmly in the group of rich creams. Its sheen reflected in her hair and suited the hint of sun-bronze that her hands and face had caught in Turkey. Its waist was fashionably dropped, and stockinged ankles that would not have been shown a few years ago now brazenly peeped above her low-heeled navy and cream shoes.

'Yes?' Jemima said, coming up behind her.

Claire shifted her gaze to Jemima's reflection. 'Yes,' she murmured. 'This is what I want to wear.' She cocked her head to one side. 'I'm just imagining my old brown coat on top of this. It will spoil the look.'

'Absolutely – there is only one coat to wear with this dress.'

As if by magic, a new garment materialised from the shadows of the salon, carried by the assistant and placed in Jemima's hands. She eased Claire into the sleeves before reverently pulling the coat onto her shoulders. 'There we are . . . perfect, don't you think?'

Claire loved it on sight and as she pushed her hands into the sleeves, she refused to regret a single pound she was about to invest in the outfit. In direct contrast to her dress, the coat was ultramarine blue – the colour she remembered from Egypt, with a belt that clasped loosely at the small of her back and a neat but eye-catching collar of floral blue and that same buttermilk colour. It fastened asymmetrically across her left breast.

'The designer's name is Eden Valentine,' Miss Dove said. 'She only makes a few pieces to please herself.'

Claire nodded.

'I've urged her to open her own salon and do you know, there was something about her smile and the way she shook her head so modestly that leads me to believe she just might. Now, you look absolutely beautiful. And when you remove your coat in the Palm Court, Claire, he will not be able to mistake your intent.'

They both smiled. Claire's was tinged with sadness. If only Jemima Dove knew that Claire's handsome date was likely a ghost, alive only in her thoughts. Instead, she grinned. 'I do love it.'

And so she'd bought it all, including a tiny new ruched ivory handbag. Not at all suitable for winter's still stubborn hold, but irresistibly pretty all the same.

Claire prayed that Saint Valentine, so keenly associated with romantic love, was somehow imbued in the Eden Valentine outfit and that the love of her life was winging his way towards her.

24

I APRIL 1919

There had been a snowfall in London but the momentary collective delight of the soft flutter of flakes had quickly darkened to a bleak mood. It had only taken overnight for the city to turn glistening, crystalline snow to a sad grey sludge that had been swept into small drifts against buildings. People slipped and cursed while drivers took it slowly with their carriages for fear of the animals creating havoc if they fell prey to the icy conditions. It had been both the wettest spring for years and arguably the coldest, with no sign of the harsh weather letting up. Forecasters were predicting that the snow would keep falling through April, and Claire began to wonder how much more punishment the world could take after war, influenza, and now a bitter winter that should be thawing by now.

She shivered as she left the Oxford Circus Underground Station, pouring out with fellow commuters from the stale, fuggy warmth below surface to exit and brave the inclement British skies. Claire looked up. The sky was a void of blizzard white but mercifully inactive. She pulled her new coat's collar closer to her neck.

Dodging horses and buses, she set off up the wide street, heedless of the sounds of traffic, people or the smell of roasting chestnuts, with her mind focused on guiding the man she loved to her.

Jamie accepted help from another soldier to alight onto the Paddington Station platform from the train, which had suffered serious delays due to the snow. The queue for a hackney cab was so long and the London Underground couldn't lure him – despite its speed – after too many years spent in the trenches. Wishing for the luxury of being able to stick his hands deep in his overcoat pockets, he ignored the strange nervous signals from an arm no longer there and the protestations of the other one leaning on a crutch. He had worked hard to strengthen that side but it would take a year at least, the doctors had warned, before he was fully adept and strong enough. A scarf wrapped around his mouth helped to keep the wind chill down as he approached one of the hackney cab drivers.

'Afternoon, sir?'

He manoeuvred his chin free of the scarf and his breath billowed in front of him; he was already wearied from exertion. 'Can you tell me the way to the Langham Hotel, please?'

'I could, yes. But I have to chuckle first if you plan to walk.'

Jamie could see the man had wanted to say *if you plan to limp*. 'I do, mate. I can't wait in this long queue. There's a woman I have to meet and all the trains were delayed today so I'm running late. I made a promise. I can't risk missing her.'

The driver grinned. 'There's always a girl behind every drama. Where did you fight?'

'Gallipoli, Palestine, all through the Jordan region. Australian Light Horse.'

'Thought you had a funny accent but I'll forgive yer because you lads were brave. I didn't think any of your lot survived.'

Jamie nodded sadly and leaned down harder on the crutch. 'Most of us didn't. Near enough a generation of fine blokes gone, left behind in the scrub of southern Turkey, but you lost just as many.'

The man nodded. 'Two of my sons are buried in France.'

'I'm sorry to hear that.'

The fellow grunted, shifted the burning cigarette that clung to the corner of his mouth and pointed. 'Head down 'ere and stay north. You're making for Hyde Park, all right?'

Jamie nodded.

'Get onto the Edgeware Road and before you reach Marble Arch, turn left onto Seymour and at the top of that road as soon as you see Regent Street loomin', you turn left onto it – the hotel is right there, opposite All Souls Church in Langham Place. If I tell you any more you'll get confused. It's more than two miles away even if you don't get lost. My advice is 'op on a bus if you can.' He grinned at his unintentional jest and coughed. 'Or flag down a ride. But anywhere is easier than 'ere.'

'Thanks, mate. I'll find it.' Jamie turned back into the biting cold. His dexterity with the crutch meant his speed had improved even if his strength was wanting, but the snow would hinder him. He was going to be late, no matter how fast he tried to get there.

'Women,' the hackney cab driver muttered as he flicked his cigarette butt away, lifted the reins and clicked at the horse to move on into traffic beyond the forecourt of busy Paddington Station.

Rifki Shahin prided himself on his ordered mind that fed into an ordered life; within its safe cocoon was protection from most emotional impact. Being forced to give up Sehr when love made it feel as though nothing else mattered had cooled his approach to life, as did having to marry a woman he shared no connection with. Her shrewish ways had taught him how to bury his romantic nature and hide in his chilled world of numbers, money, ambition. Losing his only son had seemed predictable, given the way his life had moved from the hot-blooded years of his teens to the slow decline into his seemingly cold-hearted acceptance of the misery of a life without romantic love.

Until the golden presence of Claire Nightingale had arrived to warm up his existence, Rifki Shahin had not imagined his pulse would ever quicken again. The depth of his loss when she departed left his emotions in tatters. He would find himself trembling in the bathrooms of his university mid-tutorial, or weeping silently in his large, lonely house. He had taken to lying down in Açar's bed with his son's prayer book clutched to his chest, dry sobs his only companion as he drifted into unhappy sleep. And it was Claire who had haunted those fitful hours of the night . . . her touch against his cheek, her wry smile, teasing words. That sad farewell he relived over in his mind repeatedly. If only he had kissed her. If only he had made her understand that she had unlocked the door to his desire. If only he had held on to her somehow . . .

In a different world, she had said. Claire had as good as admitted that he had ignited a longing in her too. When the invitation had come through for a sabbatical at King's College, London – no doubt promoted strongly by Professor Leavers – he had surprised himself by accepting immediately: no time to consider or calculate. It was the teenage Rifki, spontaneous and driven by his heart. It would put him closer to Claire. Perhaps her world could be different?

He would know soon enough, for today was the day that Claire hoped to be reunited with Wren. If the Australian was indeed dead, then maybe Claire, in time, would consider him. Rifki needed to know if the Australian soldier turned up – and if he didn't, then he might make another approach to the woman consuming his thoughts. If the soldier kept their long-promised date, then Rifki would not trouble the couple again. He was ashamed to acknowledge that he had silently cast out his desire, clutching his son's precious prayer book, that James Wren did not make it to the arranged rendezvous.

It was a bitter English afternoon and Rifki, dressed in the preferred dark suit of Londoners, had replaced the increasingly defunct fez for a homburg and regarded himself in the mirror of the main foyer of his university building. He checked his watch. He planned to arrive by two-thirty. It was one-fifty now and that gave him plenty of time to walk from the university to the Langham.

Shahin stepped out of the neo-classical, grey-stoned building of the embankment entrance of King's College that overlooked the Thames, and with an optimistic set to his features he began a brisk walk towards Drury Lane, heading north towards Oxford Street, Regent Street and the rendezvous in Portland Place.

———

Claire once again stood with her back to the Church of All Souls and faced the towering prospect of the golden-coloured stone of the Langham Hotel that today in the dreary weather appeared a dull bronze. She took a slow, deep breath to steady herself before adjusting her coat so it sat absolutely perfectly over her angular shoulders and glided across the road, avoiding the ice. She skipped up the shallow marble stairs and smiled at the doorman rising from a polite bow.

'Good afternoon, miss.'

'Afternoon.'

He reached to open the door. 'Let's get you in from the chill.'

'Thank you.' She smiled again, and tiptoed up the six marble steps to the grand foyer she recalled from her childhood and remembered her aunt explaining that the vast, white-tiled corridors were built wide enough to take a horse and carriage.

Mind you, darling, in terms of its practicality, what that really meant is that two ladies in voluminous crinolines could pass each other in the corridor without getting trapped.

The notion had amused her as a child and she remembered now how she had spluttered over her elderberry cordial when her aunt had recalled that snippet. But Claire was too nervous, too churned up, to be amused now. She slipped back her sleeve to look at her watch. Unbeknownst to her, one of her admirers had already arrived early, the other running late. Her timing was immaculate as always. It was nearing ten to three.

'Twelve minutes,' she muttered.

'Pardon, miss, can I help you?' one of the pageboys offered. He was dressed in the distinctive maroon uniform with polished brass buttons and somewhere at the back of her mind a thought bubbled and burst to consciousness that she was glad this sweet-faced youth had not been sent to war. If he'd been born just a year earlier she may well have attended to him in Europe or Turkey.

'I . . . er, I'm going to the Palm Court,' she replied.

He smiled, nodding to where she should head. 'Straight fru, miss.'

She already knew where it was but she smiled politely at where he pointed. 'Thank you, I might sit in the lobby a while and wait for my friend.'

'Of course,' he said and gestured to a dark velvet sofa positioned against the rich cream walls, which were gilded, and beneath an enormous silk hanging against exquisite hand-painted wallpaper. A chandelier featuring pale-pink glass shades sent a soft rose light upon her from beneath the tall ceiling with its massive detailed architraves. Exquisite plasterwork of wreaths and trailing roses danced beneath the architraves and framed decorative archways, beyond which stood Corinthian-style columns, which made her think instantly of the Column of the Goths and, of course, Rifki Shahin. She banished that memory although she knew she must walk past those columns shortly if she was going to meet Jamie at the appointed place.

No less than fifteen-thousand yards of Persian carpet has been laid in this glorious building . . . She could hear the echo of her aunt's words and had to admit that, looking at this vestibule alone, she could imagine that every floor would be palatial throughout the hotel, its tiles softened by exotic carpets. She felt as though people were watching her too closely when another page asked if he could fetch her anything.

She declined with a smile, removing herself to a quieter wing of the hotel known as the Fernery. She didn't want to go into the Palm Court too early and then be seated alone for long. Although she couldn't see Jamie arrive from this vantage, she could kill off some minutes and hope that he magically appeared and found his way to the Palm Court in the interim. She sat straight-backed in the conservatory on a plush couch, trying not to count off the minutes, the toes of her shoes just touching the panel of deep-red carpet that ran the length of this light-filled glass space. It was much cooler here but the bright green of the ferns gave it a jolly atmosphere and she was at last alone with her thoughts.

Not for long, though. She tried not to sigh when a voice interrupted her quiet.

'Are you all right, Miss . . .?'

'Nightingale,' she answered as a man drifted up. He was dressed formally but not in a uniform.

'I am the desk manager,' he said. 'Can I assist in any way? We do have a glorious drawing room if you would like to make yourself comfortable? It is rather cool and lonely in here at this time of year.'

She explained that she was simply waiting to meet a friend. 'I'm finding it rather entrancing waiting here, if that is permitted.'

'Oh my word, yes. Yes, of course,' he said. 'It's certainly a spot to take a fine aspect of the comings and goings of our grand hotel, as was the, er . . . lobby. Um, have you visited previously?'

'As a child, yes.'

'Well, although I wouldn't for a moment suggest you are much older, Miss Nightingale,' he charmed, his moustache twitching with enjoyment of his perceived flair for flirtation, 'we have made many changes to the hotel in the last decade or so.'

She smiled, not at all interested in anything this man had to say to her, but he seemed determined to keep her company. They blinked at each other as he finally finished his soliloquy. Claire had nothing to say to his meanderings; for all of his grandiose sentiments, her impression was that the hotel looked as though it had languished through the war years, which was understandable, and now appeared in need of refreshment. She didn't think she'd like to open that discussion with him, though, and instead broke the awkward pause by glancing at her watch again. She had played this scene over in her mind so many times. Claire wanted to walk into the Palm Court and feel that electrifying moment when their gazes met across the room. She didn't want to spoil that daydream – which she was sure had kept her alive at times – from being tarnished or changed. She wanted it to unfold as she'd envisaged. There were just another two minutes to go before she could let it play out and she would know whether Jamie was alive and her life complete. However, the thought crossed her mind that the manager might think she was an undesirable escort. And it now occurred that he might attribute any number of meanings to her words that she was waiting for a friend. Anxiety trilled through her.

'Perhaps I should take my table in the Palm Court. My guest,' she was careful to say, 'should be arriving any moment now.'

He bowed, even clicking his heels gently. 'Let me walk with you.'

'Thank you,' she said, and rose gracefully as she beamed him a smile and let him accompany her back into the hotel foyer. Claire glanced over her shoulder, hoping to glimpse a familiar figure, but the lobby, though busy with people with somewhere to go, was empty of Jamie.

She swallowed her disappointment and moved towards the entrance of the Palm Court where chamber music had recently struck up. 'I can find my own way,' she murmured and her companion beamed her a final smile and departed. Claire stepped past the alabaster-white columns to where the fronds of palms looked as though they were opening their hands in welcome to her. Dark shiny fingers trembled in the gust of stirred air that the gleaming silver-and-gold glass doors made as another two page boys opened them for her entry.

She could smell the overriding sweetness of sugar from the baking cakes and pastries mingling with floral scents of ladies' perfume, gentlemen's pomade and the sulfurous aroma of boiled egg that wafted out of nowhere.

'Good afternoon,' the *maître d'* said.

'Er, yes, I'm Miss Nightingale. I do hope you have a table. I . . . er, didn't think to reserve one.'

'A table for two, Miss Nightingale?'

'Please.' She looked around hopefully, scanning desperately in case Jamie had already arrived and was waiting eagerly for his first glimpse of her. 'Unless of course, he's already here,' she added, already knowing it was an empty hope. The only lone gentleman was dressed in a day suit and buried behind a large newspaper near the string quartet. She could only see his hands around the edges of the broadsheet. Jamie would be looking for her, not lost in the news headlines of the day.

The string quartet moved seamlessly into some bright Vivaldi and soft laughter from the other patrons mocked her mood.

'Follow me,' he said, with effortless charm.

He showed her towards another velvet chair – a club chair, this time, of pale green at a small table in the corner of the room alongside another matching chair. This was definitely a quiet table for two and at the other end of the room to the orchestra. She trod softly across the thick Persian rugs and caught smatterings of chatter.

'Darling, are we going to Maidenhead this summer for Ascot Sunday?'

She walked past them all and appreciated the quiet niche where she now had a view of the length of the room, especially its doors, which she positioned herself to focus on.

'Thank you, this is perfect,' she said with a sigh of relief.

'Shall I send a waiter over once your guest has arrived?'

'Thank you, yes.'

Rifki had arrived early as he'd planned and seated himself in the Palm Court near the quartet, believing that would be the least popular end of the chamber. He had presumed correctly. He was exceptionally mindful of his dark features arousing suspicions given that Britain had been at war in Turkey just a few moons ago. But he was dressed as if he'd stepped out of a Savile Row salon and presented no obvious interest so long as he remained as unobtrusive as possible.

His tea had been served and he was munching on the strangest of food called sandwiches when he'd seen the flash of golden hair as Claire arrived. He'd had his newspaper ready to hide behind but forgot to do so, mesmerised by the sight of her again, and he only managed to flick it up in time as she had naturally begun to scan the room. He'd stopped chewing, stopped breathing momentarily, and was sure it was only luck that the *maître d'* had led her in the opposite direction. Rifki watched her walk, straight-backed, to an almost secretive table at the other end of the room. She couldn't have been placed further away from him.

Swallowing at last, Rifki flapped his broadsheet again and disappeared behind it. The temptation to watch her every move was tugging at him but he remained hidden, stealing an odd glance around the side of his newspaper every now and then. He couldn't ignore the resplendent afternoon tea or it may have attracted the attention of the staff, so he reached for his tea, which was instantly flavourless. All he could taste suddenly was sage *çay* to the sounds of an Istanbul tea garden and the thrilling memory of accidentally touching Claire Nightingale.

Conversations pressed in on her.

'Really, dear? Five years, is it? Yes, of course, that's right, it *was* Cambridge. Oh well, they say we'll have a boat race next year. Here's to the Dark Blues, eh?'

The summer sporting season did seem to be on the minds of the wealthy, Claire decided. 'Thank heavens we'll have the tennis championship back on this year,' one woman bleated as a towering silver tiered tray laden with food arrived to soothe her. Talk of the Chelsea Flower Show also, she noted, occupied much of the nearby trio of women and their conversation.

It all felt alien to her. She had nothing in common with any of these well-heeled people and, though she knew it was deeply unfair to think this way, she wanted to yell at them that the end of the Great War was only months behind them. Millions dead. Thousands still dying as a result. Countless numbers of broken people and damaged lives. Surely talk of who might win the Derby this year was irrelevant? Instead she checked her watch again, knowing that she was on edge but that her well-practised calm appearance meant that no one else could guess her tribulations, and if anything she should admire the fact that these people – who had surely lost sons, brothers, fathers – were getting on with life: putting on a brave face and relentlessly going forward.

If Jamie was coming, he was now running late by six minutes, she realised, but Claire waited, as silent and still as one of the columns around the Palm Court, and hoped she appeared as unobtrusive. His transport could have been held up. Another twenty minutes cruelly passed her until she wanted to stand up and scream her fears to all the people around her, absorbed by their discussions on Wimbledon or this year's Deb ball. Her trauma, she knew, didn't show but she was tempted to stand and flee until the *maître d'* chose that moment to return with a soft glance of apology.

'The traffic, I hear, is turning hostile and to add to the congestion it's begun raining. No doubt people are running late all over London,' he said kindly as if answering a query. 'Let me organise a pot of tea for you, while you wait for your companion.'

'That would be lovely,' Claire replied, surprised by her outward composure but knowing she needed to occupy her hands, distract herself from her watch and her nervousness.

'What is your pleasure, Miss?'

She looked back at him, lost for a moment for what to order.

He immediately helped out. 'The second flush Darjeeling is most fine. The quintessential tea for a cool afternoon.'

She smiled and played along, determined not to be po-faced. 'And yet I am always persuaded by the Nilgiri Frost,' she said.

He beamed. 'Exceptional choice: ever-so-slightly grassy and with a fresh, tart apple finish.'

'Delicious. Thank you.'

The paraphernalia of tea arrived in a clinking array of fine silver and exquisite porcelain featuring an exotic bird. Claire could see light passing through the near-transparent crockery when it was laid out expertly, followed by the silver teapot and its accompanying finery. The teapot's handle was tied with a starched white napkin so that neither she nor her attendant might inadvertently burn their fingers, and in that moment she was reminded of an Istanbul tea garden, the salty smell of the Bosphorus lapping below, the cry of gulls, the purr of a cat and – before she could stop herself – a dark-eyed man who seemed entirely unaware of his charisma. But these thoughts were chased away by memories of a man with eyes the colour of woodland and his effortlessly bright smile through his pain of being wounded and robbed of his best mate. She remembered how she had given him her tea that day and his boyish delight at tasting sugar in it. Jamie, and his pleasure in the simple treats of life and uncomplicated way, was all she wanted.

In another life . . . the remembered words rode in on the scent of the steaming pot but it was the smell of antiseptic she tasted, remembering that precious first kiss with Jamie. He would come. She had to believe it. She had to trust him. He'd been held up. Traffic, rain; it was all conspiring to test them, *but he would come*.

She blinked as a waitress repeated her request.

'The tea has drawn, Miss. Shall I pour?' the young waitress asked again in a sweet voice.

'Please.'

'Lemon or milk?'

'Milk,' she answered without hesitation. After years of doing without, fresh milk in her tea felt luxurious and decadent.

'One lump?' the girl said, reaching for the tongs.

'Smallest one you can find,' Claire replied.

The doors swung back and her attention was caught, but it was two women strolling in laughing, arm in arm. They were immaculately dressed in fur-collared coats that slipped easily from their shoulders to reveal gorgeous mid-season garb of rich, bright colours and hinted towards their obvious desire to cast off winter and move into pastels and florals.

Claire bit her lip with disappointment. She thanked the waitress and began stirring her tea soundlessly as she had been taught. To keep occupied and distracted she reached for the menu but didn't read it; it lay redundant in her lap and it was only now she realised she hadn't yet removed her gloves. She spent another few mindless seconds picking those off and unpinning her hat. Claire regarded her tea, could smell the scent of the brew from the gentle steam from her cup and politely took her first sip of Nilgiri Frost.

The limping man had to lean against a lamppost to check his watch and anyone glancing at him might have seen his look of horror and guessed he was drastically late for an appointment. Jamie couldn't run, he could barely hurry with his new lopsided gait and even though the air felt frosty to breathe, he could feel his face had become moist from his exertion. He did his best to dodge the shoppers, sometimes needing to veer clumsily into the road and take care from the pandemonium of horses dragging their carriages and the loud call of drivers, their passengers talking, animals braying. It was like the press of war again . . . and just as alien after so long in the desert or quiet hospital wards.

He finally drew level with the five-storey, palatial Waring & Gillow furniture store on Oxford Street – hard to miss with its bronze façade and fussy white stonework. Why today of all days was everything, including the elements, against him? He reached the mammoth frontage of 'the Richly Stocked Dress and Drapery Warehouse' of the Peter Robinson department store that ran the length of the street to the corner and hurriedly limped around it into Regent Street, just missing hurtling into a corpulent woman leading two poodles with jewelled collars. She said something churlish but, although he had no spare arm to lift his hat, he muttered his apology and was already moving past her.

Among the abundance of advertising messages desperate for his attention – from Pears soapmakers to Piggott & Company dyes and furniture cleaners – he could finally see frontage of the Langham Hotel towering in the distance. He was nearly there. What should have taken him half an hour had taken well over an hour. Had she turned up? Would she still be there, waiting inside for him? Maybe he should have waited and tried to hail a taxi or, better still, gone to the general post office and asked for someone to call the hotel, but that would all have taken precious time . . . time he did not have. Time leaking away from his lifeline of Claire like blood from his body, killing him with each passing second he wasted not getting to the Langham as he'd promised her he would all those years ago. *Be there, Claire*, he begged the universe. *Wait for me.*

As he limped, trying to hurry, he distracted himself by imagining what he would he say when he saw her.

What would she say?

It all seemed deeply romantic, which was the whole point, he supposed. He paused briefly in the doorway of Wayre's, one of the numerous furriers that had set up shop nearby to the fashionable and huge hotel, to draw a breath. He'd pushed himself too hard for that last half mile. The sign above him read 'Grand Depot for Rich Furs and Seal Skin Jackets'. Only Langham guests, surely, could afford those. He leaned against the shopfront, took another deep lungful of London's moist air, pulled up the collar of his coat – because he couldn't use a brolly against the freshly falling rain – and ducked out of number 249. He would be there in minutes, so long as the rain and snow didn't conspire against him.

His heart began to hammer afresh but not from exertion. Now the shortened breath and tightness in his chest was about Claire. Had she stayed true to their promise and trusted that no German, no bomb, no sniper, no distance, no injury would keep him from her on this day?

Be there, Claire, he repeated silently in his mind as a mantra to distract him from each increasingly painful step.

———

Rifki glanced at his watch. It was now ten minutes shy of four o'clock. The diners had thinned but not enough to make the room feel empty and the quartet played gaily on. He peeped around the newspaper, having not read anything but a single headline repeatedly since he'd opened it. He could not even remember what that headline actually said. He knew it was about war reparations from Germany that would cripple the country. He didn't care; Germany had dragged his country into a war it didn't win and with its surge for power it had taken his son with it to his death.

Rifki pilfered another sly look at Claire. She was far prettier than the sweet waltz being delivered by the accomplished musicians nearby. She was far prettier than any woman in the room . . . in fact, prettier than any of the pretty women he had ever been lucky enough to know, except Sehr perhaps. But they were night and day. Sehr so dark and exotic, with that husky laugh and provocative manner, while Claire Nightingale was dazzling, like bright sunshine in his life that could throw light on his bleakness, untangle his complexities and make life sound straightforward. If she had taught him anything, it was that a life no matter how successful was unfulfilled without love in it: love for family, romantic love and a love for life. He knew she had discovered this the hard way too but she had urged him not to stand back from life as he had been but to confront it with all of its shadows and highlights. That's what he was trying to do now, he assured himself . . . confront what he thought he most wanted out of life . . . her.

And maybe his new approach was going to be put to the test for the time was now closer to four o'clock than was surely comfortable for Claire. He knew he should disappear behind the broadsheet but he could see the anxiety deepening in her expression, was attuned to her growing acceptance that James Wren was not going to keep this date, which she had clung to like a life raft in the ocean of her sorrows.

He thought he would feel a tremor of elation at her sad expression. Instead he felt a deep and disappointed dismay that anyone would let her down in this way. If he were that blessed soldier, no injury or hospital would keep him from her . . . only death would halt his path to her heart.

Are you dead, Jamie Wren? he asked silently into the jolly atmosphere. *Be dead, Wren, and let me live again.*

———————

Claire had not given up hope despite having the time to read closely the entire menu. Today's afternoon tea offered a range of delicate fingers of creamy hen's egg and cress sandwiches, elegant triangles of minted cucumber, and neat quarters of chicken with celery, apple and walnuts. For fish lovers there was even a sandwich of Scottish smoked salmon with a cauliflower mousse. It read too good to be true given the austerity of the war years. Fluffy still-warm scones were on the menu too, to be served with the richest of Devonshire clotted cream and thick blackberry jam with all the sweetness of late summer held within its jewel-like, shiny darkness. And then there were the cakes. Her gaze had followed one towering tiered stand of what could only be described as *bijoux*. They were indeed like oversized jewels of pink icing, yellow confectioner's custard, chocolate fancies and mouthwatering treats of tiny lemon tarts dusted with sugar or jellied tarts of hibiscus and blackcurrant, layered slices of vanilla sponge with cream and strawberry conserve oozing within, and thick sticks of shortbread with crystals of sugar glistening on top. Claire knew she'd held her breath as she watched this delicious fare being served in all of its decadence and her guilt intensified. She tempered it with her memory of Istanbul and the overwhelming number of treats that were served up on platters in the hammam. They were emerging from the privations of war too but managed to put together a feast to make her eyes bulge and her belly groan.

This was a time of celebration, she had to admit. The war was finished. The world had to look forward despite all of the destruction and desolation in the hearts of those who had lost their loved ones. She had to embrace this belief and if Jamie was not coming today, then she must show the courage that others had and take life forward, keeping her promise to herself.

She glanced up with painful understanding that she was being called upon to keep that promise to herself now. *Accept it*, she thought, bitterness finally breaking through. *Jamie is not coming*. The letters had not lied. He had died in the desert of the Middle East, no doubt charging courageously on a horse he loved that was just as brave as he. Jamie was a hero but even heroes died in war. His name would go down with the millions of others killed in action and no amount of wishing or daydreaming could change the fact he was not coming for her today.

It was time to go. She checked her watch. Four o'clock. She raised a finger, caught the eye of the *maître d'* and he understood. She stood, accepted help with her coat, returned gloves to hands, hat to head and paid her bill with a well-constructed smile on the mask she'd contrived to hide her anguish. She demanded of herself that she retain her composure and once out of the hotel she could give in to loss fully, but for now, her nurse's training served her valiantly and she betrayed no obvious sign of unravelling.

Deliberately keeping her eyes lowered as best she could, Claire blocked out her surrounds and didn't see the gentleman tucked away in a corner by the musicians signal for the bill. She didn't notice that when he stood to full height he caught the attention of several attractive women in the Palm Court. She was entirely unaware that he had eyes only for her as he struggled to neatly fold the newspaper beneath his arm, his gaze focused on where she was smiling at the *maître d'* as he opened the door to usher her out.

Once clear of the Palm Court, Claire hurried across the floor of the lobby, hoping she didn't fall on the marble. She was aware of the queue of pages again but didn't look left or right as she skipped down the stairs and out into the freezing afternoon air of London.

It was raining heavily and she quickly opened her umbrella, blocking out everyone and everything but the ground she stared at, which was blurred by her tears that joined the raindrops on the pavement running away towards the London drains. She turned her back on the hotel and hurried towards a side street. She didn't look up to see the one-armed man limping into Portland Place, his gaze fixed only on the entrance of the hotel.

Claire hit her stride, watching for ice, but dodging immediately out of sight of Regent Street, running down various side roads, not caring where she ended up so long as she could outrun her sorrow and the building that had come to represent so much of the past, present and future to her. It was no longer her happy place and she could not get away from it fast enough.

———————

Rifki had sensed her decision before she acted upon it, but it had still come as a shock to surreptitiously watch her gather up her hat, gloves and pain and leave. She stood gracefully, looking no one in the eye, least of all the gentleman in charge, who moved quickly to help her on with her coat.

He too had to move fast now if he was to catch her or he may lose her completely. He quickly folded up his newspaper, struggling slightly and marvelling at how adept the English were at this particular action. He couldn't take his gaze from Claire, even as he caught the notice of the waitress, or when he stood and reached for his homburg. He watched her every move as she swept from the room. She was gone and she was in a hurry.

Claire was gone! He was caught in a dawning of enlightenment and felt momentarily paralysed. She had accepted her soldier was dead. Claire might be available to him now: not immediately, but surely she would be delighted to see him and he could soothe away the sorrows, help her to accept what had surely been the inevitable and ultimately . . . just maybe . . . examine her admission again of *in another lifetime*. This was another lifetime opening up, wasn't it? She was free to consider him now.

Move, Rifki, he urged, *chase her; don't lose her again*. His thoughts scattered as to what he would say when he caught up with her but he knew he'd think of something. As he looked around to check he'd left nothing of his behind, the *maître d'* arrived at his table to halt him. Rifki blinked at the delay.

'Good afternoon, sir, how was your afternoon tea?'

Rifki glanced at the mostly untouched spread. 'Forgive me,' he admitted, embarrassed. 'It was more than I could eat alone.'

'But your tea is hardly sipped. Please, let me refresh the pot. And perhaps we can clear away some of the food, leave you a couple of the biscuits, or one of the sandwiches if you find the full presentation too much.' Rifki did not eat bread with mashed-up egg. It tasted like the food one fed an infant, but he smiled politely as he glanced at the door. She would have already left the hotel premises by now, be walking down Regent Street, or perhaps had swung towards Portland Place. How would he find her? He took a slow breath and stared at the kind man who was still talking. 'I understand completely. After all the limitations of the war, sir, all this colour and largesse can be overwhelming.'

'No, truly,' Rifki said, trying not to show his agitation but certain it was revealed in the way his voice was calm but firm, his thoughts racing on how he would find her. 'I must go. It has been a pleasure and next time I promise to come with a better appetite.'

The man nodded a bow in acquiescence. 'In that case, sir, let me have this all cleared away and please follow me so we can get you on your way.'

'Your receipt, sir, thank you,' the *maître d'* said a minute later, graciously handing him the folded paper with a courteous bow of the head. 'Ah, here's your coat, sir, thank you, Amanda.'

Jamie had finally arrived at the Langham and taken a few moments to catch his breath, awkwardly wipe his face dry with his handkerchief and gather his thoughts. He didn't want to arrive looking panicked. He suspected a man in uniform, especially an officer, would draw a smile and a grateful nod. A porter touched his hat and the doorman reached quickly for the handle to swing the entrance open to him as he was welcomed warmly.

'Hope it's good to be back, sir?' he enquired politely.

He grinned. 'First time to the hotel, I'll admit, but my oath it's good to be back in peacetime.'

The doorman nodded. 'Welcome to the Langham Hotel, sir.'

One of the pages grinned. 'Love your fevver, sir,' he said, pointing to his hat, which he now pulled off for good manners.

He threw the youngster a wink. 'Only the Australian Light Horse wears these,' he said, touching the feather with reverence. 'Too many who wore them didn't get home.'

'Glad you made it, sir.'

'Where's the Palm Court?' he asked, feeling a buzz of excitement erupt in his belly.

'Straight fru, sir. Can't miss it. Follow the palms. Hope she loves you, sir,' he added cheekily, making a calculated guess.

He grinned. 'I'm going to marry her today.'

'Blimey, sir! I hope she knows. I didn't see no bride walkin' in, but there have been some beautiful ladies taking afternoon tea today. Good luck, sir,' the messenger boy called to him.

'Won't need it. If she's here waiting, I know she'll say yes.' He winked again and then he was hurrying through the conveniently opening glass doors, unaware of pushing past a debonair, slightly swarthy gentleman into the Court where a string quartet was playing beautiful chamber music. He recognised it as Chopin from his family's collection of music sheets – it was a pretty waltz, which seemed appropriate as he scanned the elegant room for a glimpse of the woman he loved.

―――――――

Rifki, his thoughts scrambled, had just shrugged on his coat with help from the *maître d'*.

'With you in a moment, sir,' the man said over Rifki's shoulder to someone behind who had just entered. 'Come again, sir.'

'I will,' he said and, accepting his hat from the man, he turned and was confronted by the sight of a wounded soldier: a handsome, eager Australian if he wasn't mistaken about the uniform.

A mixture of visceral responses erupted like lava from the pit of his belly. First, the hot anger of defeat blazed through him, but just as quickly it turned to despair, floating through his mind as hope turned to ashes that emerged as bitter saliva in his suddenly dry throat. Yet even though his heart felt as though it were sinking so fast the sensation made him catch his breath inwardly, the thought of Claire's faith being rewarded brought him an unexpected smile, which was – at least – timely. 'James Wren?' he forced out, not much more than a whisper as the soldier turned towards him in surprise.

25

Rifki regarded the man who was unwittingly dismantling his hopes with his easy smile and heroic empty sleeve. He'd guided the limping, damaged soldier to an armchair in the drawing room so they could talk without too many observers while the young man had given a torrent of explanation for his lateness, beginning that morning with a car that broke down on its way to the station and then a train needing repairs that held up every train behind it. Rifki had let it flow but tuned out the man's arrival into crowded London, his slowness on the crutch he was still learning to manoeuvre, the queues for taxis, the crowded streets, the weather! He understood the man's anxiety and it gave him some precious moments to gather up his own hurts. He looked past the despicably handsome presence of Wren that even a missing arm couldn't spoil, and allowed his conscience to ask its inevitable question: *Will you tell him?*

'Were you sharing tea with her?' Wren asked.

He blinked, coming out of his thoughts. 'Er, no. She didn't even know I was here.'

Jamie frowned and Rifki drew a slow breath as he decided to skirt the truth. 'I was to meet another professor here this afternoon. It seems both of you have been beset by weather woes, Mr Wren. He didn't make our appointment either.'

He could imagine all the wheels turning in Wren's mind and was ready for the next question. 'But how do you know Claire?'

'I will tell you everything, but can I offer you anything first? You look fatigued.'

Wren shook his head. 'Just tell me what you know . . . quickly, please. I have to find her.'

Rifki began an abridged version of events and with each carefully chosen sentence he felt his bonds to Claire loosen like a ship being cast away from its moorings. He settled deeper into his armchair.

'You are Açar's father?' Jamie murmured, his expression filled with disbelief. Rifki watched the young man push his hand through hair that was still damp from the inclement weather. Inadvertently he messed the formerly neatly parted and combed style but that only gave him a rakish quality. Wren was staring past him, frowning, trying to make sense of what he'd just been told. 'How can you be here? I don't understand.' He shook his head, perplexed. 'Açar's father?'

Rifki nodded. 'Let me explain.' He told him about the opportunity to study and teach in London and of Claire's visit to Istanbul. 'This is how I know your name.' He shrugged. 'I couldn't imagine you to be anyone but the James Wren that Claire had told me about. I could hardly not introduce myself. Fate is clearly enjoying playing with our lives, Mr Wren. I am aware that I owe you my heartfelt thanks for befriending my son, accepting the responsibility of his letter and prayer book, and to Claire, of course, for returning them to us. My family became most fond of her.'

'Did you know she'd be here today?' Something flickered in Wren's gaze but it was gone in a heartbeat.

'I suppose I did, but it was also one of life's odd coincidences as my colleague chose the venue,' he lied. 'I didn't see her until she was leaving.' He hoped he'd convinced the light horseman in his dashing uniform, who made him feel so plain by comparison.

Wren studied him in a brief hesitation before smiling disarmingly. 'I'm glad she did what she did for your family . . . and for you.'

Rifki looked up sharply.

'I mean, I would like to think that someone would do that for my father. Açar was sad when he and I met that day. He wanted to tell you how much he loved you.'

Rifki's breath felt trapped as the old wound reopened inside and bled. He didn't know what to say.

'I think you're right about fate. It has a sense of humour today, pushing us all around like little chess pieces. I'm a bit confused but I'm glad we met, Mr Shahin.' Jamie smiled crookedly. He struggled to stand and Rifki wanted to help but suspected the soldier preferred to help himself. 'But now I have to find Claire,' he murmured.

Rifki swallowed his yearning. She was no longer his. No matter what his desperate thoughts plotted for preserving Claire for himself none of it felt right, certainly not taking advantage of this courageous soldier – his enemy once, perhaps, but now simply his rival for a woman who was never his to contest. If there was to be any nobility in his clandestine activity, it should show itself right now; he needed to be honourable. *Will you tell him?* his conscience demanded, and he hovered between wishing to keep Claire and knowing he could not.

'I may know where you might find her,' he said, letting the words slip before he could wrestle them back.

Jamie's expression brightened immediately. He shifted awkwardly to face Rifki square on. 'Really? Please, Mr Shahin, tell me now. The only thing that kept me alive all these years was dreaming of Claire.'

'I understand,' he said softly. 'She told me that she was returning to a friend. I believe her name is Eugenie Lester. She lives in a place called Radlett.' He shrugged.

'Loom Lane,' Jamie breathed in wonder. 'I remember that now.'

Rifki felt his throat clogging with agonising disappointment. 'Good luck, James Wren. She told me all about you and my impression is that Claire is single-minded in her affection for you. You are a lucky man.'

'I'd shake your hand if I could, Mr Shahin, but thank you.'

'*Bir şey değil*,' he said with a soft smile and yet it wasn't nothing, it was everything, damn him! He had given Jamie Wren everything that mattered in this moment.

'Perhaps we could meet again,' Jamie said, standing awkwardly.

'Perhaps, yes,' Rifki replied. He looked down momentarily, cleared his throat of its emotional pain and then fixed Wren with a soft smile. 'Claire knows where she can contact our family in Istanbul. You are always welcome and you both have our family's gratitude.'

Jamie nodded and again Rifki saw a sense of knowing flash in his expression as though he was aware of the struggle that Rifki had faced and understood honour had won out. 'To peace,' he said, before turning and limping out of the drawing room, pushing away from Shahin towards the pull of Claire.

———————

She'd stopped running and knew this only because she wasn't breathing hard from exertion. She had walked through that time without conscious thought; heaven only knew how she'd avoided being trampled by horses or jostling pedestrians. Now she came back to herself and took note of her surrounds, realising with surprise that she was standing in the Burlington Arcade behind Bond Street and off Piccadilly. She had been staring, unseeing, into the window of H.P. Truefitt, the only American shaving parlour in London. The tall, glazed arcade with its posh shopfronts let in no light, she realised, because it had already become dark outside and shops were shutting up around her, including this magnificently appointed saloon that was offering the gentleman everything from shaving, hair dressing and manicures to hats and hosiery.

She turned away and noticed one of the adventurous, and to her mind courageous, women who had opened her own salon. This one was selling millinery and she was just beginning to roll down shutters and lock up for the day too. 'Are you all right?' she asked Claire over a shoulder.

'Yes,' she replied, glad to have a steady voice. 'Just taking some air for a headache.'

'This cold will make it worse, miss. Head home, they're saying more snow is on the way. I'm lucky, I live upstairs with my stock,' she smiled with a shrug, 'but your outfit is not stout enough to withstand the night weather.'

She nodded with a sad smile and one of the Burlington's Beadles now approached. He'd obviously been watching her from his armchair positioned at the end of the arcade. She knew his job was to ensure the peace and calm was kept within the arcade; Beadles had been patrolling the arcade since it had first been built by Lord Cavendish.

The beadle waddled closer in his gold braided uniform and Claire could hear the squeak of his polished boots on the tiled floor.

'Miss . . . are you well?'

'I'm fine, thank you.'

'It's just you've been standing there awhile and we're locking up now. The millinery shop is the last to close. Everyone else has gone for the night.'

She nodded. 'Yes, I'm so sorry. I was walking off a headache,' she lied again and then ridiculously began to cry. She wished he hadn't possessed such an open face and kind voice or she might have got away without the tears. Sympathy only made her feel worse.

'Oh, come now, miss. There, there. It can't be that bad, surely?'

'It is,' she muttered, sniffing. 'Forgive me.'

'Nothing to forgive, miss. I've got myself two daughters and a wife and I've learned over the years that every girl needs a good cry now and then.'

His generosity helped and she sniffed back the tears as she looked at her watch. 'Thank you. I see I have really lost track of the time.'

'Have you got far to go?'

'Radlett.'

'Far enough.'

She nodded. 'So I'd better get started,' she said, discovering only now that her fingers and toes were losing feeling and her nose was already numb. It would be deep night before she got back to Radlett, if she could get back easily.

'I don't think you should make that journey this evening, miss, if you don't mind me saying so.' He was too loudly echoing her concerns. 'I think you should stay overnight in London.'

'But I have nowhere to stay.' Her mind began to race towards hotels, lodging rooms, but which one? She probably had enough money to cover it, she decided.

'Well, as it happens, we have a tiny room that we use for storage and making cups of tea when we're on a break. It's modest but it's just upstairs and it's got a heater and light, and a very comfy armchair. If you just need a place to put your head down, it's safe and secure. No one will bother you.'

'Mr . . .?'

'Jackson. Call me Percy, though. And before you ask why, I'll tell you it's because I do have daughters and one must be your age and I wouldn't let her walk off into the night alone so I can't, in all good conscience, let you do it either.'

'Mr Jackson, I really —'

'Percy,' he insisted.

She smiled.

'Please,' he encouraged. 'You seem upset and everything

always looks better in the morning.' He pulled out his watch hanging on a chain at his belly. 'Look at that, it's gone six, all the trains will be slowing now so you could be waiting on a chilly platform for hours.'

'That's true.' She couldn't believe she was about to accept his offer but she was exhausted and needed somewhere quiet to reflect. The thought of returning to Eugenie in her current state was unpalatable. She needed to be strong now, especially for Eugenie . . . a night to gather up the pain and put it away for good was a helpful plan. 'Are you quite sure about this?'

'I am, miss. And it would make me happier to know you're secure and warm.'

'Then thank you.'

Percy took the extra precaution of asking the milliner to accompany him when he showed Claire to the room. She gladly did so, still tutting about her fancy clothes being inappropriate for the cold evening. Claire didn't feel like explaining so she went along with it and allowed them to fuss, even accepting some soup and bread.

'You're very kind. How can I repay this?'

They both waved away her gratitude and then they were gone. She was alone with a cup of beefy broth, a slice of thinly buttered bread, a small apple and her thoughts. She sipped the broth gratefully, appreciating only now that she had not eaten since the previous evening. She had been too nervous this morning and all she had in her belly was the single gulp of tea from the Langham. Claire began to feel better for the food as she munched her apple and considered her situation.

'It's time to let him be,' she whispered aloud.

26

Once again Claire stood at the end of Loom Lane. Fresh snowfall had turned it into a fairytale landscape, with even the hedges iced with a sparkling frost that crunched underfoot. Mercifully it wasn't nearly deep enough to trouble her steps and if Claire were honest, she couldn't feel the cold right now.

She had dozed fitfully, and welcomed the chance to get busy and ready herself to travel again by rising before dawn and taking time with making herself presentable. She didn't bother with even lighting a fire, not planning to be around long enough to coax the embers back to life and enjoy the results. Because she'd rested sitting up, her hair was still in place and her eyes, though a little bruised, brightened with the splash of freezing water. She pulled on her coat, hat and gloves and was slipping out the door and down the back entrance as day broke. The chorus of birds sang chirpily but they couldn't lift her spirits. She waved back at the rubbish collectors and early workers who lifted their caps to the elegant young woman hurrying towards the Piccadilly Tube Station but she was pretending at cheerfulness simply out of politeness.

She'd forced herself to sit in the station refreshment rooms and had ordered a steaming pot of tea and some toast with butter and jam, impatiently chewing and sipping, while she waited for the first train to leave Paddington for Radlett. And now finally she was here, glad of her enforced overnight in London to gather her wits and feel strong enough to face the journey to Eugenie and whatever else came beyond that.

A golden-headed bird flitted past and settled on a nearby branch. She instantly recognised the tiniest of the winter songbirds, the goldcrest, and she knew from the warbling that this was a male and that he was busy foraging. His miniature presence, up against all the odds of a harsh winter, prey to larger birds, always on the move for food, usually a dozen hatchlings to worry about with his mate, strengthened her resolve further. If he could survive, she could . . . no, she would.

She didn't have far to walk up the lane until she was facing the familiar gate and, without pausing or taking a breath, she marched up to the door and knocked. She gave a final promise to herself that today was the first day of a new life. She was going to embrace and enjoy whatever time she had left with Eugenie.

It opened and there was Joy, a look of surprised relief ghosting beneath her otherwise controlled expression. And before Joy could speak, Claire hugged her; it helped to stop her tearing up.

'I'm sorry about yesterday. I know I would have worried Eugenie, I should have called; I decided to overnight and it's a long story why and where but I'll explain everything shortly. I'm just glad to be back. Is she upstairs or . . .'

'She's outside,' Joy murmured, as if stunned by the gushing tumble of words that had barged in with the cold.

'Thanks, Joy, I'll find her.'

'Er, Claire . . .?'

But Claire was already moving out of earshot, keen to take a deep breath, dab away the damp in her eyes and to hug Eugenie, tell her sorry tale and try not to cry all over again. She hurried out onto the patio but, discovering it empty, turned to look down the garden where she saw the familiar, rugged-up shape of her closest friend sitting in her wheelchair, facing away from the house.

Claire steeled herself to not show her ragged emotions in her expression, and moved down the stairs, careful of the melting frost, and across crunchy grass until she crouched by Eugenie's side.

'Eugenie,' she began and watched her elder's pale, tired expression ignite.

'Oh my dear,' she said, breathlessly weak. 'My darling, Claire. You had us so worried . . .' Her eyes glistened with tears of delight.

'I'm so sorry. Yesterday was —'

'Don't be sorry. I heard. I'm just so happy I got to see you one more time.'

Claire wasn't really paying attention, just glad to know she hadn't broken down at the sight of her dear friend. But she had heard the last three words. 'What do you mean, "One more time"?'

'Time ticks away, dearest, and I fear the clock sounds my bell.'

'No!' she said firmly, yet her nursing instincts were already confirming the worst. Eugenie was dying and it was happening now, so much sooner than she'd imagined . . . in these unbearably fragile moments of crystallised grass, the songs of finches, the first peeping colour of croci. Eugenie would not see spring's full burst. These were her final heartbeats – how many? Twenty more? Fifty, maybe even one thousand? Even if it was as many as a thousand, Claire calculated that was barely a quarter hour more of life. She had only just made it back in time. She knew she should begin to fuss about getting Eugenie back into the warmth, into bed, even, but she knew it would serve no purpose and in truth when the time came she too would prefer to leave life on a beautiful spring day like today, seated outside, appreciating nature's moment of rebirth, knowing that life goes on after death. Yes, she would leave Eugenie be.

Eugenie seemed to understand her private decision and gave Claire a smile of such radiance it made Claire hold her breath for what was coming. Eugenie began to speak haltingly but with clear delight. 'I did say that I hoped yours would be the last face I saw before I left to join my Eddie, but now I have another face – less familiar – but one that nonetheless brings immense pleasure to my farewell.'

Claire wondered if Eugenie was beginning to get lost in her thoughts as she slipped away. It didn't really matter what she was saying – this was goodbye and she'd seen it happen so many times previously. Rather than allow herself to feel maudlin, she let a thrill of happiness wash over her to look at Eugenie's serene smile as she moved closer to her beloved Edward. And the truth, she decided in that moment, was that Eugenie didn't need to know what happened yesterday: *Let her slip away without hearing your sorrows.* Yet, even as she thought this, something wasn't adding up. She hadn't been paying attention but her hearing was sharp. What had Eugenie meant when she said 'I heard'? Heard what? How? And from whom? How could she know anything of what happened yesterday?

Claire's questions died in her throat and her expression leapt from quizzical to astonishment to hear a man's voice sounding from the small, hidden orchard at the bottom of Eugenie's extensive garden. It was an orchard of plums, pears and apples – all of them now in flower and some of the beautiful ivory Farleigh damson petals fluttered ahead of him on the April wind as he approached.

'Strike me, Mrs Lester, you're right! It's going to be perfect for it,' she heard him say.

The voice was beautiful and achingly familiar. Its Australian twang was unmistakable and when its owner broke cover from around the hedge that hid the orchard, with blossom drifting around him and settling on his hair, it seemed to Claire that she was seeing an apparition. She couldn't say anything because she couldn't breathe in that tight-chested moment when it felt as though even her blood had ceased moving as her heart seemed to trip and stutter to a stop.

James Wren limped from beneath the shade of the trees, using a crutch awkwardly to balance on the good leg; his other was obviously injured but whole, possibly bandaged beneath his baggy uniform. She noted now that the opposite arm's jacket sleeve was tucked into a pocket to prevent it flapping. She took this all in with a single, speechless glance.

He had been looking down, carefully choosing where to place his next step in the strange, slow, hopping hobble he'd adopted. But when he looked up and saw her, she watched him lose his balance and if not for a handy tree trunk to fall against, he would have toppled sideways to the hard ground.

'Claire,' he murmured in a choked whisper.

She still couldn't speak. But she heard a deep and delighted chuckle from Eugenie, still alert, still clinging to life. 'I told you to believe, dear one. There he is. Your Jamie Wren. Rush to him. And tell him all that's in your heart.'

And she was moving, propelled by Eugenie's words, powered by shocked delight, moving on a heavenly air for she could not feel the ground, had no ability to judge the distance between leaping to action and throwing herself into the embrace of Jamie's one good arm. He'd already flung aside the crutch, relying on the tree to fully support him as he gathered her to him.

She couldn't hear, couldn't think, couldn't speak. All she could do was feel the solidity and reality of his presence. She could smell the shaving soap still clinging to his neck where she nestled and wept without shame.

'Claire, I'm sorry. I couldn't —'

She swallowed, needed to find her voice, which sounded only a pathetic whimpering.

He kept trying to explain. 'I couldn't get to you yesterday. The snow, the train, my legs wouldn't move me fast enough . . .'

She finally felt as though she had control of her speech again.

'How are you here?'

'A bloke called Rifki.'

If he'd asked her to guess, she would have said a hundred names before that one. 'Rifki Shahin, Açar's father?' Her voice shook but so was her whole body trembling from the shock of seeing him here.

He nodded, searching her face. 'He told me where to find you. He remembered you mentioning Eugenie in Radlett. And I remembered Loom Lané.'

She took a moment or two to grasp this. 'Wait . . . wait, but where did you see him?'

'He was at the Langham Hotel, taking afternoon tea, waiting for a colleague . . . And then I arrived.'

She didn't trust herself to say too much; she needed time to examine these facts. Rifki in London? At the Palm Court on the same day, at the precise time of her rendezvous with Jamie? 'I wish he'd said hello,' was all she could think to say.

'Odd that he didn't. He seems fond of you.'

The understatement in his careful words was unmistakable. Jamie knew. She didn't know how, but he knew that Rifki had come for her; there was no other explanation. However, he was looking at her with only love and suddenly nothing else in the whole world mattered more than holding Jamie.

Joy had arrived and Claire didn't know if she was more surprised to be in the arms of Jamie again or to see such a genuinely thrilled smile.

Joy took up the story. 'As soon as Mr Wren called the house, Mrs Lester sent Mr Cartwright to pick him up in his Bentley. I'm sure she called in all her favours.'

Eugenie wheezed a struggling breath.

Claire straightened to look at Jamie again; the glow from his green-brown eyes, like the orchard he'd emerged from, warmed her

369

soul and she didn't believe she could ever be cold again as long as Jamie was near.

'I didn't mean not to trust you. Every way I turned I thought I'd lost you.'

'I know,' he soothed. 'Wrong soldier, right unit, similar name . . . communications were dire in the desert and it was hard to keep track of the fallen,' he said, glancing at the empty sleeve.

'How could they get it so wrong?'

'Mine's not the first or last mix-up.'

'Claire . . .' It was Eugenie and her voice was choked. 'Come, both of you . . . please.'

Claire picked up Jamie's crudely made crutch, ensured he was steady again and together they limped the short distance to their friend. Joy pulled a nearby garden chair across so that Jamie could be seated and then Claire moved to crouch beside her dying elder. The questions of failed communications and wrong details could be asked later.

'Ah, look at you both,' Eugenie said, mainly to Jamie. 'I don't think I could be happier than in this moment to see Claire reunited with you,' she said in a hard-won, whispering voice.

'Thank you again for bringing me here,' Jamie said, taking Eugenie's now very skeletal and suddenly tiny hand. She pulled his to her chest where her heart worked hard to keep her alive for a few moments longer.

'Love her forever, James Wren.'

Claire watched him nod with misted eyes before she saw Eugenie turn with difficulty to focus a drifting gaze on her. Helplessly, she reached for Eugenie's other hand and kissed it as Eugenie continued. 'And you, my girl; he has fought for you, stayed alive for you. He is here now and needs your care and your cherishing.' Eugenie found some final reserve of strength to pull Claire's hand to her chest and cover Jamie's with it.

Claire knew they both felt it in the same moment like a charge of lightning passing through them; it was a repeat of the scene of Spud's death, both of them connected over the failing heart of someone whom one of them loved. This time it was Claire's turn, although she suspected that Jamie's fondness for Eugenie was already well established.

'Marry each other. The vicar is waiting. Joy has agreed to witness, so will Bertie Cartwright. Don't hesitate over me; be married in the orchard as we planned, Jamie, with the happiness of blossom and all of its significance of new life and fecundity.' Her expression brightened again from intense to a relaxed, resigned grin. 'It's time, my darlings,' she whispered. 'I'm tired, but oh so happy.' She looked at Jamie and nodded.

He glanced at Claire but leaned forward to murmur, 'Godspeed,' at Eugenie's ear and kissed her hollow cheek.

And she turned once more to Claire with affection. 'Don't grieve, Claire dear, because I am feeling unburdened and curiously joyous. I want to rush to Edward now – I'm choosing to. So no tears on my account, lovely girl, I've had a wonderful and long life.'

'You're the elder woman I've always lacked in my life, Eugenie. Thank you for your love and wisdom,' Claire said and kissed Eugenie tenderly several times. 'You can let go. Edward's waiting for you.'

She heard a soft sigh as her tears fell on Eugenie's cheek and she felt her friend relax beneath her lips.

'She's gone,' she murmured, pulling back to revel in the gentle smile that Eugenie had left them with.

'Marry me, Claire,' he whispered in a shaken voice.

She nodded, tearful, feeling Eugenie's warmth against her body. 'Yes. Yes, I will.'

27

Joy assured the newly reunited couple that Eugenie had, weeks previously, made careful arrangements for her funeral and burial alongside her husband. She was interred privately with only six people witnessing and, despite her friend's insistence, Claire had waited a fortnight until her sorrow of Eugenie's passing could not spoil the pleasure of her marriage.

And now spring's warmth had begun to melt winter away; Claire had watched it peel back its grip as the heads of bulbs burst fully through the once-frozen ground in a show of bright promise, the streets became more lively with people for more hours each day, and the war felt even more distant as uniforms disappeared from the everyday scenes.

She sighed with soft pleasure to see the sun light the facets of the three diamonds embedded into the rose gold wedding ring that Jamie had slipped awkwardly onto her finger yesterday afternoon in a tiny ceremony exactly as Eugenie had wished. Claire had worn the ivory silk Valentine dress that she'd bought for him. She'd added a small garland of individually threaded cream hyacinth flowers to her hair and carried gloriously scented soft white and pastel-pink hyacinths from Eugenie's garden. They'd stood with the delighted rector in the orchard for the brief ceremony. A beaming Bertie Cartwright and Joy witnessed and there was no doubt in everyone's minds that Eugenie was among them in spirit when a gentle breeze stirred a blizzard of blossom to fall like confetti as Claire and Jamie shared their vows.

Last night, after finding the funny side of how tricky it was to make love with Jamie 'armless and legless', as he described himself, they had not let his injuries prevent the culmination of years of dreaming and wanting each other.

'We're just going to have to practise,' he said with an exaggerated sigh as he rolled slightly clumsily onto his back. 'I mean every night, Claire, into training I shall go.'

Her spluttering laughter had filled the room and his amused hushing had filled her heart until she had admitted, breathlessly, 'I don't believe I could love you another inch.'

'Oh, come on, Claire. Be a sport, surely you can manage another inch. I know I could,' he said, still in an arch tone, lifting an eyebrow.

She had never known herself to laugh as much as she had in the last twenty-four hours and they were both shooshing each other helplessly before Claire remembered there was no one else in the house.

Later, with an enormous woollen rug pulled around their nakedness, Claire sipped cocoa leaning against her husband's broad chest in the seat of the window and looked out into the darkness.

'I'm sorry to burden you with a husband who isn't whole,' he whispered.

'My life is complete, Jamie,' she murmured after a contented sigh. 'I'm deeply saddened about your arm but only for you and the difficulties it presents. But in terms of us, we are whole. I want you to believe that. No injuries matter to me, only that you are here and safe and we belong to one another.'

He wrapped his arm around her shoulders and pulled her even closer to him until she could feel the full heat of his flesh and the pulse of his heart against her body. She did privately mourn the loss of his limb because she knew he was a horseman through and through, but she felt convinced that Jamie would adjust and in time nothing would stop him getting back into the saddle. She was also fully aware that they were the lucky survivors and had a lifetime of loving ahead, where others had only grief. They sat in a delicious, comfortable silence until Jamie broke it admitting that he believed Spud had been with them too in the garden, and perhaps even Açar Shahin, whose prayer book had surely saved his life.

'Eugenie told me about your trip back to Turkey after the Armistice,' he continued, stroking her hair, having already confessed that he used to fantasise nightly of being able to touch her like this.

She nestled deeper against him, amazed by how hard and flat a man's body was; she swore privately to the guardians who had kept him safe that she would never tire of the sound of his voice, or the smell of his skin, the coarseness of his chin this late in the day or the softness of his hair that tickled her breasts when he kissed them. She would never want to stop that soulful, hungry gaze of his on her body, or how making love with Jamie felt like perfection because everything about him inexplicably made her nerves trill with desire. And even as she thought this she felt the tug of her thoughts shift to Rifki, as though needing to consider him. She'd made the right decision, didn't doubt herself. Her love for Jamie consumed her – there was no other room in her world for another man, a different man. Claire pulled the rug closer about them until their shared warmth had become one and it felt as though they had melted into each other and could no longer be separated.

'So . . .' he urged. 'Tell me about your return to Turkey.'

She was glad she had her back to him even though the light was too low to see her blush. 'His father was deeply appreciative to have the prayer book returned.'

'Yes, he told me. What do you think of him?'

Claire reminded herself there was nothing to feel guilty about and answered truthfully. 'Younger than I'd anticipated. A mathematician who'd forgotten he'd once been a romantic. Broken, of course, as any father might be over losing his only son; grateful for our care, for your friendship of Açar. I met Shahin's aunts, his cousins . . . it was a memorable experience,' she admitted. 'I feel privileged to have shared it and glad to have brought something so precious to them.' She told him about extracting the book from Bernard Jenkins and his demand she return the prayer book. 'I must write to him. As it turned out, he did me a favour. Going to Turkey was the ideal distraction, gave me hope, made me realise just how much I loved you. I hope you don't feel cheated?'

'No. You did something very special, and on my behalf. Besides, it's obviously still going to be some months before I can get around easily enough with a cane. I'm just glad we achieved what Shahin hoped. I imagine being with you unlocked the father's romantic soul again.'

Was she that transparent?

'He . . .' she began but wasn't sure what she wanted to say. She knew she should say yes, perhaps even tell Jamie that Rifki felt deeply attracted to her, but in the heartbeat of her hesitation she knew such an admission served no purpose to her husband, to Rifki, or to herself. Nothing had happened for her to be ashamed of and it seemed as though Jamie knew this much anyway.

'He what?' Jamie wondered, moving his lips across the exposed column of her neck. The unbearable lightness of his touch stirred her, made her close her eyes, made her want him again . . . right now.

But he was waiting.

She cleared her throat softly. 'I was going to say that I learned from Rifki's sister that he'd loved a woman passionately but they'd not been allowed to be together. His son's death, my arrival to

375

remind him of the pain of loss and how much I loved you, well . . .
I think – hope, anyway – that he will go in search of her again.'

Jamie cupped her chin, turned her towards him and kissed her
gently. He lingered at her mouth, barely a hair's width apart as if
wanting to breathe the same air that she did. 'I'm never going to let
you go again,' he promised.

'Nor do I want you to.' She turned in his embrace to face him.
'Take me back to bed,' she breathed and opened herself only to
Jamie, forcing the ghostly presence of Rifki Shahin, which had
walked alongside her these last weeks, to let her go.

———

Claire was seated in one of the anterooms of Eugenie's home whose
single window overlooked a small strip of narrow garden that ran
down the side of the house, rimmed by a tangle of blackberry canes.
In the days since Eugenie's passing and being reunited with Jamie,
they had barely left each other's side; today was the first time, in
fact, and she was using it to write a letter she'd been avoiding. She
knew she needed to impress upon the Turk that he must bury whatever romantic notions he harboured for her, while not damaging his
fragile feelings.

Dear Rifki,

*I gather you are or have been in London. I write to you with
the happy news that I am now Mrs James Wren. My Australian
Light Horseman finally found me again and although his
injuries have permanently damaged him – as you would know
from your meeting – his love for me remains intact, as mine
remains for him. We look forward with great hope to a long
life together, including raising a family.*

*And speaking of family, I hope with all of my full heart
that this letter finds you and all of your wonderful sisters,
husbands, et al, in very good health and looking forward
to summer. It seems rather amazing that Kashifa's grandson
will be a year old come September. The time has flown.
You will all have your work cut out once he finds his feet!
And I know you will be a wise, wonderful great-uncle that
any young boy could be lucky enough to have. Enjoy him
as he grows and it is my hope that he shows some of Açar's
finest qualities to remind you that your son and the proud
blood of Shahin pumps strongly through your sisters'
children and their children's children.*

*I trust your work at the university is busy and rewarding.
I never did get to say a proper goodbye to Professor Leavers
and really should look him up . . .*

She was tempted to ask for a forwarding address to keep the
innocent conversation flowing, but thought better of it as it would
mean him perhaps feeling obliged to respond.

*My great friend and someone I loved dearly, Eugenie Lester,
passed away recently. I think we both hoped that we might
have had a bit longer together, and we'd agreed that I would
nurse her but it seems her body failed her sooner than she'd
intended it. Her generosity towards me knows no bounds,
it seems. She has left me her fine house in her will and I will
keep my promise to help set up a local clinic that she had
bequeathed the money to establish. I can hardly let her down
in this, so we shall remain in England while Jamie recuperates
and I can keep this promise to Eugenie.*

It is our decision, however, to make a home in southern Australia and we will leave by year's end to meet my husband's folks. He has warned me I am travelling at the hottest time to the driest state of the driest continent on our earth, and arguably to the loneliest corner of it. It seems his people are connected with a massive sheep station of many thousands of hectares, the size of which most of us could not imagine. Wish me luck!

Well, dear Rifki, I know you played a part in reuniting Jamie with me and for that I thank you with all my heart. I can only imagine which fates threw us together once again but I am grateful you were there at the Langham Hotel or Jamie and I might still be searching for each other. I will remember this kindness of yours forever and hope you know that you occupy a special place in my heart.

So, that is all my news since returning from Turkey and I have mentioned to my husband that now that I'm extremely familiar with the ways of the hammam we should visit Charing Cross and try out London's Turkish Baths. It could never match my special day with your family and friends, but it will be a lovely reminder of the joyful memories I have of you all.

I trust you are keeping well and remain hopeful that you have not forgotten our last conversation and that you will seek out the happiness that potentially awaits you. I was told repeatedly of the courage and fearlessness of the Turks during the battles at Gallipoli, and know you will be in possession of these enviable traits too. It perhaps only requires you to take the first brave step.

Claire smiled to herself as she was sure she could picture how Rifki's lips would thin at her audacious words.

All my very best wishes, and with love,

Claire

She sealed it before she could change her mind and slipped the letter into her pocket, feeling unburdened and convinced Rifki would read between the lines to appreciate the gratitude and deep fondness she held for him. She would post it tomorrow morning.

Claire went in search of Jamie and glimpsed him through the kitchen's window to where he sat on the verandah, writing to his family in Australia to follow up the telegram announcing their marriage.

His shoulders were hunched, face filled with concentration as he focused on finding the right words and struggled to keep his pad straight with the same hand he wrote with. He'd not once complained, not once spoken of the pain he'd endured, or the fear he'd overcome during the war years, while she had talked out all of her anguish of the time since they'd parted. He'd encouraged her, listening quietly, absorbing her pain, letting it flow over him and through him until she'd purged herself of it and wept softly in his embrace. And then he'd kissed her tenderly and told her they would now never speak of the war or anyone from it ever again. Peace, marriage, love and laughter were all he was interested in, he had impressed.

She looked at her husband, labouring over his letter to his family of stockmen, and decided she loved the broad sweep of his shoulders and the shape of his head, knew what the ridges beneath his hair felt like and the texture of the thatch that had grown slightly unruly around his ears. She would trim that for him later today and then she would kiss those ears and whisper her love to them.

———————

Jamie knew that Claire was watching him. He could feel her presence wherever she was like a ray of warmth. Since he'd first seen her crouched by Eugenie's wheelchair with that expression of disbelief, it had felt like he had emerged fully from the winter of his life. He'd cast that cloak of bleakness away when she'd rushed into his arms, weeping and laughing at once. Now it was spring in every sense and there was so much to look forward to – so much living to be done and laughter to be enjoyed. He refused to allow anything to darken the horizon of his season of joy, not least his missing arm, but especially his notion that something had occurred between her and Shahin.

Shahin was already the past. Now he had to look to the future. Claire thought he was writing to his parents, who hopefully by now were celebrating the news of him being alive, but in truth he was crafting the hardest of letters to Alice.

She was a sweet enough girl. He'd made the journey to farewell her in Melrose. They'd stood in the looming shadow of Mount Remarkable, not far from the North Star Hotel but out of sight of the pub's patrons, and Alice had cried as he'd hugged her farewell.

'You'll come back to me, won't you, Jamie?' she'd said through a teary smile as she tried to be brave.

'I'm coming back, Alice, I promise.'

'And will you promise to marry me then?'

He'd felt embarrassed to be talking about marriage on the eve of his grand adventure of war in far-off lands.

'Let's wait until I get home. We'll work it all out then.'

'You will marry me, though, won't you, Jamie? I'm going to wait for you.'

He didn't think she had much choice. So many of his peers were going too and very few had anything but war on their minds and those left behind didn't have weddings in their immediate scheme of life. Even so, there would be a queue of farming boys who would give an arm to be with Alice.

Jamie gave a near inaudible, rueful sigh at that final thought. Strange, his arm that wasn't there was itching from its slow healing as he thought about it. He hoped that sensation would pass.

He wondered what his parents thought of the telegram message that he had married Claire. He'd read his father's letter to her, astonished and touched by its tenderness, and knew their relationship would be changed as a result.

He returned to his letter and read back what he'd written.

Hello, dear Alice,

I hope this finds you in good spirits and I'm sure it also finds you as pretty as I left you. I'm imagining that you'll still be on fire alert but hopefully the rains aren't far away with autumn arriving.

I guess you've heard by now from my parents that I made it through the war and, although I left a bit of myself behind, I am glad to be alive as so many aren't.

There is something important I need to tell you and I didn't want you to hear it from anyone but me. Finding the right words, of course, is hard and I am no wordsmith as you know so I shall just say it plain and hope you understand.

The war has changed me. I look different with only one arm now. I have an injured leg too and suspect I shall always limp but I'm learning to live with both situations and I shall be fine. In fact I can't wait to try riding again when I am fully healed. But the war has changed more than my physical appearance, dear Alice. I have changed inside too and I want to be honest with you and tell you that I cannot be with you. I realise this might bring upset to your life and to your plans, and heaven knows you deserve better than me. There are so many men in the district who would fall over each other to be lucky enough to call themselves your beau and some of them more than wealthy enough – if they made it through the war too – to make a good life for you, and give you the family you always talked about.

I have met someone. It would be wrong not to tell you this. Her name is Claire and I fell in love with her when she nursed me after I was wounded in Gallipoli. I thought I'd lost her but we found each other again in England and we have married, Alice. I feel as though I should apologise to you for falling for her, but I can't make any apology for loving Claire. She is my world now and that is how I think love should be . . . like the grassfires we used to watch from afar. Remember how the flames used to consume everything in their path? That's what our love is like. She is the fire that consumes me and while I think you might hate me for telling you all of this, I have always aimed to be honest with you.

I do want to offer my regret, though, Alice, for any hurt this letter brings. Maybe in time you will forgive me for letting you down and it is probably better we both discovered how disappointing I am for you sooner rather than later.

You are such a great girl and I wish you love and happiness with the right bloke, who is surely in that queue outside your door in Melrose right now.

I'll be home towards the end of the Australian summer and hope by then you will have forgiven me, and perhaps already found someone special who has both his arms to hold you close!

Goodbye, pretty Alice, and thanks for being such a good friend.

Jamie x

He sealed it, would address it later and post tomorrow. He slipped the envelope into his pocket and looked out at the setting sun. It seemed fitting that it was closing on its horizon, setting the sky ablaze with a golden-pink that harked back to his days on Walker's Ridge when he watched Claire's ship disappearing into the light as though it was being drawn into heaven. This sky was the colour he would always associate with his wife and he was glad it was a gold-flecked pink dusk to remind him that he loved Claire so wholly that his honest letter to Alice felt right and he should suffer no regret at telling her only the truth.

He turned and saw her now, smiling at him with a look of such pleasure that he wished he could capture this moment and store it away so that he could bring it out and feel its glow whenever he felt lonely or vulnerable. There she was, Nurse Nightingale, the golden afternoon painting her in the colour of the angel he knew she was to him. He grinned back and blew her a kiss. Claire caught it and instantly tucked it beneath her shirt. Their laughter erupted into the gloaming, where swallows, newly arrived from their migration, flew their swooping flight joyfully in the lowering light as if joining their celebration of new life.

ACKNOWLEDGEMENTS

Storytellers take liberties. And if we accept that my job as a novelist is to entertain, then I'm asking that readers knowledgeable about Gallipoli will tolerate that I may have taken a few small liberties to bring you a story to escape with. That said, I have involved myself in plenty of research: from the dozen or more books I've read on everything from anaesthesia to life in Turkey at the turn of the previous century, to the various trips I've made to the Australian War Memorial and the Imperial War Museums in England. I have walked the ANZAC site at Gallipoli with an expert guide in 2013 and spent time in Istanbul, Alexandria, Cairo and, of course, London and Radlett, where so much of the non-war action takes place.

My deepest thanks to Kenan Çelik of the Çanakkale Onsekiz Mart University in Turkey, who was a wealth of information for both the ANZAC and the Ottoman perspectives and who guided me so faithfully on my visit to Gallipoli. I must also thank Cameron Atkinson from the Australian War Memorial for his patient, tireless and always cheerful help over the course of writing *Nightingale*. Love and thanks to Chris Sweeting in Hong Kong, who grew up in Radlett and gave me a wonderful guided tour and insight into its post-war layout, life and people, for helping me to find the perfect house for Eugenie but especially for sharing the secret fairy tree in the woods! Louise Furrow from California – what a star you are for helping me with the bathing scene . . . much gratitude. I'm grateful to Nick Barrington-Wells at the Langham Hotel in London too for spoiling me with a pretty marvellous afternoon tea, all in the name of research, and to Paul Gauger and his team at VisitBritain.

Thank you to the wonderful Penguin Group for its sterling support – special nod to the fabulous trio of Ali Watts, Chantelle Sturt, Lou Ryan, each amazing at what you do. Pip Klimentou, Nigelle-Ann Blaser, Sonya Caddy . . . all important first readers – thanks, your early critiques are vital and much appreciated. Wonderful booksellers and librarians around Australia and New Zealand – sincerest thanks for your brilliant support at the coalface.

Heartfelt thanks to Ian McIntosh for having my back always and to Will and Jack who never fail to make me explode into help-less laughter at least once a day, and usually at inopportune times.

The writing journey of this story was made all the more poign-ant because a member of the McIntosh clan gave his life at Lone Pine in 1915. Darcy Roberts was just twenty when he passed away and was like so many other braves who volunteered from Australia: he fought in a war not of his making, one that took place on the other side of the world. According to the family he was a gifted horseman and, like the majority of the mounted soldiers, he would have hated leaving behind his beloved horse in Cairo when the Light Horse Brigade was posted from Egypt to the Dardanelles to fight as infantry. The Battle of Lone Pine over three days resulted in some of the fiercest and most heroic fighting of the Turkish cam-paign with devastating losses on both sides, amounting to eight thousand lives given and countless injured. It's impossible not to weep when you walk through the Lone Pine cemetery, now so peaceful and picturesque.

F

BOOK CLUB DISCUSSION NOTES

1.   The opening of the novel is extremely evocative. Did it reveal new aspects of the Gallipoli story for you?

2.   When Claire and Jamie meet it is love at first sight. Do you really think it's possible to fall in love just like that?

3.   Jamie's friendship with Spud and Claire's friendship with Eugenie are critical to this story. Discuss the ways in which these secondary characters influence our lovebirds, and the outcome of the novel.

4.   Did the war strengthen or weaken the bond between Claire and Jamie?

5.   Claire begs Jamie: 'Live for me. And I will love you.' Discuss this and the role of other promises made throughout the novel.

6.   Who do you think is the bravest character in this book?

7.   The story contains a number of very powerful scenes. Which of those did you find most effective? Most heart-wrenching? Most satisfying?

8. Did you ever hope that Claire would surrender to Rifki's charms?

9. I think we all like to imagine that Rifki will find his own happy ending. What do you imagine happens to him after our story concludes?

10. How many instances of tea drinking can you find throughout the novel? What are the different functions of it in the story?

11. If Gallipoli symbolises all that is hopeless about war, why do we continue to throw our young men and women into conflict? Have we learned much about war since World War One?

12. Discuss the symbolism of the birds in the story.

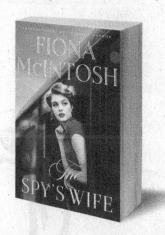

The highly anticipated new
historical adventure from
the bestselling author of
The Champagne War.

Evie, a widow and stationmaster's daughter, can't help but look for the weekly visit of the handsome man she and her sister call the Southerner on their train platform in the wilds of northern England. When polite salutations shift to friendly conversations, they become captivated by each other. After so much sorrow, the childless Evie can't believe love and the chance for her own family have come into her life again.

With rumours coming out of Germany that Hitler may be stirring up war, local English authorities have warned against spies. Even Evie becomes suspicious of her new suitor, Roger. But all is not what it seems.

When Roger is arrested, Evie comes up with an audacious plan to prove his innocence that means moving to Germany and working as a British counter-spy. Wearing the disguise of dutiful, naïve wife, Evie must charm the Nazi Party's dangerous officials to bring home hard evidence of war mongering on the Führer's part.

But in this game of cat and mouse, it seems everyone has an ulterior motive, and Evie finds it impossible to know who to trust. With lives on the line, ultimate sacrifices will be made as she wrestles between her patriotism and saving the man she loves.

From the windswept moors of the Yorkshire dales to the noisy beer halls of Munich and grand country estates in the picture-book Bavarian mountains, this is a lively and high-stakes thriller that will keep you second-guessing until the very end.